T0005948

BEST
MEN

BEST MEN

SIDNEY KARGER

BERKLEY ROMANCE

NEW YORK

BERKLEY ROMANCE
Published by Berkley
An imprint of Penguin Random House LLC
penguinrandomhouse.com

Library of Congress Cataloging-in-Publication Data

Names: Karger, Sidney, author.
Title: Best men / Sidney Karger.
Description: First edition. | New York: Berkley Romance, 2023.
Identifiers: LCCN 2022033392 (print) | LCCN 2022033393 (ebook) |
ISBN 9780593439487 (trade paperback) | ISBN 9780593439494 (ebook)
Subjects: LCGFT: Romantic fiction. | Novels.
Classification: LCC PS3611.A7824 Be 2023 (print) |
LCC PS3611.A7824 (ebook) | DDC 813/.6—dc23/eng/20220815
LC record available at https://lccn.loc.gov/2022033392
LC ebook record available at https://lccn.loc.gov/2022033393

First Edition: May 2023

Printed in the United States of America
3 5 7 9 10 8 6 4

Book design by Daniel Brount
Interior art: Phone © kustomer/Shutterstock.com;
record sleeve © Andrey_Kuzmin/Shutterstock.com;
torn newspaper © STILLFX/Shutterstock.com

For my mom and dad.
You somehow knew that one day I'd write a book.

BEST MEN

Vows

MAX MOODY and GREG LEVINE

Max Moody, the son of Phil and Joanne Moody of Plain Ridge, Ill., and Greg Levine, the son of William and Elaine Levine of Shaker Heights, Ohio, will not be married in New York City because if you ask me, Greg seriously screwed everything up. Jerk.

chapter

ONE

"WHEN THEY FIRST MET, LOVE WAS AFOOT." THAT WAS the *New York Times* wedding announcement headline my best friend Paige had jokingly imagined for Greg, my ex-boyfriend, the podiatrist, and me even though we were never engaged nor had we even remotely discussed getting married one day. Our actual wedding, in my head, wasn't exactly planned out because I don't really have that gay-wedding-planning gene, but it probably would've been a super-casual affair for three hundred and fifty of our closest friends and family on Pier Sixty overlooking the Hudson River, with Greg and me wearing tuxes while we had our first dance together as husbands to "This Charming Man" by the Smiths. Okay, maybe I thought about it a tiny bit.

This increasingly distant memory pops into my mind right now because, like a tourist, I'm standing in the middle of a busy sidewalk on Twenty-Third and Eighth on a hot summer Thursday evening, grinning at a text from Greg. I feel a tiny warm tingle in my undercarriage as I reply, Yep.

Oh, I didn't tell you? I'm still seeing my ex for sex. Wait—is that a Rascal Flatts song? Right before entering the subway on my way home from work, Greg texted, Free before dinner? which is code for "hook up," so maybe after we do the sex, we'll grab a bite at Pepe Giallo, our once favorite Italian restaurant in West Chelsea that we'd been going to since we first met eight years ago. (In fact, it's where we had our first date.) Then, over a bottle of red wine and plates of deliciously gooey chicken Parm, he'll admit he misses us and say he desperately wants to get back together.

Greg asks to meet at six thirty, in forty-five minutes, which means I'm early, so I slip into a diner called the Rail Line. It used to be called Moonstruck Diner, and I imagine they wanted to name it the High Line Diner, after the nearby High Line elevated park, but couldn't get legal clearance, so they ended up with this weird, off-brand name.

I take a seat at the counter and order an old-fashioned along with a basket of bread and butter. There's nothing weirder—or more fun—than ordering a cocktail at a diner. It's like the opposite of ordering chicken nuggets at some fancy French restaurant.

Scanning the room full of silver-haired early birders, I spot an extremely handsome fella sitting alone in a booth, texting, waiting for either his food or a companion. Occasionally, he looks up from his phone and eyes me. Doesn't he know I'm about to have complicated relations with my ex-boyfriend? I'm taken, sir.

My seen-it-all Polish server makes me the strongest old-fashioned I've ever had, and I love it as I tear into the stale bread, butter a piece and look up again, noticing Cutie in a Booth is still staring at me. This time I really clock him. He seems slightly younger than me, definitely more chiseled and somehow more New Yorky. But then, that's pretty much everyone in this city. I also notice he has a June-in-New York sun-kissed face and looks like the kind of sophisticated urbanite who wouldn't be caught dead in a mediocre diner. Unlike me. Mediocre diners give me life.

I decide to smile. I may be in an unhealthy relationship with my ex, but I'm not dead inside. Now he squints at me. Did I do the smile wrong? Was I creepy? A grizzled server probably named Margie or Bernice arrives at his booth and takes his order. Now they both look at me. Was I that obvious? A sudden thought occurs to me, so I look over my shoulder and realize he'd been reading the chalkboard of tonight's specials the entire time. He was literally looking right through me. He probably didn't think I looked as good as "Virginia Ham Steak," and he'd be correct.

Knowing that Greg doesn't like when I'm late, I finish my drink, forget the guy in the booth and leave. I arrive at Greg's place at exactly six thirty as his not-so-friendly doorman, Dario from Staten Island, who's dressed in a tight, all-black suit like a mean bouncer at a high-end gentlemen's club, lets me in. I still can't believe Greg moved into this crazy upscale building—designed by the British-Iraqi starchitect Zaha Hadid, he always likes to remind me—after we broke up. It's incredibly cool but expensive, and I don't get why you'd want to pay this much to overlook the High Line, filled with tourists staring up at you, wondering why you'd want to pay this much to look down at them.

Dr. Greg has his own private, extremely successful practice as a foot doctor in Tribeca. He always knew he wanted to become a podiatrist, even in high school, he told me. I'd always thought this was an interesting quirk, and his nerdy but compassionate determination to treat strangers' toenail fungus was one of the many reasons I was drawn to him. Some people may assume a person wanting to professionally hold feet all day has some kind of foot fetish, but it's more like Greg is one with a foot and a foot is one with Greg. He just "gets" feet the same way Cesar Millan gets dogs. Greg is New York City's number one foot whisperer.

The elevator plops me right into Greg's apartment. His own private entrance. No common hallway up in this piece. Adele's "When We Were Young" plays on his Sonos speakers with the irony right on cue. I don't see Greg anywhere. I just see his overpriced sofas and chairs and coffee tables and modern art he bought at auction all staring at me like I can't afford them, which I can't. Except for a nice-looking bottle of chilled rosé and two wine glasses sitting there, his envious all-marble kitchen is empty too. Wanting to ride my diner cocktail buzz, I sidle up to the Carrara kitchen island, pull out his high-tech wine opener and go to town opening the bottle. I'd prefer an ice-cold beer on this hot summer night, but Greg is signaling he wants to be romantic, so I don't mind hitting the pink vino—

"Stop!" Greg enters, scaring the crap out of me and simultaneously turning me on in his half-unbuttoned white dress shirt. Something looks different about his slightly exposed chest, but I'm not sure what.

"Why? It's chilled," I say. No hellos. No kisses. No "how are yous."

"I'm sort of saving it for later," Greg says with a slight smile. And slowly, I realize something that I've tried not to think of since we broke up. He's seeing someone new. Greg and I are no longer together. We're free to see other people and have been for a year. I guess this is my life now. Don't mind me while I slip into a warm bath of heavy denial.

Any jealousy I have immediately disappears as Greg grabs the wine opener from me, sets it gently on the marble and then starts mauling my mouth with his. There is nothing greater than kissing Greg. It's pure masculine warmth sizzling with electricity. But tonight feels off. It's animalistic, impassionate and rushed. Cold. We don't even move to his giant Hästens king-sized bed—made with the finest horsehair, Greg likes to remind me—as I unbutton Greg's shirt right there in the kitchen. That's when it hits me what's different about him. *He shaved his chest hair?* I've never seen or felt this on him before. It's already started to grow back as rough stubble, and I can't help but wonder who this new guy is that has such power over the usually very hairy Dr. Greg.

Quickly after he's naked and my pants are unbuttoned, I'm watching Greg watch himself pleasure both of us in the reflection of his glass refrigerator door, and I suddenly realize he's gone full Patrick Bateman from *American Psycho*. Even weirder is that I'm enjoying his transformation, but then it's over before I even know it. He finishes. I don't.

Fuck.

"Doing anything this weekend?" he asks me, completely bulldozing past what just happened and moving as far away from me as possible. No snuggling here. We're officially fuck buddies.

"That was incredible. How was it for you?" I say.

"Hysterical," he says as he moves the bottle opener next to the wine glasses in a perfectly straight line like he's a goddamned footman lining up silverware at Downton Abbey. I give him a look. A look he should recognize from torturing each other romantically for the last year plus.

"What. I'm just . . . I have something tonight," he says.

"A date?" I ask.

"Sure. I guess you can call it that." Way to keep me in suspense.

I'm going to ignore this for now, so I say, "I like the chest stubble." I don't really. "You seem . . . more ripped . . . or something. Massive pec action." *Massive pec action?* That might be the dumbest, shallowest thing I've ever said out loud, but maybe if I appeal to his superficial side, he'll call off his date with Mr. Whomever and have dinner with me, cuddle, and ask me to spend the night, increasing our chances for that coveted *New York Times* wedding paragraph.

"Thanks. I've been hitting the gym hard. Braydon has me waking up at five a.m. to do CrossFit. It's kicking my ass." *Braydon?* He sounds twelve. With all his gym talk and, I assume, dating younger guys, Greg is inching into self-parody-level gay, but he's still the Greg I once fell in love with underneath the newly acquired gym bod.

"You look great," I say. "Are you and Brandon—" I purposely butcher his name.

"Braydon. I'm seeing him after this but didn't want to be too horny."

"Got it." That explains it. "Are you guys, like . . . a thing?"

"I dunno. It's whatever for now." He seems unsure of moving on from me, which is why this is such torture. Or maybe he's just softening the blow of seeing new people.

"Cool for you." I meant to say, "Good for you," but it came out "Cool for you," so I'll go with it. I try to keep our conversation moving forward, but I can tell he just wants me to leave. He gives me the final hint by wiping down his countertop even though it's spotless, like a bartender pushing out the last drunk of the night. I wouldn't be surprised if he starts counting tips and putting the kitchen chairs upside down on the table.

"Keys, phone, wallet?" Greg recites, not even pretending to subtly throw me out now. I go through the motions of checking my pockets for all my personal belongings even though I know they're in all the right places. Then I just stare at him as he puts his clothes back on, waiting for I don't know what. But nothing comes.

The elevator dings and I'm deposited back into the building's lobby, where Dario the doorman scowls at me as if he knows what just happened. Even though we've never had one conversation ever, for some reason I feel like Dario has known every detail of my relationship with Greg. Either that or my quick visits make him suspect I'm a drug dealer.

Hookup apps aren't exactly my thing. I'm the rarity fishing for an LTR in our modern-day technology hellscape that's mostly shirtless torsos belonging to guys soliciting sex. I've probably downloaded and immediately deleted Grindr about a dozen times, but tonight as I walk back to my apartment, I'm thinking about how my ex has someone new and all I have is my phone, which is sounding pretty good right now.

I like to use the time climbing the six stories to my apartment wisely, so while I shuffle upstairs, I download Scruff. I've never tried it before, but peeking at the photos, I've gathered it's a slightly older, hairier version of Grindr. Like me.

People can't believe I live in a six-story walk-up. On the plus side, it's in the heart of the West Village on Grove Street above a mystery bookshop, it's rent stabilized, I pay a dollar fifty a month, and I live down the street from my best friend Paige, whom I see or talk to every day.

Oh. Remember how I said I talk to Paige every day? After checking my phone, I notice our last text exchange was over a week ago, and it suddenly occurs to me that she might be missing.

Delete   Archive   Move   Flag   ...

Subject: Difference Day

Moody, Max <moody.max@bpa.com>

To: Everyone
Cc: Pierce Whitman, Janet <piercewhitman.janet@bpa.com>

Employees of Benser + Powell Advertising:

It's that time of year again! As you may know, Difference Day is our annual companywide day of service, where we set aside our daily tasks and put our resources toward improving our communities together. Time to make a difference!

Whether it's mentoring young people, providing homes for adopted pets, entertaining seniors, cleaning up public spaces, and everything in between, through the years we've volunteered our time and remained committed to making an impact in the world around us for the greater good.

For this year's Difference Day, happening on August 12, our volunteers (all of you!) will create and plant new gardens. We hope you will sign up with your direct manager to lend a hand in keeping our city green.

Thank you.

Max Moody

Director of Creative Talent, Corporate Responsibility and Employee Engagement

chapter
TWO

"PRESS THE CALL BUTTON FOR HELP." EVERY MORNING AS I stare at this sign while temporarily trapped in the elevator on the way to my soul-melting job, I can't help but think it's the perfect metaphor for my tragicomic life. Especially right now: I'm surrounded by what seems like sixteen people all standing perfectly still, crammed in this moving veal pen. I'm the only person not staring at my phone. Three women are holding offensively giant Starbucks coffees. Two straight guys are listening to competing hip-hop songs on their AirPods. And the mouth breather behind me reeks of sweat and cigarette smoke and a hint of something that's possibly expired cottage cheese.

Help.

We stop on every floor until there are five of us left. I'm squeezed in the middle, while the remaining four stand in each corner, like dots on a pair of dice. The dots file out until I'm the last one of the morning sheeple to exit on the twenty-seventh floor and I remember that I'm soaking wet as my eight-year-old pair of New Balance sneakers—still holding up quite nicely, if you ask me—squeak down the linoleum. Not only is it two hundred degrees on this summer Friday and I'm profusely sweating, but it's also raining. And I forgot an umbrella.

I'm on an eerily quiet floor in the HR department, which thankfully doesn't have a receptionist. Probably the only perk of my job is that no one can see me come or go. No Carol behind a desk flipping through an old *People* magazine judging me when I'm running late. No Stephen with a Long Island accent to wish me a happy hump day. No Roz with plum-colored hair asking, "Hot enough for ya?" while playing online Scrabble and chewing her nicotine gum. Just a giant high-tech video wall that screams BENSER + POWELL ADVERTISING with an intermittent, floating generic word salad that includes "Creative Storytelling," "Diversity Works" and "Globally Iconic." Beyond the blinding wall of light is a lobby bigger than five of my apartments combined that's always empty and deadly quiet, overlooking an impressive view of the Hudson River.

After nine years here, at least I no longer have a cubicle and can shut my office door, which I always do immediately upon arriving. It's one of those sliding glass deals so anyone can see through but it's frosted with a stripe so when you're sitting down they can still see your legs. I'll take the upper-half privacy.

Don't ask me how I became "Director of Creative Talent, Corporate Responsibility and Employee Engagement." It's like three jobs smooshed together, one of which is hiring and firing people. I guess that's four jobs. I thought I wanted to be a copywriter, so Paige got me a job here when I first moved to New York and I just kept rising up the HR ranks. My whole life I've longed to do something creative, trying it all: graphic design, guitar, painting, improv, playwriting, photography, acting. I've never found the right artistic niche.

As I towel off the sweat and rain with Kleenex, I start mentally composing a text to Paige, wondering if she is, in fact, missing. Not like "have a search party and candlelight vigil" missing; just "not responding to any of my texts" missing, which is not like her.

Paige and I have been best friends since growing up next door to each other in our modest Illinois suburb just northwest of Chicago. We were born in the same hospital, a month apart, the same year. Our parents were best friends who ritualistically spent hours every weekend at each other's houses over long, boisterous dinners, bottles of red wine and cigarettes before they realized smoking was bad for you. Paige and I would eat and excuse ourselves from the dinner table to go play, then spy on them, fantasizing about what it was like to be adults and "smoking" our crayons. We lived in the same houses our entire lives until we both went to Northwestern. When we were kids, everyone imagined that one day Paige and I would get married. But me liking dudes rewrote that script.

I look at my phone, and before I can type anything, I'm pleasantly shocked to see Paige has texted me first. Our childhood telepathy in full force, minus a weeklong delay.

Lunch? she asks.

Splunch. I correct her.

On Fridays, historically, we Splunch. That is, we splurge on lunch, monetarily and gluttonously. It's almost the weekend, and I want to drop thirty dollars on a bacon cheeseburger, fried mozzarella sticks and light beer with my best friend. Also, on weekends I refuse to use the word brunch. Paige hates "brunch" too. One of the many things she and I love about each other. It's "late breakfast."

An entire minute goes by after my text. Something is definitely wrong with her.

Paige responds. *A minute and a half later?!* Finally.

Sure, she flatly says. The worst text you can possibly receive.

MAX

Don't sound too excited.

PAIGE

I am. Splunch!!

MAX

Only two exclamation points?

Well, okay, see you at noon at

Waverly then . . . I guess?

We do this thing where we pretend we don't know how to end a text.

PAIGE

Great, okay, well, sounds good to me.

MAX

Yeah, me too. Awesome then.

PAIGE

Okay, cool.

MAX

Super cool, cool. Chill.

PAIGE
Well, bye for now.

MAX
Yep, signing off.

PAIGE
To infinity and beyond.

MAX
And you as well.

PAIGE
Likewise.

MAX
Adios x 2.

This could go on for another hour (it has before) but not today. I hear the determined CLICK CLICK CLICK of executive VP–status high heels heading my way, so I slip my phone into my damp khakis. My boss slides open my glass door without knocking or caring.

"My office in five?" she asks without requiring an answer. Asking me to meet her in her office when she can just tell me whatever business stuff of the day in my own office is a signature Janet Pierce Whitman power move. She's either in her late forties or early sixties, and her eyes always dart around the room when I'm talking, like she's too high-level and impatient to listen to a peasant like me.

"You got it," I say, trying to please her.

"Home court advantage," she says as she CLICKS away without shutting my door. Janet speaks in sports metaphors that I never understand.

Walking to her corner office always gives me PTSD. Once, not even off hours—in the middle of the day—I caught her watching lesbian soft-core porn on her computer. Neither one of us ever acknowledged it, and god willing, we never will. She's the head of HR so it's not like there's anyone in HR I could've told. She didn't seem to think much of it, closing her browser and seamlessly looking up at me without a shred of guilt, almost an act of defiance, but it's a moment that will haunt me to my grave.

On the other hand, I do enjoy saying hi to my only work friend, Janet's executive assistant, Stella, who like me is a late bloomer in life and hasn't settled into her true calling. She's a whip-smart bisexual twentysomething with the soul of George Burns. Unlike everyone else, Stella is never rattled by Janet's intensity. She's been dropping hints that she'd like to become a junior copywriter, and hopefully with her upcoming one-woman show (about growing up half-Chinese, half-Jewish and called *I, Genghis Cohen*), Stella will finally convince Janet and the creative directors to promote her.

Stella's cubicle is covered in colorful, nonsensical Post-it notes that we've left for each other through the years, pretending to be a married couple; like the last one I wrote to her, which reads, "BRB out buying diapers xo Gary." No matter what time of year, Stella is always cold. Physically, not emotionally. She's never not wearing a large blanket draped over her rail-thin, barely five-foot-tall body. Today she's wearing a custom-made, fuzzy lime-green blanket emblazoned with identical photos of her pug, Cate Blanchett.

From behind her computer, she peeps me approaching. "Don't steal shit," Stella jokes as I stride into Janet's office with a laugh and a wave.

At the entrance of Janet's sprawling digs, I stop. "Before I tee this up . . . two things," Janet says, scrolling on her computer, not looking at me. "Good email about the garden volunteering thingy. Whatever happened to just tossing some Campbell's soup cans and old mittens in a cardboard box and calling it a day?" She's like a female Don Draper.

I'm becoming more interested in gardening since I've started to miss my old childhood backyard with the weeping willow and spruce trees that my parents planted when I was a kid. New York is truly a concrete jungle; I've forgotten what the color green looks like. "It was either planting gardens or giving body massages to veterans," I say.

"Exaaactly," Janet says, not listening to me or my joke as she continues to type and scroll. I know she's not listening when she says, "Exaaactly." Sometimes she's *really* not listening when she says, "Of course so," which has no meaning at all.

There's a long pause as I wait. Another power move. So I quickly scan her giant office with envy and realize I actually would like to steal shit. She has an enormous flat-screen television, two luxurious sofas you could probably only buy with a licensed interior designer, and one of those asymmetrical wooden coffee tables that looks like the side of a redwood tree, topped with a massive hardcover book about exclusive golf courses around the world. The only thing I wouldn't want to steal are her vaguely Georgia O'Keeffe–style knockoff paintings on the walls, the kind you'd see in an art gallery in Laguna Beach or some coastal town. In addition to my chair and desk, all I have is a single monastic guest chair. Now I remember why she never wants to meet in my office.

Finally, Janet stops what she's doing and stands.

"Some layoffs may be coming," Janet says casually as she swings her invisible nine iron or whatever. She's always practicing her golf swing for god knows what. I think she plays in tournaments or something? At least, that's what I can tell by the dozen or so trophies she keeps on her desk in front of her. Not in a cabinet discreetly in the corner of her office. Not even on a shelf on the wall. On her desk. In front of her. Instead of family photos.

"Oh no, why? How many?" I ask, realizing that's one too many questions for her.

"No clue," she says with a perfect swing. Despite her faults, I do love her unwavering Minnesota accent. It makes me long for home in Illinois and the overextended midwestern vowels that Paige and I naturally refined in college.

I try to fill the silence. "Is this another big one?"

Now she practices her putt. I know this from playing mini golf as a kid.

"We're not sure yet how many people are getting the axe. Sorry. Laid off." She rolls her eyes at the more diplomatic term, swings, and pumps her fist at her imaginary hole in one. She says this so cavalierly, while my heart breaks for those people unaware of their near-future unemployment status. Good people who at this very minute are earnestly tapping away on their keyboards, artfully debating ideas, naively scheduling "important" meetings, dutifully replying to clients, carefully composing a commercial script or ambitiously storyboarding a presentation. None of these people know they're about to lose their job, their livelihood, their identity. And I'm the grim reaper who has to tell them.

"That really sucks," I say to Janet as if she's the only one who can stop laying off people.

"Yeah. Lotsa folks are gonna be down for the count, but at least it'll level the playing field." There it is. Two sports metaphors in one. She stuck the landing. Her imaginary golf club disappears, and she CLICK CLICK CLICKS back to her desk, signaling for me to leave. "Let's circle back and make sure we're aligned EOD."

I take her cue and immediately go. "Sounds good, thanks." Office zombies like us say "thanks" so many times a day, it's completely lost all meaning.

"Her flat-screen is in my pants. Is that bad?" I tell Stella on my way out. She snort-laughs and pulls her blanket tighter.

"Are you going to that birthday thing next week?" she asks.

"Another birthday thing?"

"It's like a preschool. Fuckin' birthday celebrations every other day."

"I'll be the chubby kid in the corner eating crayons," I say.

"Save me a burnt sienna," she says. We both let out tiny laughs.

I make my way back to my office, down the freakishly long and wide hallways where unexplained empty offices abound, the *Shining* twins undoubtedly lurking behind every highly designed corner. I check my phone for another dopamine hit of Paige. Zero texts. She hasn't responded since my last message. There is definitely something very seriously wrong with her. Now I'm getting worried.

Phrases to Avoid When Terminating an Employee

- "I'm, like, really, really, really sorry."

- "I know exactly how you feel."

- "Will you forgive me? Pweeeeeease?"

- "This place blows anyway."

- "If it helps, I liked you way better than Courtney in digital."

- "Don't be such a little crybaby."

- "Before you pack up, I'll give you ten minutes to raid the supply closet. GO!"

- "Here's an elaborate pie chart on all the reasons why you suck."

- "Are you mad at me?"

chapter

THREE

T HE WAVERLY DINER, OUR REGULAR SPLUNCH HAUNT IN the West Village, is yet another one of my favorite comfort food joints, with its burgundy vinyl booths and framed black-and-white photos of dead people on wood-paneled walls. It reminds me of places Paige and I used to go to as kids with our parents, with its endless menu (twelve kinds of waffles!) and prominent glass display of real homemade pies and cakes. Paige's dad introduced us to the decadent tradition of dipping crispy, well-done bacon into maple syrup as my mom reminded us, "Keep your elbows off the table, Mabel."

This place is considered a "classic diner," but to me it's just a "normal restaurant." I'm sitting in a booth roomy enough for six. Most restaurants in Manhattan would never allow just two people to sit in a space like this, and that's why I'm a loyal customer.

A distracted server hovers over me.

"How goes?" She pretends to care, whipping a menu the size of a Toyota at me.

"I'm great! How are you?" We're both suspicious of my forced enthusiasm.

"Can I get you started with a drink?"

If we're doing Splunch correctly, we drink alcohol. But I'll wait for Paige before I decide how Splunchy we want Splunch.

"Just water for now, please."

"Bottled or tap?" she asks, annoyed, having been through this a thousand times. I think of adding more jokey water options to brighten the mood: pond, ocean, aquarium, holy . . . But her resting stink eye tells me to keep this exchange moving.

"Tap is fine," I say with a smile as she leaves with a frown.

Outside the diner window, I spot Paige and her purposeful walk approaching, and now for some reason I'm nervous. As she nears the entrance, I mentally highlight a list of possible reasons she hasn't been texting me like usual. Mad at me? No. Moving out of New York? No way. Taking a cell phone sabbatical? Let's go with that one.

Paige enters wearing a powder-blue T-shirt that reads "Sondheim," which only she can pull off. Her smart eyes, cute face and chaotically controlled curls haven't changed since we were kids. The only difference is her high school theater geek persona has transformed into cool urban hottie. I'd maybe make out with her if I weren't gay.

Paige spots me immediately and flashes a faux awkward grimace that makes me laugh. We almost never say hello or goodbye to each other. God forbid we should ever hug. Now that I think of it, I'm not much of a hugger with anyone. Hardest of passes.

"I'm starving," Paige says, gliding into the seat across from me.

I study her. Is she glowing? For some reason her face looks like a gold brick—shiny but perfectly polished. She doesn't look harried or sweaty or ashy or generally gray the way most New

Yorkers do in the summer and also every season. There's an air of content around her. She seems . . . happy?

"So, tell me why we haven't seen each other in weeks. You respond to my texts with like one word now," I say, breaking the headline immediately.

Maybe it's not healthy relying on Paige this much, but there really hasn't been a day since we've been in New York when we haven't communicated with each other, let alone a few days. Waverly was the first New York diner we visited together. I remember it was after a grueling marathon of barhopping when Paige was going through her cocaine phase while dating an aloof, sorta-famous anchor on MSNBC. They dragged me to some of the seediest places imaginable, sniffing out random strangers for drugs. After a series of failed attempts on the Lower East Side, Paige forced us into a now-defunct leather-and-Levi's gay bar in Chelsea called Rawhide, a place I would've never otherwise stepped foot in. She met some guy in a tank top who reeked of poppers and old cologne and presented us with a tiny bag of white powder in the graffiti-stained bathroom. MSNBC Guy tried it and immediately threw up. He declared it must've been cut with baby powder, said his embarrassed apologies and hopped in a cab home. Paige and I were left wandering the West Village, cocaine-less and hungry when we found the Waverly Diner. At 3:00 a.m., over burgers and fries, Paige and I felt the sweet relief of having ditched MSNBC Guy and the effects of snorting a cleaning agent. We decided right there that the Waverly Diner would be our go-to place, our reminder of wild times together in New York, our tradition.

Before I have another chance to ask her where she's been, Paige looks up at the server, who's back and standing at our table. This time, her previously hardened mouth is smiling.

"Hi there. Have you had a chance to look at the menu?" our server asks with a gentle tone that she hadn't used on me. And now her stink eye is gone? Paige has this effect on people.

Instead of knowing what she wants, Paige has absolutely no idea what she wants even though we've been to this place a million times. It's the thing I love to hate to love about Paige. It's the reverse Meg Ryan in *When Harry Met Sally*. I disappear into my turtle shell when Paige does this. Here we go.

"Can you make an Aperol Spritz?" Paige starts. *Seriously?*

"We sure can," the server happily informs.

"Wait—is it sweet?" Paige follows up. There's always a follow-up.

"We can make it with a little more Aperol so it cuts into the sweetness and you're left with a little more bitterness," the server explains.

"Paige. It's a diner for chrissakes," I say. "Keep it simple."

"Shush," Paige says, fixated on the full bar. "Nah, maybe I'll do a wine. I'm deciding between a white or a rosé. How are your whites?"

"You can't have white before Labor Day," I joke, not even making sense. They both ignore me.

"We have a great Chardonnay." The server points to the menu Paige is holding as if Paige can't read. "The Sancerre is nice. I personally love the Riesling but we only sell that by the bottle."

I sigh. Loudly. Again—it's a diner.

Paige has always had an uncontrollable need to exhaust all options, and it doesn't end in restaurants. Every bar, bodega, clothing store and cupcake shop, there's Paige, exploring every imaginable outcome. Once or twice it's actually been helpful. Like on our spring break to Cancún junior year of college when Paige spent forty-five minutes with the Delta gate attendant going over every possible seat configuration. Somehow she managed to wear the attendant down until she just gave up and upgraded us to first class while our poor friends sat envious in coach. I'll give her that one.

Paige slowly winds down her food inquisition and acknowledges my existence. "It is Splunch." The server grins curiously at the word. Don't try to understand Splunch, lady.

"A bottle's too much. I have shit to do after this. Can I try the Sancerre?" Paige thinks it's perfectly okay to sample different wines, like an indecisive tween at a fro-yo shop.

"Of course!" The server is way too happy about this for some reason.

"And maybe I'll try the rosé too. Why not." And we're back to one.

The server chuckles, thinks Paige is cute and quirky, then turns to me as her smile fades and all the light in her eyes immediately drains. "And you?"

I'm no longer hungry or thirsty. Am I even alive? "I'll have a Heineken," I say.

"I'll get those started for you and be right back," she says, though the perky chirp in her voice is only directed at Paige, and goes.

"She's sweet," Paige says.

"Still hates me. You know this isn't your last meal. There will be one later tonight. And possibly another one tomorrow."

"Stop. It's Splunch. Lighten up. What are you getting?" Paige scans the menu.

"Same thing I always get. Bacon cheeseburger and mozzarella sticks."

"Yum. You wanna get the mac and cheese instead and we can share that and the fried chicken?" I might kill her.

"No, because I'm having the bacon cheeseburger and mozzarella sticks."

"Fine. Mr. Grump," Paige pouts. So I give in. I'll always give in to a pouty Paige. It brings us back to being little kids and me wanting to please my next-door neighbor.

"Fine, I'll share the mac and cheese, but I'm still getting the burger and sticks."

"Ew. 'Sticks.' Okay, good. And the fried chicken."

Welcome to Max & Paige®. We laugh at how ridiculous we must sound to the people around us. Or really anyone in the world.

The server returns with drinks. I can tell immediately that she's brought the wrong beer. "You had the Amstel, right?"

"Mm-hm," I lie, not wanting to create a whole thing. I'm a simple guy. I can roll with the Paige punches.

Paige sips her wine samplings and decides it's summer, therefore, rosé. While we *share* all of our food, Paige spends the majority of Splunch getting to know the server, something she often does. Paige is the most unselfconscious person I've ever known. One of my first memories of Paige is when we were standing in our adjoining front yards and she asked me, "Wanna see me spit?" We were five years old, and I hadn't previously been aware of spitting as an art form, though I was vaguely aware girls weren't supposed to spit. She didn't care. When her bodily fluid gracefully flung from her mouth as if in slow motion, clear across the yard, I knew this girl would be my best friend in perpetuity.

After our fried food feast, Paige suggests something out of the ordinary.

"Should we go to Big Gay Ice Cream?" she asks, hopeful.

"And skip the banana split here?" I say. Waverly banana

splits at Splunch are a tradition. We must eat until we're physically ill.

"C'mon, Gay Best Friend. Big Gay Ice Cream is right down the street. I know it's touristy, but doesn't that sound good right now?"

"Ice cream is already big and gay. Like Christmas. Just get something here."

"Fine. Sheesh," Paige says, defeated, signaling for the server. She won Splunch lunch. I win Splunch dessert.

While I eat my banana split, Paige still samples ice cream flavors, deciding which one is the least fattening, which I'm fine with because I'm nestled in peak euphoria of my drug of choice: chocolate sauce. Greg actively hated chocolate, so when we lived together, I would never have it. Paige ends up ordering nothing and eating half of mine.

As we're scooping ice cream into our face holes and chatting, I realize we've been having so much fun that I've completely forgotten to follow up on the main thing that I asked her.

"So, what's going on? Why aren't you being normal these days?"

And then Paige tells me something I wasn't expecting to hear from her for at least another one to two billion years.

Types of People Paige Has Dated

- Influencer Wannabes
- Hot Nerds with Glasses
- Finance Brahs
- The Unshowered
- Maybe Lesbians
- Connecticut Commuters
- Weird Beards
- Astoria Actors (Actorias)
- Old Rockers with Faded Tattoos
- Vaguely European Accents
- He's Not Jewish?
- Upper East Side Hotel Doormen
- Shorties with Muscles
- He's Not Gay?
- Chuckle Chubbies (overweight stand-up comics)

chapter

FOUR

'M ENGAGED!" PAIGE SAYS. SHE REVEALS A SNAZZY DIAMOND
ring on her finger, which she had hidden this whole time and
I was too focused on eating to notice.

"What?!" I say with my mouth full of chocolate deliciousness.

"I haven't been texting because I wanted to tell you in person."

I try to swallow. This explains her happy, glowy face.

I stare at Paige while trying to compute her saying the words
"I'm engaged." Here, let me try again. Hang on a sec. Almost
there. One more second. Okay, nope. Does not compute. I'm
the romantic one who was supposed to get married first. Not
Paige.

"Hmmm," she says. "That's so weird because I thought my
gay best friend of all time would be a little more excited."

Plugging the last of the strawberry ice cream in my mouth,
I manage, "No, yeah, that's incredible!" I glance at the older guy
with crazy hair sitting alone in a booth across from us, drinking
a cup of black coffee and chomping down on crispy bacon. I

think, *That's me in thirty years*. Friendless. Husbandless. Endless weekdays of eating strips of burnt pork by myself.

Then just to clarify, I ask Paige, "To Austin?"

"Of course to Austin!"

"Just making sure. That's great! I like him. He has a good laugh."

"He does have a good laugh."

"So . . . when?"

"He asked me last Friday."

"No, I mean when is the wedding? Do you have a date?"

"Labor Day weekend."

"*This* Labor Day weekend? Like, in three months?"

Paige nods, excited. "I figured we should have it sooner than later so I don't change my mind."

"Smart. Are you having an engagement party?"

"In two weeks," Paige says. I can't believe this.

"How did he ask you?"

"We were staying at his cousin's place in the Hamptons, and on our last night he asked if I wanted to go to the beach before sunset. So we get there and in the middle of the sand is this gorgeous table made up with roses and like ten thousand candles. He had someone from his restaurant preparing and serving us his most popular dishes. When he showed me the customized menu, at the bottom under 'Dessert' it said, 'Will you marry me?'"

"Awww. Sounds very *The Bachelor*."

I realize I'd kind of expected this from Austin when Paige first introduced us about a year ago. Greg and I were in the midst of breaking up when Paige and Austin invited me to be their third wheel at the soft open for Austin's restaurant, Zebra (his favorite animal). Austin had been an up-and-coming chef at various trendy restaurants and was now opening his first. When I met Austin, with his wavy hair, large features and husband-material face, I wanted Paige to romance him but I also knew she was always too wishy-washy about guys and not exactly the settling-down type.

Molecular gastronomy isn't exactly my thing, so I didn't have a clue what I was eating. Octopus croquette with pickled ginger, Parmesan, and seven other things I've never heard of? Sure. Why not. I took pictures of everything and sent them to my parents. It was actually delicious, and after twelve courses, I didn't want to eat anything for an entire week. I didn't realize who all the famous people in attendance were that night until Paige rattled off the boldface names. There was a palpable buzz and energy swirling around the ornate but cozy zebra-themed room with red booths and a roaring fireplace, while the best classic rock pumped through the sound system. I did recognize a graying David Byrne from my love of Talking Heads in college, which was extremely cool.

When Austin was done cooking, the three of us huddled at our VIP chef's counter and gorged on six varieties of desserts until we exploded. It was so crowded and loud, and we just listened and laughed as Austin told us the behind-the-scenes gossip about the severely thin Broadway diva who didn't eat any of her food or the famous hip-hop artist who brought his entourage and gave the entire kitchen staff edibles.

The razzle-dazzle of the event mixed with the "Test-Tube Tequila" was starting to make my head spin, and as we all became drunker and Paige and Austin cuddlier, I took my cue to leave. Austin was a perfect host and clearly a great guy, but I said goodbye to him for what I assumed was forever, usually never seeing Paige's dates more than once or twice. So I've been happy to see Austin and Paige together for the last year, and that Paige decided to make one of the good ones stick.

I just can't believe she waited an entire week to tell me this giant news. But I'll keep that thought to myself before she accuses me of making this about me.

"So yeah, last weekend we told Austin's whole family, and I honestly didn't want to tell anyone until I knew it was the right decision. You're the first person I've told. I haven't even told my sister."

"What about Nadine and Bruce and Ron and Laurie?"

"Okay, my mom and dad and stepparents were the first people. Austin actually asked them for permission. Isn't that so weird and old-timey? But none of my other friends know yet. You're my gay bestie. Of course I wanted to tell you first."

"Congrats. Seriously."

Paige smirks, skeptical of my sincerity. "Slightly closer to an appropriate response." She looks down at the remains of the banana split. I can tell something else is coming. I brace myself. Is she pregnant too?

"So you wanna be my like maid of honor or whatever?"

I look back at Paige, half expecting to be on a prank show where she's pranking me about all of this, but there is no prank show crew anywhere to be found, so I guess I'm not being pranked. She's dead serious. This is really happening.

"Like a best man?" I swallow, tearing up a little.

When we were in third grade, Paige and I decided to have a wedding in the woods behind our backyards. We were too young to know you needed to make it a whole legal thing. We thought if an older person said some words, then we said some words, then you were married. To us eight-year-olds, marriage was a way of saying we wanted to be together forever. To declare our love for each other as best friends. Paige's older sister Zoe stood between us and slowly said, "Mawwiage . . . Mawwiage is what bwings us togethah today. Have you . . . the wing?" We were reenacting the famous wedding scene from *The Princess Bride* as I imitated Prince Humperdinck and demanded, "Man and wife! Say 'man and wife'!" Then Zoe repeated, "Man and wife," as I put my hand on Paige's mouth and kissed my own hand. This childish act of imitating a movie marriage was the only way we knew how to stay bonded for life. I wonder if Austin knows Paige is already fake married.

"You can be my gay of honor," Paige says.

"I would be gay of honored," I say.

Paige lets out a tiny, thrilled squeak and then rolls her eyes. "Ugh, I'm already exhausted thinking about all the parties."

I can tell Paige is excited but trying to not to freak me out, knowing the idea of Big Important Parties with lots of people fills me with vague anxiety.

"You'll meet Austin's best man. His younger brother, Chasten," Paige says. "He's gay too."

"You mean Jason?" I ask, thinking she has a maraschino cherry in her mouth.

"Chasten. With a *C-H*," Paige says.

"His name is Chasten? That's not an actual name. No one can pronounce that or spell it," I say. "Chasten Benchley sounds like a dean at Harvard."

"I know. It's a lot." Paige shrugs.

"Do you think the wedding should be like a big formal thing in a synagogue with a hotel reception for five hundred people, or should we make it, you know, more *me* with just friends and family at like a scummy rock club in Brooklyn or something?"

I'm still overwhelmed thinking of all the wines Paige just

indecisively sampled, not yet ready to tackle her impending wedding indecisions.

"Let's—you could . . . I don't know. We'll figure it out," I say, scratching my two-week chin stubble.

"Ohmigod, I have to go. I'm recording this song for a dumb dog food commersh." While Paige waits on her big Broadway break writing smash-hit musicals, she writes and produces music for commercials at a recording studio, which keeps her well paid.

"Me too. I have a ton of work to do right now. Oh wow, I am so stressed. Argh!" We both laugh, knowing this isn't true. It's almost never true. My job is like talking about watching paint dry. I envy Paige's creative prowess.

We leave the Waverly, and suddenly the concept of time now feels like it can be boiled down into two distinct historical periods: before Paige announced she's getting married, and after Paige announced she's getting married. Nothing will ever be the same.

Then Paige says the phrase that New Yorkers say to each other on a daily basis.

"Okay, I'm going this way."

"I'm headed that way," I say.

Despite this life-changing day celebrating Paige, we still don't hug. That's so not us. We just walk in opposite directions. "Text you later!" she yells.

Then it finally hits me for real.

"Holy shit!" I yell back at her down the street. "You're getting straight married!" Paige does the Beyoncé ring wave motion and laughs as she disappears into the subway.

I walk west down Christopher Street alone.

Possible First Sentences for My Best Man Speech

- Ladies and gentlemen, I'm Max Moody and I'd like to propose a toast.
- I'm Max Moody, Paige's best friend. And this whole thing is fucking bullshit.
- *Webster's Dictionary* defines "marriage" as the state of being united as spouses in a *consensual* and contractual relationship recognized by law.
- According to Abraham Lincoln, marriage is neither heaven nor hell, it is simply purgatory.
- As the great Oprah once said, love is a great baked potato and someone to share it with.
- I'm not losing a best friend. I'm gaining separation anxiety.
- I'd like to raise a glass to Austin and Paige, who remind me of a young Charles Manson and Squeaky Fromme.
- I'm just going to ask the question that's on everyone's mind: Do half of all marriages really end in divorce?
- To my dear, dear, dear friend Paige: How are you getting married before me? (Pause for awkward silence. Keep pausing. Pause until it's super uncomfortable.)

chapter

FIVE

PAIGE TELLING ME SHE'S ENGAGED REMINDS ME OF THE summer before college when I met her for Chinese food at Little Szechuan one rainy night to confess that my parents were going through a rough patch and briefly separated (she knew), and Paige shared that her parents were also going through a rough patch but were definitely getting a divorce (I knew). Those bombshells were something that brought us closer together forever. But Paige telling me she's getting married? Somehow this news feels like it's permanently tearing us apart.

I'm trying to escalate my excitement, but if I'm being honest, Paige isn't supposed to get married before me. I'm the one who dreamed of marrying dudes in high school when I couldn't even dare come out for fear of rejection by my friends and family. It was me who spent years completely repressed, watching everyone around me hook up, have sex and fall in and out of relationships, while I barely registered that those were even options for me. I'm the one who finally had the guts to start dating after college and come out to my family. It was me who dated around in Chicago, then moved to New York upon Paige's encouragement, met a decent guy (through Paige) and thought it was forever, only to get dumped a few years later. I'm the one who spends my days not trusting guys and living in a fog of heartbreak. I'm the one who saved a copy of the *New York Times* with the headline screaming they made gay marriage legal, hoping to one day have it framed and hung in my living room but never really getting around to it.

Before Paige met Austin, she moved through types of men as if she were deciding on what kind of wine to drink at Splunch. I'm not bitter though. We all change.

As I saunter down what was once considered the gayest street in the entire world, buzzed on Amstel and sugar, browsing the old-school gay bars and leather shops, I'm reminded of how being gay is not really my forte. Oh, I like guys *that way*, but I'm not really the kind of gay you're expecting. Anyone who knows me will agree that I'm not a professional gay and should have my gay card taken away by the gay police. I love morose eighties college rock and hate Britney Spears. I use my Brooklyn Botanic Garden membership more than my gym membership. I've seen half an episode of *RuPaul's Drag Race*. And I'm really not a fan of going to Pride parades. Not because I'm not, you know, proud or whatever, but because I'm deathly uncomfortable in noisy, large crowds.

Sometimes I think I'm still single because other gays don't know what kind of gay I am. I don't think I fit in anywhere since I'm not a jock, muscle guy, daddy, twink, bear, cub, otter, hyena, cobra, walrus or any other ridiculous label gays put on each other. (I made up those last three.) I'm a Max Moody. That should be enough for someone, right?

Sure, I'd had some brief flings before my one big relationship with Greg. Like sophomore year at Northwestern when I spotted Eddie that first time in the cafeteria plopping ranch dressing on his french fries, I thought he was the one. Not because of the ranch on the fries, which I love, but because of everything else. I couldn't get enough of his baseball-player build fitted perfectly under his Fall Out Boy concert T-shirt and his Zac Efron windswept hair circa High School Musical. He was perfect; it was as if I'd created him late one night from my 1980s desktop computer while thunder crashed outside. I also fell for him because he held up his can of Dr Pepper across the entire cafeteria to cheers me after I'd been staring at him for seventeen minutes. Paige introduced us and we drunkenly hooked up a lot but because I was still kind of repressed and ashamed of being gay, and Eddie wasn't out even though he was a theater major (wink), we pretended we were friends. We lost touch after graduation when he moved back home to Boston.

At twenty-five, Paige had moved to New York to chase her dream of writing music for Broadway and, after a few months, we realized we were neighbors for life, so she encouraged me to leave my hometown safety net for love and lust in Manhattan. When I'd arrived, Paige had a string of debatably eligible gays she wanted me to meet. But a straight girl's version of two compatible gay guys is typically different from a gay guy's version. Don't even get me started on the Racist Florist. Or the Agoraphobic Video Game Designer. Or the International DJ / Conspiracy Theorist / Hustler.

And of course, Paige was the one who coaxed me into talking to Greg one night at Splash, a water-themed bar/club that closed shortly after. He was the hot skinny ginger nerd standing alone in the corner nursing a Heineken, which is what I was drinking too. It was love at first sip. Or so I thought.

But while I was a gay on training wheels, still trying to find my balance, Greg seemed like a comfortably out gay on a racing bike careening around the Alps in the Tour de France. Where he had had real boyfriends, successful dates and *experience*, I was still living in a fantasy world and wondering what it would be like to kiss Maxwell Caulfield from *Grease 2*.

Greg and I lightly dated at first, while he was completing his residency program and I was an assistant in the HR department in the same ad agency as now, trying to figure out what I really wanted to do (still don't know). When Greg became a physician, we turned serious and moved in together. Those first years in New York I felt exhausted, not used to the rhythm of extreme urban living, not to mention sharing an apartment with another human adult.

Greg and I covered all the major milestone questions I'd dreamed about back when I was still clawing myself out of the closet.

"Can I call you sometime?" *Yes.*

"Want to go out on a second date?" *How about tomorrow?*

"So. Are we boyfriends?" *Of course.*

"What do you think about being monogamous?" *I'd love to.*

"Should we move in together?" *Finally.*

"Want to get married?" That one never came. I knew he wasn't ready—still sorting out his life as a doctor—so I waited.

Our relationship took a bad turn when Greg realized he was getting older (almost thirty-two!) and needed to dabble outside of us. He wanted to make up for all the time he'd lost studying and attending med school, so he started going out more, partying and dating younger guys. I was headed toward marriage, kids and the suburbs while Greg was spiraling in the opposite direction. After seven years together (the seven-year itch is real), he moved out and now I'm having an epically difficult time getting over our recent split. And by recent I mean one year and three months ago.

My deep Greg thoughts continue as I walk into some fancy-ass coffee shop in the West Village and order an espresso. One summer, after Greg learned I'd never traveled outside of the country, being the perfectly sheltered midwesterner that I am, we decided to go to Rome. Before that trip, I'd never regularly had any kind of caffeine, which I'd tried but never acquired the taste for. But something magical happened in Italy when we woke up that first morning and went to a local café, where I tipped that sweet brown nectar into my mouth. An addiction was born, and I've been drinking espresso ever since.

I take a seat on a revolving stool and note the list of other things Greg had turned me onto that I still drink, eat, watch or listen to is too painful to contemplate: late-night reruns of *Murder, She Wrote*, sunflowers, John Waters movies, pesto, whiskey sours and the Scissor Sisters' first album. Greg gave me all of these gifts that are now part of my DNA. Even now, this post-lunch tiny cup of caffeine obsession of mine has become so ingrained in my daily routine that I almost forget it's one of the many souvenirs I still hold on to from my relationship with Greg.

I slam the rest of my espresso and head back to the office. Feeling energized after a deadly quiet work afternoon, I decide to walk along the picture-perfect Hudson River Park into Chelsea as the golden summer sun sets. Now coming dangerously close to Greg's deluxe apartment, I resist the urge to text him, and find myself grabbing a solo dinner at our favorite restaurant,

Pepe Giallo. I can no longer determine whether I'm eating here because I like it or because it reminds me of us. After a heaping plate of rigatoni, it's almost 9:00 p.m. but I'm still not ready to go home. Between last night's encounter with Greg and now Paige's wedding news, I decide I need a cold drink.

With its long bar in the front and loungy room in the back that doubles as a performance space, Barracuda is a nearby hangout that was my favorite go-to bar when I first moved to New York. It's not pretentious and feels like any old friendly gay bar you'd find in Chicago or Cleveland. Paige and I dubbed it the 'Cudes.

It's crowded, but tonight somehow seems a little seedier than most nights. Usually, a drag show attracts at least three bachelorette parties in full force, but right now it's just a bunch of horny single guys cruising one another, turned on by the extreme heat of the summer night.

Three Dua Lipa remixes and two gin and tonics later, I spot a handsome guy chatting up three other equally handsome guys who hang on his every word and laugh at what he's saying like it's the funniest thing they've ever heard. Usually, I go for loners lingering in dark corners or gingers who look exactly like Greg, but for some reason, this guy who looks vaguely familiar has me intrigued. So I ignore him and order another gin and tonic.

After I squeeze a lime into my drink, spraying my face in the process, I look across the room and see the handsome guy smile at me. Then it hits me. Holy shit. It's Cutie in a Booth from the diner. This is the second time he's seen me being an idiot. I check for a chalkboard menu behind me, but this time he's really looking directly at me. Maybe I was wrong the first time. I smile back, grab a napkin and wipe lime juice off my chin. Next thing I know, the guy is standing right next to me.

"That's exactly what I need," he says to me, shouting over Megan Thee Stallion and motioning to the bartender, who nods and smirks like they know each other.

"Spraying lime into your eyes?" I say.

"Yes. Plus, a gin and tonic," he says, politely asking the bartender for one.

"How'd you know it was gin and tonic?" I ask.

"You don't seem like a vodka soda guy." He's right. How does he know me so well?

"Yeah, not bitter enough," I say. He laughs.

"Think I saw you last night," he says. I'm shocked he remembers. "I love a good diner." Is he for real?

"Oh, riiiiiight," I say, feigning recognition since my one hundred percent facial recognition usually freaks people out. If you waited on me at a Burger King in 2009, I would remember you. "Small world." What a dumb thing to say.

He pays for his drink and holds up his glass to cheers. "It's the only way to beat the humidity," he says, having intense, direct eye contact with me, which makes me go wobbly. This guy is magnetic.

"I can think of other ways to beat the humidity," I say, surprising myself at how simultaneously bold and cheesy I sound.

The sides of our hairy bare thighs under our shorts press against each other as we clink glasses, smile and simultaneously gulp our summer drinks. Oh, god. I'm drunk.

An hour later, after heavy flirting, we get to his place in Hell's Kitchen, and I'm relieved there's no doorman to judge us clearly having a one-night stand. How do I know this is a one-night stand? I honestly think that eighty-five percent of me going home with a stranger tonight is just to get back at Greg. The other forty-three percent is really feeling this guy. (I can't do math.)

Our hands have been massaging each other's hard-ons since we entered the tiny elevator of his building. I notice his forearms with just the right amount of dark hair. When we get to the top floor, we push through a metal exit door and stumble upstairs to the rooftop. We're now in plain sight of hundreds of surrounding apartments as he slides off my T-shirt and unbuttons my shorts. Oh, look, the entire theater district can see me in my ten-year-old underwear.

And, well, with the combination of Greg last night and now this guy, I'm a little too excited, because I finish in exactly one second. Through my boxers. It seems like all the city noise goes mute as the look on his face reads equal parts shock, disappointment and *what are you, fourteen?* And at the exact same time, we both notice an unmistakable bodily fluid has dripped from my boxers onto his shoe.

The effects of the alcohol immediately make me heavy because my head starts to pound after bending over to lift up my shorts.

"Uh, thanks?" he says.

"Do you want to—"

He picks up my shirt and hands it to me with a nervous laugh. "That's okay. I'm good."

"Great view," I say, looking around Manhattan's twinkling skyline. Anything to avoid what just happened.

He half nods, still wondering what's wrong with me.

Feeling bad that I let this guy down, I realize we never even exchanged names. Hell, we never even kissed. But I'm too mortified that I just ejaculated onto his brand-new Nike shoes and leave it at that. I awkwardly fist-bump him for some reason and bolt down twelve flights of stairs.

THE FOLLOWING MONDAY, WORK IS UNEVENTFUL SO I SPEND most of the day googling photos of plants and trees, preparing for Difference Day. Just as I'm contemplating leaving early for the day, I'm assaulted by an incoming work email written in all caps from Kelleigh, one of the office managers, telling us to !!!!!!!!!!!!MEET IN THE CLOUD ROOM AT 4PM!!!!!!!!!!!!!—a conference room where an actual puffy sculpture in the shape of a cloud hangs from the ceiling in a forced way of saying the room is for brainstorming. *Get it?* It's Chris L.'s birthday and we all "must" wish him a happy birthday, demands Kelleigh, who is very nice but her aggressive emails suggest otherwise. She also lives for office birthday parties, and I would not be surprised if she had actual pony rides.

Secretly knowing that jobs are on the chopping block and, who knows, maybe even mine, I make a point to be on time when 4:00 p.m. finally rolls around. The Cloud Room looks like a press junket for Shark Week. Kelleigh decorated the entire room in sharks: posters of great whites, paper plates and cups with little sharks, balloons in various colors of ocean blue, a shark piñata, and of course cupcakes with sharks on them. I guess Chris L., who last I checked was a grown adult man . . . likes sharks? The layoff rumor must be out because a few clumps of creatives I'd hired quietly gossip in closed-off circles. They all side-eye me and continue talking to each other as I roam, looking for Stella, who's nowhere in sight.

My search is interrupted as everyone lifelessly sings, *"Happy birthday to you. Happy birthday to you . . ."* As if the cupcakes weren't enough, Kelleigh unveils a giant sheet cake in the shape of a shark and presents it to a pained-looking Chris L. What was this budget? Maybe birthday parties are why we're having layoffs?

The birthday song is still going (it's always too slow) when Janet beckons me. I approach and she says in a low voice, "Check your email. Official kickoff in three weeks." My stomach flips. The layoffs are happening.

I grab two shark cupcakes and duck out before the birthday song is even close to finishing. Filled with dread, knowing I'm going to have to fire people in three weeks, I stop by Stella's desk to find her dead-eyed and scrolling on her computer. She's wearing a brown fleece blanket with a built-in hoodie that makes her look like baby Obi-Wan Kenobi.

"Saved a burnt sienna for you," I say and hand her a cupcake.

"I got stuck organizing fucking golf tournament travel for Janet. How was it? Why's it so effing cold in here?" Stella asks, peeling the wrapper off her sharkcake like it's the highlight of her week, because it is.

"People are starting to talk about the, uh, you-know-whats . . ." I reveal.

"The layoffs? Fuck," she says, worried, burying herself deep within her hoodie.

"You're fine. You're the head of HR's right-hand gal. Plus, she's about to promote you." I have no idea if that last part is true but I know Janet is thinking of making Stella a junior copywriter because I've suggested it a few times.

"You'd let me know, right?"

"Of course," I say, even though I'm just as scared for her job as I am for mine. We clink our shark cupcakes and take giant bites, our teeth covered in blue frosting, both knowing that something terrible is about to happen.

Paige Greendale

— *and* —

Austin Benchley

JOYFULLY INVITE YOU TO THEIR

Engagement Party

even though
Max Moody should've gotten married first
but whatever

HOSTED BY
THEODORE AND GAIL BENCHLEY

chapter
SIX

WAITING AT PENN STATION FOR THE TRAIN TO PAIGE'S engagement party in Sag Harbor, I remember I'd signed up for Scruff and immediately forgot about it. I already have one message even though my profile is still blank, so I tap the box and the guy's profile picture is . . . a meerkat standing on a log? Among the dozens of potential matches, I get a *meerkat standing on a log*. Not even a person. A small mongoose. Is "meerkat on a log" a sexual euphemism for something gross? I open the message and it simply reads: into tickling? So, to recap: a meerkat standing on a log asked me if I'm into tickling. In all lowercase. I'm more disturbed than when I accidentally click on violent porn, so I'm just gonna go ahead and toss my phone into a dumpster.

My favorite thing to do on trains, crowded or otherwise, is slip into a Smiths coma by putting on headphones and listening to their compilation album *Louder Than Bombs*. Every song, not to mention Morrissey's voice, perfectly matches the melancholy of staring out the window of a fast-moving train. If I'm lucky, I'll catch my contemplative reflection in the window, which gives the whole thing an extra-dramatic twinge. If only a single tear could slowly fall from my left eye. The only interruption I have is the train conductor announcing each stop in the most old-timey way: "Next stop . . . *Massapequa*! *Massapequa*, next stop!" Or my favorite: "Ronkonkoma! Next stop . . . *Ronkonko-maaaaaaa*!" They always stretch it out for added nostalgia.

During this time that I have to reflect on Morrissey's colorful (read: gray) words and my current situation, it's hard not to imagine how I ended up here. What is this suburban Chicago boy doing on the LIRR on his way to the Hamptons? It seems so surreal to me. I grew up in a humble middle-class town with nice houses and well-kept lawns, but the Hamptons is another planet. My dad is an adolescent psychoanalyst and my mom a journalist turned librarian, so we were comfortable, but nowhere near build-a-hundred-million-dollar-compound-with-a-helipad-on-a-private-beach comfortable. That's not even in the realm of my imagination. My childhood home is a modest split-level filled with tons of classic novels, a Brady-orange kitchen that hasn't been remodeled since the eighties and a small home office where my dad conducts his business of analyzing young minds. As teens, Paige and I used to spy outside my laundry room window to catch a glimpse of one of our high school peers who was a patient of my dad's. Luckily our high school was big enough so we often saw people from our class we didn't know, like the girl who was rumored to have had an abortion in seventh grade, or the stoner kid who got arrested for digging up graves at the local cemetery one night while he was flipping out on LSD. When I probed, my dad, always the professional, never once told me what my peers said.

I feel like I'm the only one on this train not in a group of people going to their summer shares, so in my mind, I'm pretending I'm on my way to my artist parents' Southampton beach estate, where we're having a private chef grill by the infinity pool with our lovely neighbors Billy Joel and Jay-Z. I had to slum it on the LIRR, I pretend to myself, since the helicopter was under repair, and also because I have *character*.

When I arrive at the train station, I grab an Uber, which turns out to be one of those "fun" ones covered in flashing LED Christmas lights, leopard-print everything, zany bumper stickers that say things like "You talkin' to me?" and a semi-impressive collection of vintage PEZ dispensers presumably superglued onto the rear dash. I'm desperately tuning out my very pleasant driver, who's telling me how Uber is his side hustle but his real job is managing porn stars: "Only women. Not men." Uh-huh.

When I arrive at 15 Tennyson Terrace, Sag Harbor, New York, Paige's future in-laws' holy-shit-huge house, we enter through the open gates and, thanks to my recent plant research for Difference Day, I notice the grounds are surrounded by twenty-foot walls of totemic hedge, known as privet, to keep riffraff like me out. As the driver pulls around the circular gravel driveway, I already feel exhausted and bedraggled. My Uber had literally everything you could possibly want except the one thing I needed: air-conditioning—and now I smell like a gym locker.

A preppy-looking, fresh-faced valet kid opens my car door and welcomes me.

"Here for the Benchley party?" He looks like he's sixteen years old, and I'm freaked out by how much younger and younger people are getting. It should be illegal for anyone younger than me to do professional things. It makes me uncomfortable watching NY1 and realizing I could've fathered the meteorologist. That's what almost being thirty-five does to a person.

"Yep!" I say a second before the valet starts to suspect I'm an imposter who's come to steal jewelry and fine wines.

"Right this way," my son the valet says as he points me in the obvious direction of a party where guests are welcomed through the double-door entrance, artfully covered in white and silver balloons. I thank him for his insightful directions (proud dad!) and head up the long pathway that's lit up like a runway at JFK.

As a joke, not expecting her to check her phone as the busy guest of honor at her own engagement party, I text Paige.

MAX

I'm here.

This party is all about me.

Out of habit, I wait a few moments and check my phone, hoping maybe Paige will respond. But nothing. Not even type bubbles appearing and disappearing.

As I approach the inviting yet expansive cedar-shingle home probably featured in several glossy architectural magazines, I can hear the party chatter and laughter of extremely wealthy people. It's a kind of high-pitched, rounded laughter that suggests you never have to stress out about money.

After completing my signature move of toweling off sweaty armpits with Kleenex in the all-white powder room, I enter the massive living room to find a costume party. I believe the theme is dress as your favorite WASP? All the men are wearing pastels with tiny lobsters, whales or sailboats on their pants. The women are in elegant cocktail party dresses that look like bright, flowered wallpaper. I quickly realize it's not Halloween and this is their standard uniform. This is a far cry from the people in my hometown who go out to dinner wearing *Looney Tunes* sweat-shirts from Kohl's.

"You cannot be sober at this thing." Eliza appears, shoving a flute of rosé champagne in my face. I'd prefer something stronger, but I'll take any alcohol right now, including vanilla extract or hairspray.

"Max!" Katie yells, following Eliza, as we all elbow bump hello. Besides me, Eliza and Katie are Paige's two best friends. They are both Brooklyn personified, and I love them. They met after Paige moved to New York ten years ago, and the three of them performed together pretty regularly in an all-girl rock band called Barbara and the Broccoli, which was like a cross between Hole and Haim, with Paige as their front woman and songwriter. They get the band back together once in a blue moon and are long overdue for a reunion.

"Eliza. Katie," I greet them in a mockingly formal way. And then: "Did you spike this?" I ask, holding out my glass of cham-pagne.

"Wishful thinking," Eliza says as I chug the champs.

"Let's see?" I ask Eliza to show off her painted nails, which are constantly revolving, super-detailed nail art that she has a team of ladies paint for her on special occasions after going to Tokyo once and becoming Japan's leading cultural ambassador. Tonight, her right hand is painted with the faces of young NSYNC, and her left hand is the present-day NSYNC. This is always ridiculously impressive and statement making. Although I'm not sure what NSYNC has to do with Paige getting married.

"When I want to leave, I can go"—Eliza puts up both hands and waves—"*Bye bye bye!*" Everyone laughs.

"Amazing. Thanks for rescuing me, by the way," I tell them.

"You saved *us*," Eliza says.

"I feel like I haven't seen you both in a while," I say.

"Between you and Austin, Paige has no time for us," Eliza says. "I don't know how she became the one to get married before all of us."

"Tell me about it," I say. "I see you're making waves as a business lady. Paige sent me that *Vulture* article," I tell Eliza, who is a full-time bohemian-chic fashion designer and somehow looks like all five Fleetwood Mac bandmates combined.

"It was just a blurb but I'll take it. We're opening our first brick-and-mortar soon," Eliza says.

"So modest," Katie says. "She's an empire."

The three of us pause to sip as we survey the crowd. "What's UP with all of these men in pink pants?" I ask.

"Salmon," Eliza says, correcting me with an eye roll suggesting she hates them too.

"It's like a tiny lobster convention," I say.

"Everyone looks slightly inbred and most definitely inebriated," Katie fires off.

"Inebriated Inbreds. *That's* what we should've named our band," says Eliza.

"It's a live-action *Preppy Handbook*," Katie adds.

"Paige is gonna upset their gene pool," I say.

"Have you seen her? We haven't even talked to her yet."

Across the room there's a young pretty woman wearing a gauzy, summery dress thing, like she's in soft focus, holding court with three older men with Bernie Madoff hair who look like they run various banks. I have to blink twice to realize the gauzy woman is Paige. Before I can say anything, Katie and Eliza have already left me high and dry to do shots at the bar with their boyfriends.

"There she is," I say to no one.

"Maaax!" Paige spots me and yells from across the room, her voice equally loud and husky, like Miley Cyrus after a five-day bender. With a huge inviting smile, she motions me toward her and the Madoffs.

I slink past the fireplace that's bigger than my bathroom, and I'm greeted by Paige—"You made it!"—and three aggressive hands extending at me. If this were a 3D movie, you would gasp and flinch at the three-armed Madoff beast. They're all holding identical glasses of scotch, neat, probably the only thing in the entire world I would ever have in common with them. I do like the brown liquor, and wish I had some right about now.

"Peter Close. Nice to meet you." My hands are pretty normal-sized, but one gets completely lost in Peter Close's giant rib eye of a hand as he shakes mine. Hard. *Jesus.*

"Nice meeting you. Hunter Close," the middle hand says. I notice his too-wide silk tie has what looks like little gin and tonic emojis dotted all over it. I immediately want to send his tie to rehab.

"Great to meet you. Glenn Close." The third one shakes my hand and—wait, did he just say his name is *Glenn Close*? Also, everyone here is introducing themselves by their first *and* last names, as if those mean anything to me. This is intense.

"Hi. I'm Max." I don't play along with the last name game.

But Paige does. "Guys, this is Max Moody, my very, very, very best, best, best friend from Chicago." She points to the Three Amigos. "These are Austin's uncles. His mother's brothers."

"We're all . . . very . . . *Close*," Glenn says with the worst comic timing I've ever heard in my life, clearly having done this exact "joke" a bazillion times before. How he and his brothers all manage to genuinely laugh at their age-old scripted family name pun is beyond me. I wait for the real punch line but nothing follows.

"Finance?" the first one asks me as if we're on some kind of one-word secret code. I'd say he's the alpha one, but somehow they're all alpha?

"Human resources," I say, praying I don't have to elaborate on my job.

"We're hedge fund guys." Glenn, um, Close points to himself and then his two brothers like he's choosing teammates on his junior high flag football team. I want to tell them I don't even remotely understand what a hedge fund is, but I feel like if I did, they'd immediately hunt me down for sport.

"Close Associates." One of them hands me his business card for reasons that I will never understand. It inexplicably reads:

CLOSE ASSOCIATES
We put the fun in hedge fund.

I look on the back for a tiny pink whale but thankfully there is none.

"Okay. Golf time," says the middle one.

"PGA tourney's on. You got ESPN in this dump?" the right one asks his brother as they all laugh very loudly and head toward the living room in unison. And just like that, the three-headed scotch monster in a fleece vest is gone.

"Aren't they great? So old-school," Paige says, trying to soften the bizarre triple-uncle encounter.

"They're a little Brett Kavanaugh–y," I say.

"Shhh! Stop." Paige smiles politely, not wanting to get in trouble with her future family. But then she can't help herself.

"They look like a steakhouse come to life." I let out a guttural laugh, the kind that only Paige can conjure.

"*Glenn Close?*"

"Insane, right?" She shakes her head, agreeing the absurdity of this guy's-guy sharing a name with the famous actress is too much. I need her to make more jokes but—

"There he is!" Paige says as Austin makes his appearance, giving Paige a luscious smooch on the lips.

"Hey, Max! You good?" he asks me, going in for a meaty bear hug. He does that thing you always hear Bill Clinton or Tom Cruise does where they have unwavering eye contact that makes you feel like the only person in the universe because . . . you *matter*. It feels good, admittedly. The last time I saw Austin was when he took Paige and me to a new tapas place where we each spent a thousand dollars on thirty small bites that left us starving.

"What's not to like?" I say, looking around the giant house and immediately regretting my stock response.

Right out of the gate, I'm trying hard not to be bitter about Austin stealing away my best friend, but he always makes it difficult. He's just too handsome and charming and fun. Seeing him in his element, I notice his WASPy features a little bit more than usual, but he still has the slight edge of a bad boy chef that Paige needs.

"This place is sick, right?" he says, reassuring me. "It's the Hamptons side of the family. My aunt and uncle had us all up here every summer. Now you guys can come too."

"Which room is mine?" I ask as Paige and Austin laugh. Invitations to Hamptons compounds are rare, and the longer I live in the city, the more I need to escape. I'll be their third wheel any day.

"Who needs refills?" Austin seamlessly grabs three more champagnes off a passing cater waiter's tray before we can answer, and hands them to us. He's the best host.

"Have you tried the mini empanadas? They're divine," Paige says in a half-mocking British accent that allows me a glimpse into her future self as an equally talented Hamptons hostess.

Paige grabs me and points to an older couple nibbling at the cheese table and sings, *"Summer cheeeeeeese, makes me feel fine . . ."* Austin makes a confused face but we don't have time to explain that Paige and I have had this inside competitive gag since we were kids, where we change the lyrics to Seals and Crofts's famous song "Summer Breeze" according to our surroundings. When we were kids, it was the song our parents played a lot at their dinner parties. Over the years it's gone from being funny to being dumb back to being kinda funny again. Paige wins this round.

"How's the restaurant?" I ask Austin, trying to include him.

"I'm finishing our fall menu, which is gonna be fantastic. Don't tell anyone, but the entire dinner will be served in nineties-themed plastic lunchboxes like Harry Potter and Ninja Turtles." He's immediately focused and in work mode. I'm in awe of his creative mind.

"That's amazing," I say in total seriousness.

"I'll get you tickets," he says.

"They're switching to selling tickets instead of making reservations," Paige adds.

"Like a Broadway show!" I say goofily, trying to connect their two loves.

"Exactly!" they say in unison. It was meant to be.

One of the cheese nibblers sneezes hard and loud three times fast, which catches everyone's eye. "*Summer sneeeeeeeze, makes me feel fine,*" I sing to Paige. Point for me.

"Good one," Austin says, already getting our dumb game without having it explained. He's quick.

Austin lovingly grabs Paige's forearm in a way that makes me envious. "Tell Max about the other thing," he says.

"Okay, this is super secret, but I'm up for a writing gig." Paige is giddy with excitement.

"Ever see *The Jerk*?" Austin asks. They're a well-oiled machine now.

"The Steve Martin movie? Are you kidding? Classic."

"Some producers I met at work are adapting it into a musical," Paige announces. "It's gonna have gospel, rock, disco . . . my dream project, basically," Paige says. "The movie costars my goddess of all time, Bernadette Peters."

"Paige is pitching them her take," Austin says, seamlessly nailing her industry's lingo.

"Steve Martin is writing the book," Paige adds.

I'm getting chills. "Paige. For real? That's incredible. This is what we always used to do," I remind her.

Austin smiles through his light confusion. He may be Paige's main man who now gets all of her breaking news, but he can't cut through our thirty years of friendship.

Paige illuminates him. "When Max and I were little, I had this tiny stage thing in my bedroom. It was more like a big step." We both laugh at this.

"We used to act out plays and—" I continue the story.

"Max would make up stories and I would write dumb little original songs and perform them," Paige says, finishing my sentence.

"Your songs were good!" I start belting out Paige's childhood song. "*Sand, sand, sand, sifting through the hourglasses . . .*"

"No, it was '*sand, SAND, sand*.' Emphasis on the second 'sand.'"

"Are you sure?" I genuinely ask, noticing Austin has an amused look on his face. I can't believe they're giving me this much time at their own engagement party. This moment is also awakening a feeling I haven't been able to put my finger on for a while. I used to have creative instincts when I was a kid. My torturous closeted years stamped all of that out, and somewhere I became this husk of a person with an empty job and nothing to show for it.

"Feel free to interrupt us at any point," I say, encouraging Austin.

He totally gets and loves it. "No, this is fascinating. Please continue." We all laugh.

"Seriously though, that is so exci—"

Suddenly, all the air is taken out of the room as everyone turns to the door to see something. Some*one*.

This person, this man, this unmistakably handsome guy enters the party like he's walking onto a yacht, like he's in his own badass slow-motion movie scene in his head, set to the beginning riffs of "Magic Man" by Heart. Familial looks fill Paige and Austin's eyes as this confident guy strides toward us.

"Chasten!" Paige waves him over.

"That's my brother. You'll love him," Austin tells me.

My face flushes, my body tenses, and I gulp my champagne as I come face-to-face with my awkward one-night stand.

Paige's Maid of Honor Speech, Which I Cowrote, for Her Mom's Third Wedding

Hi, everybody. Thank you all for joining us here tonight at the magical Marriott Lincolnshire, Banquet Room C. My name is Paige and I never thought my mom would find love and I would be standing here giving a speech at her wedding for the third time. I guess my mom really wanted to get married three times before any of her kids got married once. This wedding speech is actually the same one I give at all of my mom's weddings. All I do is change the groom's name. Mom, your weddings are like iPhones. There's a new one every year and a half. My mom has been married so many times, on a scale of one to ten, she's a Liz Taylor. My mom didn't vow to never marry until gay marriage was legal. She vowed to keep getting married over and over again until gay marriage was legal.

When I first met Ron, little did I know that I'd be adding another stepfather. I have so many stepdads, I can make a staircase. Ron has been married just as many times as my mom, so together their marriage licenses have been rebooted more than Star Wars. Mom, cover your ears for this one: I heard Ron is really into sixty-nining. Sixty-nine weddings. And, Breelyn, I just want to welcome you to our family and say how nice it is to have you as my twenty-fourth stepsister.

In all seriousness, Mom and Ron, I'd like to wish you both love, light, laughter and a long, healthy, happy marriage. Mom, see you at the next one.

chapter

SEVEN

CHASTEN AND PAIGE HUG TIGHT AND SWING BACK AND forth like long-lost reunited pals, which, by the by, Paige and I have never even come close to doing in all the years we've been friends. Next, Chasten hugs it out with Austin in one of the tightest bro embraces of all time as Chasten whispers something in Austin's ear that makes Austin laugh hysterically. And then Chasten whispers something else in Austin's other ear that no one can hear, which makes Austin immediately tear up. They hold each other even tighter, and that goes on for an even longer, even more uncomfortable period of time as Paige smiles at me, signaling how she thinks this is all so thoughtful and special and·heartwarming. I've never seen a smile so big on Paige's face.

"Let me guess." Chasten spins Paige around to examine her lady clothes. Fashion? I guess it's called? "Peter Pilotto."

"Nope." Paige grins like she has a secret she can't wait to tell.

"Don't say Erdem." Paige shakes her head. "Roksanda?" He

guesses again. At this point I have no idea what they're even talking about.

"Zara. Fifty-seven bucks," Paige says. Now they're just making shit up. I look to Austin for some straight-guy empathy, but he just raises his eyebrows and gives me a hard-to-read smile.

"Fuck you. I love you," Chasten zings back at Paige. Well, which is it?

"Should you maybe help me with my wedding gown?" Paige asks Chasten. Somehow I'm a little hurt by this even though I barely know what a gown is and I would be no help to Paige.

"Of course. On the way over here, I was thinking a strapless Miu Miu with like a Minkoff shoe, but now that I see you're building an avant-garde look, I'm thinking McCartney, but we'll talk. And you'll need bachelorette, shower and post–wedding reception outfits. I just saw this really great off-the-shoulder Proenza Schouler number you'd crush." Okay, I can't compete with this guy.

As Paige and Chasten speak whatever foreign language this is, I'm awkwardly standing here with an empty drink, freaking out because I don't know what to do with my hands. I'm also not sure if I'm supposed to admit to everyone that we . . . know each other.

My uncomfortable shifting finally bleeds into their conversation and naturally starts to make them uncomfortable, so they both turn to me as I stare at them, wide-eyed and confused. "Sorry. Hi, I'm Chasten, Austin's younger brother." He either doesn't recognize me out of context or wants to pretend we never met, but at least he didn't feel compelled to thrust his first and last name onto me like all of his relatives.

"Nice to smeet you," I say, accidentally caught between "see" and "meet." "I'm Max. And this is head-to-toe J.Crew," I deadpan, pointing to my suit. He laughs.

"My GBF," Paige chimes in. Always with the gay best friend.

"Hi, GBF. I've heard so many great things about you from Paige," he says, looking right at me. Now I remember from that night we met that he's also very good at the unwavering eye contact thing. It must be a Benchley brother signature move. "I'm looking forward to getting to know you. Fellow best man and all." I really can't tell if he remembers me or not, and I don't want to say the wrong thing in front of Paige and Austin.

So I say, "That's right. You're Austin's best man, I hear."

"I am. It's gonna be a blast putting this wedding together," he says, startling me. I hadn't thought of that. I glance at Paige, and she looks at me and grimaces, like she's breaking the news for the first time. I'm cohead of the wedding planning committee. I make a mental note to google "best man / maid of honor duties" later.

"It's totally caj. We'll all help. It'll be a group effort," Paige says. "My stepmom is going to want in too." After Paige's parents divorced, they each married and remarried two more times. My parents, who were best friends with hers, couldn't even keep up. It was taxing enough to make Paige never want to get married, which explains why she's had so many boyfriends until now. She's had a rough time through all the stepparents, but now her mom and dad, older and wiser, have settled into their current marriages, and Paige is less stressed because of it.

Eyeing Chasten, I notice he's in one of those designer suits that's cropped perfectly, slightly revealing his bare ankles, with each muscle of his calves, arms and chest popping. Somehow, I managed to get through ten years of being a gay man in New York without really caring about clothes, but I'm not completely fashion blind. I do know it's über-trendy for guys to have a tight, tailored suit, and I want to say his is like Tom Ford or Thom

Browne or Tommy Hilfiger or one of the Toms, but all I know is that I could never pull it off. I skew more Tommy Bahama.

Keeping an eye on Chasten as he chats with Paige, I do the gay math: I'm figuring he probably gets his hair cut every week and a half, plus he goes to the gym six days a week, and multiply his profile on three different gay dating apps, that equals exactly one thousand percent gayer than me.

His hair. I could create a PowerPoint presentation on Chasten's hair. It's that deep side part with what looks like a complicated tower of Cool Whip on top. It was a little messier the night we officially met.

Austin politely gets sidetracked by a few old pals, and as Chasten and Paige yap intimately with each other, I notice Chasten's posture is better than any human being I've ever seen. He's the next rung on the evolution of gay man.

Chasten continues mesmerizing Paige with his bons mots, and I think he can't perform like this—be this ON—all the time. I need to take notes on his social skills. Paige is turning red from all the flattery but loving it.

Chasten does that point-and-wave motion to various family members, friends and admirers like a coiffed politician as a swarm of well-dressed older women all wearing identical diamond earrings and gold Rolexes, presumably Austin's aunts, descend upon us. Chasten introduces us and the women all have names like Binny, Poppy, Topsy and Turvey, and I'm getting light-headed, so I vanish like a hangry ghost to let Paige bond with her future in-laws while I hit up the appetizer table.

On my way there, I steal my third champagne off another tray from a roving cater waiter who doesn't acknowledge me, and gulp as I dodge and weave through the massive living rooms full of happy party people.

As Paige's best man (that's going to take a minute to get used to), I'm wondering how much longer I'm contractually obligated to stay here. I love Paige, and Austin is supercool, but they're hosting and ignoring me now, as they should, and I don't see Eliza and Katie anywhere. Plus, I'm really not sure what to do about Chasten.

The invite said just cocktails and appetizers, so I'm going to have to stuff my face with miniature food before I leave. Turns out, WASPs know how to eat, because the food tables are incredible. I'm eyeing the impressive spread of mini everything: mini tacos, mini quiches, mini cheeseburgers. There's an inordinate amount of chocolate bars. One of Austin's aunts, Poppy, if I remember correctly, is currently loading her plate with a half dozen sliders.

"Bride or groom?" the aunt asks me.

"Neither. I'm a friend of the bride," I say, which provokes a high-pitched, hysterical laugh that I did not see coming. It's trailed by an equally high-pitched sigh.

"I'll have to remember that one. I'm Poppy Close," she confirms, having no recollection of just meeting me five seconds ago, which is normal for me. Must be, um, Glenn Close's wife? She looks like a tan, young Betty White after eighteen holes of golf.

"Max." I smile and shake her hand. "Moody," I follow up, trying the last name thing.

"What do you do, Max?" she asks.

I don't want to disappoint another person I meet with tales from the HR department, plus I'm now a tad drunk, so I fib and say, "I'm in . . . landscape design." I whip that one out of my ass since I'd been staring at plants and trees all week at work. Although, the profession has always intrigued me. It was either that or aspiring blacksmith.

Her eyes light up. "I've been looking for someone to redesign our Park Avenue terrace!" Oh no. What did I just do? She unsnaps her tiny purse thing and takes out her bejeweled cell phone with the ease of an older woman who doesn't really know how to work a cell phone or a tiny purse thing. "Can you put your phone number in there? I don't even know how to work that thing."

I hesitate for a second about continuing my landscape charade before grabbing her phone and entering my name and phone number in her Notes app. As I hand her phone back and am about to pop the first course of my dinner into my mouth, I hear—

"Aunt Poppy." It's Chasten. They kiss hello as Aunt Poppy introduces me to her nephew.

"We've met," I say, thinking of the *first* night we met.

"Yeah, Austin *just* introduced us. Max is Paige's best friend. Her GBF."

"GBF?" Poppy asks.

"Gay best friend," Chasten and I say a second apart.

"Oh, that's clever." Poppy smiles. I'm still unclear if Chasten remembers me. Maybe he's closeted? That seems impossible with a name like Chasten.

"You live in the city?" Chasten asks me while holding a fresh flute of champs and with lips so full and perfect they're unrelatable. It's a legitimate question since he never asked me that night. Aunt Poppy watches us, now tossing a handful of cashews into her mouth like she's a sentient popcorn-eating GIF.

"Yeah, I'm in the West Village," I say with a mouth full of slider. "How 'bout you?" I ask, playing along.

"I'm in HK."

For a split second, I have no idea what HK stands for, but then I remember that's what people call Hell's Kitchen now. Through the years, New York City gays have gone from the

West Village up to Chelsea and have now taken over the neighborhood north of that in Hell's Kitchen, migrating like horny penguins. But I can't let him get away with the abbreviation of this neighborhood.

"Hong Kong?" I ask jokingly. Aunt Poppy laughs.

"Hell's Kitchen," he says with a slight laugh. "And you grew up next to Paige in Illinois?" He makes the name Illinois sound insulting.

"That's right. Where are you from?"

"New Canaan. Connecticut. Born and raised." He grabs a stick of chicken satay and politely takes a bite while I gleefully shove another succulent slider into my face, pulling the melted cheese from the burger with my teeth like a wild animal.

"Oh, to be single and gay in your thirties in the big city," Aunt Poppy says, admiring us. "You're both so handsome." Is she suggesting we'd make a good couple?

Aunt Poppy softly touches my wrist and says, "I'll be in touch about my terrace." She gives me a conspiratorial grin, floats past an ice sculpture of a giant wedding ring and disappears into the party.

"Excited for the wedding?" Chasten asks.

"Yeah, should be a blast," I say, dipping my third slider into a fancy bowl of dijonnaise. Okay, if he's not going to say anything, I will. "Do you remember meeting at Barracuda?" I ask.

He clears his throat. "Yeah, that night was kind of a drunken mistake." He does remember. "And it would probably be very chill of us if we didn't mention it to Paige or my brother or anyone else right now." Maybe he is closeted? But all that fashion knowledge.

"Oh. Totally. I'm so chill with that," I say as casually as possible. "Plus, I'm pretty much in a relationship anyway so . . ."

He processes this. "I just think we shouldn't take away the spotlight on Paige and Austin, ya know?"

"Totally." Maybe he isn't closeted.

"Are you coming to brunch with me and Paige tomorrow?" he asks, cruising past the entire topic completely.

"Brunch?" *You mean late breakfast?* I think. "No, Paige didn't say anything about brunch."

"Oh, she invited me to start planning everything. Bachelorette party. Bridal shower . . ." he says. Right. I keep forgetting there are all those other things. Tonight already feels like an entire wedding to me.

Chasten whips out his phone quicker than I've ever seen anyone handle a piece of technology and gets lost in a text. I look into the crowd to spot Paige. I wonder if I should ask her if she'd like me at her and Chasten's late breakfast, but she's busy, surrounded by pearls and seersucker.

"Maybe she forgot to mention it. That's very Paige," I say, trying to reinsert my decades of knowing her.

"I'm assuming you'd want to help plan the wedding?" He looks me up and down again, at my old suit, probably thinking Paige needs a gay best friend upgrade. My competitive side kicks in.

"Of course. Where should we meet?" I ask.

"We're meeting tomorrow at this fun place in Williamsburg," he offers magnanimously.

"I'll be there." I pick up a mini tiramisu and offer it to him.

"Already had one, thanks," he says. I shrug and eat his dessert.

Human League's "Don't You Want Me" comes on the high-end speaker system in the garden as I steal a glance at this guy, my best man rival, who I'm supposed to pretend I've never met, and I wonder what it would be like to actually make out with him.

SONGS BY THE SMITHS

I'D LIKE PLAYED AT PAIGE'S WEDDING THAT ALSO KINDA DESCRIBE A GAY MAN'S LIFE IN CHRONOLOGICAL ORDER IF YOU THINK ABOUT IT

"THE BOY WITH THE THORN IN HIS SIDE"

"GIRL AFRAID"

"HALF A PERSON"

"PANIC"

"PLEASE PLEASE PLEASE LET ME GET WHAT I WANT"

"HOW SOON IS NOW?"

"DEATH OF A DISCO DANCER"

"THIS CHARMING MAN"

"I WON'T SHARE YOU"

"THE QUEEN IS DEAD"

"CEMETERY GATES"

"GOLDEN LIGHTS"

chapter

EIGHT

'M ON THE MISERABLE SUBWAY AND I'M HORRIBLY LATE TO
late breakfast. Sorry. *Brunch*. Why Paige and Chasten decided
to meet in Brooklyn is a mystery since the three of us all live
in Manhattan. Not only are train schedules notoriously a mess
on the weekends but also I have no idea how to navigate Brooklyn because I'm don't-like-going-beyond-a-ten-block-radius-
from-my-place years old. I know this is not supporting all my
New York boroughs, but I couldn't tell you the difference between Fort Greene and Greenpoint other than one is a fort and
one is a point and they're both green.

Not only that, but Paige lives down the street from me in the
Village, so this really makes no sense. We love telling everyone
we were neighbors growing up, neighbors at Northwestern,
neighbors as adults, and we're cosmically neighbors for life. I
wonder if we'll get cemetery plots next to each other? Nothing
bonds two six-year-olds in suburbia forever like the first time
Paige and I set up a lemonade stand and realized no one came

since we lived at the end of a dead-end street. We drank so much lemonade that fateful Saturday and agreed to set up our small, failed business the first day of every summer going forward. Even if no one ever came.

I haven't had a chance to ask Paige how or why she didn't mention this midmorning meal with Chasten. Although I'm sure she didn't say that dreaded word. *Brunch with Chasten* sounds like a Hallmark Christmas movie I'd watch for ten seconds just to glimpse the hot guy named Chasten who moves back to his hometown in the country after being a high-powered generic "executive" in the city and now wears too much flannel while chopping wood in the middle of a movie set covered in fake snow.

Two hours after leaving my house, I find the frickin' restaurant, some see-and-be-seen place called Sunday in Brooklyn, which is a little on the nose if you ask me. Why not Wednesday in Cleveland or Monday in Sacramento. C'mon, Brooklynites, you're supposed to be ironic. As I approach the restaurant, I send Paige a text announcing I'm here as I'm now realizing she might not even know that I'm joining them.

My excruciating trip jumping the pond to Brooklyn is tempered when I enter the restaurant and smell bacon and maple syrup, hearing the soothing sounds of Joni Mitchell's "Help Me." I see Paige and Chasten sitting in a cozy corner table, almost finished with their Bloody Marys that they're sipping through colorful paper (yuck) straws. Paige looks refreshed and relaxed, and is laughing hysterically at something Chasten said. Chasten is dressed in a button-down short-sleeve shirt with short corduroy shorts that make him look like he just got off the bus from Coachella. Somehow he's pulling it off? Damn him.

"Oh my god. We HAVE to go later!" Paige drunk screams

at Chasten as I approach, covered in summer sweat, marinated in a torpid hangover and topped off with a light dust of subway grime.

"Where we going?" I ask as I fall into a seat next to Paige.

"You made it." Chasten seems surprised to see me. Or it's the vodka talking. Or neither.

"Finally. Did you get lost?" Paige asks.

"Maybe I could've planned to come to Brooklyn better if I'd known this was happening," I say, trying to make Paige feel guilty.

"I could've sworn I texted you about it. Sorry, I'm crazed with everything happening right now. Don't be mad. I probably assumed you didn't want to come because you hate Brooklyn."

"I don't *hate* Brooklyn. I just don't like *going* to Brooklyn," I say.

"Same diff," Paige says.

I actually like Brooklyn since Manhattan has become an overcrowded, unbearable playground for trillionaires. "Also, why are we in Brooklyn again?"

"I was originally supposed to meet Eliza and Katie but they bailed, so I asked Chasten. Then it turned into a wedding planning thing, so."

"Where do you *have* to go tonight?" I ask, then motion to the server for three more Bloody Marys. I need to catch up.

"Nice work," Paige says, referring to my slick ordering skills.

"Paige wants to go to drag karaoke bingo barbecue at the Metropolitan later." The words roll off Chasten's tongue like he's said this exact phrase a million times before. Meanwhile, a *drag karaoke bingo barbecue*? He lost me at "drag," "karaoke," "bingo" AND "barbecue." Fine, maybe not "barbecue."

"Sounds fun," I say as I scratch my nose.

"Max's nightmare," Paige says. She's my personal autocorrect.

"It is not." I scratch my chin. I'm really trying to play along here. I don't mind drag shows, but sometimes they feel like mandatory gay fun. Like, can't we all just go bowling, grab a burger and call it a night? Don't get me wrong—I'll go out for a gay drink once in a while at Gym Bar or an Eagle beer bust, hence my meet and greet with Chasten at Barracuda, but even those places feel forced. I'd much prefer to hit up a graffiti-stained underground hole-in-the-wall, listening to some freaky band on the Lower Lower Lower East Side. I'm guessing Paige is buddying up to Chasten right now because he's a new type of gay flavor that Paige can't seem to enjoy from me.

Staring at our menus, I can't help but notice Chasten's shirt is unbuttoned at the top just enough so you can make out his chiseled chest. Sure, he has defined pecs, but I'm alarmed by the fact that there isn't a single hair popping out anywhere. He's so smooth that I'm wondering if he shaves or if there's some sort of gay laser clinic he's not just a member of but also its president. Meanwhile, it's making me self-conscious since my hairy, misshapen body looks like a pear-shaped gorilla wearing a gorilla costume. I was too drunk to notice any of this the night we met.

Our server arrives with fresh Bloody Marys and we order various styles of eggs. Paige spends seventeen minutes asking precisely how the huevos rancheros are prepared. The server has Billie Eilish–green hair, multiple piercings, and a tattoo of a pot leaf on her inner wrist. When she leaves, I sing to Paige, "*Summer weeeeeeed. Makes me feel fine . . .*" Paige fist bumps me.

"What are you singing?" Chasten asks with a laugh and a whisper of jealousy.

"Nothing. It's this dumb thing he and I do," Paige replies.

Dumb thing? It's not a dumb thing. It's our thing that Paige just belittled to Chasten so we don't make him feel bad about trying to wedge his tower of hair into our lifelong friendship. I'm fake offended but I hide my frown in a long pull of my Bloody. My paper straw is already totally disintegrated and sticking to my fingers. Can we all agree we'd rather have normal straws? Cool, thanks.

"Okay. Paige's bachelorette party. Go." Chasten speeds past our inside joke routine and careens into our main topic of today's discussion. I sigh, knowing wedding shit's about to get real.

"Yay! I'm so excited. No baby T-shirts with the word 'naughty' on them," Paige says.

"No crazy straws that spell out 'bride,'" Chasten adds.

"No penis piñata."

"No tiara shaped like a uterus."

Wow. They've *really* thought about this. I start to feel anxious and totally unprepared, like I'm forced to choose "Ancient Rome" for a thousand on *Jeopardy!* "Let's spitball some ideas. Chasten, you first." Paige clearly chooses her teammate. It's the opposite of the gay kid getting picked last in gym class. The gayest kid is the first one chosen on the wedding team. Oh, but if you think Paige has a hard time choosing which wine to drink? Try planning her wedding.

"We could do like a retro nineties slumber party? Watch *Blossom*, drink cosmos and listen to Spice Girls?" Chasten says as if he hadn't pre-thought of this idea. Point for Chasten. I can tell by the look on Paige's face that she isn't feeling this idea.

"We could do a winery. Oooh, maybe a trip to Napa?" Paige says.

"We could do a murder mystery," Chasten says.

"We could do a cowgirl-themed party on a dude ranch."

"We could do an all-pink *Legally Blonde*–themed party."

"How 'bout a spa retreat?" Paige asks.

"How 'bout a midnight scavenger hunt?" Chasten says.

"Coachella themed?"

"Movie marathon in our pj's?"

"Vegas."

"London."

"Nashville."

I haven't said a word, watching this verbal ping-pong in pure bewilderment. Paige and Chasten have found this familial, brother-and-sister rhythm, like they've known each other longer than Paige and I have, and it's starting to make me a little bonkers. Also, I'm getting the feeling that Chasten is more indecisive than Paige, if that's even possible.

"Max? Any ideas?" Paige says. Before I can think of a single thing, our late-breakfast food arrives.

"Are your scones gluten-free?" Paige asks our server, who replies with an apologetic no.

"I'll eat her gluten," I joke, which no one appreciates.

After the server leaves, Paige and Chasten both try to get back onto their train of thought as we all sip and eat. There's finally a brief opening, so I pounce on it.

"How about our diner?" I offer. They both look at me with quizzical, sympathetic faces, like I'm the Elephant Man.

"A diner?" Chasten is confused and clearly feels bad that I have zero imagination for this kind of thing.

"Yes, like we just get everyone together at Waverly Diner, have a feast, drink cocktails and call it a night." I'm not spitballing here. I'm writing this idea down in permanent blood. I've already reached my limit on bachelorette-party planning.

"Diner cocktails? Seems low-rent," Chasten says. We're both

thinking the same thing: we met drinking diner cocktails. Well, at least that's what I'm thinking.

"Exactly," I say, looking at Paige for recognition, support and a shared history of our thirty years of friendship. "Make it fun and super caj."

"Yeah, but diners are like a 'you and me' thing, Max," Paige says, gently rejecting my idea. "Max and I always go to Waverly Diner," she explains to Chasten. "We need this to be like a memorable thing with Katie, Eliza, all my work ladies . . ."

"Read the room, Max. Our friend wants a blowout bachelorette party."

"Welp, I'm all out of ideas," I say, dead serious, plowing through my four-cheese-and-no-vegetable omelet.

"You literally had one idea and it was terrible," Chasten chastises me. I'm not going to lie—this stings, even if it's true and he looks good while criticizing me.

"Should we have another one?" Chasten asks, holding up his now-empty Bloody Mary. I toss my shredded paper straw onto the table and quickly gulp down the rest of mine. I may not be able to out–wedding plan him, but I can sure as hell out-drink him.

I slam my empty drink on the table. I gulped it so fast my brain is swimming, and I like it. "Bloody Marys all day!" Silence. "Get it? Like a play on 'rosé all day'?" They both look at me expressionless, unamused, like I'm their dad.

"Yeah, that didn't work / Don't be weird," they say in unison.

I shrug and motion to our weed server for another round as we hop aboard an express train to Tipsy Town. Population: three.

Titles of My TED Talks

- "Inside the Mind of a Gay Best Friend"
- "Why I'm Awkward"
- "The Smiths versus the Cure"
- "What's with People's Clothes?"
- "It Feels like East Coasters Think All Midwesterners Are Farmers"
- "How to Be Single Forever"

chapter
NINE

ONCE SUNDAY DEPOSITS US BACK INTO THE HARSH SUM-
mer daylight, it's late afternoon and I'm completely hammered. Like overserved–frat boy hammered.

Paige glides down the street in good form; whenever she's
drunk, she's perpetually smiling and her eyes become happy
lines like a laughing Buddha.

"Did you know Angela Lansbury has hosted the Tony Awards
more than anyone?" Paige says.

"I did not know that," Chasten says.

"That *includes* Hugh Jackman and Neil Patrick Harris."

Another one of Paige's trademark drunk moves is randomly
spouting obscure fun facts about the Tony Awards.

Chasten is now wearing some kind of flowered-patterned
fanny pack slung around his puffed-out chest—a look I'll never
understand—walking in between us, oozing that same confidence and perfect posture, checking his phone for the eight
hundred billionth time—all without a single hair out of place—

and somehow looking *more refreshed* than he did sober. How is that technically possible? I look and feel like a sixty-year-old unmade bed walking uphill underwater.

We're on our way to that drag bingo barbecue bullshit thingy, and I can't help but think this is not how I would've liked to spend my Sunday afternoon. I would've much preferred to sit at the counter at La Bonbonniere, eat sunny-side-up eggs that drip down my chin and stain my Gap pocket T-shirt from 2003, maybe hit the extensive magazine shop next door, catch up on news, politics and home gardens while never actually buying a magazine, take a Citi Bike ride along the Hudson River as the sun begins to set, go home, Seamless a pizza, watch a new episode of *The Handmaid's Tale* and end my night by thinking of stress-masturbating but feeling too anxious about work the next day to get lucky with myself. I guess I can still do that last part.

I'd kill to sprint in the other direction right now and go home—anything to avoid having to go to a loud, crowded, dark gay bar while it's perfectly sunny outside—but I am the Gay Best Friend and want to support Paige and her bachelorette planning, so I'm sticking with it until the bitter end. Chasten may be currently, physically in between Paige and me, but he won't be by her side forever like I've been. I'm so lost in thought on how exactly I'm going to steer Paige back onto my team that when I look up, I'm mortified to see Paige and Chasten holding hands and drunk skipping down the sidewalk ahead of me, singing some song I don't recognize. (Fine, it's Olivia Rodrigo—gay guys are legally required to know this.) I drunkenly try to join them but realize I haven't skipped since I was four.

"What about me and *my* hand-holding?" I say nonsensically, trying to get in on the action.

I tear apart Paige and Chasten's hands and hold both of

them in mine as we three clumsily skip down the street. Then something I was not expecting happens.

Whoa.

Some sort of current rises from Chasten's hand, shoots through my arm and into my chest. Maybe it's because I'm startled by the heft of his appendage. Like his uncles, Chasten's hand is meaty and strong, but also weirdly comfortable like I've known him forever? I quickly glance over at Chasten's unblemished face, his impeccably sliced jawline, and wonder if hands can have chemistry. And is he feeling this too? My full-body rush is interrupted by Paige swatting away my hand and declaring, "Okay, this just got weird." I'm offended but relieved that the skipping segment is over for today. But I'm going to have to suppress whatever I just felt and hope it doesn't happen again.

We continue walking, the three of us with Chasten in the middle. How does he keep snagging the middle? We pass various Brooklyn coffee shops, vintage stores and nice restaurants, and I can't help but think this not-very-crowded neighborhood is a more tolerable version of the once coveted, now oversaturated West Village.

Three Brooklyn-chic moms pushing strollers with toddlers who I assume are named Jagger, Hendrix and Bowie breeze past us three drunkards, and I feel the heat of their stares as they either wonder why we're already plastered at 5:00 p.m. or are more likely wishing they could be plastered at 5:00 p.m. Meanwhile, these moms are probably younger than us. Paige smiles winsomely at them, perhaps acknowledging her soon-to-be future self. She's beating me at married life, and if she has kids before me too, I will tear her balls off. We pass a CVS, and Paige checks out our reflection in the window, which I notice is advertising toilet paper. Does that really need to be advertised?

"We look supercute together," Paige says.

"Like a reverse *Three's Company*," I say. Paige giggles, to which Chasten immediately pulls out his phone again and tap-tap-taps something.

"Show from the seventies. Hmmm," Chasten reads.

"Did you just seriously have to look up *Three's Company*?"

"Sure did," he proudly admits. *What kind of monster doesn't know* Three's Company?

"There is no hope for today's youth. None," I complain.

"You're like one year older than me. And you really expect me to know a dumb sitcom from 1977?"

"It's not dumb," I say defensively. "It makes you laugh *and* has valuable life lessons. You can still watch the reruns."

"Thanks, Mr. YouTube," Chasten says.

"How can you not know a sitcom just because you weren't born? And what are you, twenty?"

"I'm thirty-one, but thank you," Chasten says.

"So, I'm three years older than you."

"Gotcha, Gramps." Chasten gloats.

"I may be old but at least I'm fat," I throw back in his court, which really confuses him.

I want to tell him that making fun of someone's age is pointless unless you plan on magically staying the same age forever like a *Simpsons* character. But I sense Paige doesn't enjoy our age battle and this could get cattily uncomfortable if I don't nip it in the bud. Also, there's a chance he doesn't know *The Simpsons* and then I'll have to murder-suicide all of us.

"Why don't you two pretend to like each other at least until my wedding," Paige says, amused by the dueling gays but also sensing something off between us.

We pass a broken jar of mayonnaise on top of a single pee-stained mattress lying on the curb, which is somehow the perfect welcome to the drag blah blah blah bar. It's an indoor-outdoor party spilling into the sizable backyard patio full of twenty-somethings who all vaguely resemble Chasten and their female admirers. The inside is extremely loud with erratic hip-hop playing, and it's making me feel even older and more anxious than normal. It's also pitch dark, so I use my iPhone flashlight to navigate my way around, and immediately a mortified Paige grabs my phone, telling me to put it away. How can these people see anything? As we reach the crowded patio, I can finally make out humans again, and no one is wearing clothes I understand, but I'm too drunk to care right now, so I'm just going to try to get my fourth wind. Chasten is the honorary mayor here, it seems, pointing and waving at friends, acquaintances and complete strangers the same way he turned the charm on at Paige's engagement party. That's some sorcery shit I'll never have.

"So do you go by Chase sometimes?" I ask, hopeful.

"Never."

"Hmm," I say and squint in his general direction, trying to judge him, but he blows this off. I look to Paige for some inside joke recognition here, but she smiles through it, staring at the crowd, not wanting conflict. Paige and I have always joked how every single gay guy prefers to be called by his full name: Christopher. Michael. Benjamin. Never Chris. Mike. Ben. Chasten is a mouthful. Like someone who takes himself a little too seriously. Chase is cute. Like a labradoodle puppy.

"There's the world's best head of hair!" shouts a young guy who's wearing Daisy Duke denim shorts with the inside pockets showing on his upper hairy thighs, a too-tight black tank top with chest hair popping out and a hard-core porn mustache. Daisy Duke is with another young dude wearing a millennial pink T-shirt that reads SUNDAY FUNDAY, pink shorts, pink socks, pink Adidas and a soft-core porn mustache. Chasten embraces them both in a group hug/grope for what feels like forever again. Apparently, Chasten teaches a master class in hugging.

"What's up, Daddy?!" If they think Chasten is a daddy, I'm their great-great-granddaddy.

"You guys have met Paige. And this is her best friend, Max," Chasten tells Daisy and Pink, who tell me their names, which I can't hear over the Britney Spears remix. I'm startled to learn that Daisy and Pink have met Paige before. I'm really out of this loop. Those three run off to fetch more drinks, which we don't need, and leave me alone with Chasten, who's eyeing the patio man meat. After two and a half seconds of that, he goes back to fondling his phone.

"I don't even know what you do," I say, trying to get him to break up with his damn phone and keep myself awake at the same time.

"Oh, you wanna do jobs?" he asks while texting someone who's apparently more interesting than me and everyone here.

"I don't want to DO jobs. I'm just making polite conversation," I shout back.

"No need to get yell-y," he says.

"I'm not. It's just very loud," I yell back.

He throws a crooked grin at the old man. Me. I'm the old man. Even though I'm only three years older than him, there's something about his youthful spirit and bouncy walk that makes me feel ancient.

"Let me guess. Finance," I say.

"Confections," he says as I tilt my head slightly. "Chocolate. I make chocolate."

This surprises me. After meeting his finance family and

thinking Austin was the creative one, I suspected Chasten to have a linear, nine-to-five office job.

"Like a chocolatier," he says. Before I can say that's impressive, he cuts me off. "What's your whole deal?" he asks while rapid-fire texting.

"I'm in HR," I sheepishly admit.

"Oh, right. Paige mentioned. How's that going?" I wonder if Paige offered this or if he was curious enough to ask.

"It's amazing . . . just kidding, it's the worst," I say. He's still furiously texting, so I try to catch him off guard. "Is there a tiny person who lives in your phone?"

He laughs a little and slips his phone back into his fanny pack that he wears on his chest and not his fanny. That worked.

"That's funny. You're kinda funny," he begrudgingly tells me. Finally. He can't resist my charm forever.

Paige, Daisy and Pink break our moment by returning with drinks that contain blue glow sticks in them. So natural.

"What is this? A Chernobyltini?" I say with a wry smile.

Paige is the only one who sorta laughs. In general, gays get only one out of ten of my jokes, or one in ten gays get my jokes, and either way, that's why I'm painfully single and unhealthily still sleeping with my ex.

"It's vodka. Just drink it," demands Daisy.

Chasten does an awe-inspiring 1-2-3 maneuver where he (1) snaps a perfect photo of him and Paige smiling with their radioactive drinks, (2) posts it in his Instagram Stories, and (3) slaps on a "Rio de Janeiro" filter. The whole thing happens quicker than I can process that I feel bad he didn't include me in the photo, while I try to blink back my eyesight after his blinding camera flash.

Two and a half Chernobyltinis later, we grab paper plates

and line up for the barbecue behind three bald, too-skinny guys
wearing denim overalls without shirts, orange bandannas
around their necks and combat boots, who all look like they've
been lightly dipped in rainbow glitter.

I'm now double fisting two burgers, trying to stomp out my
inevitable alcohol poisoning. I have no clue where Paige, Daisy
and Pink have gone, and midbite, I look up and realize it's just
Chasten and me again. He's a quarter through a hot dog with no
bun and gently swaying to Rihanna, looking more comfortable
in his skin than I could ever imagine possible. It's magic hour as
the sun finally sets.

"I think as Paige's man of honor, I should plan her wedding
stuff," I tell him, to my own surprise.

"What are you, like a Best Man–zilla? Don't be so binary.
We can all help," he shoots back.

Before I can respond, my stomach revolts. I enjoy a bar burger
as much as the next guy, but these are one notch past frozen, so I
toss mine into a nearby recycling bin. Two righteous gays shoot me
a disdainful look for not using the correct receptacle while they
poison the air and their lungs with e-cigarettes. I feel like I'm going to be sick, so I tell Chasten I need to pee, and head to the
bathroom where a sign on the door reads "Please Use the Rest-
room That Best Fits Your Gender Identity and Self-Expression,
Betches." It's perfectly inclusive but ends on an unfortunate mi-
sogynist note. Someone really should've told management to come
up with a second draft. It's tough being a bathroom these days.

Luckily the potential throw up was a false alarm, and my
stomach settles. I just pee next to a line of guys for what seems
like an hour, into a silver trough that reeks of urine and horniness. When I shamble out of the bathroom, I see Chasten and
Paige psyching up for the drag portion of the evening. Seeing

Chasten in the shadows, I process the fact that Chasten is the best-looking guy in the room. He's smiling at me with an air of self-satisfaction, like he knows I just thought that. And now he's arm in arm with Paige.

"Chasten figured it out," Paige screams at me, handing me another nuclear drink, which, at this point, I refuse to put into my body.

"What?" I say with fake enthusiasm.

"Bachelorette party on Fire Island!" she says in her sing-song way.

"I do a share in the Pines that none of my housemates ever go to. They're either too coupled or too busy with work," Chasten explains.

"We're gonna fuckin' *murder* the Pines!" Paige excitedly says, referring to the exclusively gay enclave in Fire Island, of which I'm not a huge fan. If you put a rainbow gun to my head and I had to choose which gay mecca vacation town best fit my personality, I would say I'm more of a Provincetown.

I've only been to the Pines once before, with Greg over a disastrous but gloriously sunny Labor Day weekend back in our late twenties. Greg started making money as a doctor, so he rented a house for a week, which is tough to do since all the houses are mostly shares that are rented for the entire summer. He overpaid for this magnificent house, right on the ocean, ground zero in the world's most famous gay summer camp. That Saturday morning, the beach was already packed full of men in Speedos, tanning, walking, playing volleyball or posing in small cliques, chatting and laughing. Unlike these guys who were waxed and bronzed from the summer spent on the beach, I was pasty white from a lifetime of avoiding the sun, with gobs of dark hair turned white from sunscreen. Greg and I set up camp with our towels and umbrellas on the beach, right in the back of our house. As someone who does not like the spotlight, I felt like we were center stage in a play about Fire Island, starring us, with an audience of hundreds. Greg loved it but I couldn't get used to it.

"Fire Island sounds great," I lie, worrying the paper straw (again!) in my glow drink and thinking I can't let this guy win. I'm going to have to come up with a better alternative plan.

"September beach vibes! You guys are gonna catch a million dicks," Paige squeals. Wow. Now she's really drunk.

"It's starting!" Daisy shouts as the music gets louder and an announcer introduces the first drag act. The lights go down and a single spotlight pops on a drag queen named Tina Tartar, who's wearing a red sequined onesie and lip-synching to "I'm the Only One" by Melissa Etheridge while writhing in a kiddie pool full of champagne. I air hug Paige goodbye.

"You're leaving?" Paige complains.

"Don't be so midwestern," Chasten says to me, sensing the drag show is too over-the-top for me.

"Don't be so . . . East Coast–y," I say, before he goes back to hooting and hollering with the rest of the crowd.

I tell Paige I can help with the bachelorette party, but she says Chasten and I can plan it together. She's clearly straddling the line of including her lifelong friend and an obligation to include her future brother-in-law. She realizes my uneasiness at being forced into this new friendship with Chasten and then tries to reassure me. "You know you're my number one, right?" I look at her like she's drunk, because she is. "Seriously, he's family by marriage but you're like *family* family."

"Have fun tonight," I reply, avoiding all human contact, as Paige waves me off and turns back to the show.

I try to fist-bump Chasten goodbye, and he goes in for an

uncomfortably warm embrace. Then I get the full Chasten effect as he presses his lips to my ear to say something.

"Just remember one thing," Chasten says.

"What's that?"

"We can never make out." He pulls back, his face in mine, grinning.

I make a fake mouth gag noise that comes out more over-the-top than I'd intended, like an immature kid, as I wave and weave through the cheering habitués toward the exit.

It's now dark outside and I can already feel a hangover approaching. I collapse into my Uber, slam the door tight and shut out the world. I'm staring out the window of the moving black Prius as we head over the Brooklyn Bridge, back into the urban forest of Manhattan. There are so many new tall buildings, it's like a secret group of architects are conspiring to erase the sky.

I'm trying to forget that Chasten is moving in on my best friend by thinking of all the things I need to do this week: fire people at work, feel bad about firing people, try to usurp Chasten's bachelorette party idea and if not, live with the dread of having to go to Fire Island again.

Checking Paige's Instagram Stories, I see she's already reposted Chasten's photo of the two of them and captioned it, "NewBFF" and "#Paige&AustinMeant2Be."

As Kelly Clarkson sings, *"What doesn't kill you makes you stronger,"* on the radio, I wonder if I'm being replaced, thinking how quickly Chasten has ambushed my friendship with Paige and all the ways I'm going to take him down.

SONGS WITH NUMBERS + WHAT PAIGE AND I HAVE THAT PAIGE AND CHASTEN DON'T HAVE

"SUMMER OF '69" AND
EVERY SUMMER AFTER '93

"A THOUSAND MILES" AROUND
THE MALL WE WENT TO AS KIDS

"EDGE OF SEVENTEEN" PLUS EVERY
AGE BEFORE AND AFTER THAT

"99 RED BALLOONS"
AND SPLUNCHES

"TWO TICKETS TO PARADISE"
AND SEVERAL SKIING TRIPS

FIVE HUNDRED TWENTY-FIVE
THOUSAND SIX HUNDRED TEXTS

chapter

TEN

MONDAY MORNING HITS ME LIKE A BULLET TRAIN ON FIRE as I wake up bleary-eyed, smelling of vodka and barbecue, with a hangover that feels like a jackhammer living inside my head. Also, there's a literal jackhammer outside my window now. What a perfect way to start the workweek. They're renovating the old town house across the street into something fancy in what looks like will take the next ten years. Luckily, I have an office job to escape to every day, because if I worked from home I would go insane, save for the semi-hot construction worker I glimpse out my kitchen window every now and then while eating my morning granola.

Right now, I'm pretending the soothing sound of the jackhammer is my white noise machine, because I'm in too much pain to hop out of bed. Checking my phone, I see Paige hasn't texted me, and now I'm convinced she's one hundred percent moved on from our friendship. She's always been a night owl—one of our few differences—and historically I wake up to one of her darkly funny texts she sends at 2:00 a.m. Paige is probably the only person on the planet who can make me emit audible laughter from a sentence on my telephone.

Our rock-solid friendship now feels as shaky as the construction site across the street.

Maybe Paige has built-up resentment from when we first met as kids, five-year-olds living next door to each other with only a single row of shrubs separating our childhood bedrooms. Our parents always said we'd one day get married. Before realizing I was gay, I never once thought Paige and I were anything but friends, soul siblings, partners in crime. Our friendship reached a crossroads our freshman year of high school—the time our hormones started peeking out from behind the curtain and pushed us center stage. The Winter Formal dance was coming up in less than three weeks, and neither Paige nor I had a date yet. I distinctly remember we were watching *Frasier* on her big-screen TV in her basement, and I was laughing while Paige couldn't understand what was so funny about a white, divorced, snobby, balding Freudian psychiatrist and his younger brother who's the total opposite—a white, divorced, snobby, balding *Jungian* psychiatrist. Little did I know the show was basically gay as hell, featuring gay actors, written by gay men with a main character who was straight but . . . loved opera, enjoyed gourmet dining and even sang his own theme song? As I was laughing and Paige wasn't getting yet another pretentious joke referencing a famous Belgian detective, she grew impatient during the commercial break and started wondering about the upcoming school dance.

"Who are you taking to the formal?" she asked.

"I have no idea. Who are you taking?"

Paige shrugged. The weight of her seemingly casual gesture didn't dawn on me until years later when I realized she had been previously thinking about this dance way more than I was. I thought it was just an excuse to have dinner at a restaurant with friends, without our parents, pretending we were adults, and then blow off steam in our high school gymnasium while everyone gyrated to Third Eye Blind. But Paige clearly saw this night as her first real romantic encounter with a boy. The night had a title and a theme, and it gave everyone an official excuse to seal the deal with another pimply, horny fourteen-year-old. It was a rite of passage. Paige's excitement and intrigue grew the more we talked about it.

"Let's write down on a piece of paper who we're each going to ask, and read them at the same time."

"Um . . . okay," I said, keeping one eye on the wacky antics of Frasier's incorrigible dad.

Paige quickly grabbed her red spiral notebook and ripped two pages of lined paper, handed me a purple Magic Marker, and took a big swig of her Pepsi Twist—Pepsi with the artificial twist of lemon, a favorite in the year 2003. I hadn't thought much about who I was going to ask to the dance. I was, after all, a repressed gay kid to the point of almost being asexual. Forget "almost." I was asexual. I didn't believe kids my age "made out" or "went to third base" or, if you were Darren Cooper and Allison Rattner, "had sex." I knew I had some sort of inexplicable fascination with Patrick Duffy as the dad in *Step by Step* while other boys my age had a thing for Suzanne Somers. Sensing Paige might understand my crush on another freshman named Nate Gimbel, who was captain of the wrestling team, broad shouldered, square jawed and had an unusually manly quality about him for a fourteen-year-old, I wrote down his name. There were honestly a couple of girls I probably should've written down—three different girls actually asked me to the dance, but I told them I was waiting—for what, I didn't know. But for some reason, at that moment, I had trusted Paige with my deeply held secret: that I was, in some weird way I didn't understand, attracted to Nate Gimbel.

So I wrote down Nate's name, folded my piece of paper three times and then folded it once more, as if prolonging any kind of embarrassment I might've gotten after Paige opened it. I looked up, and Paige had already written hers down, folded it once and was staring at me with hopeful, excited, even dreamy, eyes. I didn't know at the time what on earth she was thinking until we swapped papers and both greedily opened them at the same time. I read whom Paige had written down. It was . . . *me*? My stomach did a backflip into a pool of Pepsi Twist. My heart fell to the floor. I took my foot out of my mouth. This was not going to end well as she read, "*Nate Gimbel*? That male himbo captain of the wrestling team?" Paige looked at me with different eyes. Like she was looking at a stranger. I triple checked her piece of paper with the simple word "You!" and my heart broke for her. We were best friends, next-door neighbors, hermano y hermana. Not . . . boyfriend and girlfriend. I was shocked. She even drew the dot on the bottom of the exclamation point into a tiny heart.

Paige's wheels turned before finally spitting it out. "Are you . . . g-a-y?" She actually spelled it out. I couldn't tell if the look in her eyes was disappointment, heartbreak or both. This wasn't me coming out as gay, this was me coming out as vaguely knowing I had interests outside of girls, Nate Gimbel specifically. Now I understand this was my circuitous way of admitting to my best friend that yep, I'm gay.

"Um . . . well, yeah. Sorta . . . I guess?" I said, swallowing, nervous.

"Oh my god."

"What?" I asked.

"Oh. *My* god."

Now she was scaring me. I felt like I was about to lose my best friend and our parents would become sworn enemies.

"Oh my god, oh my god, oh my god. My best friend is gay!" Paige jumped up and down like a *Price Is Right* contestant winning a patio furniture set. "I can't believe I have a gay best friend! This is all I ever wanted!" Was she serious?

"Are you serious?"

"Yes!"

"I had no idea you were gonna pick me. You're not upset?"

"No. It wasn't like a romantic thing. As if," Paige said defensively. I believe that, as kids, Paige imagined we'd end up married, and when I disappointed her by outing my puppy love for a male wrestler, she stamped those thoughts down. She was genuinely happy to have a gay best friend but frustrated we couldn't evolve into something more. Either way, she tried to move on and cemented in her mind that, from now on, I was her Gay. Best. Friend. It was a role I found myself growing into, after I finally admitted to myself I was full-on gay, which came later in college.

The jackhammering outside continues so I pretend I have the most annoying alarm clock in the world and peel the covers off to start the day. With renewed energy to prove to Paige that I'm her *best* gay best friend, I've decided to throw a wrench into Chasten's Fire Island bachelorette plan.

I hop in the shower, get dressed, eat granola while staring at the one semi-hot construction worker and text Paige. I'm going to prove that I can plan her wedding by taking her on a secret outing that she can't refuse.

Quotes from Paige That Have Made Me Laugh Out Loud

- "Have you listened to Dr. Death podcast? It's so gross. I love it."

- "Let's move to LA and live the dream. Hiking Runyon Canyon. Eating salads at the Grove. Murdering Sharon Tate."

- "Oh, nothing. Just eating organic cheese puffs and hate-watching TikToks."

- "I got so drunk last night I turned into a pile of bones and gore on our banquette."

chapter

ELEVEN

AFTER WORK, I SLUMP INTO AN UBER SINCE MY HANGOVER has gotten progressively worse throughout the day and I can't imagine standing in a four-hundred-degree oven slash subway right now. Driving past the sticky throngs of people walking in the early evening summer heat, I feel comforted by the air-conditioning that I've asked my Uber driver to crank to eleven, which he didn't seem happy about. But now we're stuck in slow-moving traffic along the West Side Highway—why we went completely off the grid, I have no idea—and I'm regretting that I promised Paige a second chance to plan her bachelorette party. Instead, I'd much rather be at home, eating clumps of Kraft shredded cheese out of the bag over the kitchen sink and calling it dinner.

Paige is supposed to meet me at Waverly Diner after work, and in true Paige fashion, she's late. I should rephrase that. I'm on me time, which is always early. Paige is on Paige time, which is always fifteen minutes late.

I decide to stand outside the diner since it's early bird special time and I don't want to steal a table from a hungry senior. Scrolling through Instagram, I see a former art director named Shawn, someone I was in charge of hiring a few years ago, posted a screenshot of a conversation he had on Grindr. It's not so much as a conversation as it is a horrifying glimpse into modern gay dating.

sup.

Nada. You.

just back from my uncle's funeral and horny af.

Nice.

It's amusing, but posting your conversation from one app onto another app seems like technology eating itself.

"Hey, freak!" I look up from my phone when I hear Paige. Chasten is by her side. What the fuck. This outing was supposed to be just the two of us, the way I win Paige over with my brilliant idea.

"Hey, guys." I rearrange my face from surprise to excitement.

"I brought the wedding expert," Paige says, referring to Chasten, instantly derailing any self-confidence I thought I had going into tonight.

"I'm not an expert. Although, I've been to like five hundred weddings, so I guess I qualify as an expert at this point." He registers my blank stare and complete indifference, so he tries to soften his stance. "I'm more like a freelance consultant."

"He wanted to check out the competition," Paige says.

This feels like an ambush. Like Paige doesn't trust me any-more and needs a second opinion. In reality, this was supposed to be my shining moment where I swoop in and win Paige back by playing into the nostalgia of our deep friendship. Chasten is just an obstruction. A handsome obstruction but an obstruction, nonetheless.

"Well, this is my idea for your bachelorette party. Should I give you the grand tour?" I'm trying to present this as something exciting and new. A fun idea. Paige laughs, knowing what's in store. Chasten seems skeptical, but he's giving me the polite benefit of the doubt in his raised-in-fancy-Connecticut-nice-boy way.

Inside the Waverly Diner, there's a smattering of Bea Arthur types sitting in booths with Norman Lear types. A sea of white hair and fedoras. All tired eyes are on us crazy kids as we enter. "So, I was thinking we could have a big dinner with all of your friends in this section," I say, pointing to the front section of the restaurant, wildly gesticulating like an overly enthused tour guide. I make sure I'm only addressing Paige at this point be-cause I don't want Chasten to think I'm opening up the floor to his questions and concerns. "Then we can move to that section and you can open your gifts," I say, with a flourish of my hand to the back section. Okay, there's no such thing as giving a grand tour because the place is comically too small but that was part of my joke to Paige. She laughs but Chasten doesn't. I ad-dress him. "Get it? Because it's only one room?"

"No, I get it. But . . ." Chasten turns to Paige. "Is this what you want?"

"It could be fun and quirky," Paige says, unsure but giving me just enough encouragement to continue.

"We could even do little theme booths somehow," I say with crazed intense eye contact to really sell her on the idea. "Like, remember that corner booth that one time when we were so drunk, we sang every single song from *Rent* until four a.m.? Or over at the counter where we spied on Dolly Parton having dinner with her two gal pals?"

"And that wall of fancy-smelling perfume," Paige says, finishing my sentence.

"Yeah, and she had a team of bodyguards waiting outside."

"I remember that. Aw, so many good times here," Paige remembers fondly. "I like this idea." I'm smiling.

"You do?" Oh, shut up, Chasten. Paige turns to hear him out, and I can already feel her start to slip away. "I mean, I get that this place has all the memories, but this sounds like it's more about both of you than just you."

"Yeah, that makes sense," Paige says, clearly waffling every time a different argument is posed. "And remember we had some not-so-good times here too."

"Like when?" I find that hard to believe.

"Like that booth when your parents were in town and that mirror fell on your mom's head. Or when we saw a rat run inside?"

"See?" Chasten says, satisfied.

"*Alleged* rat. I don't know. I think the good times outweigh the bad."

"Oh, for sure," Paige decides, maybe coming back to my side again.

Before Chasten can interject, I have to sell my idea once and for all, so I finally address him. "It's not about me and Paige. It's about Paige and the many sides of her dining life. This happens to be one of her favorite places in New York."

"That's true," Paige agrees, swinging to my side again as she watches a harried server carry out two blue plate specials.

"Yeah, but it's a *diner*." Chasten's face contorts into a mixture of disgust and impatience.

Paige laughs. "Chasten's got a point."

"Yeah, but Paige comes here with all of her friends and family when they're in town. It's not just like, for me."

Paige agrees with me. "True."

"Are you planning on renting out the whole space so it's just Paige and her party? If not, that could get complicated."

"Right, good point." Paige swings back to Team Chasten.

"We can ask how much it would be to rent out the whole place," I counterargue.

"Yeah, why not," Paige says, back on Team Max.

"Are you three here to eat or what?" a confused hostess says as the three of us become aware that we're just hovering in the entrance, surveying the place like we're ghosts of diners past.

"Sorry, we're just deciding." Paige smiles, charming the hostess, who lets us continue casing the joint for the time being.

"You'd really rather do a diner than Fire Island?" Chasten asks.

"We just need options," I say, speaking for Paige.

"If you want options, I'll give you options," Chasten says.

"What do you suggest, Chasten?" And I've lost Paige again.

WE'RE NOW SOMEWHERE IN THE NO-MAN'S-LAND BETWEEN Soho and Tribeca, entering a packed outdoor bar/restaurant with a pink neon sign out front, filled with actual palm trees and real sand to look like a jungle. My inner thoughts are stamped out by the Beyoncé that the DJ has pumped up at ear-damaging levels. I feel like a foreigner in my own city among the too-young, too-hip crowd who are pretending like this seemingly pop-up restaurant has been here for eternity, while Chasten looks completely in his element yet again. I'm sure my shitty New Balance sneakers are not cutting it for this summer-chic crowd, and I couldn't care less. It's weird seeing tropical trees with twinkling nighttime skyscrapers filling out the backdrop in the distance. Throughout the sprawling space are dozens of cabanas, bohemian patio umbrellas, reflective pools and several bars that serve exotic drinks with four hundred ingredients each. There's also a mysterious mist that's unleashed from several corners of the restaurant every seven minutes, which could be water, oxygen or CBD. Hard to tell.

"Isn't this amazing? They re-created my favorite restaurant in Tulum."

"It's unbelievable. I love Tulum!" Paige could not be more excited.

"When have you ever been to Tulum?" I ask, incredulously, fearing Paige traveled somewhere without me that I'm not aware of.

"In my mind, Max. *In my mind*," Paige says as she makes a wild double hand gesture you might see a cheesy Las Vegas illusionist toss out. She and Chasten laugh at my expense.

"Oh, you have to go to Tulum. It's the best. You and Austin should honeymoon there." Of course, Chasten has been to Tulum. He invented Tulum. "Have you been to Tulum, Max?"

"No." Why would he ask me that other than to make me feel bad?

"Well, now you have," Chasten says as he leads us around.

One of the water/oxygen/CBD streams explodes out of a wall again, this time directly into my face, and I start coughing at the smoky, sweet taste, so now I'm worried I'm going to start hallucinating.

The sense memory of this place takes me back to the time Paige and I had our first and only falling-out, on our Cancún trip during spring break in college (Northwestern Neighbors). Paige and I were firmly entrenched in the school's theater crowd—even then she knew exactly what she wanted to do with her life, while I was floundering in my cliché "communications" major after realizing theater wasn't for me. We were both part of a group of friends dubbed "The Broadway Bunch." It was fun being the only nonwannabe actor in the group, since as an outsider I wasn't caught up in their petty competitiveness over winning the lead in *Into the Woods*. Each of them was so clearly defined by their onstage persona, offstage. There was Margot, the ethereal blond ingenue who projected a naively sweet shine but was secretly manipulative and could be downright mean. Angus, the chubby, larger-than-life, hilarious Nathan Lane in training, always sweating and using physical comedy to get a cheap laugh. Teddy, the exceedingly handsome, tall Brit, was cast as the lead in everything but wasn't as witty or bright as his accent suggested and often misused the word "untenable." And Olive, the magnetic, overly effusive red-haired star who was everyone's best friend and could outsing, outact, outlaugh and outdrink anyone. Every night during our Cancún trip would end with all of them sitting in a single-file line, giving each other back rubs, rolling around in a cuddle puddle or just blatantly pairing off and having sex while I tried to steer their attention away from their horny selves to the TV that I was flipping through in our cheap hotel room. "Look! *Sex and the City* in Spanish!" I was too repressed to even get in line for the back rubs despite their aggressive cajoling.

After four days and nights of endless Sondheim references, breaking out into choreographed musical numbers on the beach and drunkenly fake arguing in improvised Shakespearean iambic pentameter, I couldn't take another night of the touchy-feely Broadway Bunch. I didn't hate them, but as the only non–theater major, I couldn't fully connect. One night, I'd read about a cool-sounding gay club on the outskirts of town and told Paige I was going to dislodge myself from hanging with the theater geeks for our last night and check out this local bar. I still wasn't officially out, and even though our theater crowd would theoretically be the easiest group of peers to tell I was gay, I just wasn't ready to announce it to anyone other than Paige. Taking a cue from our overly dramatic friends, Paige drunk smirked like a main character in an Elizabethan play receiving scandalous gossip that Mr. Titherington was coming to town.

"What kind of club?" Paige asked.

"I dunno. I read about it. Just a cool-looking club that we haven't tried." It was a club called La Bomba, which I'd discovered in the back of a free magazine of local Cancún hotspots. The hunky, hairy model they used in the ad to promote it caught my eye.

"Why can't we all go?"

Because there's a hunky, hairy guy who goes there I want all to myself, Paige, why do you think?

"It's just something I'd like to try on my own," I said in a down-low voice, trying to diffuse the speeding train of Paige's curiosity and keep this between us. The gang was too busy letting servers slam tequila directly into their throats to hear anything at first. But then Paige took it personally.

"I'm sure everyone would be okay with whatever kind of club it is," Paige continued, now dancing around the word "gay." I could tell she was feeling threatened by my desire to forge into unknown territory without her.

"I'm sure too, but I'm also sure it's something I need to see for myself."

"Well, where is it?"

"I have to map it and probably get a cab."

Paige pushed back her newly braided hair and stopped eating her sizzling beef fajitas. "I'm not letting you go somewhere outside of town *alone*, Max." Paige was trying to take her frustration with me in a new direction in faux concern for my safety. "Your parents would kill me if you got murdered." And now Olive was catching a whiff of drama and wanted in.

"Murdered where?" Olive leaned in.

"Nowh—"

"Max wants to go somewhere on his own," Paige said, blowing my cover.

"Have you gone loco, mi hermanito?" Olive, of course, couldn't help incorporating overly pronounced Spanglish into our conversations.

"That's what I said," Paige said. Now one by one, everyone was in on the conversation, escalating the theatrics and narrowing my chances of escaping solo.

"What kind of club?"

"A discoteca?"

"I wanna dance!"

"It's our last night. We all have to *beeeee togetherrrrr*!"

"Es una lástima if we split up!"

"Just tell us. Is it a gay club?" Paige said. *You did not just out me at Señor Frog's*, I thought. Paige was drunk and she didn't care if she let it rip. These were her people now and they shared everything. I looked around the table, and everyone was now

frozen midbite or midsip, waiting for my answer. Olive and Angus probably knew I was gay before I did. I suspect Teddy questioned my hetero-ness because frankly, I questioned his. And
Margot was too self-involved to even think about me for one
second.

I didn't think I'd react the way I did, but stomping out of
that Señor Frog's and into a cab alone to go to Cancún's hottest
gay club never felt more liberating. Sure, I was mad at Paige and
possibly never speaking to her again. That's when I'd realized I
read the days wrong. Gay nights were Thursday nights, not Friday nights. I got my jueves and viernes mixed up. But that forty-
five minutes to and from the bar, with just a whisper of danger,
made me feel freer and more alive than ever, like I could go
anywhere and do anything. I promised I'd one day come back to
La Bomba on a Thursday night.

My freedom buzz ended the next morning at the all-
inclusive, unlimited omelet bar at our hotel where I silently
waited in line for my omelet (red peppers, onions, cheddar
cheese) among the hungover theater kids who were full of regret
from god knows what sexual combinations they all formed the
night before. Paige and I wouldn't look at each other while we
all ate in uncomfortable silence. Later, at the airport before we
boarded our plane home, a miasma of resentment hung between
Paige and me. I was mad she outed me in front of people I'd
never see again after college, which I didn't realize at the time.
And Paige was mad at me for making her keep a secret since
high school. She also didn't like that I had this secret double life
without her, like I was supposed to explore my own gayness
with her. As we walked to our gate, we heard the faint strains of
a John Lennon song until it came into clear audible focus. A
group of wandering Deadheads with tie-dyed T-shirts and

acoustic guitars were sitting cross-legged on the floor, randomly singing "Give Peace a Chance." They had attracted a healthy crowd of people who were singing along, global citizens all of us. As we stood to watch and sing along, of course Margot, Angus, Olive and Teddy started wildly dancing like hippies and chanting along with the Lennon tune, quickly becoming the stars of this show. Paige and I were left alone, watching this beautifully spontaneous moment erupting before us, begging us to "give peace a chance." We looked at each other and couldn't help but laugh at the simple message, and our first huge falling-out ended right there in the Cancún International Airport food court.

"Remember when we went to Mexico and got into a huge fight and then we heard those people sing John Lennon and we made up?" Paige asks me back in the Tulum restaurant. I smile as the three of us sit at the bar, knowing how much Paige and I think alike. We both laugh and eternally bond at the memory all over again. Chasten's got nothin' on me now.

I'm Gay. Ask Me Anything.

- When did you know you were gay?
- When did you come out?
- Were your parents cool with it?
- Were you bullied in school?
- Did you ever date women?
- Have sex with a woman?
- When did you first have sex with a guy?
- Be honest, do you consider yourself completely gay or a little bi maybe?
- Do you believe in monogamy or would you want an open relationship?
- Do you want to get married?
- Thought about having kids?
- Would you adopt or use a surrogate?
- Do you think it would be easier as a gay dad to have a boy or a girl?
- Do you watch the Housewives?

chapter

TWELVE

OVER SHOTS OF MEZCAL (SIP, DON'T SHOOT), PAIGE IS doing that thing where she asks all the questions that people love to ask gay guys when they're getting to know us on a deeper level, specifically what it means to be gay.

As Paige conducts her intense Q and A with Chasten, she's gone into full Oprah mode, with a mixture of admiring concern and genuine curiosity, frequently nodding her head to telegraph that she's engaged and present, injecting a quick laugh here and there and narrowing her eyes every now and then to really sell her excellent listening skills. She even puts two fingers together on her lips and nods profoundly.

I'm just sitting here, Oprah/Paige's audience of one, listening and waiting for a commercial break so I can stand up and stretch. Paige has asked me all of these questions multiple times through-out the years, as if my answers would change or develop, which they have, and I usually have to maintain patience while Paige does her thing. I know she's coming from a good, genuinely curious place, but there's a slight undercurrent of me thinking how straight people are lucky not to have to answer a question like, *When did you find out you were straight?* It's a luxury not to even have to think about that. But I'm not going to get all righteous about it because on the other hand, it makes me feel even luckier to be part of a club where we do get asked these questions. After all, who doesn't want to get interviewed by Oprah?

By the way, heteros aren't the only ones asking these questions. Before Greg, I went on a few torturous, not-quite-right dates with enough guys to know that gays pose these exact same interview questions to each other·all the time when getting to know one another, specifically halfway into our poached halibut entrée, after the third sip of our second negroni on a first date.

Even though I've endured listening to Paige ask Greg these questions when we first started dating and then every random gay we ever met along the way since college, later living in Chicago and then New York, I'm actually intrigued and moved by Chasten's answers. He knew he was gay when he was six years old and he watched *The Best Little Whorehouse in Texas* on cable, laying eyes on a strapping, hairy Burt Reynolds and being equally interested in the musical number in the football team's locker room and seeing them snap their towels at each other's butts. He was lucky enough to have the most understanding older brother of all time who couldn't care less that he was gay even though he had·buddies who did care, but Austin would always stand up for him if they cracked hurtful jokes. Before Austin graduated from high school, he founded a gay-straight alliance club and became a huge gay advocate, turning their once conservative, private high school in Connecticut into a leading supporter of LGBTQ rights, that goddamned saint. "What a sweetie." Paige melts.

Chasten's first kiss was his freshman year of high school

with his lacrosse teammate Fergus, identical twin of Connor, who was also gay and whom Chasten made out with a year later. Chasten never dated girls, nor did he have sex with girls, and was out and proud to his peers all throughout high school. Although, he did have a drunken "experiment" with his best friend Sarah one night their freshman year at Yale during a Halloween party dressed as Steve Carell and Catherine Keener from *The 40-Year-Old Virgin* just to see what it was like (not good).

His first full-on sex with a guy was a year later, when he dabbled as the on-staff poet for the school's overly pretentious upstart literary magazine called *Cacophony*, where he slept with the equally pretentious editor-in-chief William (don't call him Bill!) one night after a St. Patrick's Day party. Chasten ended up writing a poem about the experience for the magazine, and when everyone gossiped about his first love's identity, he got fired for outing the closeted William.

Chasten is not even remotely bi.

He believes in monogamy and notes that a lot of gay couples have secret open relationships with rules like (1) no kissing, (2) no second dates and (3) no anal. But Chasten doesn't judge.

Chasten very much wants to get married, and what he's looking for in a guy is mutual trust, laughter and impromptu dance parties to Yaz's *Upstairs at Eric's*. Wait, I was not expecting this answer. Now he has my full attention.

Chasten wants to have kids, or a kid, through a surrogate probably, but he wants to wait until his business is more established and secure.

Chasten wants to have a boy or a girl, and it doesn't matter which one because he just wants to re-create the cozy, tight-knit, loving family he had growing up.

Out of all the gays I've heard Paige interrogate with these same stock interview questions, Chasten gives responses that feel different somehow, and more than a few of his answers make me swoon, which I cover by ordering three more shots of mezcal (this time shoot, don't sip).

It takes us a little over thirty-seven minutes to order food. "What's the difference between a tostada and a tamale? . . . How spicy are the spicy smoked tacos? . . . What's 'ajo'?" Because, Paige.

Now, with the mezcal and various tacos throwing a fiesta in our stomachs, a group of twentysomethings sit uncomfortably close to us, none of them acknowledging us old people. They're all dressed like a fake rock band in a movie. I'm ready to leave.

If I had known I was going to go out three nights in a row, two on school nights, I would've napped for a week prior in preparation. I'm beyond the point of exhaustion.

"Wanna hit this rooftop party?" Chasten asks. *Please god, no,* I think.

"Hundred percent," Paige says immediately. For me, this is all too much. They're like convicts just out of prison who want to do everything they possibly can before violating their parole and having to go back in.

"Oh my god. Rooftop party? That is so my scene. Count me in," I say sarcastically. Paige laughs and rolls her eyes. Without missing a beat, Chasten motions for the check as the server immediately heads to our table in a seamless gesture that has happened to me exactly zero times, no matter how hard I've tried. Before Chasten wins this round by paying for all of us, I hand the server my entire wallet and everyone looks confused. "Just kidding," even though I'm not. I'm drunk and tired and accidentally forgot to remove my credit card.

"Are you all right?" Paige asks, not buying my "joke," which I wave off.

"Psshhht. Of course. Where's the party?" I ask, trying to plant myself farther in between the two of them.

"It's in Tribeca. Just down the street," Chasten says. "You sure you want to go?"

"Of course," I say, when all I want to do is sleep for a week.

This time, the three of us walking down the street, I firmly secure the center of this platonic threesome. We're not holding hands and we're not skipping down the street.

Before we get to the party, Chasten leads us into a nearby bodega, where I bet he needs to buy chewing gum to mask his taco breath with cinnamon.

"Is this your second idea for Paige's bachelorette party?" I ask with a smirk. "The fly strips are a nice touch."

"Ew," Paige says as the three of us dodge strips of dead flies hanging from the ceiling in the store's effort to protect the extensive selection of stale Milano cookies.

"Yes, I was thinking all of Paige's friends can meet in the refrigerated section and then party our way up to the cashier. If we're lucky, we'll have a special appearance by a bodega cat." Chasten is a good-natured sport as Paige and I laugh. To my surprise though, he passes the gum section and heads to the water section, grabbing three bottles and handing them to us. "Gotta stay hydrated." It's a thoughtful gesture on this incredibly humid night, I must begrudgingly admit. I take one, annoyed that he's right.

As we wait behind three Tribeca teens all with the same shoulder-length hair, all holding skateboards and buying energy drinks, it hits me.

"Paige, why don't we do a destination bachelorette party?" I suggest. Part of this idea is to bring Chasten down a peg. "Why go to Fake Tulum when we can go to Actual Tulum?"

"I kinda like that idea," Paige says.

"I don't know if we want Mexico in the middle of the summer?" Chasten is low-key offended I just dinged tonight's outing.

"That's true." Paige swings back.

"Mezcal by the beach beats mezcal by the Holland Tunnel heading into Jersey."

Paige smiles, knowing I'm right.

Chasten pays for our waters, and we head toward Greenwich Street in the toniest area of Tribeca.

We walk past garbage bags on top of garbage bags, which, after nine years of living in Manhattan, I'll never get used to. I remember when I told my parents I got a job and was moving to New York, the first thing my dad said was, "Manhattan is full of garbage," while my mom reminded him that's where they met.

"The fact that New York always reminds you of garbage first and not where we met is just . . ." When my mom is bewildered, amazed or in general awe of something, she lets her sentences trail off. "Your dad doesn't remember we met at his cousin's wedding and I am just . . ."

"Of course I remember we met at Stacy and Kevin's wedding at Tavern on the Green," my dad said as if reciting a grocery list. "I asked you to dance when they played a Temptations song. I'm just saying New York *also* reminds me of garbage."

"It would just be nice to have our memory of meeting in New York without picturing a mountain of garbage for once."

"Tell that to the New York City mayor." My dad pretended to joke, but he was serious and this was their way of skirting the issue of me leaving Illinois. Now they're just happy I'm New

York City street-smart, which basically means knowing how to coil away from people standing on sidewalks holding clipboards and adapting the mantra "If I can smell you, you're too close."

"Lovely," Chasten says as we pass the pile of trash. I guess my dad and I aren't the only ones who find this repulsive. "I just think if we want a destination bachelorette party, we should do something a little closer," Chasten says, subtly sliding in a "we" as if he's the one getting married now. Pretty soon he's going to start talking about "our wedding dress."

Paige and I follow Chasten into an exclusive residential building as a doorman lets us in. There must be a League of Extraordinary Doormen who all get the same playbook on how to behave because this one reminds me of all the uptight doormen at Greg's building. Doorman is New York City's finest superhero. Faster than a speeding repairman! More powerful than a local dry cleaner! Able to keep an eye on tall buildings!

"How are ya, Mr. Chasten?" the doorman asks.

"Great, Paul. How are you?" Of fucking course Chasten is on a first-name basis with half of this city's fancy doormen.

"Humid out there but AC's nice and cool inside here, so I can't complain." Paul presses the elevator button and motions us inside with a welcoming face even though I swear he just eyed me up and down as if I'm the weak link of the bunch.

"Thanks, Paul," Chasten says as the doors close on us. "Bachelorette party option number four."

"I like it already," Paige says.

The elevator dings and we're on the top floor. "I like to give options." Chasten looks at me when he says this. The doors open, and I'm not sure which is louder: the music or the party people shouting at each other. Who throws a rager like this on a Monday night? "Let's find the birthday girl," Chasten shouts at us, and I guess birthday girls living in Tribeca penthouses have parties like this.

We snake our way through the mixed crowd of uptown, downtown, gay, straight, formally dressed, super casual, young, old, babies and even a few dogs as Chasten says hi or hugs one out of three people and animals. I would be relishing in the picture-perfect New York moment of every demographic colliding inside a giant apartment with an expansive, sparkling view of the Hudson River at night if I weren't so tired.

We step onto a wraparound terrace that's easily fourteen of my apartments combined filled with even more people, a built-in grill with an outdoor kitchen, and some kind of retractable roof that presumably covers the outdoor space when it rains, all outlined by giant hedges, shrubbery and various other plants that conceal the fact that we're in the middle of a city. My plant envy is in full force right now. At first, collecting laid-off employees' plants and taking care of them in my apartment made me feel like a cat lady except with plants, but now I'm really starting to love it. Seeing this urban garden reconfirms my burgeoning extracurricular activity and inspires me to take my plant game to the next level.

Chasten bear-hugs a young, radiant woman in her thirties who looks like a downtown Kate Middleton with skin that was grown in a Goop lab by the world-renowned scientist Gwyneth Paltrow. Chasten introduces her as his cousin, and she might be the nicest, friendliest person I've ever met and looks like she would own a cool art gallery in Tribeca or something.

"This is my cousin Evelyn. This is Paige and Max," Chasten shouts even though it's quieter out here and he doesn't really have to, but he's clearly "on."

"Nice to meet you, Paige and Max." Evelyn bear-hugs us both. Runs in the family.

"Evelyn owns the coolest gallery and design store in Tribeca," Chasten informs us. Bingo. I usually have a one hundred percent accuracy rate when guessing people's professions or recognizing celebrity voiceover talent in commercials.

"I love all of your greenery," I say stupidly.

"Oh, thank you. My mother and her landscape architect are control freaks," Evelyn says as she turns to look at her terrace landscaping like she's never even considered it before.

"See those two VC douches?" Evelyn conspires with Chasten, leaning into him. "They're gonna be your angel investors. They're my cousins on my father's side."

"Right on."

"We'll talk more later. Go get drinks. I gotta find the birthday boy, Ben." The gracious Evelyn waves at us and leaves to sprinkle her magic fairy dust on other guests.

"So what do you think of the space?" Chasten says to Paige.

"Oh my god. It's stunning," Paige says. "I don't think you'd want my rinky-dink bachelorette party here though."

"Why not? It's made for entertaining. I've already spoken to Evelyn about it. She's cool with it."

"Really?" Paige says, clocking the square footage and imagining where she and her friends would hang out, probably.

As we walk to one of the four bars Evelyn has set up throughout the place, I think it's all a little much for me. Chasten has immediate access to parts of this city I've never even seen before. Whereas the only thing I have to offer is some ancient diner. I wish I could do more for my best friend, but I'm limited in my suggestions. And I can't help but wonder if Chasten is just showing off.

"Sparkling water with a lemon," I say to the hunky, runway model–esque bartender. I try to jazz it up by asking for sparkling and lemon so he's not disappointed I'm just ordering water. Chasten and Paige keep the Mezcalapalooza going. I officially can't keep up with these kids.

"So your choices are your little diner." Chasten nods to me as he condescendingly says this, thank you very much. "Tulum in the city, Evelyn's dope rooftop or Fire Island."

"Or actual Tulum," I remind them.

"This is amazing, you guys. Why can't we do all five?" Paige laughs and sips. I'm now realizing what a horrible mistake we made in giving Paige options.

"Which one will it be?" I ask, knowing there's no immediate answer to this question and I will have to ask Paige at least a half dozen more times.

Paige starts typing on her phone.

"Are you phoning a friend?" I ask.

"I'm starting a group text with the three of us so after we can obsessively weigh the pros and cons of my bachelorette party location." Paige has always needed a codependent decision maker. Me. I'm her codependent decision maker. I suppose now she has two, if Chasten is game for that sort of thing.

"Oh, I can't wait," I say to Paige as my phone nudges my thigh through my khakis.

It's me Paige. Now the three of us are connected! She punctuates her text with a family emoji. Great. Now I'm going to have to compete with Chasten's wit and charm in text. I create a new contact for Chasten in my phone: "The Brother," making sure he and Paige don't see my secretly derogatory nickname. I showed him!

"I'm still leaning toward Fire Island for you," Chasten reminds Paige. I really hoped this idea had gone away.

Paige is visibly overwhelmed with all of the Chasten options, but I know her well enough to see that she's now heavily leaning into his original idea.

"What about real Tulum?" I remind her again.

"I love that idea, but does it seem a little far for a bachelorette party?" Here comes the Paige Indecisive Tour. I have a front-row seat and backstage pass. "I mean, I'm only inviting a few friends, and I don't know if they'd all commit. Eliza's opening her store soon, so she's focused on that. I know Katie's getting her dance studio ready for the fall. My sister has three kids and won't want to fly from LA twice. My high school friend Erica is pregnant and can only fly once. Cori is a cheap-ass and probably won't want to spend the money. And Nina would go but we're all flying to Big Sur for her wedding this fall so I don't want to step on her destination-wedding toes."

"Well, that settles that," Chasten says, thinking Paige is done.

"Of course, my ladies all deserve a nice vacation somewhere on a beach . . ." Paige has to start with the cons and then list all of the pros. It seems like she's talking to us, but in reality, it's a monologue, and she's speaking to herself out loud. It's not that she's not open to input, it's that no one's opinion is as assertive as Paige's inner voice so don't even try. I'm kind of resigned to the fact that Real Tulum is out of the question, so I'm tuning out all the reasons why Paige thinks it's a good idea because she will inevitably talk herself out of it.

". . . and that's probably why we should keep it in New York," Paige concludes. I nod like I was definitely, totally listening.

"Those are all good and valid points," Chasten agrees. Oh, he was actually listening to her this whole time. How adorable. "So . . . Fire Island?"

"I'll sleep on it," Paige decides without actually deciding anything. The two of them order more drinks while I order an Uber.

Types of People I've Dated

- Eddie from college
- Greg

chapter

THIRTEEN

SEVENTY-EIGHT TEXTS. THAT'S HOW MANY MESSAGES I wake up to in our newly formed group chat between me, Chasten and Paige. It takes me half an hour just to read through all of them, and I realize this is not even a group text because I was sleeping the entire time. It's just a string of late-night messages between Paige and Chasten in which they couldn't care less if I responded. My favorite one that made me laugh out loud is a GIF that Paige sent of Julianne Moore crying in the movie *Magnolia*, and under it Paige wrote, "Actual footage of me tomorrow with a hangover." At least I'm not the only one. But then Paige goes on to list more pros and cons of each bachelorette party locale while they bounce *even more* ideas back and forth. I feel safe and comforted knowing I was asleep for all of that.

A couple things I'm noticing about Chasten in this thread is that he uses a lot of emojis and says "haha" too much, but on the plus side, he's funny in text. Or maybe I just haven't gotten to know his sense of humor in real life yet. A couple of his retorts to Paige's retorts made me breathe a tiny puff of air out of my nose, which constitutes a genuine laugh. My scrolling and reading are interrupted by a text from my boss:

JANET
Meet me in the Cloud Room at 9:30am?

It's unfortunate that I've allowed Janet to text me at any hour of the day, but here we are. I'm slightly disturbed that I'm losing Paige to Chasten even by text, but I have to get ready for work.

BY THE TIME I FINISH UP AT THE OFFICE AROUND 9:45 P.M., I just want to crawl under my bed and cry forever. Today was absolutely brutal, and it had nothing to do with planning my best friend's wedding.

The first person I had to fire this morning was Melinda, who had been with the agency for the last twenty-two years. She was the only person who always wore her laminated ID card around her neck as if she were constantly walking in and out of secured doors and needed her "swoosh" (our nickname for security cards) at all times. Or maybe it was her badge of honor. Her role was general manager, and she was everyone's favorite matriarch, therapist, handywoman and sounding board. She had the one and only key to the well-stocked supply closet and never once abused her duties as the gatekeeper. She was good for a black felt-tip pen or a shoulder to cry on. If someone had a rough day personally or professionally, Melinda was your go-to, and as I heartbreakingly told her that her job was terminated, the roles reversed. She started to cry a little at first, which progressed into uncontrollable sobs the more it sunk in that she would wake up tomorrow with no supply closet key, no cubicle to decorate with "funny" little quotes on wooden plaques and nowhere to go outside of her one-bedroom apartment in Turtle Bay. After she went home forever, she left behind a hanging fern that she kept dangling from her wall that I promptly took to my office and will replenish in her honor.

When I thought it couldn't get worse than having to fire Melinda, the agency's next victim was Cheryl, the alpha account executive from Queens who projected an air of old-school professionalism in her perfectly put-together cashmere sweaters, pantsuits and gold accessories. No one ever saw Cheryl in the same outfit twice. Cheryl relished in her famous catchphrase "Work hard, play hard," which she threw into every meeting or casual conversation, as if this frequent reminder were some new, uniquely outrageous saying she had just invented on the spot. She was overly prepared for every meeting, always the most vocal, with the loudest laugh, and she drank everyone under the table while looking like a flawless Italian mob wife. She considered herself an agency lifer and was blindsided when I broke the news to her. For the first time ever, she had nothing to say, no perfect rebuttal, zero momentum to keep our meeting going forward. Not even "Work hard, play hard." It was tough for me to see her disoriented, unraveling as she walked to clear out her office. She left behind a purple orchid, which I've adopted.

Mateo was a brilliant senior art director who started as an invisible grunt drawing storyboards in the art department and then rose within the creative department. Originally from Madrid, Mateo wallpapered his office in comic books, stacks of old board games, *Star Wars* figures and every vintage toy from Magic 8 Ball to Slinky to dozens of Rubik's Cubes. We used to joke that it would take a moving truck to haul his stuff away and that he kept adding more stuff so he could never get fired. When

I broke the news, he shrugged in a confident but not cocky way, both of us knowing any agency would scoop him up overnight. He sweetly said he enjoyed working with me. I asked him if I could have his Chia Pet.

Tatiana was a delightfully weird British VP creative director who wore thick nerd glasses, had a posh accent, and shared my love for the Smiths. She was not so secretly trying to springboard out of the ad world to become a sitcom writer and was always placing in TV-writing competitions. Some of the higher-ups frowned upon her extracurricular desire to write dumb TV shows instead of writing dumb car commercials, but she had no self-edit button and couldn't stop talking about it. I loved when she would come into my office and shut the door because I knew she had fun gossip about our coworkers, like the time she'd heard Steph screaming at her mother-in-law on the phone for feeding her son peanut butter or informing me every time Geoff hoarded leftover free bagels in his messenger bag. Tatiana said she'll either move to LA to write for TV or go back to London and work with people with disabilities.

Chloe was super young and came from crazy money—her dad invented the pool noodle—so she didn't need her job as a junior copywriter, but the look on her face when I told her that she was let go registered a deep insecurity that she'll internalize and think she'll never be good enough. I feel like she'll carry the weight of this day forever.

Edwin did not take the news well. He was known for being somewhat of a loose cannon, and no amount of HR training could have prepared me for his response. He was one of our newer research directors, he had a hacking smoker's cough that appeared when he laughed, and he smelled like several ashtrays. Morning, noon and night, Edwin stood outside next to the revolving doors, smoking, resentful that he had to leave the building for his addiction. When I broke the news to him sitting across from me in the conference room (keep the terminations on neutral ground), Edwin pulled out a cigarette, lit up, took the deepest inhale I've ever seen and blew a giant, fuck-you plume of smoke directly into my face. I didn't tell him to put the cigarette out for fear of what he might do next, so I awkwardly let the scenario play out until he silently walked out of the conference room, blowing smoke rings in his wake. I sort of respected him for that.

After that, it was almost noon and my next bloodbath wasn't until one thirty, so I escaped the building for a much-needed lunch break. The firings started weighing on me, and feeling like a sponge to these wildly different reactions from these unfortunate souls made me realize why doctors have poor bedside manner—if they dwell on the bad news, it will kill them.

Across the street is Just Salad, where people wait in a ridiculous line that overflows out the door, holding stupid plastic orange reusable containers they purchased for a dollar for one free topping on each order. You have to know EXACTLY what ingredients you want tossed into your miserable salad and then be prepared to shout them ("Spinach! Kidney beans! Grilled chicken!") in fear that you'll annoy the salad artists and they'll ignore you. For this reason, I chose a ready-made chicken Caesar, which I pecked at while staring at my phone. I had zero appetite and my energy was depleted. It took me a solid four minutes before I realized I was just zoning out to the home page of apps on my phone and not even looking at anything.

After I nibbled a few croutons to keep up my energy for the rest of the afternoon, my text messages finally came into focus, and I saw the Paige and Chasten group chat had ramped up to sixty-four more messages. Scrolling through, I skimmed the highlights:

CHASTEN

Yay! Fire Island it is!

PAIGE

Margs and dildos on the beach!

CHASTEN

All the men are gonna be hot AF

PAIGE

SPF 69, bitches!

CHASTEN

haha ☀️🥒

PAIGE

Where's Max?????

CHASTEN

Prolly reading this and judging us.

My eyes hurt from all the abbreviated words, emojis, animated GIFs and videos they sent to the group, and it was pointless to even contribute now because fourteen different conversations had started and stopped since this morning. At least it seemed Paige had landed on Fire Island for her bachelorette party, and planning a wedding seemed quaint right now compared to the rest of my afternoon, which I would spend stripping people of their livelihoods, health insurance and unlimited supply of yellow highlighters.

I looked up to see Stella sitting across from me, munching

on her own gross salad. I didn't recognize her at first without a blanket.

"Uh . . . how long have you been sitting there?" I asked her, realizing I'd been in a phone hole.

"This much," Stella said and pointed to her half-eaten spinach, Cajun chicken, cucumber, carrots, blue cheese medley. "I heard it's happening."

"Yeah. Not fun. Like, for anyone."

"You look exhausted."

"I'm honestly not cut out for this job. It really sucks they made me this person."

"Can you . . . am I . . ."

"You're safe," I reassured Stella. I had checked the list of employees given to me by Janet, who got it from her faceless higher-up, who created the list with a team of number crunchers, and thankfully I didn't see Stella's name. I barely know what goes into the making of the list of people we have to let go. I'm guessing it's a combination of salary, staff redundancies and the impending possible merger.

"Are you sure?" Stella asked, with fear and relief competing in her eyes.

"I'm sure." The truth is, I was sure she wasn't on the list but I'm not sure there isn't going to be a second list. Or a third. Or fifth.

"Ugh, thank god. I honestly don't know what I would do if I got fired. I would have to move back home with my mom in Sausalito. Which is the saddest sentence a grown adult could possibly imagine."

"It sounds like a nice escape from New York, if you ask me."

"Are you saying it might happen?" I could see the stress of layoffs has caused Stella to hang on my every word.

"No, no, no. I'm not saying that. You're safe. Like I said. Your job is perfectly safe. You're not going anywhere." I tried to give her some comfort. A weight lifted from her shoulders, and she seemed somewhat relieved for the time being.

"Okay, I trust you. I'm so glad we're friends," she said with a hint of a smile.

"Me too. We'll make it out of this alive," I said.

"Scary shit, huh?"

"Yeah, it's the worst."

"I heard Melinda was fired. And Tatiana, who I love. Edwin too. But I won't miss his ciggy breath."

"Confirmed. All of those. But you didn't hear it from me, and I can't comment on anyone I have to terminate this afternoon and the rest of the week," I said.

"I respect your privacy at this time," Stella said, and we both sort of laughed but knew it wasn't funny at all as we chomped with an air of dread on our wilted lettuce.

The morning seemed tame compared to the afternoon, when I wielded my rusty axe and chopped the heads off two dozen more people, some I knew and adored, others I didn't know at all and had been looking forward to getting to know more. So many of them had given their blood, sweat and tears to the agency, whether they had been working there for twenty-five years or had started last month.

Kimmie was a senior account executive who landed a ton of new business and was praised for her former life as a professional ice skater who qualified for the Olympics but had to quit when she tore her ACL. Graham was a broadcast producer from South Africa who was also the front man of an experimental rock band called Loose Meat. Yvonne, a Mormon from Utah, was a strategic planner who always reminded people she used to be a serious lawyer before switching to this "crazy ad biz." Pradeep was a media planner from LA with a deadpan sense of humor who dabbled in improv, and when he was in his twenties he won a red Jeep on *Wheel of Fortune*. Rodney was in design, had flesh tunnels in both earlobes and would talk to you way too close, but somehow that was okay because he had a soothing voice. Daniella was in legal, had a vague European accent, wrote mean-sounding emails and was rumored to have been moon-lighting as a dominatrix. Hannah was a fast-talking junior copywriter from Kentucky who worshipped horror movies and ate microwaved popcorn every day for lunch. Murad was a proj-ect manager who was insanely tall and often joked that when he sat at his desk in his office, his feet would obstruct the hallway. Kelvin was in research, had a limp, always seemed borderline sexually inappropriate and was the in-office Ping-Pong champ.

This is the in memoriam of people I had to fire today (set to Sarah McLachlan's "I Will Remember You"). Some made huge impacts, others contributed the best way they could, and a few just collected a paycheck. I was half-afraid that when I left tonight they'd have formed a line outside the office, waiting to murder me with various Clue weapons. Before I went home to-day, I stared at the stash of plants I'd collected from people's offices after they left, including ferns, orchids, a fake bonsai, hanging spider plants and Mateo's Chia Pet.

I've decided to buy a new plant for each and every person who had to leave us, as my own personal way of honoring them. Of course, these wonderful people are not dead and I'm sup-posed to fulfill my duties without emotion, but it feels to me like a profound loss. I had to excavate the building today, but I'm the one left gutted.

Rejected T-Shirt Ideas for Paige's Broadway-Themed Bachelorette Party

- Ease on Down the Rosé
- God, I Hope I Get Lit
- Wavin' through a Hangover
- I Am Not Throwin' Away My Tequila Shot!
- Let's Get Wicked Drunk

chapter

FOURTEEN

'M ANOTHER SWEATY MESS. MY BACK HURTS FROM LUGGING around a too-full weekender bag. I'm slowly becoming claustrophobic from all the people closing in behind me. And I'm anxiously starting to believe I'm going to miss my train. Welcome to Penn Station in the summer. Oh, and everything smells like pee.

I'm staring lasers at the giant train schedule board trying to remember which stop the lady behind the counter told me is my transfer to Fire Island. *Babylon? No, Jamaica. Or was it Babylon. Could be Jamaica though.* Then I remember it's Babylon because I'd told myself to remember the name that sounded farther away. Babylon sounds like a fifteenth-century BC location, while Jamaica sounds like I can fly there on Delta.

Once the train schedule board *flip flip flips* to my destination, the herd of zombie summer people uniformly springs forward, on their way to devour track thirteen. How they all immediately know where to find track thirteen is some weird Long Island

Rail Road sixth-sense shit I have yet to develop. This is a completely uncivilized and unsettling summer ritual I wouldn't want to repeat every weekend, and once we locate the train, the zombies sprint to any open car, trying to find an empty seat, not caring whose brains they have to eat to get one. That's when the self-satisfied nine-to-five workers—whether their collars are blue or white, heading to their suburban homes—crack open a well-deserved Black Cherry White Claw, sip and smugly stare at all the suckers who got left behind and have to stand.

When we reach Babylon, not Jamaica, I exit the train in search of my connecting train, where I wait on a platform for the next fifteen minutes. I start to panic, second-guessing myself until I see small gaggles of gathering gays doing the same thing, to which I breathe easy knowing I'm headed in the right direction. One foursome wears bandannas around their necks, which I recognize as a summer fashion statement but seems more like the uniforms of sleepaway camp kids in a buddy system.

The next train has a slightly quieter, more civilized tone even though the same crush of people fights their way on—some go upstairs! Downstairs! Right! Left! The air-conditioning is on full blast so my sweat has evenly caked my entire body while I'm sitting in a T-shirt and shorts, freezing. I look around at all the smart gays on their smartphones, wearing their smart sweaters, fully prepared for this unexpected arctic blast of cool air, and I realize I'm a novice.

The one time I'd made this LGBTQ rite of passage to Fire Island Pines with Greg resulted in a ridiculously delayed trip on our way there. We were both FIP newbies, so neither of us knew what we were doing, like right now. I followed Greg's lead since he had done a share one summer but only went out once because he was always on weekend shifts at work. Greg didn't appreciate all of the rules his eleven other housemates had, including "You must always have breakfast, lunch and dinner together" and "You can never go to 'tea' without the entire group." When I questioned if "tea" meant English breakfast or chamomile, Greg explained that "tea" is cocktail hour and that there were two "teas" every day: Low Tea was between 5:00 p.m. and 8:00 p.m., where everyone gathered, freshly showered after a day on the beach, and drank fourteen-dollar drinks in plastic cups at the Blue Whale, overlooking the boat dock. After that was High Tea, when you would go upstairs and drink more rounds of fourteen-dollar drinks. At every dinner in their house someone was assigned to cook, to assist the cook and to clean up. After dinner, it was then optional for anyone in the house to go out dancing. There were two options: Sip-n-Twirl, a casual, easy breezy gathering where people swayed and socialized while a DJ spun fun summer remixes. After that was the Pavilion, with hard-core music that lasted until 4:00 a.m. After I listened to Greg tell me about these activities, we both realized we'd some-how missed our train (Jamaica, not Babylon).

Since back then he was romantic, Greg had planned ahead and surprised me with gourmet sandwiches that he made at home. We sat cross-legged on the train platform, sharing our tuna on whole wheat, and prosciutto and Brie on ciabatta, not caring we weren't going to make either Low Tea or High Tea. It was the two of us against the world back then, but those days are long gone.

Before sliding into my long weekend, I vowed to focus on Paige and not check work emails, so I decide to peek one last time before I figuratively throw my phone off this speeding train. Scrolling through, I see lots of "Farewell" emails from many of the employees I let go. All of them professional, explaining that they're leaving the company and how to reach them going forward, which I read with a giant ache in my stomach. The last email in the bunch, from Cheryl, has the bluntest of blunt subject headings. It simply reads GOODBYE. All caps. With a period that looks like it was stuck there in anger. I can't blame her. I'd be pissed off too. Her email reads:

ALL,

First off, it behooves me to state the obvious. I was fired. Not laid off. Not let go. Fired. Okay???? So next time you hear about someone getting FIRED, you should be scared. Be very scared. Because the person after that could be YOU!! The constructs of society were built on capitalism . . .

As I read Cheryl's manifesto, I notice several people have already started lining up to exit the train so, taking their cue, I follow suit. The second the doors open, we flood out the exit, down an off-ramp where people are not afraid to step in front of me and completely cut me off. Once I'm in the parking lot of the train station, there are several vans waiting, and I see most of them are already filled with passengers as the drivers load up their bags and drive away. There's now one left, and the kind middle-aged driver spots me and waves me over. She smiles at me, the first timer, with wrinkled lips and eyes that have seen a thing or two.

"Your lucky day. We got room for one more," she says as she grabs my bag and tosses it on top of everyone else's. I pay her seven dollars in cash, hop into the van and see every single seat is taken, with the middle row full of standing people. So I grab the nearest strap and hang on for dear life as our plucky driver swerves around corners toward the ferry. It's hard to imagine a less relaxed way of traveling to your relaxing vacation. Sadly, I have one more mode of transportation before I can even come close to a beach.

We reach the ferry, and even though I'm the first one out the door, somehow everyone has grabbed their weekend bags and lined up to buy tickets to the boat before me. So many colorful bags, high-tech coolers, little red wagons full of farmers' market produce—we're suddenly on Planet Summer. The ferry is packed full of all the people I'd brushed up against on the trains and van. It's like an all-star gathering of my fellow commuters: Guy with Oversized Sunglasses and Shirt Unbuttoned to His Navel! Woman Who Thinks She's Sarah Jessica Parker! Twentysomething Couple Who Just Had a Fight and Are Trying to Make the Best of It! I stand inside the boat, sandwiched in the middle of everyone's luggage lined up like soldiers about to storm the beach, cursing Paige and her wedding.

As the ferry slowly docks and the cute boat hands on the other side swing open the doors, I feel the sunshine smack my face and realize that I forgot sunglasses.

"Maaaaax!" I hear the distinct wailing of Paige calling my name. I wasn't expecting to see anyone greet me at the dock, but here she is with Eliza and Katie. They're all barely recognizable in their caftans, hats and sandals.

"Where are your bougie matching bridesmaids' T-shirts?" I ask them, my way of saying hello.

"Chasten's bedazzling them back at home as we speak," Paige says.

"Bougie Bedazzling is the name of my new boutique," Eliza says. We all laugh, and I feel bad they have to whiff my classic summer scent: Complicated Body Odor by Max Moody. On the way to Chasten's house, Paige informs me that Austin paid for a luxury SUV to take them to the ferry, bypassing the several hours of the poor man's commute I just had to endure. They just went to the market and stocked up on loads of fresh vegetables, fruit, meats and fish for grilling and of course booze. Paige wants to keep it casual beach chic and not have anything fancy. I'm sensing she's reacting to her shmancy engagement party in Connecticut that Austin's parents threw for them and deciding she's the boss on this one. Rolling my little suitcase over the wobbly boardwalk—no cars here—it feels like a kind of strange version of Oz but instead of ruby slippers, you wear flip-flops. Actually, some people wear ruby slippers here too.

We arrive at a gated house you can't make out behind the trees, and I'm shocked to see that the gate is a little bit busted and not working properly. Is Chasten's perfect world not so perfect after all? When Paige opens the gate, the answer to that question is apparent: Chasten's world is perfection. A long private boardwalk is surrounded by a beautifully manicured garden filled with lavender; baby's breath; pink bergenia; and red, gold and yellow zinnias just in the first few steps. My knowledge of gardens has grown so much in the past couple of weeks that I'm able to tick off the names of each one out loud, but the girls laugh and pretend they're not impressed. Beyond the rainbow of flowers comes an enviable garden full of basil, sage and mint, and as we pass by, I rub my fingers on the rosemary for a powerful whiff of the herbal delights. The house is a ridiculously sized modernist glass-and-wood monolith centered on the beach. The front door is open, and Chasten effortlessly prepares lunch in an apron and no shirt.

"You made it!" Chasten greets me, wiping avocado off his

hands onto his apron and engulfing me in his bear hug. I don't hate it.

"I did, indeed."

"Would you like a drink? Aperol Spritz? Pimm's Cup? Frosé?"

"Mimosas too," Paige says, spraying herself with some fancy brand of sunscreen I've never seen or heard of.

I'm overwhelmed with all the beverage options and look around the voluminous house with golden sunlight pouring through every window, door and skylight, and can't believe this is Fire Island. It feels more like what you'd expect in the Hamptons or the South of France or heaven. Large patio walls open completely onto the expansive deck with an infinity pool overlooking the goddamned ocean, which sparkles like blue-green diamonds.

"I'd love a Pimm's Cup," I say, choosing the one I barely know. The fresh scent of ocean air is rivaled by the smoky aroma of Chasten's grilled shrimp. I want to tell him that serious chefs aren't shirtless, until he points out the lunch spread he's putting the finishing touches on: a caprese salad with fresh heirloom tomatoes, four different kinds of quiches, and the mimosa bar with your choice of orange, blood orange, pomegranate or mango juice. "I thought your brother was the chef," I say in awe of everything.

"Runs in the family," Eliza says.

"It's nothing. I just whipped it together."

"It took you longer to get here than for Chasten to make all of this," Paige says, making me feel guilty somehow?

"Looks incredible," I say about the feast. I never would have imagined Chasten putting this much effort into someone else's big weekend. He seems so . . . Chasten-centric. And there's something refreshing about his attention to food, which Greg and I never bothered to care about or made a focal point of our relationship. Whenever we had dinner with other people, Greg would always say, "I'm a total foodie," and then proceed, without fail, to order a medium-well hamburger or the simplest pasta dish no matter what type of restaurant we went to. Even though my culinary knowledge is limited to middle-of-the-road diners and the midwestern staple of meat and potatoes, I was always more open than Greg when it came to trying new things. For our third anniversary, we went to Eleven Madison Park (my idea), and he actually ordered a side of buttered noodles, which he made his main dish. I laughed then and thought it was punk rock to order a kid's dish off menu at a three-star Michelin restaurant, but now I realize it's kind of immature.

Paige leads me outside to say hi to her two other bridesmaids, who are on the patio sunbathing. These two are Paige's work squad. Nina, originally from Ireland, in her forties, sits shrouded under an umbrella, wearing huge sunglasses and loose-fitting white linen clothing that covers her entire body, while reading a book. She's a hugely successful voice-over artist who does everything from audiobooks to Zoloft commercials. We chat about the weather for a few minutes as Nina informs me of the various sunscreens she has for the weekend in case I'd like to borrow some.

In a completely opposite tableau, Cori is sprawled out on a unicorn raft, floating in the pool, wearing a bikini and worshipping the sun. Cori is a no-nonsense Texan and producer extraordinaire where Paige works, and loves to party. They're both several mimosas in. The always competitive Cori tells me she wants everyone to get into the pool already so we can have chicken fights.

The only ones missing are Erica, Paige's other best friend

from high school besides me, who's six months pregnant and still lives in suburban Chicago, and Paige's older sister, Zoe, who has three kids and lives in LA. Both of them couldn't fly in for the bachelorette party and again later for the wedding.

After laughing with Nina and Cori about how insane our new living situation is, with the swimming pool, ocean view and modern five-bedroom house, and how we should probably make a music video, I walk to the end of the deck to take in the view of the beach. It's a perfect day with clear blue skies, and it occurs to me just now how deprived we are of the sun in the city. The lulling waves foam onto fresh sand, and I take a profoundly deep breath, trying to release all of my tension, anxiousness and hyperconnectivity.

My moment of Zen crashes to a halt when three golden Adonises in Speedos cross the beach in front of our house. The three of them apparently have the same gym routine and turn in unison to size up the house. I'd say we all make eye contact for a brief moment if I could see behind their sunglasses, and I think one of them smiles at me until I hear Paige yell, "Max! C'mere!"

Back inside, Paige hands me a mango mimosa and shows me which room I'm sleeping in. It's a beautifully decorated upstairs bedroom painted in sea-breeze light blue with magazine-quality furniture. There's a king-sized bed and a bathroom that connects to another equally sized bedroom. "That's your bathroom with Chasten," Paige informs me as I mentally shuffle through all of the bathroom rituals that I'll have to share with him. *Are we going to see each other naked? Or worse, brushing our teeth?* "Are you cool not facing the ocean?"

"Of course," I say, sipping my fizzy cocktail. "You should get all the ocean views. This is your bachelorette party."

Paige sits down on the bed, staring into space. Oh no.

"What's wrong?"

"Nothing," she says. "It's just all hitting me at once and it's so overwhelming." Paige looks up at me, studies my face. "Can I tell you something you promise not to tell anyone?"

"What?" I ask. Paige doesn't say anything for a while. We just listen to the crashing ocean waves.

"Are you sure?"

"Stop. Just say it. What?"

"Well, if I'm being honest with you. And myself. I'm not sure I want to go through with this." My mind starts churning and I can't believe what I'm hearing. This is so Paige.

What Your Favorite Version of Paige Says about Your Personality

CHILDHOOD NEXT-DOOR NEIGHBOR PAIGE

You're nostalgic. You long for a simpler time.

MUSICAL THEATER MAJOR PAIGE

You're a giant dork.

EARLY NEW YORK PAIGE

You're an undiscovered artist. You love red meat and cocaine.

BRIDE-TO-BE PAIGE

You're a romantic at heart but you're not annoying about it.

chapter

FIFTEEN

FUCKING STRAIGHT PEOPLE. I REALIZE I'VE BEEN ON FIRE IS-
land for three and a half minutes, so I normally wouldn't pit
straights versus gays, but goddamn. I'm too painfully aware of
the history of same-sex marriage not being legal, so the idea of
canceling a wedding shouldn't be as easy as buying and sending
back the wine. It's a privilege to question whether or not she
wants to get married. Paige gets an engagement party, a bachelorette party, a shower, a wedding. She's lucky. I spent the better chunk of my twenties wanting only one of those things.

Jesus. I just made her moment all about me.

"You're not sure you want to go through with this . . . bachelorette party weekend?"

"Not just the weekend. The whole . . . thing. The wedding
thing."

"The *wedding* thing? No. This is not like workshopping food
at a restaurant. You've ordered your entrée. Now you just have to
eat it and not have any buyer's remorse."

"I'm serious, Max. This isn't me being indecisive. This is real." Paige's eyes fill with tears, and I know she's struggling. She discreetly wipes away a tear. It fills me with heartbreak to see her like this.

"I forgot my sunglasses," I say, trying to defuse the emotion with something to distract her.

"Are you serious?"

"Yeah, I just never wear them in the city—"

"No, I mean, I'm having a heart-to-heart with you about not wanting to go through with this huge event, and you're like bringing up sunglasses."

I snort-laugh. Paige laughs too. Now we can't stop. We die giggling.

Paige's indecisiveness has infiltrated her whole life. When we were growing up, she couldn't decide on gymnastics or ice-skating, piano lessons or guitar, the fuchsia Formica bedroom set or the red convertible Toyota Celica. Why her mom continued to give her options, I'll never know. One summer, Paige went to three different sleepaway camps in Wisconsin, Michigan and Maine, doing a two-week stint at each, unable to decide before going back home. But Paige wasn't a brat about any of it. Just a product of her upbringing. Paige's mom had plenty of disposable income—thanks to marrying up three times and an excellent divorce lawyer, she could indulge Paige in all of her whimsical decision-making. Maybe Paige's wedding is her last big indecisive hoorah before she gives her indecisiveness the boot. Wishful thinking.

"Don't tell anyone what I just told you," Paige says as we walk along the boardwalk into town to find a pair of sunglasses for me. I should mention that "town" in the Pines consists of a grocery store, disco, bistro, café, flower shop, wine store, hardware place, and a couple of clothing stores, all packed into a very short stretch where the ferry docks.

"I won't," I say to Paige with meaningful eye contact, making sure she knows I'm here for her. It feels good to have Paige back on my side as her only confidant. "But shouldn't you, like, figure this out soon? I mean, if you need to start canceling things?" Paige says this is why she wanted to get married so quickly, so there wouldn't be enough time to second-guess herself. As Paige speaks, all I hear is flippity-floppity sounds fast approaching behind us. I turn to see two very hairy, very sweaty guys on our heels, only wearing Speedos, flip-flops and lime-green wristbands, pulling a red wagon full of bottles of rosé.

"S'cuse us," they say with smiles as we let them pass. There's only room for two people side by side on all the boardwalks, and these guys are in a hurry to drink their pink wine somewhere, so we happily let them pass.

"Oh, the shops are straight that way, right?" Paige asks one of the Speedos.

"You mean gayly forward, yes," one of them says. We laugh and thank them, and as they forge ahead, we see each of their phones sticking out of the backs of their Speedos. Paige and I silently look at each other with slight smiles. And then a tiny rust-colored Cavapoo runs between us to catch up with her daddies.

I'm scanning all the random beachy items the store sells—an eighty-dollar candle that smells like "Paris After the Rain," an all-white cashmere tote bag with the words RAINBOW FLAG embroidered on it, a massive coffee-table book full of silver daddies—while listening to Paige continue. "It didn't hit me at the engagement party because I was with him and we were IN IT. Ya know?" We both go silent as we quizzically eye a magazine called *BUTT* with two farmhands in seventies mustaches chewing blades of hay on the cover. "Is this vintage or now?" Paige asks.

"No clue. What were you saying?"

"Just all the momentum of our engagement party kept me in it to win it, and now we're here and Austin's not here and I'm just like . . . contemplating everything."

"That's your first mistake."

"What?"

"Thinking."

"Oooh! Sunglasses!" Paige says joyfully, pointing to a small display by the counter. I point to a dark pair of classic-looking ones and ask the model-handsome store clerk if I can see them.

I try them on, look into the mirror and say, "I'll take them." Paige whips her head and looks like I'm insane.

"What are you doing? Don't you want to try some other ones on?" The model cashier takes my credit card, I slip on my new sunglasses, and we walk out of there.

"That's how you make a decision," I say to Paige as she rolls her eyes and sighs.

"I need like five thousand more mimosas."

"Same," I say and gulp, realizing I didn't look at the price of the sunglasses. I hope I didn't just drop a small fortune to prove a point.

We walk back to the house along the ocean, which looks like a tourism commercial for a gay beach. Six shirtless guys, sweaty and playing volleyball. Three guys snapping photos of each other, pretending they're supermodels, splash around in the water. A couple in matching straw hats, holding hands while they walk. Everything looks sepia-toned in my new sunglasses. On Paige's advice, I've taken off my New Balance sneakers and socks and I'm barefoot. The lush sand feels exfoliating under my city-swollen feet. It's a beautiful summer Friday outside but I can tell inside Paige is a wintry mix of uncertainty, doubt and a million other Paige demons that she's wrestling. There are so many more things I want to tell her: You've made the right decision. You should be so happy that you've found the rest of your life. Think of all the horrible creeps you'll never have to date again. But I remember my mom would always remind me as a kid when Paige grew quiet like this, "Let Paige be Paige." This is her thing.

Instead of giving her advice, I bring up our past misadventures together as kids. The time she broke her collarbone doing a cartwheel and a week later I sprained my ankle on the trampoline in her backyard. Our junior year of high school when our parents went out of town and we both got drunk for the first time by chugging vodka straight from the bottle until we threw up. The stray cat who wandered into my garage one fall whom we lovingly named after Grizabella from *Cats* only to realize she was possessed by an evil spirit from hell, so we let her go. It's nice to continually remind ourselves of our shared idiosyncratic experiences.

For a moment, we walk in comfortable silence, half in the water and half out, listening to the waves, feeling the city dissolve, pondering what's to come. Paige checks her phone.

"Just in time," she says. "Chasten has brunch ready." I notice she's saying "brunch" a lot more now.

After single-handedly making a delicious *late breakfast* for seven people, Chasten deserves a little credit. Or maybe I'm just mango-mimosa drunk. We're all sitting at a circular table with an umbrella on the patio, just having finished eating, laughing and dishing. Paige's doubts have been temporarily muffled by her closest group of friends, and I'm thinking maybe Paige shouldn't be alone with her thoughts, like, ever. The ladies head inside for afternoon power naps before we start drinking and eating all over again in a couple of hours. I tell Chasten to take a load off and float in the unicorn raft while I clear the dishes. "That was so good," I say, and mean it.

He smirks at me. "You're just saying that."

"I would never fake compliment someone," I say, trying to reassure him. He refuses to sit, and the two of us go back and forth from the patio to the kitchen, weaving around the table and each other as we clean up.

"I can never tell if you're being sarcastic." Could there be a worse thing to say to someone who's trying to be sincere?

"Are *you* being sarcastic?" I ask sarcastically. I can feel him staring at me blankly while I collect the cloth napkins with tiny watermelons on them. We try to move past this pregnant pause by grabbing the large bowl of uneaten cherries at the same time. Our hands almost touch. It's weird. I swallow, nervous. Was that an accident? I avoid any eye contact, let him take the bowl, and start stacking the salad bowls.

"This is such a great house." I try to break the silence and smooth over the moment we almost touched.

"Yeah, we've been renting it for a couple of years, but everyone is getting so busy now with work and settling down with husbands and stuff. I'm not sure I need to come back here year after year the way I did in my twenties. There's more to see, ya know?"

"Totally," I say, wondering if I missed out by never doing a Fire Island share with all the gay friends I don't have while he's probably been using "summer" as a verb since he was a baby.

"So did Paige tell you?" he asks as we both hold stacks of

dirty plates, having eye contact with each other for the first time since the cleaning began.

"Tell me . . . what?" I raise my eyebrows. There's no way Paige shared the information that she's debating calling off her wedding when she just made me swear on my life not to tell anyone.

"Oh, if she didn't bring you on board, then never mind."

"Wait—she brought me on board. I'm way on board. She brought you on board too?" I have no idea what board either of us is on.

"About the . . ."

"Wedding. Yes. What about it?" I blink twice.

He squints. "Are you sure she said something to you?"

"She said she's not sure—"

"That she wants to go through with it." There it is. Paige is fully talking out of both sides of her mouth or whatever you call it. "We're going to have to do something about it," Chasten says.

"We?" I say, insinuating he and I are an ocean apart. "Like what?"

"I dunno. Team up. Make sure she's not second-guessing herself. You know how Paige gets."

"Yeah. I do. I've known her since I was five."

"Right. I forgot you own her."

"I don't own her. I'm just saying we go further back than you."

"Now you're being defensive."

"I'm not defensive," I say.

"I can't have my brother's fiancée deciding she doesn't want to marry him on my watch." He has a point. If I hosted Paige's bachelorette party and she decided to call off the wedding, I'd feel guilty too.

"So, what do you think we should do?" I've been so used to

seeing Chasten as my rival, it doesn't feel right to suddenly be on the same team. We've firmly established our roles as the best man and the man of honor who definitely did not have a terrible hookup the first night we met and definitely are not into each other that way.

"We have an entire weekend to turn her around. We're going to have to put our heads together."

I look up at him and can't help but think, *Didn't we already try to do that on your rooftop?*

I can't fall asleep during designated nap time, so I read the rest of my painfully sad work goodbye emails, then join an "NYC Native Plants" discussion group on Facebook. I get sucked into a long thread where plant people start arguing about different kinds of garden soil, and I laugh to myself, thinking that the stakes for plant drama could not be lower. After that, I switch social media apps and discover the happier, less argumentative world of Plant Instagram. I didn't realize how many plant nerds there were, and I guess I've become one. Plantstagram is full of all kinds of people, from high-end interior designers to farmers showing off. This inevitably leads me to #PlantDaddy, where there are gobs of cute guys posing with their green loved ones. I make a mental note to start my own Plants of Instagram account after I get home and can take photos of my little collection. Next, I exhaust every news, pop culture and angry Karen article until there's zero content left to consume. I'm googling Jennifer Aniston's net worth when there's a knock on my door.

"Greetings!" I say, feeling empowered by my new beach domain and realizing how I could get comfortable in a bedroom like this, the sounds of the ocean waves drifting softly through the open windows past the framed watercolors of seashells on the wall opposite my king-sized bed.

Chasten enters through our Jack-and-Jill bathroom, which startles me because I forgot that was there and thought the knock was coming from the main door.

"Just a heads-up," he says, taking off his shirt. We get it. Your body is perfect. "I'm hitting the shower, so . . ."

With the long white curtains billowing in the breeze and golden afternoon sunlight backlighting Chasten, he looks like some kind of angel sent from heaven.

"Hello?" he says.

I shake whatever thoughts I'm having out of my head. "Cool. Yeah. No prob. It's all yours."

"I thought a little more about Paige and what to do."

"I'm sure she's just stuck in her regular old indecision mode."

"I want to make sure. Maybe we play a game or something. Like 'How Well Do You Know the Groom' shit."

"Quiz her about Austin?"

"Could be fun, right?"

I'm not sure. "What if she gets something wrong, wouldn't that remind her of how well she *doesn't* know him?"

"We'll keep it light and easy. All the little reminders she loves about him. Keep the focus on him and not some random male stripper or something."

"We're not having strippers, are we?"

"Not for Paige," Chasten says with a smile and a forced wink. He tosses his shirt in a ball on the bathroom counter, turns on the shower and strips to his God-given nothings. The door is slightly open, and I can see him in the mirror. I wonder if he's leaving the door open on purpose.

The Six Questions Everyone Asks Each Other in Fire Island

1. When did you get in?

2. Where are you staying?

3. Who are you staying with?

4. How long are you here?

5. Half share or quarter share?

6. Are you going out tonight?

chapter

SIXTEEN

AAAAAND SUDDENLY I'M FEELING GUILTY, LIKE I'M SOME-
how cheating on Greg. Sharing a bathroom with Chasten
has given me the false sensation that I'm in a monogamous,
live-in relationship with a new guy. I haven't shared a bathroom
with anyone before or after Greg (except for college roommates),
and now I'm finding myself imagining what it would be like to
actually be in a relationship with Chasten. Maybe we have this
whole not-telling-Paige-about-our-hookup thing wrong.

Forget Greg. Let's say he's completely out of the picture.
What would life with Chasten look like? He'd cook a lot, for
one. I'd come home late from the office and there he'd be, shirtless under his apron with a funny saying on it like "You Had
Me at Jell-O." He'd greet me by putting a pig in a blanket in
my mouth or some other fancy hors d'oeuvre that I don't
know about because he's the chef and I'm me. I'd sip a cocktail
that he invented inside our beautiful but not over-the-top
summerhouse—maybe in the Hudson Valley or a laid-back part

of the Hamptons like Montauk. There would be a fire because of course it's October and the leaves are blowing and piling up outside and winter is in the air and "This Charming Man" by the Smiths would be playing on vinyl. Oh, and there'd be decorative pumpkins artfully scattered throughout the house. Saturday morning I'd wake up in bed to him surprising me with coffee and muffins or a chocolate croissant that he'd made from scratch while he'd teach me all about what kind of chocolate went into the pastry. He'd surprise me with a trip to the Ivory Coast because it has the world's best cocoa beans and—oh my god, what am I doing?! I'm projecting an entire life onto this person whom I've had a horrible one-night stand with and am now pretending that I hadn't met before so I won't ruin my best friend's wedding. Predicting my romantic future with someone is exactly the kind of assholery I've done with Greg for the past decade, and look where that's gotten me.

Why do I do this?

My pathetic thoughts come crashing to a halt as I hop out of the shower and hear the sounds of the Weeknd mixed in with the cackling laughter from downstairs. It's crazy that a group of six women somehow all showered and got ready for the night before me, but I ended up finally falling into a nap. What's a group of bridesmaids called? A school? An army? Let's go with a cackle.

Walking downstairs I see all the women look amazingly done up in perfect beachy evening wear, ready for their Instagram portrait close-up. Chasten is with them in a fresh, perfectly fitted dark T-shirt and contrasting floral shorts, and I now realize I don't have a "Friday night outfit" like everyone else, but I'm okay with that.

"Good morning," Eliza says sarcastically. Everyone turns to see me, hair still wet and a sheepish smile on my face.

"Hurry up and do this shot. We're gonna miss tea!" Paige says, holding out some clear liquid in a red cup and already dropping the Fire Island Pines lingo. I'm relieved to see she's not wearing a bridal veil with tiny penises on it. Yet.

"What is it?" I ask.

"Tequila!" three of the girls say in unison.

"The good kind." Chasten shows me the bottle of some stuff I've never heard of. "No hangovers."

"You do shots?" Paige asks, quoting a line from *Sixteen Candles*.

"Come on, wolf it!" I say, finishing the bit from our favorite movie.

"Woo!" Paige cheers. While the girls sip and primp, Chasten tilts his head, looks at me funny.

"Don't tell me you've never seen *Sixteen Candles*." He doesn't say anything. Just a smirk. "Oh, Jesus. Don't tell me you've never *heard* of *Sixteen Candles*!" I say, now emboldened and feeling the sweet warmth of that top-shelf tequila coursing through every cell in my body.

"It's my favorite John Hughes movie." He slams his tequila and pours us each more. Color me shocked.

The cackle of bridesmaids walk and talk and laugh ahead of us on the boardwalk, all carrying their "roadies," or to-go cups, of tequila in red plastic cups. These ladies are feeling themselves on this all-gay island community, and they're ready to party. Chasten and I walk a few feet behind them, listening and laughing along with them as they discuss their ideal playlist for the night.

"I want Donna Summer."

"I hope it's like an all-seventies disco mix."

"Oh my god, no, I want full-on hard-core gay dance music."

"I thought she was going to say 'porn,'" I say to Chasten, making him laugh. Hearing the faint sounds of music coming from one unique house after another, seeing a few deer leap through the woods, feeling the sun approaching its descent in the distance with a slight ocean breeze sweeping past us, I realize I'd forgotten how magical it is here.

"So do people actually drink tea at Low Tea?" I ask as a joke.

"No. It's supposed to be ironic. Like English teatime."

"I know. I was kidding."

"So was I."

We pass a couple of guys in their seventies with tan, leathery skin, carrying beach chairs and umbrellas. They pass us with smiles, looking like they're going to have a romantic dinner after a relaxing day at the beach. The girls are now so far ahead of us and must've taken a turn somewhere because we can't see them anymore. It's just the two of us on this boardwalk that stretches along the houses right on the beach.

"You ready for the questions?" Chasten asks.

"Questions about the bachelorette party?"

"No, *the* questions. When you walk into tea and start mingling, everyone asks you the exact same six questions."

"I don't think I'm aware of the questions."

Chasten lists The Questions in the typical order of their appearance.

"Maybe we should have T-shirts made with "The Questions" on the front and our answers on the back," I say.

Chasten lets out a big laugh. "That's actually hysterical," he says. He got one of my movie references and now he's getting my jokes. What is happening right now?

"Do you want to go to all of the teas?" he asks.

"Is that another one of the questions?"

"No, I'm genuinely asking. I didn't know if Paige had that planned out."

"I think we were just doing Low Tea, then dinner, then play it by ear. Aren't there only two teas?"

"There are basically like four teas now."

"Four?! How?"

"There's Low Tea, which we're going to now. Then High Tea right after that. Then Mid Tea, which sort of overlaps Low Tea and High Tea. Then Lina Tea."

I look at Chasten, waiting for him to explain what Lina Tea is.

"Lina was the DJ who used to spin that tea, but she doesn't anymore, so it just morphed into Whatever Tea."

"Got it. I think." I don't get it. I'll probably never get it.

As we walk, Chasten says hi and hugs no less than six different people and kisses three of them on the mouth hello. He's the mayor of this gay town.

We turn the corner onto a boardwalk creatively called Fire Island Boulevard, and now we see all types of gaggles of gays beelining for the party that is Low Tea. A few impossibly young ones pass us by at a weirdly fast pace, clearly amped up on something more than Red Bull and vodka. I can hear a *thump thump thump* in the distance and wonder if it's one of the song selections the girls were discussing. I suspect we won't hear any Smiths playing tonight. The club music is getting louder and louder as we approach the harbor where the entire community has congregated, and now it sounds like a raging party. Walking along the water by the boats we see the girls in the distance getting pseudo-catcalled by guys as the entire bachelorette party walks into tea like supermodels strutting the runway. The guys eat them up.

"Let the games begin," Chasten says with a furtive sigh like he's done this a million times before. A small knot of social anxiety in my stomach grows as I see just how many people are at this thing. The main patio is completely packed with bodies that are so crowded in, they're unable to move. People literally spill outside of the venue like penguins falling off a melting iceberg. Inside the restaurant, which is cleared nightly to make room for a dance floor, colored lights swirl around even more sweaty bodies.

"Come," Paige says, putting her arm around me as all of them get swallowed by the crowd before us. I hesitate for a second, not wanting to elbow my way through the masses, but Paige, who knows I shudder at the thought of crowds, pulls me up the few stairs and suddenly we're in the deep end of the petri dish—there's no going back. As Paige holds my wrist and guides me through the sea of freshly-showered-from-the-beach people like I'm her pet, I turn to see a too-serious Gen Zer ask another equally earnest Gen Zer, "When did you get in?" And they begin to rattle off The Questions (in exact order!) as we sail past them.

The rest of our gang is nowhere in sight, so Paige leads me immediately inside, which is where the dance floor is, and I shake my head no. I mime drinking two very large drinks and Paige nods, knowing I'd prefer to hit the bar first, which has several chaotic lines mixed in with the crowd.

When did you get in? How long are you here?

I take a firm stance near the far corner, where it's slightly less crowded. Paige follows me like she's my pet for once. I'm secretly proud of myself for not wearing flip-flops and instead opting for sneakers, now that I'm feeling dozens of feet stepping on my toes. We stand behind two mammoth men in their fifties who are shirtless, wearing their muscles like armor, protecting themselves as they head into battle.

"What should we get?" I yell over the Demi Lovato.

"Is there like a cocktail menu?" Paige asks.

"Oh my god. No. We're not doing this."

"Doing what?" Paige looks at me in disbelief, as if she's forgotten our entire lifetime together.

"This. The indecisive dance. It's tequila, vodka or gin. That's it."

"Fiiiiiine. Sheesh!" Paige pouts. She wants options. "Maybe we should stick to tequila."

"How 'bout margaritas?" I ask, trying to give her at least one option.

"Oooh, good call," she says as a guy wearing a purple crop top that reads BORING AF turns from the bar messily carrying two giant toxic, orange-colored drinks, spilling them all over his hands and everyone around us. Something tells me he's anything but what his T-shirt suggests. "Yum. What are those?" Paige asks him.

"Planter's punch," he says like she should know better. Like Paige is the tourist and he's the native on the Island of Fire.

"What's in it?" Oh, cool. Paige is treating this random guy like a server at a restaurant she can ask a million questions.

"Alcohol," the guy responds with a laugh, wisely shutting down any follow-up questions we might have. "You should try 'em," he says to me with a playful smile as he gets sucked into the vortex of the shifting crowd on his way to find his friends.

Half share? Quarter share?

Before Paige can ask another question, I pull her toward a rare opening at the bar. A bartender who looks underage, underdressed and undernourished is frantically busy messing up drink orders, and I can see some of the locals on the front line are not having it. One demanding older gentleman with an eighties mustache who looks like an extra from *Longtime Companion* is teaching him how to make what looks like a proper gin and tonic. "Lime. Not a lemon, sweetie."

Where are you staying? Who are you staying with?

I grab the poor, inexperienced bartender's attention before a half dozen other pushy patrons. "Can we get two planter's punches?" The kid barely nods and he's off, pouring the ready-made mixes into plastic cups.

"Wait—I thought you were going to ask for a menu," Paige says. I throw her a dead-eyed stare and focus on the bartender who's pouring seventeen different kinds of alcohol into the other alcohol and topping it off with alcohol. A splash of alcohol and a dollop of alcohol.

After Paige and I clink cups and sip, we both squint, feeling this sting of orange poison hit the backs of our throats, which immediately makes me drunk. Back at the house, the tequila had given me a nice buzzy mellow high, while the planter's punch has made me jacked up on sugar.

Howlongareyouhere?Areyougoingouttonight?

Surveying the crowd, everyone is wearing tight T-shirts or tight tank tops that look like placeholders that will eventually come off at some point later tonight. A select few of the guys are wearing polos (tight) and pastel shorts (short) and look like they've taken a detour from the Hamptons. One guy twirling to the music alone in the corner wears a tennis-white seventies terry cloth headband, and that's pretty much it. The music in his head doesn't match the music that's actually playing, but we love him for letting his freak flag fly. Looking around at all the hard-core mingling makes me wonder how anyone couldn't find love here. There are enough choices of men here to make the most indecisive person on earth happy.

Which reminds me. I turn to ask Paige if she sees the girls, but Paige is now a large, bearded blond daddy wearing a John Deere cap with a dolphin tattoo on his shoulder. He sips his Corona Light with a lime and smiles at me with refreshed lips. Realizing I've lost Paige, I smile back and scan the crowd. It looks like I'm pretending to look for "my friend" and avoiding this nice guy. It takes me back to my Chicago days of popping into gay bar after gay bar, looking for "my friend" and leaving out of fright before chatting anyone up. The thought of those days makes me shudder now.

I spot our bachelorette party by a rainbow wall backdrop, posing for photos, so I smile *see ya* to the blond and head over there. Several twinks, daddies, otters, tinkers, tailors, soldiers and spies later, I've reached the rainbow wall but the girls are gone. Now it's just five self-possessed guys, all posing for the perfect shot, all under the spell of getting future likes, all wearing matching T-shirts that are stylishly shredded on the bottoms and read "145 Bay Walk," which is I guess their house address? A summer share with merch. That's new to me.

I can't find the girls anywhere, not even Chasten, so I wade back through the crowd and head toward—where else would they be—the dance floor.

Now I can feel the *thump thump thump* of the music in my entire body and don't recognize whichever diva du jour is singing. The sun has begun to set, and the DJ is spinning aggressive dance music. A deep cut. The second I enter the periphery of the dance floor, the DJ finally drops the bass of the track, and the crowd unanimously goes wild. Someone accidentally twerks into me, causing me to drop my drink and spill the remainder of my planter's punch everywhere. Thankfully, everyone is too hyped up on the music to feel my drink on their bare legs.

I look around and realize I haven't seen Chasten since we got here. I'm assuming he's holding court with his constituents somewhere, acting out his mayoral duties. Then, in the exact middle of the dance floor, I spot the girls, who have appropriately gone wild. Despite the negative reputation that bachelorette parties usually get when they infiltrate a gay space, these women are cool bachelorettes and have, not surprisingly, become the life of this party. Eliza and Katie are grinding away in an A-list gay sandwich, Nina and Cori, both shockingly great dancers, hold their own and elicit cheers for their moves. Paige is in the middle of them all, still nursing her planter's punch with eyes like slits, probably wanting to drop some Tony trivia, and I know she's having a blast.

I slowly back away, hoping that none of them see me.

The sunsets in Fire Island are epic; I remember from that time Greg and I were here. We'd have dinner around 6:00 p.m., walk right past the craziness of Low Tea, watch the sunset and go home to have a quick drink before bed around 10:00 p.m. Greg kept telling me we were doing Fire Island wrong, but I didn't care. It was fun to be here with him, and our romantic bond was alive back then, so none of the guy candy tempted us. Like a *Titanic* cliché, we held on to each other as the sun set and the last tiny dot of fiery red orange disappeared. Every night it was our favorite show to binge.

Squeezing myself out of the crush of bodies at Low Tea, I walk to the end of the marina to grab a front-row seat to the sunset. There are about a half dozen guys sitting on the dock with their feet dangling over the calm water in the bay, plastic cups still in hand. A few of them look intimate, like couples, and could be in either thirty-year or thirty-minute relationships. I sneak glances at them while I stand and watch the sun, realizing this nightly ritual feels different alone, without my guy version of Kate Winslet to clutch from behind.

That's when I see Chasten sitting at the very edge of the pier, shockingly alone, staring at the light show and sipping his drink. He doesn't look sad or lonely or anything. Just content. A side of him I haven't seen before, since usually each side of him is surrounded by people. He looks so comfortably alone, I'm deciding if I should leave him that way or say hi. That's when I have an idea.

"This morning. Staying on the ocean. With my best friend and her bachelorette party. Leaving on Sunday. Not sure if I'm going out tonight."

Chasten turns with a big, broad smile, knowing exactly what I'm talking about.

"Your answers to The Questions."

"Did I get them all?"

"You forgot half share or quarter share, but that doesn't count since you're here for the weekend." We both laugh and stare at the sun performing its finale for the night.

"Can I sit?"

Chasten scoots over to make room, and I plop down next to him, relieved to have a seat after what feels like hours of standing and roaming. He hands me his drink to offer me a sip, and I take it. The sky and clouds surrounding the sun are filled with amber, apricot, fuchsia, lavender and flaming crimson.

"The sun is such a show-off," I say.

"A little too overconfident, if you ask me."

And then. Out of nowhere. The sky darkens. Clouds roll in.

The summer evening glow turns almost pitch-black. A downpour. All the fair-weather sunset gazers run for cover, as if their beachwear can't handle a little water. Chasten and I just sit there, a competition of who will get up first. Neither of us wins. Or we both win. Either way, we're not moving. The rain is a much-needed cleanser from the heat, the night, the everything. It feels good.

And then the skies clear; the rain stops. The breathtaking, rose-colored sky is topped off by a magical rainbow. All of the colors are represented in front of us and, if I'm being cheesy, all the colors of the rainbow are behind us, dancing away at Low Tea. If I didn't know any better, I would think Chasten and I are experiencing what feels like, dare I say, a romantic moment. Before I can process this, all of the sunset watchers return, half-wet but mostly dry from taking cover from the rain. Dozens more Low Tea revelers run out to the pier, surrounding us.

Chasten and I are soaking wet, in our same positions. We turn to each other.

I wonder if he's thinking what I'm thinking.

Chasten

Sup?

Hi.

Hey! Let's totes chillax sometime
in the city sans Paigerooni.

I liked your shirt last night.

Paige. Am I right? 😬

You're from Connecticut. Do you
know this guy Peter I work with?

Question: Do you enjoy food?

chapter

SEVENTEEN

Fuuuuuuuuuuuuuuuuuuuuuuuuuuuuuuuuuuuuuuuuuuuuck. Seriously. Fuck.

What did I do last night? I got too close to the fire and flirted with Chasten. This was not the plan. We were supposed to stick to our story: we've never met and we never had an awkward one-night stand. It wasn't even a one-night stand. It was just an embarrassingly terrible non-hookup. Chasten and I agreed to not fall prey to our initial attraction to each other. I'm "still in a relationship" with Greg, and we don't want to overshadow Paige's wedding. The trouble is now I can't stop thinking about what almost woulda coulda shoulda mighta happened.

Here's what happened: After the heavenly rainbow during Low Tea, we moved to Middle Tea, which is basically the exact same group of people who migrate next door and do the exact same things (stand around, pose, ask The Questions, drink) around a pool, which was fun. We finally caught up with the girls, who were fairly drunk by that point and all decided to switch to drinking water. "Gotta stay hydrated," Katie drunkenly kept re-peating to herself and to no one in particular in between sips.

Before heading home for dinner, we popped into High Tea, where it's the same people in a *different* location, standing around, posing, asking The Questions and drinking. I made everyone laugh by suggesting they should eliminate all the teas and there should just be one big Super Tea. It was funny when we were drunk, *okay*?

Unable to drink and stand around anymore, and with no more teas left, we all went home in a group around 9:00 p.m., Chasten grilled skirt steak and had a bunch of elaborate salads pre-prepared.

Every. Single. Girl. Passed. Out.

They all went to take a quick disco nap before eating, and none of them woke up. So Chasten and I let them sleep, and the two of us ate his delicious meal alone. Between the poolside feast, the gloriously decorated, candlelit dinner table and the almost full moon shining above us into the ocean, I have to say it wasn't not romantic. We surprisingly were able to drink more alcohol throughout dinner, keeping a bottle of rosé going. Paige took a break from "napping" to say hi, eat a piece of skirt steak and drunkenly drop in conversation, "Did you know that Har-old Prince won the most Tonys of anyone?" Her narrow eyes looked even more ridiculous than usual.

"Twenty-one," I said, disappointing her and ruining her Tony trivia game.

"You're zero fun," said Paige. She burped a little, not caring who saw, a kaleidoscope of mixed drinks making itself known in her stomach. "I think I need to go back to bed. We're gonna have more fun tomorrow, right?"

"'Cause we didn't have enough fun today," I said.

"G'night, Paige," said Chasten.

"Bachelorette party! Woo!" Paige punctuated her guest appearance with a limp fist pump in the air and disappeared upstairs.

"I picture her muttering Tony factoids in her sleep," Chasten said, opening another bottle of rosé.

"Instead of sheep, she counts how many times Sondheim was snubbed."

Knowing our common denominator was in bed for the night, we were suddenly faced with getting to know each other. Just us. So I went for the jugular.

"When did you come out?" I asked.

He gave me a look. "Are we really doing this?" As much of a cliché as I know it is to ask another gay guy his coming-out story, and since Paige never specifically asked Chasten this question during her "interview," I genuinely wanted to know this person better. Chasten seemed game as he sighed and laughed to himself at the memory.

"I came out to my parents and Austin when I was eleven. I declared a 'family meeting' to officially announce I was gay and then proceeded to list all the reasons why that was okay in a funny, kid version of a PowerPoint presentation I drew in Magic Markers on rainbow-colored construction paper. My parents were convinced it was just a phase until years later when Austin walked in on me and my high school boyfriend about to have sex in my bed."

"Go on," I say with mock overenthusiasm. He laughed.

"I was literally in the middle of lubing up and there was a knock on my door."

"No," I said in horror. "It seems worse for a sibling to walk in on that than a parent."

"Hundred percent. But Austin is Austin, so of course he immediately didn't care. He was like, 'Pizza's here. Don't forget to wear a condom.'"

"And that's why we love Austin."

"What about you?"

"I was at an outdoor James Taylor concert with my parents."

"Go on!" Chasten said with even more mock enthusiasm, which made it even funnier. "Also, ew."

"He's my parents' favorite singer. Anyway, James Taylor was in the middle of his classic 'You've Got a Friend,' and the emotion of it all just hit me. I'd been torturing myself about it my whole life, just avoiding saying I was gay even to myself."

"That's so sad."

"Right. I thought I needed to face whatever fear came along with saying, 'I'm gay,' out loud. So what better way to come out to my parents than on a perfect summer evening at Ravinia, listening to James Taylor over a picnic dinner while wearing bug spray?"

"So you said, 'I'm gay,' just like that?"

"In the middle of the songs, I said, 'Mom, Dad, I too have seen sunny days that I thought would never end.'"

"You were doing dad jokes in high school? Cringe."

"Oh. Always."

"What did they say?"

"They shushed me 'cause they wanted to hear the music, obviously, so I had to wait until the whole concert was over."

Chasten and I laughed at the absurdity.

"They took it well. James Taylor finished his two encore numbers, and the three of us just sat there as everyone around us packed up their picnic baskets and folded chairs and walked to their cars. We sat in this giant, empty field, the stars over our heads, talking about it all. Plus thousands of mosquitoes. They said they knew."

"The mosquitoes?"

"My parents." We shared a smile.

"We're lucky. Having families that accepted us."

"Yeah. It's rare," I said, struck by a hopeful feeling that Chasten had referred to him and me as a "we."

The conversation between Chasten and me continued to flow with the rosé. We'd discussed the worst jobs we'd ever had: me dressed as a hot dog, handing out flyers for a Chicago-style hot dog place; Chasten interning for his local city hall, where they assigned him to remove roadkill. We'd discussed if either of us had a tattoo, what kind we would get: me a molecule symbol on the space between my thumb and forefinger; Chasten a Harry Potter lightning bolt on his right tricep. We'd discussed a country we've always wanted to go to but haven't: Japan for both. We'd moved on to the topic of ghosts and if we believed in them: yes for both. We shared ghost stories: me the time in college when I lived in an apartment off campus that was supposedly haunted by the building's old maintenance man who accidentally died there years prior. My roommate was gone for the weekend and the refrigerator door kept opening on its own. Chasten the time he was in his college library late one night and asked the librarian a question, and after she answered, she vanished into thin air as he saw her spirit evaporate like a hologram.

For some reason, this didn't feel like the normal job interview Q and A on a first date. Our answers were overlapping more and more now, with funny coincidences, similarities and both agreeing on things I would've never thought in a million

years we'd see eye to eye on. I'd been attracted to Chasten physically when we first met, but because of our weird agreement, I
knew it wouldn't develop past that. But getting to know him has
thrown a wrench into that plan.

After dinner and endless conversation, we switched from
rosé to whiskey, and I was surprised my body could still absorb
any more liquid. It was getting late, and the only thing left on
the official Fire Island agenda was to go to the underwear party
and dance until four in the morning, then maybe end up in
someone's hot tub for late night / early morning shenanigans
and then finally go to sleep. We'd decided to wait until Saturday
night to hit the Pavilion and dance the night away when the
girls were able to join us. The beach looked like it was lit by its
own natural disco ball of a moon, so we decided to have a quick
walk. Our quick walk turned epic as we strolled from one end
of the Pines and back, stopping just short of the Meat Rack, the
late-night outdoor hookup spot. Anyone watching us would've
thought, *That's a nice couple having a romantic walk on the beach.*

"Let's sit for a sec," I said. We found a spot between the
water and the dunes, sat and stared at the moon staring back at
us, its reflection gently shimmering on the water. If we were
romantic with each other, this would've been so romantic.

We heard the faint strains of Joni Mitchell's vocals mixed in
with some dance song playing inside a small house party nearby.
*So, I bought me a ticket. I caught a plane to Spain. There were lots of
pretty people there, reading* Rolling Stone, *reading* Vogue . . . We
both agreed what a great lyric that was and what a shame this
hyper dance song was exploiting it.

"What's your favorite opening line in a song?" I challenged
him. To my surprise, he answered right away.

"That's easy," he said. "Madonna." I roll my eyes a little too hard at that one. *Madonna? Really?* Everything was going so well but this answer was so . . . basic. Anything romantic I was trying to suppress disappeared completely like the boardwalk deer at night.

"Madonna? Oh god." I couldn't resist letting him know I didn't approve.

"You're such a music snob. Don't you even want to know the lyric?"

"What is it? *Bitch, I'm Madonna*?"

He shook his head. He wasn't going to answer now.

"Okay, sorry. Just tell me," I said, sipping my whiskey from my red cup.

He looked out into the ocean. "*I made it through the wilderness. Somehow I made it through,*" he said like he was quoting Sylvia Plath. And then it struck me.

"Holy shit. That *is* good," I had to admit. I don't think it was the whiskey talking because it did sound like poetry. "I never thought 'Like a Virgin' could move me that way." I looked at Madonna (and Chasten) in a whole new light.

"So? What's yours?"

"Oh, right." I had to think now that he derailed me. Then I remembered why I started this game. "*I am the son . . . and the heir . . .*"

He waited for more. "That's it?"

"Yeah."

"What's it from? Who sings it?"

"The Smiths."

"Of course it's the Smiths. Now who's cliché."

"You don't get it? The *son* and *heir*?"

"The double meaning. A pun. I get it. Pretty good. I love puns."

I'm shocked. Greg never got that one. And he hated puns.

"*We could leave the Christmas lights up till January and this is our place, we make the rules*," Chasten sang with a perfect voice.

"Taylor Swift? Jesus." I shook my head.

"You know it!"

"*Midnight, it's rainin' outside, he must be soaking wet.*"

"*Home is where I want to be, pick me up and turn me 'round.*"

"*Sugar magnolia, blossoms bloomin', head's all empty and I don't care.*"

"I never pegged you as a Deadhead," Chasten said.

"Never thought you would've got that one."

"I had a brief Dead phase in college."

"So did I."

"*Fourteenth Street, the garbage swirls like a cyclone.*"

"Who's that?" he asked.

"Ani DiFranco."

"*I just took a DNA test, turns out, I'm a hundred percent dat bitch.*"

"Lizzo," I said. He was impressed I knew that one too.

Then he did another one. "*It's Britney, bitch.*"

"Tough one," I joked.

"I just realized *Bitch, I'm Madonna* is the inverse of *It's Britney, bitch.* Or maybe a response?"

"Gay Musicology 101."

"*Do you ever feel like a plastic bag?*" he said.

"I'm not sure if that line is good or bad. And I think Katy Perry borrowed that imagery from *American Beauty.*"

"Oooh. Deep."

It's fun we're connecting this way. I never thought Chasten would have this much music knowledge. Another thing Greg and I never shared. He tolerated my music, but if I hadn't been in the picture, Greg probably wouldn't have listened to music at all.

We stared at the glow of the moon, its stillness.

"What are you thinking?" Chasten asked me.

"Honestly? I'm still hung up on that Madonna lyric. It's too good."

"*You're hung up . . .* " he sang.

"Another Madonna song," I said.

"Someone's a closet Madge fan," he said.

The moon. The warm sand. The soft breeze. Our connection. It was too perfect. The whiskey demon overtook me, and I instinctively turned to him, leaned in and—

"Stranger danger!" we heard someone shriek at us and turned to see what looked like a twelve-foot silhouette of a drag queen behind us, standing at the top of the boardwalk platform stairs leading to the beach. She led a small entourage, laughing, drinking and lord knows what else.

"Are we interrupting you two lovahbirds?" she said sweetly but inaccurately. I didn't know what I was leaning in for. A kiss. A cuddle. A friendly shoulder-to-shoulder collision. It wasn't planned. All I know is that it was interrupted by a large person wearing a prom dress and a very long weave.

The drag queen slipped off her heels and proceeded to strut the beach like she was a severe supermodel in a fashion show that no one asked for while her hangers-on cheered and hollered. For the first few moments, I could barely pay attention because I was still electrified by what almost just happened between me and Chasten. But her impromptu show took an unexpected comical turn when she catwalked directly into the ocean waves, pretending not to stop until her entire body, weave and all, disappeared underwater. When she reappeared after thirty seconds, long enough for us to grow scared she was gone forever, we all burst into applause. She told us to catch her show in Cherry Grove the next night and said her goodbyes, repeating our new "lovahbird" moniker.

Any chance of romance was gone. But my whole body felt reenergized, a fire in my heart reignited even though nothing happened. And I couldn't stop thinking about it. That manifested itself during our walk back to the house when I tripped on a loose piece of boardwalk, almost falling off the edge where the white lines are painted so idiots like me don't fall. Chasten didn't see me as it was too dark and he was a step or two ahead of me, so I picked up my pace and pretended like nothing happened.

As we continued to walk, my regret over turning our friendly night into something more hung in the air like the strains of music we heard bouncing from house to house. Maybe Chasten hadn't known what I'd tried to do. I barely knew.

The night couldn't have ended on a more profound note.

We reached the front gate to our house, which was jammed shut. I tried jiggling it, Chasten tried forcefully prying it open, but it wouldn't budge. So I took out my phone to use the flashlight. Before I could find it, Chasten caught a glimpse of my screen saver. It's an old photo of Greg and me, where I'm smiling but Greg is holding his hand over his face. I don't know why I've never bothered to swap it out.

"Is that him?" Chasten asked.

"Who? Oh. Yeah. That's Greg." I took the picture early on in our relationship and kept it as my screen saver ever since. Wallpaper that needs to be torn down.

"Kind of a weird picture, don't you think?"

I looked at it like I was seeing it for the first time. You can't see Greg's face at all. Maybe I read too much into it last night, but part of me wondered if that was intentional on my part. Like deep down somewhere I never really thought Greg should be in the picture. "I guess I thought it was funny at the time." I stared at the photo a few moments longer before finding my phone flashlight and successfully getting us in through the gate.

Spent from the long day and night, Chasten and I muttered good nights and went to our separate bedrooms.

CHECKING MY PHONE THE NEXT MORNING, IT DAWNS ON ME that Greg hasn't texted me once since I've been here. Not that I've reached out to him either. What do dads say at weddings? "I'm not losing a daughter. I'm gaining a son." I'm not losing Greg. I'm gaining . . . me time? My self-esteem? A chance at a future boyfriend? Maybe I'm ready to admit it's my turn for all of those things. Streaks of early morning sun pour through the window in my bedroom, and I'm basking in it, something I'm never able to do in the city since my apartment gets little direct sunlight. The sound of the jackhammer being replaced by the ocean waves isn't so bad either.

Staring at the sun rays, I replay last night's events, wondering what would've happened if we weren't so abruptly interrupted by the cast of *RuPaul's Drag Race*. Would we have made out? Would it have been horrible? Would it have changed the course of my life?

After soaking up the warm sun and ocean breeze, I head down into the kitchen, where the entire first floor is filled with the smell of fresh bread, and I wonder if our resident baker

Chasten even went to sleep last night after I left him. I pause in front of the oven and take in a deep, exaggerated breath.

Turns out Chasten and I are the only ones who enjoy the quiet of the early morning as I stumble onto the pool deck, where I find him perched on a lounge chair reading a serious-looking hardcover book. I'm wearing my new sunglasses, which I'm still getting used to, and take in the sun glistening off the slow-motion ocean waves.

"Whatcha readin'?" I ask him. He shows me the cover, and I read it out loud. "*Gettysburg: The Last Invasion.*" Interesting. "Any good?"

"Just cracked it open." I stare at him for a moment too long. "What?"

"No, that's just not what I'd expect you to read."

"What did you expect?"

I think about this and don't know the answer. "Maybe something . . . lighter?"

"Like *People* magazine?"

"Somewhere between *Gettysburg: The Last Invasion* and *People* magazine."

"I'm a history nerd," he says with a shrug.

"I had no idea." A waft of deliciousness hits my nose again. "So, you're baking up a storm and just casually reading a giant history book at the same time?"

"Pain au chocolat," he says, ignoring my compliment.

"That's 'good morning' in German or something, right?" I joke. He laughs . . . at me? With me? I can't tell which one.

Back in the kitchen, Chasten puts on oven mitts and takes out a hot tray of freshly baked croissants, and I can't believe my eyes. They're perfectly flaky, buttery and chocolaty looking.

"Holy crap," I say. "You made those from scratch?"

"I did," he says, as if this is not a big effing deal. Making chocolate croissants from scratch deserves a gold medal in my book. He puts more in the oven and carefully takes out the hot ones, placing them artfully in a decorative basket. I turn to see an even more impressive spread than yesterday's laid out on the patio table. Bagels, cream cheese, two different kinds of frittata, strawberries, blackberries and blueberries, Bloody Marys and—"More mimosas?"

"Those are Bellinis," he corrects me. "Freshly chilled peach puree." Of course. Why wouldn't it be?

"You're an early riser," I say, trying to play it cool and not shower him with too much love for his culinary talents.

"Yeah, a lot to do for Paige today."

"I like waking up with the sun if I can."

"I usually do too."

Yet another thing I find so refreshing about Chasten right now. That's something I've never loved about Greg but came to accept. He always slept in late. You'd think a successful doctor would be a morning person but not him.

Before we can both silently process our seemingly romantic time together and acknowledge how much neither of us realized we have in common, I hear one of the girls padding downstairs.

"Is someone baking bread?" Eliza asks, shuffling into the kitchen.

"Pain au chocolat," I say, like French is suddenly my first and only language. "And it's all Chasten."

"That is the smell of heaven," Katie says, walking down the stairs a few minutes later. The girls discuss how amazing it is to have Chasten the chocolatier, and I'm feeling useless. Everyone eventually joins us at staggered times.

Sitting at a table next to the pool, I notice all the girls are wearing various accessories to hide the fact that they're hungover. Sunglasses. A baseball cap. Those patches under their eyes that I guess are eye-lift, antiaging things? These items only highlight the fact that they're hungover. Paige wears a white silk monogrammed robe that her mom and Ron sent her as a gift. We all "mmm" and "yummm" over Chasten's hangover brunch, laughing over key WTF moments from the night before, piecing together drunken blackout moments and excitedly talking about our dinner tonight.

"I love the fuck out of these croissants," Paige says with her mouth full, not caring she's on her second one.

"Has Austin made them for you? He taught me his technique."

A moment goes by as we all watch Paige start fanning herself like she's too hot or she's breaking out into an allergic reaction. None of us know what to do.

With that, Paige bursts into tears and runs inside.

Fire Island versus Provincetown

Fire Island is a cat.
Provincetown is a dog.

Fire Island is an egg white omelet, hold the toast.
Provincetown is an all-you-can-eat surf and turf buffet.

Fire Island is a banker.
Provincetown is an artist.

Fire Island is Calvin Klein.
Provincetown is Tennessee Williams.

Fire Island is all, "Heeeeeeey, bish."
Provincetown is like, "'Sup, bro?"

Fire Island is a sailor.
Provincetown is a Navy SEAL.

Fire Island is a waxed twink.
Provincetown is a hairy bear.

chapter

EIGHTEEN

O N MY RUN AFTER BREAKFAST, I NOTICE SOMEONE HAS scribbled out the "B" on a street sign that reads "Bass Walk." Fire Island humor.

Every other boardwalk I'm jogging along this morning is perfectly bouncy, which puts a spring in my New Balances. I'm profusely sweating out last night's tequila, now mixed with SPF 30, trying to cleanse myself a little before we drink more tonight. The sky is crazy blue with a few puffy clouds dangling overhead, which reminds me how far away I am from the Cloud Room at work. I feel a pang in my stomach at the thought of the people I had to let go, a harsh contrast to this beautiful day.

Paige was laughing and perfectly fine after a good thirty-minute crying jag, so I felt okay to leave her for some me time. Eliza and Katie consoled her by crying with her. Chasten offered to name one of his new chocolate bars after her. And I talked her off the ledge by reminding her she's not giving up her old life. I told her it was like she can't decide between the fettuccini with clams and the penne with meatballs so she orders *both* dishes. All of this seemed to simultaneously calm her down and make her hungry for Italian food.

While running, which I rarely do, I imagine all of the ghosts of Fire Island with each passing house. Chasten gave me the provenance of certain houses on our walk last night. He said you have to pass on the history of the community to each newcomer.

Calvin Klein built that house, then David Geffen bought it from him. One time Madonna and her boy toy Warren Beatty stayed at that house with her brother. Jerry Herman, the Broadway producer, owned that one. Chasten went to a late-night party that required you to be naked in that one on the bay.

I imagine who occupies these summer shares full of environmental lawyers, real estate brokers, magazine journalists, social media managers, architects, ballet dancers, hotel managers, fitness instructors, soap opera head writers, bank vice presidents and tech CFOs. I imagine what's inside these *Architectural Digest*–y modernists structures filled with skimpy bathing suits, glitter, wigs, dumbbells, yoga mats, weight benches, protein shakes, barbecued chicken breast leftovers, ketamine, chocolate edibles, beach chairs, expensive sunglasses, rainbow beach umbrellas, espresso machines, pool rafts, zero carbs, glow sticks, party wrist bands and bottles of rosé outnumbering bottles of sunscreen. I imagine what goes on inside these places full of adrenaline-fueled one-night stands, messy drunken hookups, impromptu hot tub mini orgies, dramatic breakups, birthday parties, selfies, group photos, wedding proposals, hurricane warnings, arguments over grocery receipts, pre-tea fashion shows, post-tea dance parties, liquid dinners, Broadway sing-alongs, movie nights, prestige-TV-streaming nights, rainy day board games, disco naps, Memorial Day excitement, Fourth of July bashes and Labor Day tears having to say goodbye to another perfect summer "in the books," as they say on the 'gram.

My heavenly run is interrupted when I turn the corner and spot a deer standing dead center in the middle of the boardwalk, looking directly into my eyes. I stop and stare back, trying to communicate to her that I've come in peace and everything is going to be okay. A smile forms on my face before the elegant creature leaps back into the woods like a prized show horse.

Back at the house, I float in the pool on an orange raft, wearing my new sunglasses, staring up at the cloudless blue sky, wondering how I can spend more time here in the future. I'm Dustin Hoffman in *The Gayduate*. Some kind of bird oddly chirps in the distance. It sounds like *birdy, birdy, birdy*. A jumbo jet silently soars overhead.

Chasten and the girls are extreme lounging on the pool deck and secretly judging guys as they cross in front of the house on the beach. "That one's a six and a half . . . I'd say he's a nine in Pittsburgh but a seven in New York." They joke they should hold up signs with numbers on them.

I hear a giant splash in the deep end and Chasten comes up for air, his normally perfect hair now a glistening, wet, perfect mess. It's frustratingly cute on him. He casually swims back and forth, circling my raft, head above water. We exchange raised eyebrows.

"This is where I live now," Katie says with her eyes closed from her lounge chair, clearly thinking what I'm thinking.

"Maybe we should all move here together," Paige says, sipping on Chasten's homemade Arnold Palmer with an alcoholic kick and a colorful straw that's not in the shape of a penis.

"Can you imagine?" Eliza says. "That would be the worst sitcom ever."

"Or the best," Paige says.

"Shouldn't we hit the beach at some point?" I suggest.

"I'm too hungover to move," Cori says through a heavy sigh.

"We're already on the beach," Katie says.

"Yeah, but we need to at least feel the sand under our feet," I say.

"Do they serve cocktails on the beach?" Nina asks.

"Don't say 'cocktails,'" Cori says, massaging her temples.

"You just did," one of them quips.

"The beach is so not for me. Sand is too sandy," Eliza says under her giant floppy hat that covers her entire face.

"It'd be nice to go for a swim in the ocean," I say.

"Max, you're literally swimming now!" Katie shouts.

"Can we not yell?" Cori curls up into a fetal position.

"We don't have to do everything in a group," Paige, our host and maker of the weekend rules, declares. "If some of us want to go to the beach while others want to stay here, that's totally fine. I'm a chill bride-to-be."

"Right," Katie says.

"Good, because I need to eat my way through this hangover," Cori says. "Is there more cheese?" Cori asks as she peels herself off the lounge chair and waddles into the kitchen.

"I'd hit the ocean for a swim," Chasten says.

Moments later, Chasten and I are the only two out of the group brave enough to walk the five seconds around the house and down the path to the beach. The only things I'm wearing are my bathing suit and a T-shirt with no shoes because this is how you dress in Beach World.

The beach is fairly crowded—peak summer—with the usual suspects of volleyball players, paddleboarders, loungers, walkers and an occasional jogger. It didn't even occur to me to jog on the beach this morning. I'll have to remember that one for tomorrow. Chasten stops to kiss hello no less than seven people.

The sand is lush, white and soft but extremely hot at first under my feet. I'm sort of walk-hopping along, not wanting my soles to linger too long to roast. I make it to where the sand meets water to cool my burning feet off. I look out, and the first thing I notice is how big the waves are right now. This is not what I was expecting for an easy, delicious dip, so I hesitate at the water's edge, scanning the vast ocean in front of me. Of course, Chasten bounds through the water and just dives right in, like he's a fearless cologne commercial.

"Come on! Dive in!" he says, doing an effortless backstroke swim past me as he is one with the giant waves. I'm not sure where he ends and the water begins.

"Are the waves bad?" I ask, seeing that the waves look, in fact, bad.

"Don't be so midwestern."

"Stop it!" I say with an exaggerated flat Midwest accent.

He laughs and swims underwater, like a show-offy killer whale at SeaWorld. He's right that midwesterners and New Englanders have a different relationship with the ocean, one of our many differences. We like swimming pools. They like the sea. We like deep-dish pizza. They prefer thin crust. We say "pop" or just an all-encompassing "Coke." They say "soda." We love meat and potatoes. They tear into lobsters and, like, shuck oysters or whatever you call it. I once read that Katharine Hepburn jumped into the Long Island Sound near her home in Connecticut every morning for a brisk swim, in every season.

I am not like Katharine Hepburn.

I've never been a strong swimmer. At best, I'm an Olympic gold medalist at floating on a raft in the shallow end of a small pool. Okay, fine, bronze. Maybe. The beach, the waves, the ocean: all too much for this midwestern, landlocked boy. When I was a kid, my parents took us to the beach maybe twice, and that was on Lake Michigan three towns over. Sure, it's called a lake, but it looks no different than an ocean. The name alone—Lake Michigan—is completely confusing for anyone outside of the Midwest. It's shared by four different states yet named after only one. The water was too cold, too unpredictable, and what lurked beneath the surface was too . . . unknown. Once, my parents decided to have a day at the beach. I remember my mom buying an actual wicker picnic basket hours before at Kmart, complete with a red checkered picnic blanket. My dad had a history of playfully putting me on his shoulders when he was feeling leisurely, so the beach was no different. Only this time, he wanted to try it in the water, since I was reluctant to swim anywhere—at the local public pool, at our aunt and uncle's condo in Florida, even the bathtub. Who wants to be soaking wet? So, my dad put me squarely on his shoulders and walked directly into the lake. It was the perfect way for me to experience "swimming" since I didn't have to actually be in the water. He bobbed up and down, lightly splashing my feet while my mom prepared the picnic. A wave must've crashed into him, because he lost his balance, and I flew off his shoulders and got sucked into the water vortex. The next thing I knew I was on the beach in my mom's arms, coughing up water. I can remember the look on my parents' frightened faces, and we never had another beach picnic again.

To this day, I still have wave PTSD. But the refreshing water in front of me plus wanting to prove I'm not a basic midwesterner to Chasten causes me to whip off my T-shirt and slowly walk into the water, like Virginia Woolf. The water is actually freezing in contrast to the fiery temperature outside. A short wave comes in, striking my legs gently and splashing my upper body in a spritzy sort of way. This isn't so bad. Chasten expertly does the sidestroke, watching the water-phobe with laughing eyes. He's staring at me now, at my shirtlessness, and suddenly I'm self-conscious. He looks better than I do, physically. It's just a fact. But I can't think about that now as another wave collides into me as I freeze, like a firmly settled one-hundred-year-old building.

"You gotta just go for it," he says, like it's the easiest thing in the world.

"What if a big wave comes in?" I ask.

"Swim under it." His instruction doesn't compute. Swim under a big wave? Wouldn't this trap me? I'm clearly very good at physics.

"What about the undertow or whatever?"

"Don't be ridiculous."

"Chasten's Ocean Swimming Lesson number forty-seven. 'Don't be ridiculous.' So helpful." He laughs at this and blinks, looking at me in a new light.

"You're funny when you're scared shitless."

With that insulting prompt, I sink lower and lower in between waves so my body gets used to the frigidness until finally I'm fully under, genitals, shoulders and all. It's not so freezing once I'm there.

"See? Easy. Now try this," Chasten says, doing a somersault underwater.

"Not gonna happen." He proceeds to do a handstand, and some dolphin-like swim move, which, if I remember correctly from high school gym class, is called the butterfly?

I'm moving farther from the shore, treading water now, almost floating. *It's just a larger version of a swimming pool*, I tell myself. My body adjusts to the ocean, and it feels like a warm bath in parts. The sun is shining, and an extremely attractive man is swimming next to me. It's heavenly, this feeling. Like paradise.

Part of me wants to see this spark between Chasten and me grow, to drown out the other part of me that hangs on to the lifelessness of my relationship with Greg, I think.

All of a sudden, I see Chasten holding his swimsuit and putting his head through one of the legs. *Is he wrapping it around his neck?* He looks at me with a mischievous little smile. "What?"

"What what. What is going on right now?"

"Au naturel. Feels amazing. You should try it."

"I'm good, thanks."

Chasten dives underwater, swims and resurfaces on the other side of me. He's naked. With his bathing suit around his neck.

"The shy, reserved midwestern act is becoming monotonous. C'mon. It's Fire Island. This is what everyone does."

"Everyone does not—" I look at the three guys directly across from us, glistening smooth muscles, each of their necks encircled by their tiny bathing suits.

The waves taper off; the water calms. It becomes like glass in front of me. It's incredible.

"It'll make you feel alive," Chasten goads me further.

"Swimming in the ocean doesn't make you feel alive enough?"

"Just try it," he says, fake exasperated. "You wanna be a zombie your whole life, Moody?"

Fuck it. When in Fire Island. I struggle to untie my bathing suit while treading water at the same time. A strong swimmer I am not. Katharine Hepburn would hate me. Also, apparently,

I'm not a very good multitasker. Chasten swims back and forth around me like a shark who's hungry for someone to make a fool of himself. Just as I'm about to give up, the knot in my string tie comes loose and my suit sails off my waist and down my legs, and I'm fully naked.

"My parents would be so proud to see me skinny-dipping in Fire Island," I say sarcastically.

"You did it!" Chasten says. I must say it feels good, liberating. "Don't forget to put your suit around your neck," he reminds me.

As I'm about to ask, *Why can't I just hold it?* suddenly, a giant wave crashes over me, and before I know what the hell is happening, I'm sucked underwater, involuntarily twisting and tumbling like a load of laundry in a high-speed washing machine. The water pulls me down. My face scrapes the rocky ocean floor, heating up my left cheek. I swallow a half cup of watery sand. My legs flip over my head in a move that would rival Chasten's water ballet. Just when my head comes up for air and I'm able to sip a drop of oxygen, a follow-up wave swallows me whole. I guess my hand unclenches my bathing suit because I'm now holding a fistful of water as the wave's momentum propels my body to shore. I'm now stuck feetfirst in the sand like a sad beached whale. The foamy water covers my body and then disappears like a magician seamlessly pulling a tablecloth from under a table setting. I'm lying on the beach. Completely. Butt. Ass. Naked. No bathing suit in sight. I wipe my eyes clean of salt water and sand and seaweed and who knows what else and see Chasten exiting the water like Daniel Craig's James Bond, laughing at me, magically snapping his bathing suit back on himself.

Before I can manage to stand up, I squirm and flop around a

little, seeing gaggles of no-carb-eating gays dotted all around me, snickering, whispering, and covering their mouths in shock over my epic skinny-dipping fail. As if in slow motion, Chasten runs to grab an acquaintance's beach towel (of course he knows the guy). It feels like an hour and a half of me sprawled out on the beach naked before he returns with the towel and wraps it around me. I'm simultaneously mortified and turned on as Chasten hovers over me, water dripping from his lips onto my sand-encrusted cheek. He smells like salt water and sunshine and other manly smells.

I'm definitely not flashing back to our romantic moment last night on the beach. For sure I'm not wondering if this could be our moment. There's no part of me that can taste his lips. I can't even imagine feeling his stubble on my stubble.

Of course, I am doing all of those things.

We lock eyes for a moment before he snort-laughs.

I'm thankfully now swaddled in some guy's red, white, and blue striped towel, and when I begin to stand, I see some short dude with a thick gold chain around his neck slow clap off to the side, in mocking amusement. This triggers the rest of the on-lookers, at least a dozen, to erupt into applause, hoots and hollers. I know they're not mean-spirited, but I'm too embarrassed to remain on the beach, so I walk back to our house with my head hanging low, hearing the faintest sounds of Katharine Hepburn's ghost saying, "And don't come back!"

Chasten follows me.

"It's not that bad . . . no one cares . . . it's Fire Island . . . everyone's naked all the time . . ." He's sweet and supportive, but I just need to go home and put on some clothes and decompress from the embarrassment.

The rest of the evening we have fun skipping all the teas and hanging out by the pool, cocktails in hand, as Chasten makes another gourmet dinner and six kinds of chocolate desserts, followed by an impromptu dance party to nineties hits. The girls all hear about my naked beach horror show and laugh it off, not understanding the magnitude of it all until we decide to go out dancing later at the Pavilion, where everyone either shouts from afar or comes up to me, wanting to say hi to "the naked guy."

Luckily, I don't take myself too seriously and try to enjoy the pseudo-fame. Paige thinks it's hysterical. The girls are using my new status to try to charm their way into free drinks. "Have you heard about our friend, Naked Guy?" Chasten's declaration of "Everybody's naked in Fire Island" doesn't exactly hold water, though, if *I'm the one* everyone has dubbed Naked Guy.

The Pavilion is packed with lots of glow sticks decked out in sweaty bodies. The music is on fire—one fun pop song after another. Everyone gets a kick out of me and Paige mouthing all the words to each other. We gyrate in one big bachelorette group, letting in the occasional onlooker glomming on to our fun. By 3:00 a.m., the unbridled bridal party has finally found complete synergy, synchronicity and success.

Until the walk home.

After 4:00 a.m., the sun is itching to make itself known. The girls walk a good thirty feet ahead of us until they disappear into a thicket of dark woods.

Chasten slows down a little. "So last night . . ." he starts. Uh-oh. What about last night? I thought that was behind us. I told myself he never knew I was going in for a kiss.

"Yeah?" I say, trying to remain as neutral and unsuspecting as possible. *What on earth could you be talking about?*

"It seemed like we were about to have some kind of moment."

"A moment?"

"Yes."

"Oh, yeah. That."

"I felt it too."

"Felt what?"

He looks at me, seeing right through my facade.

"Oh. That," I say, finally relenting.

"That. Yeah, so. It can't really happen."

"I get it. I was drunk and caught up in the moment, I guess. I'll respect our rules."

"It's not really about any rules."

"Then what's it about?"

"Given Paige's wedding jitters, we have to be careful not to steal the spotlight. Make this about us."

"True. But she seems in a better place today. No tears," I say. He nods, agreeing.

"The other thing is . . ." he says with too long a pause. "I started seeing someone. And I don't want to fuck it up."

We continue walking as I try not to break my stride, startled by how much this hurts.

Sentences Paige and I Have Said That Could Also Be the Title of Our Memoir

- *I Can't Decide between the Salmon or the Trout*
  —by Paige Greendale

- *I Don't Really Want to Go to Brooklyn*
  —by Max Moody

- *Comedy Girls Love Dresses with Pockets*
  —by Paige Greendale

- *Why Does Everyone Have a Cool Job but Me?*
  —by Max Moody

chapter

NINETEEN

ACK IN THE CITY, THE JACKHAMMER OUTSIDE MY WINDOW has gotten louder. My welcome-home song. I wouldn't be surprised if it hadn't stopped the entire time I was gone. Somehow it sounds more powerful, like the Hulk, gaining strength as it becomes angrier.

Speaking of the Hulk, I spot the one semi-hot construction worker climbing the scaffolding across the street. To cope with the sound of the jackhammer, I'm pretending that he's a porn star that I've dubbed Jack Hammer.

The commute back to the city was a complex set of emotions of feeling heartbroken about something that never even was, mixed with the fun we had with Paige and the euphoric sense of a beach vacation. But when the Long Island Rail Road filled up with loud, sunburnt passengers from other Fire Island communities and every other stop along the way, my dreamy beach bliss started to wear off until we finally arrived in the grimy oven of Penn Station.

"Last stop!" the conductor yelled at my face, spraying me

with saliva and his Queens accent. Okay, not really. It was over the loudspeaker, but that's how it felt.

Heading to the office, I'm excited to show off to my coworkers the souvenirs I picked up over the weekend, including my uneven, splotchy red tan, dozens of mosquito bites all over my legs and alcohol overconsumption. I usually wear pants to the office, but a heat wave has descended upon the city, so no. Today is Shorts City, baby.

Even though I was only gone for the weekend, returning to my daily commute and into the swing of things in this city feels like culture shock. There are more people in a hurry, more batshit crazy bicyclists and more urine odors than I remember. My empty boardwalks to nowhere and endless pristine beach have been replaced by streets jammed with impatient cars and cigarette butt–littered sidewalks. Even the elevator to my twenty-seventh-floor office seems completely unnatural now. *We travel to work vertically in a mechanical box stuffed full of other people?* This Monday morning, I need all the coffees.

While answering dozens of emails and making sure there's no more hate mail or potential death threats from disgruntled, laid-off employees, I look up from my computer, startled to see Stella standing in the doorway of my office.

"Jesus. You scared the crap outta me." I inhale a deep breath. "Legit horror movie scare."

"Sowwy."

"You're so quiet. You're like a cat."

"Take *meowt* for lunch?" she asks, pawing the air like a cat, I guess, and then wrapping her cold self tightly in a giant hand-crafted quilt.

"Good one. I should probably stick around and see what Janet has in store today."

"She's out all next week." This is the equivalent of hearing your parents are going out of town when you're in high school.

"Oh, party time. Salads, anyone?"

When Janet is out, Stella can relax and actually go to our crappy salad place rather than stay chained to her desk. The fact that this is an actual thrill for both of us is what makes working in an office so tragic.

"Yas, queen-sized comforter," I say. "Where's she going?"

"Nanfuckit." Janet has a summerhouse in Nantucket that Stella and I have definitely never googled before (four bedrooms, three and a half baths, 2,196 square feet, 2.5-acre lot, 3D tour not available).

"Doesn't she usually go the week after Labor Day?"

"I guess she's going early this year?"

We both look at each other, wondering if this has any greater meaning. I silently decide first it does not.

"New blanket?"

"Yeah. I found it at this cool flea market in Williamsburg. You like?"

"Looks warm."

"Feels like they jacked up the AC today. I'm freezing."

"Probably 'cause of the heat wave."

Stella sits in my only chair, cradling her knees. She pulls a giant coffee thermos thing that appears taller than her out from under her blanket and sips. I have no idea what else she's hiding under there. A heat lamp? A blow-dryer? A live chicken?

"So . . ." she says, burying herself in a sip of hot coffee. "Any more news?"

"About?"

She lowers her head and looks at me with are-you-joking eyes.

"Oh. The layoffs."

"Beach brain much?"

I glance at my computer. "I was just catching up with emails after being away." I see nothing alarming and look back at Stella with a genuine smile. "Everything seems okay."

"Phew." Stella exhales with some lingering dread and holds her mug out for me to cheers but I don't have a drink so I fist-bump it.

"It's safe to assume you're good."

Relieved and getting the real information she came in here for, she stands and lets her blanket fall onto the chair so she can smooth out her heavy sweater and wool pants. Wool pants! Today is the hottest day of the year. She's that cold.

"'Kay. See you on the flip side." She re-swaddles herself in her blanket like a giant, self-sufficient baby.

"That's it?"

"Oh. Sorry. How was your friend's bachelorette thingy or whatever this weekend?"

"It was a blast. Thanks for asking."

"You're funny. You look tan." And with that, she swaddle-waddles out of my office and down the hall.

———————————

THE NEXT COUPLE OF DAYS ARE DREADFULLY SLOW, SO I SPEND them watching videos on how to make your own garden, gaining tips and tricks for Difference Day and my own burgeoning hobby. I set up my own Instagram profile called @TheReal RobertPlant and fill it with photos of all the fired plants I'd taken home.

I further busy myself with going to the bathroom, getting coffee from the kitchen, drinking said coffee and then going back to the kitchen and washing my mug. My bathroom breaks include standing at the sink and listening to the daily radio station they have pumping in there. Sometimes it's a hard-core rap song with inappropriately explicit lyrics, other times it's some white cis-male straight comedian from the eighties with offensively outdated jokes or a disturbing true-crime podcast about a gruesome murder described in graphic detail. The bathroom should come equipped with a trigger warning. I've flagged this as problematic to Janet a couple of times and she said she'd go "full-court press" on Carl, the guy who controls the loudspeaker, but nothing's changed.

I kill more time by going to the seventh floor to live vicariously through the creatives who've had their work produced on television, in magazines, on billboards, in movie theaters or online. It's usually fun to see their wacky props collected from various commercial shoots: a giant stuffed walrus wearing a T-shirt that reads "Born This Way," a six-foot-tall syringe, a neon sign in the shape of a burrito. Even their clothes are more interesting here. Funky sneakers, artsy eyeglasses, shirts with fun prints on them. One woman even has pink hair. Pink!

Without the creatives, there would be no advertising. The world doesn't need strategists or account servicing or someone who lays people off. This business thrives on ideas sprung from the imaginative minds I wish I could emulate.

But my heart sinks seeing how many offices are now empty. What have I done? This once buzzy beehive has turned into a cost-effective graveyard. A few random art directors and copywriters I pass look at me with uneasy smiles and fear in their eyes. I shouldn't take random walks around the office during massive layoffs. I feel like an evil slumlord handing out eviction notices.

After my tour of the bombed-out creative floor, I head back to my office, when I get a text from Chasten. At first, I assume it's wedding related, but it's a link to Madonna's video for "Like a Virgin" with nothing written before or after it. I laugh inside and think Paige probably won't get this since he and I talked about the first line of that song alone, but that's when I inspect the text. He didn't send it to our group text with Paige. Just to me, alone. He had to remove Paige's contact, add me to his phone contacts and message me and only me directly. I smile, thinking:

A. He's still seeing that guy and just a tease.

B. He feels bad that I tried to kiss him or whatever, so this is my consolation prize but he's still seeing some other dude.

C. I'm overthinking a friendly gesture.

I click on the link and watch the Madonna video. That first line really is everything. Then Madonna frolics in the canals of Venice with . . . *a lion who turns into a man wearing a lion mask? I guess?* I listen to the lyrics, wondering if Chasten thinks he was lost until he found me.

Without wasting time, I fire back my favorite opening lyric by sending him the Smiths' video of "How Soon Is Now?"

I sit back and wait for his response. Nothing. As I'm about to busy myself with more work emails, he sends me the Taylor Swift video with his favorite first line. I'm grinning ear to ear.

I want to text him back and ask if he's sure about this guy he's seeing. I want to stalk all of his social media accounts and see this other guy's photo. I want to tell Greg that our fuck-buddy situation needs to end because I found someone new and it wasn't working for me anyway. I want to tell Paige about my first encounter with Chasten and how we awkwardly met and maybe now we're smoothing it over by sending each other cute music messages right now. But no.

Meteors must be heading to earth. Planets must be spontaneously combusting. A hole in the space-time continuum must be slowly tearing apart. Something irregular has to be happening for me to have this level of self-control right now, because when it comes to guys, I've never played it this cool. Once, in college, there was a guy whom I routinely sat behind in my classic film studies class. I fell under the spell of his perfectly coiffed goatee and Cubs hat. He was so Chicago. In class, we'd watch a different classic movie from the forties, fifties and sixties. But I was so distracted by this guy, my first college crush, that I'd end up watching the back of his head. I tracked every move he made, absorbed his laugh, how he sighed, the way he shifted in his seat. I'd mentally mark which position the few strands of his black hair fell through the back of his baseball cap. I began to imagine sitting next to him, laughing together at Tony Curtis and Jack Lemmon's screwball antics. I wondered what it'd be like to slowly take his hand in mine while our fellow students around us were none the wiser. My fantasy continued with us inside my dorm room discussing how much we both loved *The Philadelphia Story* as we snuggled on my futon. I'd brush my fingers through his goatee, feeling its soft yet rough edges, gently kissing its outline. We'd slowly undress each other, button by button, but not before I'd wrap a sock around the doorknob, signaling to my roommate not to disturb us the way he did every other night with his girlfriend.

If you didn't know I was a young gay guy yearning to figure out how to date someone, you would've thought I was some kind of sick stalker. I wouldn't dare say hi to him out of fear he wasn't "like me." One time, *Rebel Without a Cause* was starting, and I couldn't spot Goatee Guy anywhere in the classroom until I turned to peer down the same row as me. He was sitting six students down from me, and at the same time I looked, he finally looked back at me. He smiled. I melted. My heart glowed like E.T.'s.

That night over wings at Buffalo Joe's, I told Paige about it. With one more class before summer, she convinced me I should say something to him. As I sat in that last class, watching *Casablanca*, Goatee Guy was nowhere to be found. I never saw him again. For all I know, he dropped out. Maybe he transferred to another school. I remembered seeing he rode a purple Trek mountain bike, and every time I saw one in a bike rack, I'd wonder if it belonged to him. Despite the emptiness, I was excited to know I was able to feel something that resembled romance after my repressed high school years. The idea of him became the prototype for a future boyfriend.

After sending Chasten a video of Yaz's "Midnight," I don't hear back from him, so I chalk up our exchange as a one-off thing. A friendly gesture and nothing else. It was literally two days ago that Chasten told me he's seeing someone new. Two days. Why wouldn't I respect that and move forward with my own (non) love life?

It's time for me to snap out of my Fire Island hedonistic haze and back into reality. It's time to triple down on Greg. I wait until Wednesday to message him.

MAX

Back from FIP. Dinner tonight?

He replies an hour later.

GREG
Sure.

It's so obvious he misses me. I knew all it would take is a little physical distance for him to realize that what he wants is right here waiting for him.

MAX
Pepe Giallo? 7p?

Before sending, I have to look up the name of the restaurant to make sure I'm spelling it correctly. I can never remember if it's one *l* or two, and I don't want to get it wrong with Greg because since day one he's always corrected my horrific spelling. He made me self-conscious to never type *u* in place of "you." When giving my zip code over the phone, he corrects me when I say "oh" instead of "zero." It's a whole thing. It sounds like grammar bullying but weirdly, I've always found his quest for perfection kinda nerdy cute.

Deep down, I know I'm subconsciously testing the romantic waters by suggesting our favorite place together. It's not exactly a trick question, but I am curious how he'll respond to this loaded suggestion. Fine, it's a trick question. He'll say he's not eating carbs. Or he doesn't want heavy Italian. Or can we do later because he has a thing earlier?

GREG
Perfect.

Wait, *what*? That was too easy. Is Greg finally coming around? Maybe he's dropping the arrested-development act and has decided to act age appropriate.

MAX

Yay! Can't wait!

I delete this before sending. *Calm down, Max.*

MAX

Great.

That's better. No exclamation point. One elusive yet upbeat word followed by a nice, patient, mature, not-needy-at-all period.

It's almost lunchtime so I check my work email one more time, hoping there's nothing. I'd suspected Janet was being too quiet all week. I hadn't run into her at all, and the few times I walked by her office, her door was closed in what appeared to be heavy conversations with people above her, the higher-ups I rarely see. I can either ruin my lunch by reading her email now or ruin the rest of the afternoon by reading her email after lunch. I choose the former.

Max,

As you know, next week I'm OOO.

God, I can't stand that. Just say you're out or out of office. Anything but "OOO." Who decided this was okay?

Going forward, we'll need you to do a little more heavy lifting. We've identified a new round of names which I will deliver to you ASAP.

She loves an acronym.

In my absence, I'll need you to conduct meetings next week.

Next round of layoffs? I hoped this shit was over. Now I'm on pins and needles, waiting for this Hunger Games list where no one wins. Lunch ruined.

As I exit the elevator, I get a text from Paige saying she's in my hood and wants to grab lunch. She doesn't have time for Splunch. Just a regular old lunch. I suggest my favorite neighborhood crappy salad place.

While we're crunching and munching (spinach for me, kale for her), the music is earsplitting today, which fights with the chopping of the salad noises, so we have to basically shout at each other.

"I was in a weird place, I guess. But I'm better now," Paige explains her mini meltdown in Fire Island.

"I'm glad," I say.

"Yeah, don't tell Austin until we're like married for ten years with a couple of kids. I don't want him thinking I had any doubts."

"Of course not. I would never. It's natural to have doubts though."

"What?" She leans in closer to hear me.

"I said it's natural to have doubts!" I yell back.

Paige nods as we both finish our salads. I'm happy she's continuing with the wedding even though I secretly knew she would.

"What are you doing this Saturday?" she asks.

"I'm super busy ordering in Seamless and bingeing a limited series based on a docuseries based on a podcast based on a magazine article. Why?"

"Wedding. Dress. Audition," Paige says with a little squeal and expectation in her eyes, like it's going to rain pink balloons.

I take a deep breath and try to build some excitement to match hers. "Oh. Cool. Yeah," I say, averting my eyes. Paige instantly recognizes my lack of enthusiasm.

"Oh, Jesus. Can you just once be a cliché gay and worship fashion with me?"

"Are wedding dresses technically fashion?"

Paige looks at me with dead-eyed disappointment.

"Actually, it's fine. Maybe choosing a dress isn't something you really need to join me for." She says it in a way that makes me think she's not mad, just relieving me of a duty I'm not suitable for. Like a mom telling her high schooler he doesn't need to unload the dishwasher. I'm admittedly relieved. I would be totally useless in a shopping montage. I have no opinion on . . . what are they called? Dresses? "I really don't need a storybook wedding at all," Paige says. "No need for a gay best friend here. Nope." I'm not playing into her guilt trip. Not today.

"Maybe we can meet after for dinner? You can tell me all about it."

"That's fine. Chasten will help."

"Chasten? He's not your man of honor."

"I know. But he knows his shit when it comes to clothes and shit."

My initial rivalry with Chasten bubbles up within yet again. *I'm* Paige's best man. *I'm* her gay best friend. *I'm* the one who helps her with wedding gowns and holds her hair when she throws up and tells her she's not fat.

I'm her everything.

"I'll help you with the dress" is something I thought I'd never say.

"Oh, sure, nooooow you want to go now."

"I just have extreme FOMO."

"I've never known you to have FOMO. If anything, you have JOMO."

"JOMO?"

"*Joy* of missing out. You just want to go now that you know I asked Chasten."

Wait. Does she suspect something romantic between us?

"You are totally competitive with him," she adds. Phew. But also true.

"I'm your best man of honor man or whatever so I should be there." The line to get into the salad place predictably snakes down the block. The visual of workers wearing corporate creative chic while holding their orange reusable bowls makes me cringe. It's an adult lunch box. Paige and I see the impatient people eyeing our table, so we stand and toss our garbage.

"I'm still hungry AND I lost my voice," she says.

"Salads blow. I should've gotten a chicken wrap. Where to now?"

"I have this recording I have to do down the street. Thanks for meeting me."

As we squeeze past the hangry nine-to-fivers on our way out, I feel an incoming text on my leg. I sip the rest of my iced tea and check it, thinking it's probably an "emergency" from Janet. A smile must've creeped onto my face as I read the text because Paige tilts her head, wondering who's charming me on the other end.

"Are you gonna tell me who's making you smile like that?"

It's another music video from Chasten. "Truth Hurts" by

Lizzo. I can't tell my best friend that we've abandoned her in the group chat and started our own. I snap out of it and look up at Paige.

"Oh. Just a dumb tweet from someone at work."

Maybe it's best I don't reply to Chasten's text. So I can protect myself from what could possibly turn into another rejection.

Choose Your Own Max Adventure

MAX'S JOB

A. Complete twenty-five years of employment to receive a whopping three months' paid vacation.

B. Go back to school and become a nurse practitioner or something.

MAX'S FRIENDSHIPS

A. Create a signature cocktail for Paige's wedding called "Nobody Came to Our Lemonade Stand When We Were Kids Cuz We Lived on a Dead-End Street" (vodka, lemonade, bitters).

B. Help Stella become a junior copywriter even though that place sucks.

MAX'S HOBBIES

A. Nerd out more with plants and flowers.

B. Actually use your gym membership and become a muscle gay.

MAX'S LOVE LIFE

A. Continue torturing yourself with Greg.

B. Follow your heart to Chasten.

chapter

TWENTY

TONIGHT'S DINNER WITH GREG WAS WEIRD. AT PEPE Giallo ("no Diet Coke, no skim milk, no decaf coffee, only good food"), we carbed out on fried calamari, antipasto, pasta, bread and two bottles of red wine. The restaurant was packed full of locals, and we had a corner table in the window that felt removed but also put us where exiting strangers glanced at us with smiles, sensing years of chemistry between us. It felt like we were a couple again. Seeing him still in his blue doctor scrubs straight from work felt nostalgic, even if he told me he just got fitted for larger ones because his muscles have grown so much.

Throughout pappardelle with sausage in spicy tomato sauce, we reminisced about trips we'd taken together (Hawaii, Rome, Rio, skiing in Vail with his parents, renting a possibly haunted lake house in Wisconsin with mine). We'd discussed my unfortunate layoffs and the fact that, thanks to summer, his office has been seeing a lot of flip-flop-related casualties lately. We laughed about a botched three-way we once almost had after I'd dragged him to a Morrissey concert in Asbury Park. We fondly winced over how similar our moms are, always adding an *s* to words that don't have one. "Hi honey, sorry I missed your call. I was at Target's . . . Have you seen the latest episode of *The Crowns*? . . . What's with that actor Leonardo Carpagios?" We bonded over both of our dads sighing heavily more than ever and, with a whiff of sadness, agreed how odd it is to see our parents growing older, as actual fragile human beings who might not be with us one day. Throughout the dinner, Greg deferred to me on everything from what we ordered to our topics of conversation, even dessert (tiramisu). He wasn't the newly detached, preoccupied Greg. He was the old, interested and interesting Greg.

We ended up back at his place and had even more to drink—whiskey sours with fancy cherries that Greg always has stocked. I just assumed none of the usual fuckbuddy sexy sexy would happen tonight since our stomachs were both loaded with high-caloric Italian meats. Did we just eat our horniness?

But then, like a demonic entity, the whiskey sours somehow took control of our bodies, and before I knew it, we were wildly making out on his sofa like it was the first time we'd met. This time last year we had stopped kissing altogether. We (he) had established more of a transactional relationship that usually in-volved only the lower portion of our bodies and nothing else inti-mate. It seemed lip-on-lip action became off-limits the second we were no longer boyfriends. At least, I'm guessing this was the fake rule he'd made up and never verbalized. But this was something new, animalistic, like our mouths were devouring each other.

After we moved to his bed (where he thankfully, for once, didn't mention its Swedish origin), we undressed each other in between lip locking. His AC was cranked up, so we immediately slipped under his covers for warmth and our kissing melted into cuddling. For some reason, at that moment, we both decided not to progress to sex. We stayed locked in an embrace that spoke to our decade of being together. We caressed each other's backs, slid our mouths on each other's necks. It was gentle, intimate, cozy.

Meanwhile, our whiskey sours and red wine came knocking, and we had to break up the love fest to use the bathroom. He went first. Lying in his actual bed for the first time, I started to remember what it was like living together. How I used to say, "Can you bring me the stuff by the thing," and he'd know exactly what I was talking about. How right before we went to sleep, I'd be in bed reading my phone or a book or a book on my phone and he was in the bathroom obsessing over his nightly hygiene routine (microderm exfoliator, two-minute foot massage, moisturize everything). After almost twenty-five minutes, he'd inevitably burst out of the bathroom with thoughts on the *Dateline* or *48 Hours* murder mystery he'd forced us to watch. (He was a little too interested in the coroner's reports.)

I'm sitting here in bed, laughing to myself about how ridiculous each of his murder theories sounded out of context, half expecting Greg to burst out of the bathroom with a new one right now.

The bathroom door finally opens, and Greg jumps onto the bed without any true-crime thoughts, but he laughs when I remind him of his beauty routine and he says, "Yeah, that sounds like me."

I give him a wet smooch and head to the bathroom. Looking around his vanity (and inside his medicine cabinet, obv) it occurs to me that I've never really been this close to Greg's inner sanctum in his new apartment. We usually have our quickie in the living room and I clean up in the generic guest bathroom in the hall. I'm poking around his skin and hair regimens and don't recognize a single label. Saddleback Extra Strength Daily Mud Peel? Greg has taken his products to another level without me. Just when I thought he was feeling like home again, when I stop and look around his new personalized pharmacy, even his new towels that we didn't buy together, it slowly dawns on me that this person feels like a stranger.

I shut his medicine cabinet quietly so he can't hear me, and decide once again I'm overthinking this casual night of fun. But we ate at *our restaurant*. We *kissed*. He didn't look at himself once in the mirror while doing any of this. It's a mixed bag of emotions, so I stare at my naked self in his expensive-looking mirror. *Get a grip, Max. Also, don't talk to yourself in the third person, Max.* Maybe, I think, I can steer us back to the way we were.

Hopping back into Greg's bed makes me feel all warm and cozy again, and even though none of these pillows, bedding or duvet cover are familiar to me, it's okay. If this night is a rekindling of what we once had, I can grow into them and make all of *his* stuff *our* stuff again. It's just stuff.

Greg is sitting up against the plush headboard, intently messaging someone on his phone with his furrowed-brow-concentration face.

"I missed you in there," I say, just like when we first started sleeping in each other's beds, as if taking a bathroom break could really cause someone to miss another person. He doesn't look up. I study his body language, which is completely different from before I went to the bathroom. Like all of the lovey-dovey coziness has evaporated. I decide to ignore this and press on.

"Now. Where were we?" I jokingly say, mocking bad soap opera dialogue.

"One sec," he says, still typing. I sigh and give him some space, lacing my hands behind my head. My limbs can go anywhere without touching him. It's total luxury. Staring out the window at the illuminated High Line, I don't stop myself from imagining this could be my view with Greg by my side.

"Is this a California king?" I ask, interrupting his virtual conversation. He doesn't respond, so I probe deeper. "What's the difference between a California king and a regular king again?" Still no response. He's so focused on his phone it's crazy. "Are you doing a work thing?" I ask. He vaguely nods like he's not even listening to me.

I scooch closer, rub his smooth chest with my fingers. I don't even care that he shaved. I grab a pec, pull it toward me, hard, trying to get his attention.

"Ow," he says.

"Sorry."

I lightly massage his other pec, which is a little bit sexual and a little bit to see how much he's been working out. Answer: a lot. I lightly kiss his neck. I grab his hard-on over the comforter. He responds just a little bit, finally glancing at me with a grin.

"That feels good." I'm trying to resume our kissing-palooza, resisting all temptation to take it below the belt. See how long we can last. "Hang on," he says, sitting up. He straight up stops me. Almost pushes me off.

"What are you doing right now?" I ask.

"I'm chatting with this hot twink," he says so casually. I sit up, peer over his shoulder and see he's been on Grindr this whole time. In shock, I turn to look at him, lit by the glow of his phone as he types. For a moment, I feel bad for this person who's so desperately trying to recapture his lost twenties he spent in a monogamous relationship, now paralyzed by arrested develop-ment. His interrupted horny youth rolls off him in waves.

Then I flash forward to me pouring gasoline all over his bed and lighting it on fire à la one of his *Dateline* murder mysteries. Spoiler: I did it.

"Are you kidding me?" I'm not the jealous type at all. I know that he's been seeing lots of other people since we broke up while I've been seeing . . . plants? But this here and now is ridiculous. We'd had a moment. We just had an entire night of moments. He processes the horror on my face and grabs my wrist lovingly.

"Hear me out," he says, trying to calm me down.

"You're seriously on Grindr right now?"

"I'm not on Grindr."

"Then what's that?"

"It's Scruff."

"Oh my god."

"What. I was just checking my messages."

"Just checking your messages or cruising for sex?" He opens his mouth to say something, but nothing comes out. He opens it again. Nothing. I've stumped him.

"Well . . . both," he says, scratching his nose. "It's this guy I've been chatting with for a while, and he's finally here. He's visiting from LA," he tells me with a complete straight face. As if this night meant absolutely nothing to him.

"What about all the kissing we just did?" I ask, gauging if we were on the same intimacy page. Whether this positive shift in our fuckbuddy status felt real to both of us.

"I don't know. I guess I was just in the mood to kiss some-one." Operative word: "someone." I'm livid right now. But I can't move. I'm frozen.

I finally turn away from him and stare at his dumb flat-screen TV hanging in the corner like it's a friggin' hospital room. "I wanted to see if maybe . . ." He pauses, careful with his words. Whatever he's about to say, I'm on the fence. "Would you maybe want to have a three-way with this guy?" he asks.

I slowly turn to look at him with a blank expression. He's grinning like the horny devil emoji come to life. "We can make up for that one botched three-way we had after the Modest Mouse concert."

"Morrissey," I correct him.

"Huh?"

"It was Morrissey. We just talked about it at din—never mind." I get out of bed and start putting on my clothes.

"I take it that's a no."

"Not only is it a no, but it's also a fuck you," I say.

"What? What did I do wrong?" His level of stupidity is shocking. He has sex brain fog.

"I thought this night was like special or whatever. Our old restaurant, kissing . . ."

"Oh, Jesus. What's with you and the kissing. It's just sex. C'mon. Don't be so heteronormative. This guy is hot. Look." He hands me his phone to check out the photo. It's just a young, hairless, shirtless guy standing at the top of a hike somewhere in LA. It makes me sad thinking how many hundreds of guys like this he's looked at on this phone.

I go into their DMs and start typing.

"Are you responding?" he asks with a little bit of hope.

I type, I have a micro penis, hit send and chuck the phone back at Greg. He reads it in shock as I calmly walk out the door as if nothing ever happened.

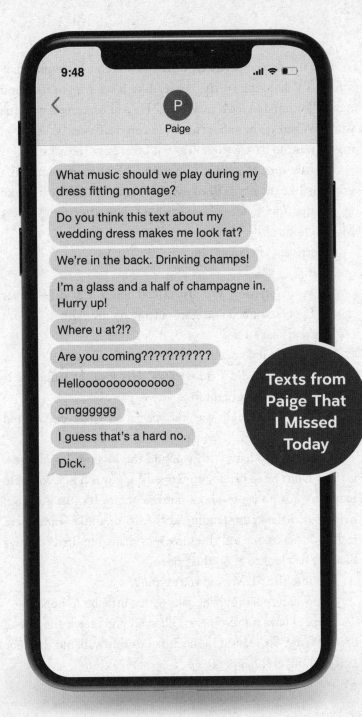

chapter
TWENTY-ONE

MY APARTMENT IS A GREENHOUSE. I SPEND MOST OF TO-day trying to put The Greg Incident out of my head and focus on nurturing my children, the plants. In addition to the potted orchids and various cacti I've collected from work, I've made at least four trips to the Flower District, scooping up more greenery than I know what to do with. I had to stuff my newly purchased plants in a series of Ubers whose drivers became increasingly annoyed, especially the one to whom I suggested there should be an "Uber Plant" option. He was not amused.

For the first time in my life, I'm feeling fulfilled by a hobby. It's unimaginable what this will look like a year from now, and I'll probably be swallowed whole by a giant bloodthirsty plant. I laugh, remembering in college when Paige starred as Audrey in *Little Shop of Horrors*.

Speak of the devil, I check my phone and see a text from Paige that I somehow missed. Actually, there are *ten* texts from Paige that I missed. Shit.

My face turns white. I slowly put down my phone knowing how badly I just fucked up. Today is Paige's wedding dress buying day. I've been too knee-deep in my new hobby to remember. Did I subconsciously forget about it because I don't like clothes? Paige is going to think I'm the worst gay best friend.

Rather than text Paige, I quickly toss on some decent-looking clothes and a baseball cap and head to the subway to meet the wedding crew on Madison Avenue. I'll have to come up with a good excuse on the way. Janet called me into work? Greg had an emergency appendectomy? My plant ate me?

The train uptown stops at Forty-Second Street for about a minute too long. I can say the trains were running late. Maybe? Then I wouldn't be totally lying.

After the train spits me out on Seventy-Seventh Street, it immediately strikes me that I'm in a foreign land. Uptown is so clean. There's no graffiti. All of the apartment buildings come equipped with uniformed doormen wearing ties, caps and white gloves. It's virtually empty since I'm guessing all the residents are in either the Hamptons, Martha's Vineyard or Nantucket for the summer. The few families I see out for a stroll look like their babies go to private pre-pre-schools. Every store looks fancy as fuck.

Now that I'm a sweaty, smelly mess from the humidity, I feel stares from passing well-to-do Upper East Siders like they know I come from—ew—downtown. Across the street, I see a heavenly store with angels and doves flying out of it and dresses like swirls of white cotton candy in the window. This must be the place.

As I extend my finger to ring the doorbell, the door opens. Katie, Eliza, Cori, Nina and Chasten walk out, beaming full of laughter and champagne. I hold the door open as each of them makes their way out, one by one.

"She said yes to the dress and no to Max," Katie says, leading the group.

"Fashionably late?" Eliza says next.

"You're in trouble," Nina says in a singsong way.

"Gay of honor fail," says Cori. "We missed you in there," she adds, to soften the blow.

Chasten just smiles and puts a hearty hand on my shoulder, like he's relieved to see me. Like he's had enough estrogen for one afternoon. But he also knows he won this round.

And then Paige makes her way out of the store, finishing her champagne, making the three salespeople laugh, probably with one of her famous witticisms, carrying a giant pink shopping bag full of something. She's wearing some kind of rose-colored lipstick with her eyes done up, and she's softer in a way I've never seen before, like she's auditioning for the role of bride-to-be. I miss one event and she's turned into a completely different person. Paige's smile evaporates upon seeing me, and she turns stone-cold sober.

"S'cuse us, sir. We were just leaving," Paige says in perfect Paige parlance. With her entourage in tow, Paige walks down Madison Avenue as they all turn back to look at me like I fucked up.

"The trains weren't working," I blurt out, desperate. "I mean . . . they were but, mine was late. A little? You know how messed-up weekend trains are." Paige continues to walk without looking back.

Chasten falls behind the girls with me. "Maybe don't make it worse, my dude."

Something within me ignites hearing him say the words "my dude." Maybe it's his possessive "my," or maybe it's the butch-sounding "dude," but whichever it is, I can't help but notice the afternoon Upper East Side version of Chasten is looking very good right now. But knowing the best man on the groom's side is at the bride's dress fitting leaves me full of regret since this is historically the territory of the maid of honor, me.

He and I walk as the caboose behind the girls in silence for a minute, and I'm not sure where we're going next, but I can't believe I missed the entire dress thing. Maybe if I explain to Paige over a Splunch that I've found this great new hobby that I love and got so immersed in, she'll be happy for me and won't care I missed this milestone.

Sadly, this isn't the first time I've disappointed Paige. Like the time when I missed her starring as Millie in *Thoroughly Modern Millie* our junior year of high school because I came down with the chickenpox the night before. Or the time our senior year when I got us pulled over for speeding down Lake Shore Drive in her dad's Audi that I'd convinced her to take out for a spin, and her parents grounded her for three months.

Paige has had her fair share of disappointing me too. Like when she blew off my oh-so-important seventh birthday party because she was deathly afraid of clowns, so her mom had to act as her substitute party guest. Or our senior year high school ski trip to Wisconsin when we were forced to buddy up but she chose her crush Josh Liffowitz over me.

Max & Paige®. Disappointing each other since 1989.

Before I know it, the girls are climbing into their own Uber. "You'll meet us there?" Paige says directly to Chasten and only Chasten, not even glancing my way for a split second. Wow. She's that mad.

"See you there," Chasten says with raised eyebrows and, like a gentleman, making sure the girls are inside the car before shutting the door for them. "What the hell happened to you?" he says, immediately turning to me for the dirt.

"I don't know. I was doing a whole project thing in my apartment and I lost track of time, I guess."

"A project thing? Like plant stuff?"

"Yes. How did you know?"

"My aunt called me and asked if you were any good. But Paige told me you're not a landscape designer."

Oh god. I've completely forgotten about my drunken lie to Chasten's aunt. I don't know how to respond to this, so I redirect.

"Am I kicked out of the wedding party?"

"Paige was pissed off all afternoon. She really let your absence get to her."

"What would I have done anyway? I don't know anything about wedding dresses."

"You're her bestie of honor. Her platonic soul mate. Her older brother."

"She's actually four months older than me."

"She was disappointed. She just wanted you there. She kept interrupting us to curse you out. It was like she couldn't even be present in the moment."

"Way to make me feel worse."

"I wasn't the one talking bad about you."

"She tarnished my good name?"

"Yeah, with about a hundred different other names."

"Like what?"

I lead Chasten down Madison Avenue, away from the scene of the crime.

"I don't think you wanna know."

AFTER TALKING AND STROLLING WITH CHASTEN, NEITHER OF US realizes that we've just walked over twenty blocks. The sun is setting between the tall buildings looking west down a long avenue, and the sky fills with a hazy orange glow. I'd snap a photo of us in this complimentary light, but that'd be weird.

We meet The Paige Gang for dinner at the Modern, which is MoMA's restaurant—a work of art in itself. The seven of us sit at a round table and there's a noticeable elephant in the room, which Paige sets the tone for because she's currently not speaking to me. Reading our menus, everyone points out something. Paige responds, "Yum," to everyone else, but when I say, "The branzino looks great," Paige silently concentrates on the menu and won't even look my way.

Near the end of our first course, I can't take it anymore, so I spoon the rest of my watermelon gazpacho down my throat, take a calm breath and clear my throat.

"Paige," I say, demanding the attention of the entire table. Now that everyone is looking right at me, I clam up for a moment. I've lost what I was going to say. But when Paige finally looks up at me with indifferent eyes, I can see genuine hurt, and I'm the only one who can make this better. "I'm sorry. I honestly was not thinking this morning, and I'm sorry I missed today."

"There are no accidents, but whatever," Paige says as she stabs her salad.

"I really didn't do it on purpose. I wanted to come. It sucks that we can't get that moment back."

"Yeah, it does. But we don't have to do this in front of everyone."

I look around the table, everyone looking back and forth at me and Paige like they're watching a sad tennis match.

"Do what? I'm saying I'm sorry."

"It's fine but you have to realize that I could've chosen another great friend of mine to be my maid of honor." Paige mo-

tions around the table, daring to include Chasten. "But I didn't.
I chose you. We've known each other for thirty years, and we
have to be there for each other and make that effort for one
another even when we don't want to."

"You're right. I fucked up. Call me an asshole if you want."

"Just . . . don't do it again. Okay? Asshole?"

The tension finally breaks, and everyone laughs a little. I laugh
too but I'm slightly shocked at how seriously Paige is taking my
wedding duties. I'm going to have to step up my game.

Two courses, six bottles of wine and a hundred and forty-
seven laughs later, Paige officially decides it's time to go karaok-
ing. This event wasn't on the wedding festivities docket, but
everyone knows Karaoke with Paige is a blast.

We travel to the ends of the earth to a subterranean dive on
the Lower East Side that has the distinct odor of stale beer
mixed with millennials desperate for attention. Paige loves this
place because it's known for its extensive song catalog. Rather
than mingle with the masses in the overcrowded main room,
who are currently singing "Pour Some Sugar on Me" by Def
Leppard, Paige takes her talents and us to a private room where
she can explore some more refined musical tastes. We let Paige
have the first two songs because, well, she's the best singer out
of all of us. She intros with Liz Phair's "Fuck and Run," and
follows up with Simple Minds' "Don't You (Forget About Me),"
complete with the Judd Nelson raised fist at the end. I tell her
she's amazing, but I'm also trying to get a few brownie points
from her. I even compliment her on the narrative she's trying to
tell with her song choices, and she's impressed I got it.

While this is all going down, I'm pressing a sticky button
covered in plastic that calls our server into the room. I order
Jäger shots for everyone—a favorite of Paige's and mine in col-

lege. Chasten informs me that this is a uniquely midwestern beverage choice as all of the East Coasters make faces and complain while Paige and I down the shots like champs. More Paige points for bonding over nasty alcohol.

Next up, Eliza sings a cute rendition of "Our Lips Are Sealed" by the Go-Go's before Katie struts her stuff to "Beautiful" by Christina Aguilera. "Written by my frickin' idol, Linda Perry!" Paige informs us as she slams another Jäger shot and points to the intercom thing for me to order more for everyone. This reminds Paige to take the stage yet again as she belts out "What's Up" by *the* Linda Perry band, 4 Non Blondes.

"And so I wake up in the morning and I step outside and I take a deep breath and I get real high . . . " Paige sings.

All of us can't help but chime in on the chorus. *"I said, 'Heeeeeeeeeeeeeeey!'"*

Chasten and I check each other out as we sing, seeing if the other actually knows the lyrics. I'm delighted to report that he knows this one. Turns out, he has great taste in music.

Next, Cori and Nina are up. They do a stunningly hilarious and somehow moving rendition of "Shallow" from *A Star Is Born*. Nina sings the Bradley Cooper part and Cori sings Lady Gaga's. We all double over laughing when Cori and Nina together sing the middle part vocal run, *"Oh, ha-ah-ah-ah, ha-ah-ah, oh, ah, Ha-ah-ah-ahhhhhhhh!"* butchering not only the lyrics but also the harmony.

Feeling duet inspired, I nudge Paige and point to our favorite karaoke song in the book—further effort to get back on her good side. Paige nods like an earnest jet fighter pilot taking instructions from her pit crew. When Cori and Nina finish their song, Paige and I stand in supercool, I-don't-care poses as everybody bobs their heads to the synth-pop beginning of "Don't

You Want Me" by the Human League. I'm up first with *"You were working as a waitress in a cocktail bar. When I met you . . ."* I sing with the dead seriousness of a 1980s British new wave pop star. I hand over the mic to Paige, and she follows my part with her side of the story: *"I was working as a waitress in a cocktail bar. That much is true . . ."* We sing our hearts out, and *The Paige and Max Music Hour* is a huge hit as everyone cheers.

After our song, in a Jäger-emboldened move, I grab the mic from Paige, type in my solo number and wait. I'm not sure what I'm thinking with the song I'm about to sing because it's not just a favorite of mine but it's also a nod to this virtual music fest that's been happening between Chasten and me. While the girls pore over the songbook, I wait for my cue and down my fresh Jäger. Suddenly, those recognizable first guitar licks from the Smiths power up and I sing, *"I am the son . . . and the heir . . ."* I do a little back-and-forth sway dance like Morrissey and steal a glance at Chasten. He smiles into his drink and knows our secret game is on.

When my love letter to Morrissey (and possibly Chasten) is over, Chasten swipes the mic from me and dials in his song. If my Spidey senses are correct, he's about to sing Taylor Swift's "Lover." Sure enough, he pops his collar and croons the tune. The girls weren't paying attention to me, but now that Chasten is singing and we can all hear his undeniably great voice, they look up from the giant songbook and perk up. I'm getting chills hearing Chasten nail the falsetto parts and watching him do dance moves I've never seen before, with his chiseled star quality only adding to his show.

Is there anything this guy *can't* do?

His performance is so good, the girls all peel themselves off the red vinyl booth, drinks in hand, and whoop it up for the natural-born pop star in front of us. We all look out the small window of the door to our booth and see that Chasten has single-handedly attracted a small group of fans. Our group screams, loving this front-row seat and backstage pass all in one.

Little do any of the girls know that my song was for Chasten and his song is for me. Chasten even looks right at me when he sings, "*You're my, my, my, my lover.*" I watch the rest of his amazing performance and can't stop grinning. He follows this up with the most soulful encore of "Purple Rain."

"Wasn't this written by Sinéad O'Connor?" Katie jokes.

"No!" Paige says, simultaneously understanding the joke but making sure no one believes anyone other than Prince wrote this song. "Prince all the way, babies!"

As Chasten settles into his song, complete with accurate air guitar that somehow comes off way cooler than I'd imagine, I wonder if he's been performing like this his entire life. I see him as a little kid, trying to stand out from under the shadow of his older jock brother who was equally handsome and charming but had the edge over him in sports. I imagine eight-year-old Chasten on autumn Connecticut nights at home, making his mom and dad light up with laughter over dinner. I can see fifteen-year-old Chasten at the local country club wearing his little preppy suit and tie, all pinks and greens, holding adult conversations with his parents' friends before sneaking sips of gin with his buddies at the bar given by a bartender from the other side of the tracks who's not much older than them. I imagine Chasten lounging by the pool in the summer, munching on club sandwiches with french fries, listening to his friends talk about Ashley or Kaitlyn's boobs while he sneaks glances at the muscly blond lifeguard named Hunter or Bradford. I think of Chasten's friends exceeding in lacrosse while all he wanted to do was make the perfect dessert. I imagine Chasten disappointing eligible Yale girls left and right while making out with a guy in his British lit class. I see him moving to New York, looking for love, wanting a Matt Bomer from *White Collar* in the streets and a Matt Bomer from *Magic Mike* in the sheets.

Chasten punctuates his performance with an identical Prince passion-scream flourish. His hips swaying side to side have had me mesmerized the whole time—I've never seen hips attached to such a meaty butt move like that so perfectly. All of us stand behind him on top of the booth, cheering, and pointing at that butt popping through his shorts. We're in awe of our karaoke rock star silhouetted by the glow of the cheap TV monitor, and when he finishes, we all agree to end the night on this high note.

When I go to shake Chasten's hand out of genuine impulsive fandom, I remember his hands are the size of oven mitts, which I'm sure come in handy as actual oven mitts when he's performing his culinary arts. I catch myself wondering how they would feel all over my body. The weight of them. The heft. Their strong embrace.

I am—and I can't stress this enough—inebriated.

Spilling out onto the sidewalk, we're met by dozens of enthusiastic people on what looks like an organized midnight bike ride through the city, their tires decked out in colorful spinning LED lights, their eclectic clothes glowing in the dark and dozens of balloons tied to their handlebars. It's like Burning Man on wheels. Our seven faces lit by the free-spirited love parade, we cheer them on. I see Chasten checking his texts, then he politely says good night to the group, and it hits me just as the moonlight bike commune passes that he's still seeing someone else.

Fake Restaurants That Stella and I Invented and Wish Existed

- Meat Barn
- Salads n' Things
- Snacks in the City
- Bacon McBacon-eria
- Shit Shack
- Cincinnati Bar & Grill & Bar Grill
- Five Guys inside Me

chapter

TWENTY-TWO

"MEET THE GAY WILLY WONKA" IS THE HEADLINE I READ over coffee and more coffee as the ubiquitous jackhammer continues outside my window. "Gay Willy Wonka" seems redundant to me, like "gay Christmas" or "dead corpse." I'm not suggesting Willy Wonka was gay, but his whole vibe was a little . . . queer maybe? The purple overcoat? The top hat? *That bow tie?* He sang. He danced. He was unmarried and loved snozzberries. Who's ever heard of a straight guy loving snozzberries?

Once I get past the homobait headline, I scroll through the *New York* magazine article Paige just texted me about Chasten and his chocolates. Throughout all of our wedding planning, he has not once mentioned how he's becoming the next Willy Wonka. Even lightly googling him a few times at work, I wasn't aware that his chocolates are so in demand. According to this article, he has a small chocolate factory in Brooklyn. His chocolates are sold everywhere from West Hollywood to Walmart to the West Village. Oprah recently had his chocolates on her annual list of favorite things. He's now getting an offer from Hershey to buy him out (still in discussions).

He's way more modest than I thought. I would've been screaming this information about myself to every man, woman and pigeon on the street. *Willy Wonka & the Chocolate Factory* (the original) was one of my favorite movies as a kid, so I'm especially impressed with this comparison. Not like there are a ton of famous fictional characters who peddle chocolate to compare him to. Like if he specialized in fried green tomatoes, the press would have no choice but to call him the gay Kathy Bates.

The photo of him accompanying the article is so good-looking, I sort of swoon at the handsomeness. In tiny print it reads, "Men's knit Oxford shirt by Ralph Lauren, brushed twill pants by James Perse, Red Wing Heritage Classic boots." His hair is perfect. It also makes me chuckle to think this article basically says, "Wear these specific clothing items if you aspire to make successful high-end chocolate too."

After studying Chasten's face for three whole minutes, I decide to text him a congratulations. I keep it short and casual by saying, Congrats! with one restrained exclamation point. I'm assuming he knows what I'm talking about, unless there are other amazing things happening in his life this morning that outdo a major magazine writing a glowing tribute in which they professionally styled you and took numerous photos of you posing on the High Line. He immediately writes back, Thanks, friend!! with two exclamation points, and now I'm wondering if I should've added a second one. Am I dead inside? I am, however, happy that we've graduated to "friend" level and aren't stuck in our precious frenemy rut. I'm feeling good about our change of status.

While I'm staring at Chasten's text, I get another incoming from Paige. She's all over me this morning. I wonder if she misses those five minutes she was mad at me for being late and is now trying to make up for it.

Paige's text reads, Also, I have news . . .

The little animated dialogue bubbles are on, and I hold my mug of coffee in midair, caught in suspense. After thirty seconds, a text comes through from Paige, asking me to coffee before work, which she never does. Avoiding another potential wedding-atastophe, I immediately say yes.

———————

WE MEET AT PASTIS, WHERE I FIND PAIGE SITTING OUTSIDE wearing huge glamorous sunglasses and rockin' an all-beige Lululemon yoga get-up. She's doing her best "bride-to-be getting in a quick yoga sesh before meeting her gay bestie" look.

Paige sees me crossing in the middle of the street and yells, "Guess who I'm meeting next week?" The reason she wanted to meet in person has already revealed itself before I even sit down. The quiet morning solo diners around her turn to see who this loud person is yelling at someone in the street. Paige does not give a shit what other people think about her. I envy that.

"Um . . ." I keep my voice lower than hers, expecting Paige to take my cue, and try to think of the most wedding-ish thing. "The flower people?" Paige shakes her head. "A harpist?" I ask, taking my seat.

"Of course you would think all weddings have harps."

"Don't you want one?"

"Soft pass."

"A hip woman rabbi we'll all become best friends with after the wedding?"

A server arrives, and I order more coffee for myself. Paige asks for a skim latte, then changes her mind and asks for just sparkling water with a wedge of lemon.

"No, you dope. It's not wedding related. For once."

"Okay, is it a work thing?"

"Steve Martin!" Paige blurts out, unable to keep me guessing any longer.

"What."

"I know!"

"You're meeting Thee Steve Martin, the daddy of all daddies?" I weirdly had a crush on his hairy chest when I would see him with Dan Aykroyd in the "Two Wild and Crazy Guys" sketch on reruns of *Saturday Night Live*.

"He is kind of the original daddy."

"Totally. That chest hair was everything."

"Oh, Jesus. Now that's all I'm going to be thinking about when I meet with him. Thank you for being my horny gay best friend."

"Anytime. Wait—are you pitching Thee Steve Martin?"

"What if I call him that in our meeting? 'Hi, Thee Steve Martin. Oh, thank you, Thee Steve Martin.'"

"Can you just tell me if you're pitching Thee Steve Martin already."

"Maybe? He's meeting three songwriters including me. I don't know if I'm pitching my take for his musical or if it's just a general. He's writing the book and lyrics, so we'd collab."

"This is insane. And amazing." I'm genuinely happy for Paige. "*You've been waiting for this moment . . . all your liiiiiife.*"

"Thanks, Phil Collins. I know!"

"So how are you going to prepare?"

Paige points to a young woman sitting across from us.

"*Summer kneeeeees, makes me feel fiiiiiine . . .*" Paige sings. I look and see the woman has bruises on her legs.

"Good one. Tell me how you're gonna prepare."

"I'm just gonna wing it like I did with the producers."

"I forgot. You're Paige."

"Every time I've prepared for something like this, I never get it. That musical about Thomas Edison?"

"*Howard the Duck the Musical?*"

"A waste of three months writing songs about anthropomorphic space birds."

"At least you dipped your toe into the Marvel family."

"Yeah, look where that got me. Anyway, I'm freaking out. This could be huge. Just meeting him is enough."

"You're meeting him after the wedding, I hope."

"A week before. It's nuts." Paige checks her phone, and her thoughts shift elsewhere. "Speaking of which, are you doing your man of honor duties?"

The server arrives with our beverages, and Paige steals a sip of my coffee before I can even touch it.

"Do you want your own?"

"No, I just wanted a sip of yours."

"What do you mean my 'man of honor duties'? Have I missed something? Other than the first half of you saying yes to the dress?"

"You missed the *entire* thing. You just came for the dinner and karaoke."

"Fine. I know. So what else am I supposed to be doing?"

Paige looks horrified that I'm asking this. "I don't know. Like, every wedding should have little surprises throughout. Stuff that the wedding party organizes."

"So, in addition to completing the list of tasks I'm supposed to do, I have to—"

"There's never been a 'list of tasks.' Sheesh. If it's work to you, then forget it."

"I'm sorry I'm not vision-boarding your wedding. Just tell me what you mean."

"I don't know. Surprise me. Just be a normal gay guy and come up with something creative and wedding-y."

"Like choreograph a dance that everyone in the wedding party does as they make their entrances, and post it on YouTube?"

"No. Do NOT do that. For the love of Christ."

"Okay. I'm not sure what you want."

"Forget it. I want *you* to want to make little surprises. I shouldn't have to tell you. That's why they're surprises."

I grin through gritted teeth. "Okay." Even though I don't have the slightest clue what she's asking for. "I'll think." I'm not sure how my entire personality has boiled down to "gay best friend of woman getting married."

"Cool. I gotta go do yoga. I need to lose five hundred pounds before the wedding."

"You're crazy."

"I'm kidding. I'm doing it to de-stress. This wedding shit is a lot. And my parents are coming in a couple weeks."

"A couple weeks? Isn't that early?"

"They're spending a week here before the wedding. The wedding's in less than a month, dude!"

"Oh my god. I'm so not ready."

"*You're* not ready?!"

"Which parents are coming?"

"My mom and Ron. They're staying at the Carlyle. My dad and Laurie are coming right before the wedding."

"Your mom at the Carlyle. That tracks hard."

"I know. She thinks she's all fancy. Meanwhile, she grew up dirt poor."

"She married well."

"Thrice," we both say in unison.

"Must be nice to spend gobs of money on a hotel room and not offer a single penny for my wedding," Paige says as she stands, checking her phone. "Shit. My Lyft went the wrong way," she says as she walks away from the restaurant.

"No goodbyes?" I yell as Paige heads east on Gansevoort.

"Love ya!" she says and waves without looking back.

———————

PAIGE AND CHASTEN BOTH GETTING INCREDIBLE CAREER NEWS is extremely inspiring but also depressing. I know I shouldn't compare myself to them. My so-called career isn't even in the same genre as either of theirs. I'm telling myself not to internalize any of this and just be happy for my friends. It's exciting to know two people who are making headlines and creating culture. But something is nagging me to face the empty void that is my work life. It's worse than an empty void. I have a job that actively diminishes people for the betterment of a large, faceless corporation.

After my coffee with Paige, I hop on a Citi Bike because now I'm running late. Even though Janet is out this week, I still have to put in the face time. I slip in my AirPods and peddle to work, listening to Morrissey's "We Hate It When Our Friends Become Successful."

There's always a lightness in the air at work whenever Janet is out of the office. It's actually pleasant. Lots of people have taken off for their summer vacations. It feels like that one time

I took a creative writing class for summer school my sophomore year of high school. All of the established rules of the school, like needing a hall pass for the bathroom or eating lunch on campus, were lifted and it felt like anything goes. I'm half expecting to see our stodgy CFO wearing Bermuda shorts with his nose covered in white sunscreen.

Inside my office, I see a new Post-it note on my wall from Stella that reads, "Remember to pick up Brandyn from tuba practice." I laugh, tear it off and see another note under it that reads, "Lunch @ 12?"

Walking through the creative floor hallway definitely has "trigonometry teacher isn't here so we're going to leave early" vibes. I hear music coming out of more than one office—Ed Sheeran in one, Band of Horses in another. There's one art director who listens to hard-core death metal with his door shut, and today he has it on extra loud. A few creatives are already playing Ping-Pong and it's not even noon. I'm sure no one is excited to see me—Janet's minion—roaming the halls again. But I try not to appear as if I'm checking on anyone, which I'm not. "I'm not like those other HR people. I'm a cool HR person!" I want to scream, but no one would believe me. Not after the job insecurity havoc I've wreaked.

When I arrive at Stella's desk, she's not there—just a fleece blanket wrapped around her chair as if she's evaporated—so I write two Post-it notes. A jokey one reads, "Don't forget to pick up Jonah from karate." I place one under it that answers her question: "Lunch @ 12. Soho?"

Lunch in Soho feels like an urban hike in relation to our office, which is as far west as you can go before hitting the Hudson River. Lunch in Soho means crossing the threshold of Sixth

Avenue, into another dimension that is South of Houston. Lunch in Soho signals that you have time on your hands.

One of my favorite spots in the office is the kitchen on the creative floor. Any chance I get, I'll escape the tiny HR floor kitchen, which inexplicably has one sad, outdated, off-brand coffee machine called Mixpresso, whatever that means, and that's it. We don't even have a vending machine.

The creative floor kitchen, on the other hand, is clearly the favorite child. With a giant colorful faux Lichtenstein painted on the back wall, the white marble counter houses at least ten glass cookie jars full of salty and sweet snacks including my favorite red licorice Nibs. The double fridge is stocked with beverages of your choice, and a long dining room–esque table with thirty orange chairs, to provide a pop of color on the slate-gray concrete floors, encourages communal meals. There's even four kinds of beer on tap. Hovering over the table is a woven wooden structure, like a dome, so you feel like you're nestled within a womb.

One of the three microwave ovens closes, where I find Stella wearing a faux-fur white blanket and taking out her regular mug with David Letterman's face on it. She blows on her hot tea and doesn't see me coming.

"Cold enough for ya?" I startle her, and she makes a high-pitched squeak, almost spilling her tea.

"Maxi-Pad! You scared me," she says, blowing on her tea. "Don't do thaaaaaat." How she can hold a hot mug of tea while keeping a giant blanket around her is some expert-level shit.

"I left you some very important notes."

"Okay. I'll check them."

She blows on her tea some more. She studies me expectantly. I immediately know what she's telepathically asking me.

"Before she left, she emailed me." We both know exactly who "she" is. We don't even have to say her name.

"What'd she say?"

The look on Stella's face is so distraught, so fragile, I can't bring myself to tell her the truth. It's not right to terrorize her while she's in this state. Even though Janet told me more layoffs are happening, who knows, maybe they won't. To use a Janet expression, I decide to pivot.

"The layoffs are basically over."

"*Basically?*"

"They're done. There shouldn't be any more."

Stella, as always, is reluctant to celebrate this tiny bit of good (not entirely true) news.

"That's good, right?" She sips the tea she drinks every day to warm herself up.

"Yeah. Stop worrying."

"She emailed me this morning asking me to book Jet Skis for her rug rats."

"Aren't her kids teenagers? They can book themselves."

"She misses me."

"See? Codependent. She can't live without you."

Stella's shoulders relax, and her face brightens into a smile.

"I'm gonna go watch vids of grizzly bear attacks at my desk, then I'll come to your office and pick you up for our lunch date."

I steal a recycled paper coffee cup full of Nibs and tell Stella I can't wait. It feels like I dodged a bullet for now.

Back at my desk, I spend the next hour and a half posting photos of my plants on Instagram, noticing I'm gaining a few followers, and texting with Stella about where to have lunch. Stlunch? We go back and forth, making each other laugh with more fake restaurant names.

I even have my feet up on the desk with the door open—an act of defiance I pointedly never do when Janet is in residence. It feels like I can do anything. I almost feel like breaking into her office and licking all of her trophies. Ew.

After Stella and I settle on SUGARFISH for lunch, I have about thirty minutes before she picks me up, so I decide to do something semi-work-related by researching plants for our upcoming Difference Day. Only eight people have replied to my email signing themselves up, which is embarrassing considering there are like two thousand people working here, give or take the fifty that were just forced out. I imagine people are anxiously laying low until they know which way their job fate takes them.

It's two minutes to noon, so I check my work email one more time before Stella scoops me up. That's when I get my first real work email of the day. It's from Janet. Of course she's sending me work emails while she's on vacation at her Nantucket manse. Why wouldn't she? Does she want me to make sure Stella has scheduled her kids' Jet Ski times?

Max,

We're going to go ahead and tee off this next round of terminations starting this week.

How callous of her to include a sports reference in the same sentence as employee terminations. It sounds so casual and playful. Like, "Oh, let's play a round of golf while we fire people. Hold my putter while I lay off Anthony in digital."

I scan the list of names that Janet and her shadowy band of higher-ups have generated. Each name is more familiar than the next.

This time it's the lower-level support staff—the people who *really* can't afford to lose their jobs. There's Duncan, the guy who listens to country music in the mail room. Marissa, the assistant producer. Betsy, Fabriana, Luis.

Then my heart sinks. My face goes white and I feel a shiver up my spine as I read the final name on this dreaded list.

Stella.

The Five Stages of Grief from Someone I Lay Off

1. Seriously?
2. I Guess It Just Wasn't Meant to Be
3. Sure, You Can Have My Plant
4. I Hated This Place Anyway
5. Fuck Off, Max

chapter
TWENTY-THREE

EXACTLY ONE SECOND AFTER READING STELLA'S NAME ON the list, as if on cue, she appears at my door. I hurriedly quit out of my email, toss on a fake smile and think about setting my computer on fire.

She looks at me suspiciously for a beat and then: "Shall we?"

While we wait in the lobby, I stab the elevator button a half dozen times out of anxiousness. I need to keep preoccupied, because I'm not sure how to break this impending awful news.

"Chill. That doesn't even do anything when you hit it like that."

"I know. I'm just starving."

"Me too. I'm gonna eat the fuck out of a spicy tuna roll."

On our walk into Soho, Stella practices some funny bits she's been adding to her one-woman show, while my mind silently interrupts her.

Should I tell her on our walk?

"But that wasn't the first time I'd seen a dick inside my sorority house."

Should I tell her before we sit down to order?

"Out of ten bridesmaids, I was the only one not named Katina, Kayla or Kylie."

Should I wait until we eat and then tell her?

"What parents wouldn't want a daughter with a unibrow whose résumé highlight includes working at Ross Dress for Less in Sausalito?"

Should I wait until we're on professional turf and tell her at the office?

"Are you even listening to me?"

Should I tell her that I'm spiraling?

"What? Yeah. Totally. Ross Dress for Less."

"You haven't laughed once. I haven't even seen one of Max's famous droll smirks."

"No, yeah. I like it. It's all very entertaining."

"Entertaining? That's like when Kevin Costner called Madonna's performance 'neat' in *Truth or Dare*."

"So, you're Madonna and I'm Kevin Costner. Got it." At this point, I'm just trying to keep up.

Since I'd rather go to a diner—I'm not a huge sushi fan—our feast at Blue Ribbon includes all the basics. Neither one of us is adventurous enough to try anything outside of the standard fare, but it wouldn't matter anyway because I'm just going through the motions of eating at this point. Each dish that goes by where I don't tell Stella about her job feels like a betrayal. The miso soup tastes like shock and denial. Every bite of edamame comes flavored with guilt. The spicy tuna roll tastes complicit. I'm numb by the time we share the bento box with the mochi ice cream.

Honestly, I didn't think this was going to happen. Not this way. Stella is a trusted brand name at the agency. She's been Janet's right-hand woman for four years now after Janet cycled through as many assistants as she has trophies on her desk. I wonder if Janet planned her vacation around knowing that Stella was about to go. That's very Janet, not wanting confrontation. But why would they vacate Janet's executive assistant role? Maybe Janet knew if Stella stayed, she'd have to make her a junior copywriter and bump up her salary. It's all such an evil chess game.

We finish our dessert, and I'm listening to Stella tell me how she can't find anyone on the dating apps. Just the way she talks sounds like a hilarious stand-up act. But then the conversation turns dark when she tells me she's been making the same salary for four years with no raise and her rent in Crown Heights keeps going up. She wonders aloud if I've heard Janet mentioning her promotion. At that moment, I need to swallow, but I don't want Stella to see it and think it's a tell that I'm lying. Luckily, her curiosity is interrupted by the entire restaurant going completely dark, as if an alien ship has suddenly descended onto Spring Street.

Everyone turns to the windows and sees the wind picking up. Garbage swirls in midair. Pigeons scatter. Street signs rattle. A large tree branch flies by as we all gasp.

"Is it supposed to rain?" Stella asks as we both check the weather app on our phones. And then we hear a loud crack as it starts to drizzle, which turns into a heavy downpour. It's a steady rain that looks like it's not going anywhere soon.

"Sake, anyone?" Stella asks.

"We could," I say.

A bottle of sake later, we're standing in the doorway outside the restaurant and it's almost 3:00 p.m. The sky is basically pitch-black, and the rain has turned to hail. I can't think of a more appropriate form of weather, which is at turns weeping for

Stella and violently hitting me for not telling her the news yet. I'm not drunk but maybe a little buzzed and definitely full of dread.

"Should we run?" she asks me as we eye other umbrella-less pedestrians across the street huddled under various awnings. The rain has completely turned my mood into morose sadness, so I turn to her and slowly nod my head yes.

As we run through the streets of Soho, hopping over puddles, dodging tourists in ridiculous ponchos and almost getting hit by a guy wearing all camouflage, inexplicably riding a little girl's pink dirt bike, we make it back to the office. My light khaki shorts are now dark brown and matted to my legs, and my New Balance sneakers are like tiny swimming pools. Stella is shivering, her teeth chattering. She's reached a new level of cold that I've never seen before, to the point that I'm thinking she needs medical help.

"I need tea and Sour Patch Kids and a blanket," she tells me.

When the elevator opens to our floor, I decide I need to pull the bandage off.

"Meet at Friday Night Lights after?"

"'Kay," she says as we walk in opposite directions, soaking-wet ghosts of our former selves. This is the last time we'll ever go to lunch again as coworkers, I think.

"Friday Night Lights" is what Stella and I call the bleachers, which are about thirty wooden stairs, the architectural design centerpiece of the agency. They triple as a casual, common work space, an auditorium for agencywide meetings and a stairway that connects the seventh and eighth floors. They remind Stella and me of high school football bleachers, and we go there half expecting to see office colleagues making out under them.

Usually Friday Night Lights is popular, but luckily today it's just the two of us sitting dead center in the empty bleachers. It's a fitting place to tell Stella, my work wife, that it's time we saw other people. Informing her in my office is a power move I don't want to employ. Breaking the news at her desk is humiliating since she's in an open space and anyone can hear her.

Stella stares at me, doe-eyed, holding her David Letterman mug, chomping on her candies, her brown fleece blanket tightly wrapped around her body and her long brown hair still wet. Somehow she started talking about a pregnancy scare she'd had recently with a one-night stand and how maybe she should just be a single mom, and suddenly I can't hold it in any longer.

"Janet emailed a new list of names."

Stella cracks a half smile and immediately knows what I'm about to say. It's like covering your anxiety with a laugh. The existential dread is too much, and instead of giving in to her own vulnerability, she's masking it with humor. Either that or it's a sense of relief, finally knowing her future.

"Okay, byeeeee," she says. It's a funny response but loaded with pain and anger.

"I didn't even tell you who's on the list."

"It's okay. I know I am." She adjusts her blanket, draping it just below her shoulders.

"I'm so sorry."

"It's fine."

I'm kind of tearing up a little. Am I taking the news harder than her?

"Seriously. It's okay. I'll be okay."

If I say anything, I'm going to start to cry. She's consoling me at this point.

"It's fine, Max. You didn't do anything wrong." I sit there in anguished silence, lump in my throat. She asks me in a tiny voice if I want a Sour Patch Kid and I shake my head no. We both stare into the gigantic screen hanging from the ceiling in front of the bleachers, obnoxiously playing an endless loop of commercials we produced.

"I'm totally fine," Stella says, over and over. Neither of us can move.

RETURNING TO MY DESK, I FEEL AWFUL, SO I FALL INTO A Google hole of "how to surprise the bride on her wedding day." For a short while, I find comfort in my "best friend of the bride" role. But after about forty-five minutes of wedding blogs ("FOB stands for Father of the Bride"), registry sites ("Fund our honeymoon!") and Pinterest lists ("750 Great Ring Bearer Ideas!") I develop a headache. I decide to decompress in our lobby, which is still always empty and maybe even more so now, where I like to clear my mind and stare out the window into the Hudson River. The rain has finally stopped, and there's a heavenly pink dome around the city. That's when I make a decision.

I need to leave early.

I'll take a Summer Monday, which is not an actual thing. Since Janet isn't here, the rest of her list is going to have to wait. The Stella Incident has forced me into realizing we're all just on borrowed time—with work and life. Right now, I need a serious escape. I act like Paige does not have a million things on her plate and text her:

MAX

Wanna hang? 🍪🥛🍸🍸🍸

Paige writes back the worst word in the English language.

PAIGE
No.

I'd rather someone use the positive-sounding "I cannot." Or even the empathetic "sorry." Anything but "no."

I wait too long for her to elaborate and then finally:

PAIGE
Can't. Sorry. So busy with work then
have cake tasting with Austin.

It sucks having a best friend that's getting married. Premarrieds are no fun. They can't think of anything except their wedding. But I understand. I'm just jealous.

I give her a passive-aggressive thumbs-up, which is somewhere between "no" and "K" on the Worst Texts List.

My dopamine system gets slightly stimulated when I see a new text from Paige.

PAIGE
Given any more thought
to a fun surprise?

For your wedding? I reply.

PAIGE
omg

Not yet. See, I easily could've said a flat-out "no," but I softened it. I will, I add. I wait for ten seconds but this concludes our texting for now. Usually, Paige tosses in an inside joke bit, but she's too busy for that right now.

The weekend rolls around and I busy myself with renting a tuxedo for the wedding, but by Saturday afternoon, I just can't bear being alone right now, so I decide to text the next best thing to Paige.

MAX

Hey Chasten. Want to meet to
discuss wedding surprises?
Answer yes or yes.

He responds immediately, which means he's either into me or he's on the toilet. Or both.

CHASTEN

Stepping up your bridal party game?

MAX

Kinda. Mostly just need to
blow off some steam.

CHASTEN

I could use a smart cocktail. 😉

MAX

Smarttails on me.

CHASTEN

Hahaha. Nice! How's 5pm?

With an hour plus to kill, I walk uptown along Hudson Street through Chelsea into Hell's Kitchen to meet Chasten. Along the way, I'm questioning why I'd decided to reach out to him. I'm not sure if it's because I diligently want to turn up my man of honor duties or if I just need a friend today. Or maybe I just want to be with him.

Two sips into my margarita at Arriba Arriba with Chasten, I decide I want to be with him. This no-frills Mexican joint that's been in Hell's Kitchen forever is perfect. Its menu is basic enough, and it has just the right flair of disco ball kitsch inside. The highlight being that the frozen margs are as big as your head.

Throughout chips, guacamole and burritos (also as big as your head), I tell Chasten how Paige has requested a surprise element for her wedding.

"If she's asking for a surprise, then it's not a surprise," he says.

"That's what I said."

"Plus, of course she wants a surprise. Every wedding should have one."

"I didn't know it was a thing. Any ideas?"

"You're asking me to do your job?" He motions to the server. "Two more, please?" I eye his margarita and see it's empty. Mine's half-full. The server lingers, waiting to see if I'm going along with Chasten's order.

"Oh, I'm still—"

"He'll finish it by the time you bring us two more," he tells the server, who nods, grabs Chasten's empty glass and goes. I gulp mine and stop just before brain freeze.

"I thought you'd have some cool ideas. Your mind is so creative." *Why did I just say that?* I need to smooth over the cheesiness. "Congrats again on your article, by the way."

"The one in *New York* mag?"

"Was there another one?"

"Oh, a bunch of outlets picked it up."

"Outlets," I say, gently mocking him.

"You're right. That sounded awful. I'm not tooting my own horn, if that's what you're thinking. And you brought it up!"

"I'm impressed. That's all I wanted to say. And I love chocolate."

"Oh, good. I usually don't trust anyone who doesn't like chocolate. Dark or milk?"

"Dark," I say. Chasten shoots me a poker face, and I can't help but wonder if I just answered wrong. "What. Wrong answer?"

"I'm just kidding. I'm not judging you. Of course dark chocolate is the right answer. I thought a midwesterner like you would say milk though."

"Preferring dark chocolate is the one fancy thing about me. I'm kind of a choco-snob."

"I'll have to bring you to the factory sometime."

"I'll need a golden ticket first," I say. Chasten laughs, which is nice because he's probably heard that a million times.

"I've never heard that before," he says. We both laugh as the server brings two fresh margaritas. I toss my paper straw aside and gulp the rest of my first one down. That sweet tequila hits, and the pang of laying off Stella bubbles up again as I make a mental note that the next person I need to fire is Greg.

An Ideal Romance Depicted by the Greatest Closing Lyrics of All Time

1. *I can't be near you, the light just radiates.*
   —"Malibu" by Hole

2. *There's a part of me hoping it's true.*
   —"Dance Yrself Clean" by LCD Soundsystem

3. *'Cause I've been waiting on you.*
   —"Seasons (Waiting on You)" by Future Islands

4. *It was a good lay.*
   —"Suedehead" by Morrissey

5. *Nobody loves no one.*
   —"Wicked Game" by Chris Isaak

6. *You ought to give me wedding rings.*
   —"The Book of Love" by the Magnetic Fields

chapter
TWENTY-FOUR

THANKS TO CHASTEN, I WAS TODAY-YEARS-OLD WHEN I learned that mole contains chocolate. I had no idea. We both order the chicken mole entrée in honor of this fun fact. Did he just expand my food horizons?

"I'm not drunk. You're drunk," I say, completely out of the blue for some reason. Chasten grins at my random outburst.

"So, what did you have in mind for Paige's wedding surprise?" he asks.

"Oh. That. Ummmm." I sip my margarita. "I got nothin'."

"I went to a wedding once that had a surprise Cirque du Soleil performance."

"Paige has a phobia of acrobats. Acrobataphobia? She can't look at anyone double-jointed or too bendy. Clowns too. She wouldn't come to my seventh birthday party because I had a clown."

"That's so sad. What about a psychic?" he asks.

"Is that too obvious?"

A Sia song comes on in the restaurant.

"We could hire Sia," I say.

"I'm sure she's an easy get." We both laugh. "What if we did like a reveal or something. Like their wedding date printed in an elegant font on all the chargers."

I have no idea what a charger is. "Yes. I love that idea," I say with zero acting abilities, which he sees through right away.

"You don't know what a charger is, do you?"

"Yeah? Maybe?"

"Okay, what is it?"

"Chargers are . . . like usher . . . people? . . . Who charge into the wedding and show you where to . . . sit." He's uncontrollably laughing at me.

"Why can't you just admit you don't know it?"

"I just went with it and then got buried in my web of lies. What is it? Like a phone charger?"

"A charger is like the decorative place setting under a dinner plate."

"Ohhhh. Wait—that seems redundant. Why would you need a plate under a plate?"

"Let's forget that idea." He looks at my empty plate. "Did you taste the chocolate in the mole sauce?"

"Yes," I say. "Dark, not Hershey's."

He looks at me with slight trepidation. "Do you . . . would you want to see the factory now?"

"The chocolate factory?"

"Yes. Consider this your golden ticket, Charlie."

"I'd have to ask my four grandparents all living in the same bed head to toe."

"Maybe your grandpa can chaperone you."

I laugh, breaking our Willy Wonka bit. "What about Paige's surprise?"

"Eh, we'll figure something out."

NO ONE I KNOW IN NEW YORK OWNS A CAR. CHASTEN, I GUESS, is like no one I know because we're currently driving in his red convertible Mercedes circa 1984 with the top down. Looking up at the tall buildings lit up at night and feeling the wind on my face as we cross the Williamsburg Bridge is a new perspective on the city that I'll never forget. When the jackhammer outside my window seems unbearable, I'll think of this moment. I'm even a little envious that Chasten can experience this thrill ride whenever he wants, and I'm assuming he's used to it, but by the look on his face, he loves it, basking in the warm summer night air along with me.

Morrissey's morbidly sweet lyric pops into my head, *And if a double decker bus, crashes into us, to die by your side is a such a heavenly way to dieeeeee*. I don't know if I entirely abide by that line, especially because Chasten and I are most definitely not a thing, but at this very moment, I get it.

"If the factory weren't in Williamsburg, I would never keep a car in the city," he says.

"You don't have to apologize. The suburban Chicago kid inside me is impressed."

"Wait'll you see the city skyline on our way back."

We turn to grin at each other as he sees a break in traffic and floors it.

When we walk inside Chasten's Chocolates and he flips the light switch, it's much smaller than I'd expected. It's a tiny storefront that could probably fit ten people, max. The dark wood paneling is lit by sepia-toned sconces that make it feel like we should be sipping whiskey in a private club in Italy or something. This is clearly the establishment of a chocolate connoisseur, I think as I study the shelves that are lined with individual chocolate bars, showcased and spotlighted like expensive bottles of wine at auction or works of art in a museum, each one more enticing than the next. Brown Butter Milk. Vanilla Bean Toasted White. Spring Salted Dark Milk. They come from faraway locales like Peru, Dominican Republic and Madagascar. This ain't no Everlasting Gobstopper shit.

"These are incredible. I want one of each."

"You got it," he says, fiddling with the bars that are packaged in muted, refined colors with stately gold lettering.

In a bid to win over my heart, Chasten brandishes a fancy tin canister of my favorite childhood candy with an adult twist: Dark Chocolate Bourbon Espresso Malted Milk Balls.

"Oh my god, are these like Whoppers?"

He laughs. "Can you sound more midwestern saying that? 'Whaaappers,'" he laughs and repeats to me in what must be an exaggerated Chicago accent because I really hope I don't sound like that.

"Whaaappers were my favorite growing up. Not to be confused with the Burger King variety."

"Mine *toooh*, doncha know," he says in another bastardized version of a midwestern accent.

"Okay, I'm not from Fargo."

"So, this is my little neighborhood emporium," Chasten says, sweeping his hand back and forth along the shelves like a hot male QVC model.

"It's incredible. Do I get a discount?"

"I have to know you at least a year before you qualify for friends and family." I must be making a sad face now because he feels forced to follow that up with "I'm kidding."

"No, yeah, I know."

"We're hopefully expanding now that there's some buzz. Probably opening a store in Manhattan and one in Connecticut."

"Gotta scale the biz."

"Wow. You really know your corporate lingo."

"I've seen *Shark Tank*."

Chasten shakes his head at my expense and takes out a humongous set of keys. He unlocks a secret door made of shelves and, not unlike Willy Wonka himself, motions for me to enter. I make a face indicating I hope he's not a serial killer and walk inside.

It makes sense why the storefront is so tiny because the factory itself is massive, what I'd imagine an artist's raw loft to look like in Soho in the nineties. There are dozens of silver cylinders and tubes and pumps and large vats and rubber hoses and cocoa beans of all shades of brown. There are maps of the world tacked to the walls, presumably pinpointing where his next batch of beans is coming from. Up until now, cynical me chalked up a rich kid's dream of owning a chocolate factory as pure privilege, but seeing all of this take shape in such an impressive way, I realize it takes a certain type of creative prowess—and madness—to actually wrangle this. It's one thing to talk about but another to actually do the thing. My eyes have nowhere to settle as I'm taking in the mechanics and moving parts of making chocolate. Chasten stands, eyeing me with an open-mouthed smile, arms crossed, relishing in his divine creation. I am Charlie. He is Willy.

"I want to try one." Wait—I'm turning into Veruca. "And I want one now!"

"Want to see how it all works?"

Before I can answer, Chasten is already flipping on switches, winding levers and turning dials. He's almost a different person, in the zone, all with a passion I wish I could identify within myself.

He takes a giant burlap sack of beans, spreads them on an industrial-sized cookie tray and sifts them, looking for defective ones. Next, he scoops up a giant mound and pours it into what looks like a coffee grinder that a giant would use. It rumbles and growls to life until a spigot pours a thick rope of perfectly heated melted chocolate into a massive stainless steel mixing bowl, sending off a heavenly scented aroma reminiscent of when I was a child and my mom made fudge brownies from scratch.

Chasten removes a tray of shiny brown sheets and admits the process takes much longer—days or weeks—than this. But he snaps off a piece of chocolate anyway and hands it to me. It's warm and full of a million complex flavors that Chasten recites back to me like a gourmet grocery shopping list.

We sit on plush velvet sofas in the back, designed for customers who actually pay for a private chocolate tasting, and eat several samplings of different bars over glasses of expensive red wine.

After my crash course in mixing cacao, fat, sugar and milk, our conversation lapses into comfortable silence. The warmth of the red wine mixed with the chocolates in my belly has lulled me into cozy happiness. When I look over at Chasten, he swirls his wine, contorting his face into a contemplative expression.

"What?" I ask.

He looks up from his wine. "What?"

"Nothing, you just have this look on your face."

"Do I? I'm just thinking, I guess."

"About chocolate?"

He laughs and sips. I know he's probably not thinking about chocolate, but I'm trying to keep it light.

"Do you think you went into chocolate because it's an alliteration with Chasten?"

"I could've gone into cheese."

"Or Cheerios."

"Oooh, like a whole shop full of different-flavored Cheerios."

"That would be so good."

The same lull in the conversation happens, and I catch Chasten doing the contemplative swirl thing again. And now I'm tired of keeping things light.

"How's the boyfriend?"

Chasten tilts his head, surprised I'm asking.

"You mean the guy I've been on a few dates with?"

"Oh, so not 'boyfriend'? Has he been demoted?"

"Not demoted. Just hasn't been promoted to boyfriend status yet."

"'Yet.' So, it's hot and heavy, huh?" I'll admit, I'm prodding him. Trying to get him to reveal his love life. Hearing him explain to me that the guy in question is someone he's "exploring more" and "getting to know his vibe," I have a sudden flashback to the night we first met. Actually, flashing further back to the moment I laid eyes on him. Sitting alone in the corner booth under that bad diner lighting with a slight grin on his cute face while I balanced my weight on the stool at the counter, trying not to seem obvious. If I actually allow myself to process the purity of that moment, something about his kind face and warm features felt like home. The irony is that I'm still not sure if he actually noticed me or if it was the food menu behind me that he found so attractive.

I'm realizing at this moment how complicated our relationship grew from there as I listen to him speak about the guy he's seeing. A bit of dread creeps in when I think that our romantic sliding doors may have closed forever.

He caps off his talk about the other guy with "I don't know. We'll see."

"That sounds promising," I say, trying not to sound sarcastic but genuinely hopeful things will work out between him and this guy.

"Well . . . I mean . . . yeah, I don't know." He sounds hesitant now. Like he wants to say more, open up honestly, but doesn't know if he trusts me.

"What?" I wait in silence for him to elaborate. His eyes on mine.

"No, he's great. It's going well," he says while scratching his chin.

I go silent. Stare him down.

"Why are you looking at me like that?"

"You said, 'No, he's great.' Not 'yeah, he's great.' You started with a no, which is a sign that something isn't right, maybe?"

"Okay, fine. I mean, yes, he's great. You're reading way too much into this. He's a high-end realtor, so he's super busy all the time."

I nod. "Sounds . . . fascinating."

Chasten looks up from his wine, makes eye contact with me again.

"Have you ever, like, kissed someone and . . ." He trails off, sighs, swirls.

"And what? He has bad breath? Beard is too rough?"

"I wish it were one of those. No, have you ever kissed someone and felt . . . absolutely nothing? Not even nothing. Less than nothing. Like negative chemistry."

"Yikes. Um. So, this is what you felt—or didn't feel—from this guy?"

"The second our lips touched, nothing. Zero."

He stares at me, hoping for a reaction. I hold in a laugh under an uncontrollable smile.

"It's not funny. Like, I had to keep kissing him to make sure there was really nothing there. It was like kissing wet cardboard."

"And this is the guy you want to keep seeing?"

"Maybe it was the one time? I'm willing to explore."

"Yeah, you said 'explore' twice. You're the Magellan of tongue."

He laughs. "Just feeling out the relationship a little more."

I nod and glance at his full lips. *They're kissable*, a voice pops inside my head to let me know. Yes, they are kissable. And at that moment, I remember again we'd never actually kissed that night we met. We went straight below the belt. Straight for each other's junk. Bypassing anything affectionate.

I'm looking around the room. The chocolate factory has silenced and gone to sleep. As we continue to polish off this bottle of red wine, the wee hours of the night arrive, and all this talk about kissing has summoned a palpable level of intimacy between us that I didn't see coming. Through Chasten's deep sighs and contemplative wine glass swirls, I wonder if he feels the same. We catch each other glancing at one another.

"What about you?" he asks. I know what he's getting at, but I play dumb.

"What about me what?"

"How's your husband?"

"He's definitely *not* my husband," I say, clenching my jaw.

"Demoted?" he asks, letting out a quick high-pitched giggle that I have not heard from him before.

"We were never married. Life partners I guess? But not anymore." I stop, testing the waters to see if he'd like to know more or move on to the next topic.

"Why not anymore?" he asks. His curiosity is a turn-on. Not just because he's asking about me but knowing he's not just interested in talking about himself. And also, maybe because he's asking about me. There's a familiar, relaxed air of openness between us now, so I go for it.

"It just . . . hasn't worked in a while." I look at him, seeing perplexed concern in his eyes. "Living together all those years was great. Then we broke up and he got his own apartment. We kept the sex alive. Sorta. Then he started fucking any living thing under the age of thirty while I waited for him to get that out of his system."

"And has he?"

"Nope. Actually, he's more fully committed than ever."

Chasten probes deeper into my relationship with Greg, and I launch into how we met because of Paige, how we bonded over being two suburban nerd outsiders who hadn't yet found their sea legs, living in New York.

Chasten wants to know more about my identity outside of Greg, which I'm happy to answer. I tell him my highlights and lowlights in college, with Morrissey as my secret boyfriend telling me to *stretch out and wait* and *it's not like any other love, this one is different because it's us.* How I wanted to pursue theater, but seeing Paige nail a dramatic Mamet monologue in our freshman year acting class made me realize then and there I would simply never have what it takes. Our Q and A is better than a first-date interview. It's intense. Honest. It's the therapy session I didn't realize I needed.

He wants to know what shaped me as a kid, so I show him the home movies in my head of a dreadful summer at sleepaway camp in Wisconsin. To this day, the sound of cicadas in the summer brings back the trauma of my first day of camp, having explosive diarrhea after a tetherball match that I epically lost. I tell Chasten that no matter which activity—volleyball, archery, canoeing—I was usually the least athletic. As a joke, one of the junior counselors (probably seventeen at the time but seemed to me like an adult) drew a fake award for Worst Swimmer Ever on a piece of paper and had a little cruel mock ceremony to present it to me. Everyone laughed. I went along with it and vowed never to write home to my parents about it.

"My only saving grace at camp," I tell Chasten, "were the commandos."

"Going commando? Like not wearing underwear?" Chasten asks.

"They were these midnight escapes our counselors called 'commandos,' like a military thing I guess. They'd surprise wake us one night at exactly midnight, and we'd have to quickly dress in all black, then walk a mile to the abandoned area of the campgrounds, where there was an unused shed on the lake."

"This sounds very horror movie," Chasten says.

"It was. Our cabin of boys crammed into this creepy shed with a girls' cabin, and the counselors told ghost stories about supposed local serial killers. They scared the hell out of us."

"Did you complain?"

"I actually loved it because it put all of the campers on equal footing—no one was immune to ghost stories. But then the next morning we'd have to wake up super early and play flag football or T-ball or something equally terrifying. The fun activities were scary and the scary activities were fun."

"Your T-ball trauma sounds like Disneyland compared to my childhood horrors," Chasten says. "When I was ten . . ." He stops. "I just realized I haven't told anyone this in a while." His tone turns serious. I can tell he's slightly nervous because he looks down, wiping away invisible dirt on his thigh. I hold eye contact with him and listen, silently letting him know he can tell me anything. "When I was ten, I was diagnosed with rheumatoid arthritis," he says. I try to hold in any type of reaction and let him continue. "The complications from it were so bad, I developed pneumonia and just . . . well, I basically almost died." I'm silent. Taking this all in. You really never know what a person goes through. I want to ask him questions, but I don't want to interrupt.

"Growing up as Austin's younger brother didn't help. He was an all-star athlete, and here I was this broken, gay disappointment to our rugged, blue-blooded father. I thought for sure I was the runt of the family and that I wouldn't survive this, so I decided I had nothing to lose and finally told my dad that I was gay."

"The kid PowerPoint presentation?"

"With the Magic Markers. It actually later paved the way for a better relationship between me and my father. Ironically, I ended up learning to live with the disease and not let it define me." I look into his eyes with a warm smile, so happy he's opened up. And even happier to hear that he isn't the perfect East Coast guy I thought he was.

I tilt back the rest of my wine, bite the last of a chocolate bar—dark with white chocolate marbling that resembles paisley—and gaze out the window, noticing the sun starting to rise, reminding me of all my responsibilities with work, the wedding, my life, and what I'm going to do with this new dimension of my relationship with Chasten.

But first, sleep.

Every Phone Conversation on the Subway Ever

"Hello?"

"Hey. Where are you?"

"I'm on the subway."

"What?"

"Let me call you when I get out of the subway."

"I can't hear you."

"Can you hear me?"

"What?"

"I said I'm on the subway."

chapter

TWENTY-FIVE

TODAY IS THE DAY THAT I END THINGS ONCE AND FOR ALL with Greg. The decision has been made. No more friends with benefits. No side piece. No fuckbuddies.

This is not some overnight epiphany. I've been brooding over it for too long and have slowly come to realize how completely callous Greg has been toward our relationship. The nostalgia of who we were has finally worn off. This is the final wake-up call on the relationship snooze button I've been hitting for years.

This morning I'm burping some of Chasten's Chocolates, which is a gross but nice sense memory of our epic night. Even though it feels like Chasten and I can't be a thing right now, I'm happy knowing I can connect with someone like that on a deeper level. It made me realize how *not* connected Greg and I have been. It's made me realize I've basically been alone this whole time.

But my first thought this morning when I woke up wasn't about Greg at all. I woke up imagining little Chasten in a children's hospital room, struggling with rheumatoid arthritis, feeling like that wasn't even the worst thing he had to deal with. He had to face disappointing his dad by telling him he was gay. It's heartbreaking to think of what he went through, but I feel grateful knowing he was open to sharing.

A woman who looks like she thinks she's Fran Lebowitz stares at me on the subway as I nonchalantly try to unstick my balls from my leg. It's full-blown August, and I can't wait for this one hundred percent humidity shit to end. I'm not exposing myself to you, Fran. I'm adjusting my junk. Frankly, Mrs. Cranky, you're the creepy one for looking.

One stop in and I'm composing my breakup email to Greg in my mind.

I think we should stop torturing each other.

Walking south on Hudson Street, it strikes me that it's been a minute since I've felt like I'm walking on air full of happy little clouds. Even the jackhammer outside my window this morning didn't bother me. Instead, it sounded like an animated bluebird chirping, "Good morning, sunshine."

Janet is back from her vacation today, which means my Chasten high is about to wear off. When Janet returns, I'm the first person she'll conjure into her office, so not only do I want to get there early, but I also want to make sure this week is over fast. With Paige's wedding coming up, I'll have to take a couple of days off prior to the weekend activities, and I want to make sure Janet sees I can get all of my work done.

I'm still bitter that Janet left and made me fire her right hand, Stella. There's no doubt Janet did this deliberately to avoid any confrontation with the person she's closest to. Right now, I'm contemplating contacting Stella to check in on her. Calling seems weird since we've never talked on the phone outside of the office. Texting seems passive-aggressive. Emailing too formal. I could DM her on Instagram? I don't want to disrupt her collection of sunset pics with my incoming missive about work. It's settled then. I'll fax her.

Maybe it's best I leave Stella alone right now. Our HR management training emphasized the Kübler-Ross Change Curve, also known as the five stages of grief, when an employee loses their job. I'm sure Stella is stuck in the frustration/anger portion at the moment and most of that is probably directed at me. Rightly so. I'd hate me too.

Settling into my desk, I start typing out my breakup email to Greg.

Greg. Nine years and three weeks ago we met and started something special.

This is stupid. He'd probably shrug off my breakup email and immediately switch over to texting a fuckbuddy, so for my own peace of mind, it has to be in person.

I've barely been inside my office for one minute when Janet is already up my ass with an email. Subject line: PLEASE , COME TO MY OFFICE!!!!

That's it. There's nothing in the body of the email. Just four demanding exclamation points and a weird space before a weirdly placed comma.

Padding down the long stretch of hallway from my windowless hole to Janet's lush corner suite, I brace myself for the wrenching sight of Stella's empty desk. As I pass by Stella's sad chair and bare cubicle, it stares back at me, silently whispering, *How can you do this to us?!?* I get it, desk. I get it.

Just as I'm about to knock on Janet's fully frosted door—it's actually written in our workplace handbook that EVPs get fully frosted doors while regular schmoes like me get half-frosted—something catches the corner of my eye. Turning to look, I see a pink Post-it note in the upper right corner of Stella's empty thumbtack board. I step closer and see on the note a hand-drawn bouquet of sunflowers. Under them reads, "I wanted you to have these, Max." It's the first time Stella hasn't jokingly called me Gary or Jerome or another fake husband name. She called me Max and drew flowers in honor of my plant collection. Her final leave-behind. Great. Now I'm emotional as Janet slides opens her door.

"Why are you just standing there?" she says, darting her eyes back and forth from Stella's desk to me. "Come in."

She leads me into her office, presumably to get as far away from Stella's desk as possible, and tells me to take a seat. She bears absolutely no sign that she's been on vacation—no tan, no serenity. She never does. I picture her wearing SPF 500 and a ridiculous floppy hat, stabbing out work emails under the world's largest umbrella while her kids and wife cajole her to join them in the pool.

"How was your vacation?" I ask. Someone has to acknowledge it. This is my gift to her, to spend five seconds basking in post-vacation bliss. But I know she won't bite.

"It was fine. I'm very concerned that you haven't been doing what was asked of you while I've been off-site." *Off-site*. Jesus.

"What do you mean?" I know exactly what she means. Firing Stella ruined me. There was no chance in hell I was laying off two dozen more people. And now we both know she couldn't have told Stella the news herself.

"I'd given you an explicit list of people. And by the looks of it, you've only notified one employee."

"Yes, Stella and I both took the news pretty hard, so. I was going to complete the rest of the list this week."

Janet blinks. This doesn't compute with her cold robot soul. "Max. I realize this can be cognitively overwhelming, but as a key representative of the agency, you have to remove emotion when eliminating employees. It may not be best for the individual at hand who was let go, but it's what best for the company."

"But the 'individual' is Stella. Your longtime assistant and my best work friend." This is like trying to reason with a nonhuman.

Janet closes her eyes, breathes in and out. To her, I'm a child nuisance who will never understand the adult's point of view.

"Max, what do you think I was doing the whole time I was off-site?"

"Getting . . . a sun tan?"

"Incorrect. I was working. My vacations are never vacations. While you're in Chicago celebrating Christmas every year, what do you think I'm doing?"

"Also celebrating Christmas?"

"I'm at the office. I don't stop. I never stop." Yes. And that's because they pay you ten times more than me. But also? This is your choice. It's why you don't know your kids' names. "I'm concerned, Max. I'm really rooting for you. But you have to advance your game now." Here come the sports ball metaphors. "If you want to take home the gold, like me, this is where I need you to pinch-hit." I'm, um, not sure that even makes sense.

"Okay, I'll get started on the rest of the list ASAP. Oh, Difference Day is this weekend. Should we maybe put a pause on that while—"

"Absolutely not. We want to keep office morale up through

this difficult time. But also, not fully acknowledge it's a difficult time, if that makes sense." Nope.

"Yeah," I lie, keeping my eyes trained on her trophies.

Then it occurs to me that she may be a teensy-weensy curious about Stella, so I throw her a bone. "Stella was okay, by the way. Not great. But she took the news like a champ." I even throw in a sportsy saying so Janet thinks I'm relatable. But there's a vacant look in her eyes as she just stares at me without blinking, impatient. I realize now that she doesn't care about Stella. She probably never cared about her at all, really. I was hoping Janet would convey one percent of compassion. But no.

"Thanks for letting me know, Max. I have no doubt Stella will land on her feet. And it's not like she has a family she has to worry about." As she says this, there's nothing behind her dark eyes. What a spectacularly shitty person on wheels. "Sidebar: I'm so glad you've decided to step up to the plate, especially if you want to slide into a position like mine one day." She plasters on a bizarre smile.

It hits me. Right here and now. I don't want Janet's job and I never did. I don't know what job I actually want, but I know it's not hers. Not that. I want to be the opposite of her. But in order to keep my job, I need her to *think* I want her job. So I placate her.

"Thanks so much, Janet."

"You got it. Now get back out there and score one for the team."

I mime swinging a baseball bat with a fake laugh like an idiot and exit, doing a heavy eye roll toward invisible Stella for old times' sake.

The rest of the week traumatizes me as I spend each day "eliminating" everyone on the list. It's taxing on my psyche, trying to not let the emotion seep through. I'll never need to say the words "reorganizing," "unfortunately" and "COBRA benefits" ever again.

The only things getting me through each day are the iced lattes I'm chugging bi-hourly, texting with my mom and dad about staying with me the week of Paige's wedding and my one lunchtime pit stop into the men's shop at J.Crew in Soho. I decide to cheer myself up by buying a new fall-colored plaid button-down shirt. Not that I get off on buying clothes, but Chasten's fashion-forward outfits have inspired me. I have designs on all of us taking a trip upstate in October to a pumpkin patch on an apple tree farm where my new shirt is perfect for sipping hot apple cider after picking six rotten apples for a sixty-five-dollar entrance fee.

Even though I blew off Greg that night he proposed a three-way, I still want to honor our years together with some mature closure, but I decide to put meeting Greg on hold until the weekend. I don't need the added stress this week. He'll just have to wait. That'll show him.

chapter

TWENTY-SIX

AFTER THIS WEEK, I HAVE LITTLE MOJO LEFT, BUT I'M EX-cited that it's Friday and I'm supposed to have dinner with Paige and Austin. All day she had texted ideas on where to go, but she was debating herself because I was too busy laying people off to reply.

I finally put her out of her indecision misery, making a reservation for three at the Odeon at 8:00 p.m. Sometimes I just have to be the daddy in our relationship. And since Austin is joining us, I thought I'd step it up from a diner and choose a traditional restaurant.

Walking north on West Broadway from the subway, I try to delete this week from my brain and focus on imagining drinking an old-fashioned and the fact that I can hang with the soon-to-be newlyweds. It'll be a nice change of pace to see Paige with Austin in between formal milestone events.

Seeing its unmistakable bright red neon sign outside, I remember the Odeon is a cozy comfort throwback to old-school New York.

I stop in the restaurant's vestibule to text Greg:

MAX

Free after dinner?

Would love to, he immediately replies.

He thinks this is code for sex. He does not know I'm pulling the plug.

Inside the perpetually bustling bistro, I see all of the buzzy people drinking booze, unwinding after their workweek, fitting for my crap mood. Before I give the host my name, I spot Paige and Austin canoodling in a corner booth. I'm on time and it's frankly jarring to arrive somewhere *after* Paige. This never happens. Another bonus point for Austin, who is most definitely responsible for improving her punctuality. As I wind through the white tablecloths, I spot a third head sitting opposite Paige and Austin. My knees buckle slightly when I realize it's Chasten, and I'm filled with that same warm glow I felt before Janet ruined my week.

"Maaaax!" Paige yells across the room as everyone in the restaurant turns to see. Squeezing into the booth next to Chasten reminds me our bodies have not been this physically close since the night we, um, met. Our legs lightly touching each other through our chinos is a nice familiar feeling.

Before we can catch up, our handsome server arrives. He has a "Sam Rockwell's younger brother" vibe with a resting "I'm an actor" face. After he coolly takes our drink orders—old-fashioned for me, martinis for Chasten and Paige; a Vieux Carré, a whiskey drink I hadn't heard of, for Austin—and saunters away, we all settle into each other.

"Chasten was just telling us about his hot boyfriend." Great cold open, Paige. As if I don't feel alone enough, staring at the glamorous couple-to-be across from me, now I have to hear how wonderful things are going between Chasten and Mr. High-End Realtor.

"A. He's not my boyfriend. And lastly, I think we're probably not seeing each other anymore," Chasten says. Not what I'd expected.

"Oh no," Paige says with genuine concern. "I didn't know that's what you were saying."

"Sorry to hear," Austin says.

"Yeah, no, it's fine. It hasn't been that long," Chasten says as a busboy delivers a basket of bread and a carafe of ice water for the table.

"Why?" I say, trying to cover a smile as I pour water for everyone.

"Why do I think we're not seeing each other anymore?"

I nod, buttering a piece of warm bread, settling into *The Chasten Show*.

"I don't know. I've messaged him a bunch and he's not replying. Whatever. As I said, it's fine. The chemistry wasn't there."

"I guess you'd mentioned that before," I say with my mouth full.

"Wait. When did you mention that?" Paige asks. Oh, shit. Did I just out my outing with Chasten?

"What do you mean?" I ask, playing dumb.

"I've always been around when you two are together, and Chasten never mentioned that. Unless you guys . . ."

I turn to Chasten and he kinda shrugs my way, which I take as a silent agreement that it's okay to tell Paige.

"Max and I were doing some secret planning for you guys, and we happened to be near the chocolate factory, so I gave him a quick tour," Chasten says before I can.

Paige's smile lights up the room as our drinks arrive. "You sneaky little wedding planners." Interesting to note that Paige sees us as her wedding planners in this scenario and her radar to see us as actual human beings who might have a thing for each other is temporarily broken.

"Salut!" Austin holds up his glass to cheers.

"Cheers!" we all shout over the crowd noise, eye contact all around, and clink.

"The guy was so good on paper, ya know?" Chasten says before taking his first sip. He's clearly not over this dude because I thought we'd already landed that plane. The conversation about how Chasten was fooled into thinking this guy was the one lasts for the next few minutes until we order our starters and entrées. It still came down to having no sexual chemistry between the two and, given his recent ghosting, Real Estate Man probably had figured that out first.

While Chasten continues, Paige kicks my shin under the table and darts her eyes to the side, which is the universal signal to discreetly look at a celebrity walking into a restaurant. Of course, we all turn our heads at the same time, embarrassing Paige, to see a celebrity wearing thick black artsy glasses and a rumpled dark T-shirt, with his head down, walk past with two chic women, both carrying designer bags, who look like mean publicists.

"Could you guys be any more embarrassing?" Paige says.

"Is he famous?" Austin says.

"Um, beyond," Chasten says.

"Babe, it's Jake Gyllenhaal," Paige says.

"*The Bourne Identity*, right?" Austin sincerely asks, craning his neck to watch them own a corner table. The girl and the two gays scowl at the straight Austin for not knowing this is incorrect. "He's married to JLo?" Austin fake asks.

"Okay, you're bad with pop culture but not that bad. He was in—"

"*Brokeback Mountain*," we all say in annoyed unison.

"The producers are talking about him for the show," Paige says.

"He came into the store once," Chasten says.

"You guys should say hi," Austin says but no takers.

"That's a good New York celebrity sighting. Usually, you just spot a judge from *Law and Order*," Chasten says as everyone except Austin laughs knowingly.

It hits me that my life is lame compared to my friends'. They're hobnobbing with New York's finest while I'm killing off people at work and torturing myself about ending things with someone who couldn't care less.

"What's Greg up to tonight?" Paige asks innocently, as if she's read my mind. It's been a while since we've discussed our complicated relationship status. I can tell she's not had a second to even think about us until this very moment.

"Not sure, actually," I say.

"How are you guys doing?" Paige has a tinge of worry in her eyes as she says this. Austin and Chasten listen intently, waiting to see how I'll answer. I start to sweat.

"We're good," I say. Why did my inflection just go super up on the word "good"? Why am I pretending things aren't over? Now I have to commit to my charade. I glance over at Chasten, who flashes slight disappointment over my news.

"That's great," Paige reassures me. "Can't wait to see him at the wedding." She really has no clue how south things have gone.

Our actor/server returns to take our orders, and the conversation about Greg naturally, thankfully, ends. As Chasten orders, I see Paige and Austin dip pieces of bread into olive oil and feed each other, oozing pre-newlywed status, and I think, *I want that*. Not the bread. Their love. But also maybe the bread.

I see Chasten noticing their lovey-dovey act too, as Paige and Chasten melt into one and order dishes to share. Paige's quiet hiccup debating her commitment a few weeks ago is gone; now they are the very definition of love. They're so blissfully into each other that everything around them, including us, is noise pollution. Chasten and I drain our cocktails in uncomfortable silence and ask the server for two more before he leaves to play it cool while chatting up his fellow actor Jake.

On the street after dinner, backdropped by the Freedom Tower, where the World Trade Center used to be, we all hug goodbye. Conversation during dinner of course veered heavily into Paige and Austin's wedding, including weird out-of-town relatives they'll have to deal with, music selection and, snore, catering.

Before we can exchange niceties, Austin whisks Paige into a giant black SUV Uber like Prince Charming and his carriage, leaving Chasten and me alone.

"Such a cute couple," I say as we wave goodbye to them.

"Disgustingly cute," Chasten says.

"Like, throw-up cute."

"Projectile-vomit-on-my-bare-feet cute."

"There could be worse things projected onto your feet."

We both laugh.

"So, what are you up to now?" I ask.

"Just gonna head home as a newly lonely spinster, I guess."

"You deserve better than Mr. Realtor."

"You think?"

"Someone who looks good on paper or in an Instagram photo doesn't translate to someone you connect with. You have more soul than that. Which is probably why you had no chemistry. Your souls didn't match up."

We are both surprised by me saying this, but Chasten takes it in. I stare at his handsome face in the red glow of the Odeon neon and find myself wishing we could redo the night we first met.

"And you? Going to your boyfriend's?" There's an implication in the way he says this, suggesting this isn't a good idea.

"Yeah. I'll probably head over there now. So."

"You fellas want some ice cream?"

We turn to see a smarty-pants-looking girl who can't be more than twenty-one, sitting behind a makeshift ice cream bar just outside the Odeon's entrance. Intrigued, and having skipped the dessert options—because Paige, wedding—Chasten and I move closer to the stand, where I notice she's holding a tattered paperback copy of *The Virgin Suicides*. My kind of girl.

"We got strawberry, vanilla, chocolate mint, peanut butter, espresso, banana graham cracker, sea salt caramel. And chocolate. Chocolate's my fave. All homemade. Oh—and sorbet if you like boring."

"I'll try the chocolate. In a cone, please," Chasten says.

"He knows a thing or two about chocolate," I tell her.

"Are you like a chocolatier or something?" she asks as her eyes go wide. "Wait—I recognize you from that *Vulture* article! No way!" she fangeeks out. "I stan."

"Thank you," Chasten says, shooting me a mock-furious

look. Suddenly, I feel a sense of pride to call this accomplished human my friend.

"I'm training to be a pastry chef," she says as she scoops his ice cream and hands it to him with a timid smile. "Don't judge me if you hate it. Not like I made it." She looks at me. "How about you?"

"I'll have the same," I say.

Chasten sniffs his like a wine sommelier studying a cabernet. Satisfied, he licks it, analyzing the texture, and approves. "Good chocolate," he says with a smile to the ice cream woman.

"Right on. I'll tell Chef. Enjoy, you two," she says and goes back to her book.

We turn the corner, slightly north of the restaurant on quiet White Street, and grab a seat on a bench along the wall, the word CAFETERIA now above our heads in glaring red neon, a relic from the seventies.

"Do you really think it's good, or were you just saying that?" I ask.

"It's amazing." *Lick.* "I thought it would be slightly chalky." *Lick.* "But it's freshly made." *Lick.* "Almost like frozen chocolate mousse."

"I love it," I say, not knowing how to describe it any better than the chocolate master. We sit there. Both licking our scoops with our feet swaying back and forth, like euphoric kids with their summertime treat. I lick, and watch his sage-green eyes process someone else's confection as his manly, pronounced Adam's apple glides up and down with each swallow. It looks like it could cut you. In a good way. He catches me looking. I swallow.

"I should get to, uh, Greg's," I say.

He responds by unfurling a mysterious smile. "Yeah, it's getting late. I should get a car."

We don't move though, stuck to each other on this bench like magnets. In between licks, Chasten wants to say something but holds back.

"What?" I ask, trying to pry it out of him.

"I don't know. Why do you let this guy torture you?"

"What do you mean?" I know exactly what he means, but I want to hear it from him.

"I just think you deserve better," he says, staring at his ice cream cone, deciding where to lick next.

He takes another lick and looks up at me. There's a lot of uncontrollable smiling happening right now between us. "But anyway, you have a boyfriend who you need to get home to." He's sticking with my story and now I have to. Buzzkill.

The faint sounds of "Five Fathoms" by Everything but the Girl get louder and louder as a minivan taxi slows down in front of us, letting out a friendly beep. The driver turns down his music a smidge and nods, asking if we need a ride.

"I guess I'll hop in. Are you heading up?" We both stand, still licking.

"I'm gonna walk a little. Have fun. G'night, Max."

"Night, Chasten."

I pull the heavy taxi door shut, and the driver turns Everything but the Girl back up and speeds through Tribeca and up the West Side Highway into West Chelsea. I chomp down the rest of my sugar cone, staring at my nighttime reflection in the taxi window, knowing with absolute clarity what I have to do next.

More Realistic Wedding Vows Than "Until Death Do Us Part"

- "Until admitting you've never seen *The Breakfast Club* do us part."

- "Until commenting on your favorite celebrity's social media posts nonstop do us part."

- "Until getting really into collecting snakes do us part."

- "Until jogging in jeans do us part."

- "Until always saying 'whole nother level' do us part."

- "Until being rude to restaurant staff do us part."

- "Until changing your ring tone to 'Who Let the Dogs Out' do us part."

- "Until Greg do us part."

chapter

TWENTY-SEVEN

GREG SMELLS AMAZING. WHAT IS HAPPENING RIGHT NOW? He's someone who never wears cologne, and I'm someone who doesn't even like cologne. This new-and-improved Greg scent is releasing some kind of sex pheromones that are making what I'm about to do very difficult right now. On top of it, he's looking buffer than ever. How weak of me if the big guy (penis) got in the way of the bigger guy (brain). I can't let myself down and not tell him we need to officially end things.

"Finally, you're here," Greg says, breaking out a fresh bottle of rosé. "I was just about to text you," he says as his eyes go from my eyes to my mouth. "What's on your mouth?" I go to wipe my mouth with my hand, but Greg grabs my wrist before I get there and says, "Wait." He moves in closer, presses his crotch against my leg. He rubs his middle finger on my lips and then smells his finger. "Is that . . . chocolate?" I nod. "Ugh. I hate chocolate." He pulls away and washes his hands immediately. How could I have ever slept with this monster?

Wetting a paper towel, I wipe my mouth clean. "Yeah, I just had the best chocolate ice cream ever."

"On a diet, are we?" he asks sarcastically.

"You fat-shaming me now?"

"I'm kidding. You're not fat. I mean, I'm not saying you shouldn't *not* hit the gym a little more often maybe." I blink at him, confused. Somehow, I went from turned on to turned off in three seconds flat. He grabs the meat of my ass playfully and crosses the kitchen.

"Isn't rosé full of sugar and carbs?" I ask.

"Yeah, but today's my cheat day." I groan internally and hope to Morrissey I never hear anyone say that ever again.

"So, Greg . . ." I start before I lose my momentum again.

"Yes, Max?"

"I just want to thank you."

"For . . . ?" He pulls out his dumb high-tech bottle opener.

"I guess . . . thank you for all these years we've spent together. And thank you for all the sex this last year. But mostly I want to thank you, right now, in this very moment. Thank you for showing me exactly who you are."

He's frozen in place, listening to me. Like a frightened animal with ripped abs. "What does that mean?"

"After we broke up and we continued . . . whatever this is, you've showed me over and over exactly who you are. And I never believed you."

"Okaaaay," he says, not sure if this is good or bad.

"Until now."

He places the bottle opener around the rosé and presses a button. We stare at each other while a weak buzzing sound slowly unleashes the cork. It's taking way too long. It's still going. And going. When the cork finally pops, he says, "I'm not following you."

"I'm ending things between us. This is it. No more hookups. No more fuckbuddy situations. No more wishful thinking on my part. I'm just . . . done." He stares at me, blinking. I stare back, not blinking.

In what feels like extreme slow motion, I watch Greg pull three wine glasses from the cupboard and set them obsessively, compulsively, evenly next to each other. He looks up and smiles as normal speed resumes.

"Fine. But let's be done after tonight, because I just planned a really hot three-way for us. Is that cool?" Wow. He genuinely thinks this is just like any other night our libidos overlap. He pours rosé into the three glasses as his intercom dings. I look at him like he's lost his mind and, feeling sorry for him, head for the elevator.

As I step inside and press L, he stares at me in complete shock with an expression that reads he can't believe I'd have the strength to do this to him. He says, "Are you being serious right now?"

The elevator door shuts.

———————

IT'S EARLY SATURDAY MORNING AND I'M INDULGING AT JOE, MY favorite coffee shop on Waverly Street and Gay Street, a real street name in the West Village. I'm chocolate carbo-loading on a chocolate croissant, chocolate scone and the largest-sized hot chocolate available, even though it's ridiculously hot and humid outside. On my walk home, I stop at Magnolia Bakery for a few chocolate-on-chocolate cupcakes for an afternoon snack later.

Not to sound dramatic, but after ending it with Greg, I feel like I'm no longer under the spell of a sex cult leader. I've found freedom and I'm having all the chocolate I want.

Suddenly, I see chocolate everywhere. There's a chocolate bar store over there, a bus shelter ad for Godiva chocolate, even that dog poop on the sidewalk kinda looks like chocolate! I'd love to connect with Chasten right now, but the adult thing to do is let the emotional dust from breaking up with Greg settle. Truthfully, the party's been over for years now and I just need a Dustbuster to suck up the glitter stuck in between the floorboards.

Leaving Greg's building last night, I cringed, running into the too-tall twink in the elevator whom Greg had set up as our third. Thankfully, the poor guy barely registered me—clearly anyone over thirty is invisible to him, so no way in hell did he suspect I'd just left Greg's apartment. In my mind, I pretended I lived in the building and was in a hurry to meet my high-powered attorney wife named Wendy for opera at the Met and didn't have time for polite eye contact. I vaguely nodded toward Dario the doorman as I made my swift exit and wondered if that was the last time I'd ever see him.

My first instinct is to call Paige and tell her Greg and I are finally kaput. But she's heard that before, and with her upcoming wedding, she won't have time to deal.

Instead, I park myself on a bench in St. Luke's church garden to munch on my chocolate croissant and nurse my hot chocolate in the flaming hot sun like a weirdo. This little hideaway on Hudson, connected to a church, has a paved pathway snaking around a garden full of brilliant flowers and trees. Breathing in the air as I stare at the lavender gladioli under a bright blue sky is the calming nature therapy I need right now. It's also giving me inspiration for Difference Day, which is in about an hour.

This oasis was always my go-to spot after a fight or breakup with Greg. Each time I'd have tears in my eyes, willing the flowers into telling me what I'd done wrong, blaming myself for our failed relationship. This time, my eyes are dry and the flowers are filling me with a sense of peace.

On the walk east along Commerce Street, I spot an interesting poster outside Cherry Lane, the off-Broadway theater near my apartment. I look closer and see it's Stella's one-woman show coming in September for three nights only. I'm smiling with chocolate-stained teeth, just like Stella would've wanted.

Arriving at the senior living community in Queens, I'm shocked to see the turnout for Difference Day is even more dismal than I'd expected. Clearly, I'm radioactive. There are literally four other people here. Janet is a no-show. Office morale, my ass.

Introducing themselves: Devra, a suburban mom strategist with a thick Long Island accent; Rafael, a heavily tatted hipster designer; Shane, a quiet bear freelance editor; and Harper, a smiley junior account executive who's a dead ringer for a twentysomething Ina Garten. They're all dutifully wearing their ill-fitting, extra-large turquoise-colored Difference Day T-shirts, which Janet had the art department make. I drop my cardboard box of a hundred "just in case" T-shirts to the side and mentally note the dumpster I walked past on my way in.

We get to know each other with painful small talk and Devra breaks out Tupperware containers full of homemade sugar cookies that look like yellow daisies. All of us fill up on too many cookies as the garden center delivery truck unloads the flowers and greenery we're planting today. Everyone's face goes white when they see how much work there is for so few people. When Devra informs the group that she has to leave early for her niece's bat mitzvah, I reassure everyone to just plant whatever we can and I'll alert the community maintenance crew that we're short-staffed.

We start digging, trimming, hoeing and planting. Just when it starts to feel like a botanical haven, I hear a tiny sneeze from Harper. Everyone says, "Bless you," and she rapid-fire sneezes for a good ten seconds. It's enough to make everyone stop and turn, but she reassures everyone she's okay, and we get back to work.

An hour later, as the sun microwaves us, Harper seems short of breath, to the point of wheezing. Her entire face has blown up like a balloon. One eye is a straight line, the other eye swollen to the size of a tennis ball, like it's about to pop. Her lips are purple and huge, like a plastic surgery addict holding a magnifying glass to her horrifically botched lip injections. Her cheeks are splotchy red. I'm frozen in shock because Harper doesn't seem to feel her face morphing into Jabba the Hutt's little sister.

"Oh my god. Harper."

"What?"

"Your . . . Are you okay?"

She's wheezing a lot now. "Oh . . . yeah . . . I guess I'm . . . allergic to . . . certain flowers? I never . . . knew . . . that . . . about me."

She forces out a tiny laugh, and her wheezing increases until she drops her pruners and holds her neck like she's choking. Because she is. Her throat closes up and her entire body turns red, breaking out into hives, like she's growing alien reptile scales.

"We need help!" I yell. Everyone around us turns to see the commotion, filling with anxiety, feeling helpless, staring. A nurse pushing an elderly woman in a wheelchair from the retirement community turns to see as Harper falls on her back, gasping for breath.

"I think . . . I'm . . . fine. Really . . ." What Harper says does not match the crime scene on her face. "We thtill have to do the . . . rhodo . . . dendronth." She's trying to deflect from the situation at hand by commenting on the flowers, but her tongue is so swollen, she can't even speak. The nurse lifts her head gently in her lap, telling her to remain quiet as I call the paramedics.

"You have an EpiPen, baby girl?" the kind nurse asks. Harper shakes her head.

"Just slide that under to elevate her legs," the nurse calmly says to Devra, who lifts Harper's legs onto the box with the T-shirts. At least they came in handy. The nurse checks Harper's pulse, comforting her. We all hover over the surreal scene as an ambulance screams in the distance.

The fear in our faces is interrupted when Shane looks up toward the parking lot and asks, "Is that . . . Kurt?"

Kurt is a permalancer IT specialist at the agency. Was. I had to let him go because a new rule prohibits permalancers, freelancers who are permanently full-time staff but without benefits. It's nice of him to show up to help even though he's an ex-employee, but it's also awkward. He was an extremely helpful computer whiz who always fixed the problem whenever anyone had a technical issue. He was quiet, maybe disturbingly so. And right now, I see he's exiting his SUV as a cloud of smoke and heavy metal pours out.

"Why's he carrying a bat?" Devra says, growing frightened. For a split second, I wonder if he mistook this Difference Day for that time Janet had organized a fundraiser for local Little Leagues where we all played softball. But that was four years ago, and Kurt is not here to play. We all quickly stand up from helping Harper and back the fuck up. But Kurt is laser focused, coming straight for me with crazy hair and murder in his eyes, like an unleashed villain in a comic book. He pushes me down onto the grass, hard, and the wind is knocked out of me. It hurts like hell. Everyone screams as Kurt gets on top of me and holds the baseball bat to my neck, basically choking me.

"You're a fucking bastard, ya know that?" he says with an evil quiet so close to my face I can smell his coffee breath and feel a little spit. His eyes are glassy like he's stoned. I think, *This is exactly what the HR orientation warned us about: disgruntled employees.* I'm supposed to thank him for his feedback, which I don't think is appropriate in this moment. So I'll move to the second step, empathize with his frustrations. But wait, this is beyond frustration. I'm moving straight to the part where I manage to say, "Please get the fuck off me, Kurt," as Shane rips him off and they fall into a wrestling match, each throwing nerdy, weak punches. Luckily, the paramedics have arrived, and now three buff men with medical experience are intervening. Poor Harper, still flat on the ground, has enough generosity to ask if I'm okay as I nod, trying to stop my entire body from shaking. This went from Difference Day to What the Fuck Just Happened Day.

LATER, WE ALL LEAVE THE HOSPITAL SPENT, PARTIALLY FROM being in the sun all day but mostly from the dramatic events. I'm thankfully left without a scratch, just trauma that may haunt me for a while. I realize how much worse that could've been. Kurt could've had a gun. I don't want to press charges. His firing was punishment enough. I'll have to meet one of the agency's lawyers, I'm sure. I still can't believe that happened. Kurt was so polite and quiet in our exit interview. Always the polite, quiet ones.

I feel bad for Harper, especially since I was the one who caused her to go into anaphylactic shock because of my flower selection. But at the hospital, we find out that Harper is allergic to hazelnuts, which were in the cookies that Devra made. The hospital is treating her, keeping her there for a couple more hours.

At home, I crumple into a ball on the couch before ordering a large pepperoni pizza and wrapping myself in a *Golden Girls* marathon. The jackhammer outside persists even at this dinner hour on a weekend. It's now accompanied by several hammers and some kind of sawing noise, producing a symphony that's the official soundtrack to New York City. I can barely hear Dorothy and Blanche insulting Rose. I take a bite of pizza and attempt to exhale.

And then, as if this day couldn't get any weirder, someone shows up at my door. It's Julia Roberts.

PLEASE JOIN US FOR A ROMANTIC

Bridal Shower

HONORING OUR FRIEND PAIGE

⁓

DUMBO HOUSE
(Dress as your favorite rom-com character.)

HOSTED BY CHASTEN BENCHLEY

TWENTY-EIGHT

T'S NOT THEE JULIA ROBERTS. BUT A LOOK-ALIKE. SHE'S standing at my door with a Richard Gere look-alike, both slightly out of breath from walking up the six flights. They collect themselves and reenact the famous scene from *Pretty Woman* when he gives her a ring in a tiny box, and as she grabs the ring, he closes the box on her hand and she laughs with her famous Julia Roberts smile and guffaw. They don't exactly nail the performance, I'm afraid to admit. It's like watching a cheap Elvis impersonator or seeing wax statues of celebrities—something is just a little *off*. Once they finish, Richard Gere hands me a large envelope. Without saying a word, the two impersonators smile and leave just as weirdly as they arrived.

Ooooookay.

Plopping down on my couch, I wipe my greasy pizza fingers on a paper towel and read Paige's bridal shower invitation.

What. The. Literal. Fuck. How was I kept out of the loop on this? Especially something so elaborate as a costume party. Not that I wanted to complete all of my man of honor duties. But I at least wanted to be *asked* to fulfill them.

I stab Paige's name on my phone, and it rings until it sends me into her voicemail. "Hi. It's Paige. Please don't leave me a voicemail because who checks voicemails, am I right? Theeeeenks." I hang up and read the last line of the invite.

HOSTED BY CHASTEN BENCHLEY

Welcome to the Twilight Zone. My best friend has flipped the script on me and sided with her fiancé's best man. She has publicly outed Chasten as her new gay best friend. I want to text Chasten, asking how they planned this without me. They really must've thought I would suggest our diner again. The fact that they even hired *Pretty Woman* impersonators is impressive, but I'm boiling, thinking about how much planning had to go into this. Without me.

Instead of wallowing in this, I'm going to go all out and find the perfect costume. I decide on Lloyd Dobler from *Say Anything . . .* , starring my hometown hero, John Cusack. I was a one-year-old when it came out, but I remember my parents having a DVD of it so when Paige and I were in junior high, we watched it obsessively. I really connected with Lloyd even then. He was an unassuming underdog with great taste in music. What's better, he carried the iconic boom box, which can be my prop I'll use as my distraction to leave Paige's party early. "Sorry, Paige. My arms are getting tired and I can't hold this boom box over my head any longer so I'm gonna head out and also thanks for excluding me on the planning of your bridal shower."

I spend the rest of the weekend foraging for the perfect Lloyd Dobler trench coat and boom box at every dusty vintage

shop in the East Village. There was even an early bird Halloween pop-up shop I popped into with no luck. The coat I finally
found is a little beiger than I'd hoped, but it'll have to do. Since
Paige completely iced me out of the shower planning with no
warning, I decide not to contact her again and just show up to
the party as if nothing has happened. I'll just shower her with
love while hoping we're hit by a meteor shower.

DUMBO House is the Brooklyn outpost of Soho House,
the private, members-only social club. I've only been to the one
in the Meatpacking District when Paige took me to the after-
party for the opening of her off-Broadway show *The Squid and
the Whale: The Musical*. Who could've ever predicted a show with
twelve plucky songs about divorce would close after three weeks,
but Paige wrote all the music and of course I supported her.

Entering a shopping mall–type building where DUMBO
House is housed, I give my name at the front desk and wait for
the elevator next to a woman dressed like Holly Golightly. She
introduces herself as Colleen, the receptionist where Paige
works, and I tell her how much respect I give her for dressing as
Audrey Hepburn in *Breakfast at Tiffany's*, a movie I hadn't
thought of as a rom-com until now.

The elevator plops us into an expansive space full of people
drinking and mingling in a casual clubby atmosphere. Immediately, Holly Golightly gets swallowed up by three friends exiting
the bathroom, all dressed like characters from *Clueless*.

I spot a tiny chalkboard sign perched on the bar that reads,
"You're just a person, standing in front of a sign, asking where
Paige's bridal shower is. (It's by the pool.)"

I wade through the club full of Brooklynites lounging like
rock stars on designer drugs but who are probably more like
aspiring podcasters on plant-based diets.

Entering the terrace overlooking the East River, I see the sun set beyond the silhouette of the Manhattan skyline, and we're flanked by majestic views of the Brooklyn Bridge and Manhattan Bridge. The swimming pool is dotted with dozens of tea-light candles. A DJ spins the Cure's "Friday I'm in Love." The bar is full of wine glasses printed with funny rom-com sayings like "You had me at merlot." It's an Instagram paradise. I shoot a quick panoramic video on my phone to commemorate the moment, bitter I didn't help plan any of it.

I hear gaggles of women talking loudly and laughing. Paige's voice dominates somewhere, but because of the costumes, I can't make out which one is her.

Spotted in the crowd is a woman wearing a white bridal gown and gym shoes like Julia Roberts in *Runaway Bride*. By the bar are two girls dressed as Drew Barrymore and Adam Sandler from *The Wedding Singer*.

Now I'm seeing some characters that I don't recognize exactly. Is she supposed to be Diane Keaton from *Baby Boom* or Sigourney Weaver from *Working Girl*? That one is, I don't know, either the titular character from *Muriel's Wedding* or someone from *My Big Fat Greek Wedding*. And there are several amorphous Meg Ryans who seem to be mashing up *When Harry Met Sally* / *Sleepless in Seattle* / *You've Got Mail*.

Wearing this unforgivingly thick vintage trench coat, I'm hit by the early evening humidity like a nonconsensual embrace. At the bar, I grab a plastic glass of rosé. Drink in one hand and my boom box in the other, I naturally gravitate toward Katie and Eliza and their pink explosion. Katie is dressed as Reese Witherspoon from *Legally Blonde*, while Eliza is Molly Ringwald from *Pretty in Pink*. We all poke and prod each other's costumes, complimentary and impressed. I hold up my boom box with one hand for the full Lloyd Dobler effect, and they die laughing.

"Did you help plan this?" Eliza asks with an eager smile, unknowingly twisting the knife further into the wound.

"I did not," I say, not wanting to elaborate. The question stings.

"Really. Has her old gay been replaced by her new gay?"

"I guess?" That question stings even more, and on so many levels.

The three of us stare at the partygoers, ranking the costumes. Third place goes to one of Austin's aunts, dressed like Marilyn Monroe from *Some Like It Hot*. Second place goes to some woman who is half–Nic Cage in a tux, half–Cher in a dress from *Moonstruck*, which I would never have gotten, had Katie not figured it out. First place goes to a woman sitting on the edge of the pool with I-have-three-nannies-but-I'm-exhausted-and-here-to-party energy. She's wearing a mermaid costume: Daryl Hannah from *Splash*.

The professional level of costumes everyone has brought tonight is such a pure delight that I'm almost forgetting I'm upset with Paige. But the longer I can't find her, the more resentment kicks in.

All of a sudden, the *Splash* girl jumps into the pool, flouncing her mermaid fin and spraying guests with water, clearly drunk and maybe even on something.

"I'll have what she's having," Eliza says dryly, referencing everyone's favorite rom-com movie quote.

"Good one," Katie says. We all laugh when *Splash* Girl gets out of the pool, now looking like a wet Rachel McAdams from *The Notebook*.

"My people!" Paige appears out of nowhere wearing a blond,

tousled wig, a leather jacket with a leopard-print bustier thing underneath, dark sunglasses and a studded leather dog collar. I barely recognize her; she looks like a smeared version of Courtney Love. I'm confused about which rom-com character she's supposed to be (Katherine Heigl from *Knocked Up*?) but I'm trying not to show it. Then Austin appears next to her wearing a black spiked wig, the same dark sunglasses, a matching studded dog collar and a leather jacket over a ripped white T-shirt with drops of fake blood on the front. I slowly put together that they're . . .

"Sid and Nancy!" Katie says.

"Was that a rom-com?" Eliza astutely asks.

"Technically not a romantic comedy," Paige says.

"More like a romantic tragedy," Austin says.

"We're the guests of honor, so fuck it. We make our own rules," Paige says.

"But in a creative way." Austin backs her up, and they give each other a quick smooch.

"Just no murdering each other at the end of the night," Katie says.

Then Austin breaks out a fake syringe and does his best Sid Vicious snarl with a cockney British accent, "Fook rom-coms! Eat a dick, you motherfoockers!" He's scarily in perfect character.

"Okay. We don't need to go that aggressive," Paige lightly pats him on his leather shoulder.

"Yeah, that was too much," Austin admits.

As the sun slowly melts away, I have an idea. I'm not going to *say anything* (!) until Paige acknowledges that she and Chasten left me in the dust and planned this party without my knowledge. Paige can call me Alanis motherfuckin' Morissette because I'm about to be the black fly in her chardonnay.

"Did you guys grab any of the mini Wagyu tacos?" Austin asks.

"He made them and they are divine," the proud pre-wife says.

"Who called them Wagyu tacos and not 'You Complete Beef,'" Eliza says as everyone stares at her blankly. "Get it? Like 'You Complete Me'?"

"Yeah, no, we got it," Paige says. "We just hate it."

"I didn't get it," Austin says. "Kidding. Even I got that one."

Okay, screw not saying anything. For my own sanity, I need to call Paige out on forging ahead without me, and it doesn't matter who hears it.

"How's the wedding planning going?" I ask.

"All good except for some centerpiece drama. Our flower person is not exactly cooperative and I think they may quit," Paige explains.

"Are you being indecisive on flowers?"

"Me? Naw."

"This is such a cool party," I say sarcastically even though I genuinely think this is truly an amazing goddamned bash. Paige gets that look in her eye. That look that speaks to decades of our friendship where she knows something is up and I'm holding back.

"Oh, for fook's sake. Are you mad at me, love?" She says it in a British Nancy Spungen accent—sounding more Dowager Countess of Grantham—to cut the edge off our building tension. But now I give her *my* look. My look that tells her she can't get off this easily. She recognizes it and wilts. Even our friends can detect what's happening between us.

"Shall we . . . ?" Eliza waves her half-empty plastic wine glass to Katie and Austin, to which they all nod in agreement.

"We're gonna . . ." She mimes drinking to me and Paige as the three of them head to the bar.

"Now wha', swee'ie," Paige says, still in Nancy character.

"Okay, no cockney accent," I say.

"Sorry. Now what, sweetie," Paige says in a midwestern accent, to which I plow through.

"I'm not mad, but I'm pretty mad."

She sighs. "Look. This whole thing just sorta happened."

"Really?" I motion to the dozens of candles, the themed bar, the little food passed around on trays, the elaborate costumes and the entire gorgeous setting. "This? This just magically happened?"

"You're my gay best friend, but face the facts, you're not the best at wedding planning. You even admit you don't have the gay wedding gene."

I down the rest of my wine, my head swirling with a thousand emotions. One for each tea light surrounding the pool.

"Why do you need to call me your gay best friend all the time?" I snap back.

"What?" Paige asks.

Something crystallizes inside me that's sporadically haunted me for years, like a lazy ghost, and it's surfacing in this moment. The party isn't the real problem. This goes deeper than that. "I just don't know why you have to say *gay* best friend."

"What do you mean? You are my gay best friend."

"Our friendship has lasted decades and you've boiled me down to my sexual orientation."

"So . . . you don't want to be associated with who you love?"

"That's literally not what I'm saying. At all."

"You've barely wanted to participate in any of my wedding festivities. I mean, do you even want to go to the actual wedding?"

I start sweating under this itchy, heavy trench coat. I place my boom box on a lounge chair and think about taking the coat off but I don't. "You're deflecting. I'm asking you to clarify why, since that time in high school I told you I liked Nate Gimbel, you insist on referring to me as your 'gay best friend.' Why can't it just be 'best friend.' Or better yet, just Max." I notice others are staring. "I don't want to be the gay best friend my whole life."

Bewilderment settles on Paige's face. "How long have you been thinking this?" she asks, defensive anger bubbling.

"Forever. But it's really come into focus with all this wedding stuff."

"*Wedding stuff*"?! Seriously? You did not just say that."

The Max and Paige Spat is escalating in a way I wasn't expecting. I catch Eliza, Katie and Austin cringe-watching from the bar. "You've wanted this wedding to be over the second I told you about it. I've given you outs at every turn, and that's why we decided not to bother you with the shower. I knew you've had a lot going on with work. I thought I was being helpful. I want you to find happiness the way I have." Her tone changes to something softer. "I think you should really get to know Chasten."

"Wait. Why? How is this about Chasten?"

"I never wanted to force anything. But you two—you're perfect for each other and you don't realize it. I just want you to figure out your life."

I'm floored. "I don't need the hetero hero to figure out the tragic gay guy's life."

"Oh god, that's not what I'm saying at all. And please don't hetero-shame me."

"That's what it feels like. Our whole life you've been playing matchmaker. You introduced me to Greg and look how that worked out. We finally broke up for good."

"You did? Then this is the perfect time for you to date Chasten."

"I don't want to date Chasten! Stop trying to take credit for every guy I date. We already had a horrible hookup before you even introduced us anyway."

"What? When?" She's angry and hurt. "Why didn't you tell me?"

"I don't . . . We didn't . . ." I'm caught.

That's when Paige pushes me into the pool.

I can't say the water's not refreshing in this August heat, as I submerge in the shallow end, wondering how I ended up here and not wanting to face the embarrassment from the crowd when I get out. After coming up with a dramatic inhale of oxygen, I see a large, meaty hand, with just the right amount of dark forearm hair, extended, helping me out of the pool. Frazzled and soaking wet, I stand and look up to see someone dressed exactly like me, Lloyd Dobler. Only the dry version. It's Chasten. By the look on his face, I can tell he's just heard that whole thing.

"Nice costume," he says. "And don't worry. I don't want to date you either." He disappears into the crowd.

Mortified, I cross the terrace, past the onlookers, and back inside toward the elevator. A woman dressed like Awkwafina from *Crazy Rich Asians* exits the bathroom and sees me. "*The Matrix* wasn't a rom-com, dude." I look at my beige trench coat, now darkened and damp and realize she thinks I'm Keanu Reeves.

"And you're appropriating someone else's culture, but thanks for rom-com-splaining me." The elevator dings, the doors open and I storm inside.

My Man of Honor Speech to Paige

chapter

TWENTY-NINE

T'S 2:00 A.M. AND I'M RAGE GARDENING. AFTER I CAME HOME and obviously couldn't fall asleep after tonight's fiasco, I had the idea to transfer my overflowing apartment garden to the unused rooftop space on my building. In a complete frenzy, I'm repotting plants, adding soil and making a mess. A full moon lights my way, and I'm taking out all of my anger on my only real friends, these poor plants. I'm a reverse Mommie Dearest: instead of chopping down a rosebush, I'm furiously planting a juniper tree. All I need is some cold cream and a white headband.

It doesn't feel good that I let down Paige at her own bridal shower, but it also didn't feel good getting shoved into a swimming pool. I'm mortified Chasten overheard what I said, and feel awful if I hurt him.

But I'm not giving a speech at Paige's wedding. I'm done being her best gay. And I'm done with weddings.

Sunday early afternoon rolls around and I finally get out of bed to face the world. It's cloudy, drizzly and humid, but I fight

the elements and spend the afternoon hitting up Home Depot
and the Container Store to find as many boxes, pots, planters
and gardening tools as I can gather to throw all of my energy
into my new rooftop garden.

When I arrive at the office on Monday morning, my stomach flips when I see Janet with Carla, the president of the agency
and a meaner, leaner-looking version of Janet, hovering outside
of my office, speaking in self-important hushed tones even
though the entire floor is literally a ghost town and there's no
one around to hear them. They turn and smile at me with their
mouths but have pity in their eyes as they "invite me" to the HR
conference room. I joke and say I forgot to RSVP, but neither of
them finds that funny. Or maybe they didn't even hear me.

Sitting at the oval table that's the size of a submarine, overlooking the Hudson, Janet and Carla sit far away from me and
look at me as though I've done something extremely wrong. This
is worse than getting called into the principal's office in school.
It's like getting called into the office by *two* principals in identical charcoal-colored pantsuits. I immediately feel guilty.

Janet defers to Carla to kick off the meeting. I'm not sure
which one is the good cop yet. "Max," Carla says, letting out a
pained sigh. Now it's becoming clear. The guy who fires people
is about to get fired. "On behalf of Benser and Powell, I would
like to extend my deepest apologies." My breathing resumes to
slightly normal, and my hands unclench the chair's armrests as
Carla goes on to tell me that what happened on Difference Day
was not my fault and they're not holding me accountable for
anything. In fact, Janet finally chimes in once she gets a terse
nod from Carla to sum up the meeting, they are giving me two
weeks' paid time off. Clearly, this is an attempt for me not to sue
the company—not like I would—but I'll take it. The meeting

ends with Janet saying something about "taking one for the team," and "sitting on the bench," and "a time-out," but I've tuned her out.

With less than two weeks before Paige's wedding and now all this time off from work, I throw myself further into my roof-top garden. So far no one from the building has any idea what I'm doing, and I'm hoping if our slumlord sees how beautiful it's becoming, he won't start chucking all of my hard work into a dumpster. Like the R.E.M. song "Gardening at Night," for some reason my plant muse only strikes me when the sun goes down, which causes me to sleep most of the day.

The following Monday, I sleep until about noon, when my doorbell wakes me up. (I've gotten so used to the jackhammer outside, I don't even hear it anymore.) I open the door and find . . . my parents? I friggin' forgot they were coming.

"Mom. *And* Dad," I say, as if I'm trying to convince my groggy-eyed self that they're actually standing in front of me, at my door, in the flesh. They have on the cheeriest of smiles and the matchiest of outfits. Both wearing similar turquoise polo shirts tucked into khaki pants, they often claim they don't wear identical clothes, but that's what happens when you've been married for forty-two years. When they see my confused smile, their faces fall.

"He forgot we were coming," my mom says to my dad. Moms always know.

"I told you to remind him," my dad says.

"I did remind him. I called him but he never returned my messages."

That's another thing they do. They talk to themselves as if no one else is in the room, happy in their own little bubble.

"I never listen to voicemails," I say.

"I told you," my mom says to my dad. We hug and I let them and their oversized, matching rolling suitcases in, when it hits me they're staying here for a week. The first time they visited me in New York, I booked them a room at the Standard Hotel along the High Line. They weren't used to the wilds of urban living. We'd done our time with weekend trips to Chicago when I was a kid, but New York was a different animal. Even though they had spectacular floor-to-ceiling views of the Hudson River, they couldn't get past how small the room was, how the hallways and elevator were too dark and how a cheeseburger cost thirty dollars. The first night, my dad slipped and fell and hit his head on their bathtub, causing him to bleed all over the white sheets, and my mom couldn't sleep because of "sex noises" in the room next door. So they've stayed with me ever since.

I'll sleep on the pullout sofa and give them my bed, which is bigger. But we won't have to debate which overpriced restaurant we can't get reservations to because, like me, my parents love a good diner.

While we eat tonight's Waverly Diner specials and my parents indulge in Welcome to New York cocktails—a white wine for my mom and old-fashioneds for my dad and me—they ask all about the wedding. I don't have the heart yet to tell them Paige pushed me into a pool and basically disinvited me to the wedding, but they sense something is up.

After dinner, walking to "Big Gay Ice Cream's," as my mom calls it, she finally slips into hard-boiled detective mode and investigates. As a former journalist for our local hometown newspaper, she knows when something stinks. She asks me a version of "So where were you the night of Paige's bridal shower?" and when I hesitate to answer, my dad chimes in.

"I knew he wasn't telling us something," he says to my mom.

"Oh, I knew the second I laid eyes on him," my mom says to my dad.

"Okay, come on. You guys have to include me in your conversation if it's about me and I'm standing right here."

We sidestep the Mount Everest of garbage piles on our way into Big Gay Ice Cream's. My mom gives my dad a look not to say anything about the garbage, so I chime in. "New York may be dirty, but at least it smells like urine," I say as they laugh and we walk inside the insanely loud joint. In a true *Freaky Friday* body swap, my parents think it's adorable how loud and aggressive everything in this city is while I just shake my curmudgeonly head.

The next couple of days I play tour guide to my parents, which inevitably turns me into a tourist. We walk through Central Park and eat hot dogs and hot pretzels while sitting on the ledge of the Bethesda Fountain. We brunch at Sarabeth's on Fifty-Ninth Street and browse Bergdorf's. We walk through Lincoln Center and catch a free outdoor ballet festival featuring underprivileged kids. We walk the entire length of the High Line while I tell them about my shitty job. We gawk at the Oculus. We tour Little Island and see a Wanda Sykes stand-up show at their free performing arts amphitheater, annoyingly dubbed the Amph. We eat "dim sums" at a place in Chinatown my mom found in the *New York Times*. We visit the too-crowded Chelsea Market, where I tell them about Greg over gourmet grilled cheeses and crepes. We ride Citi Bikes to Battery Park and eat outside at Pier A, where we have Bloody Mary shooters, oysters and fish and chips while staring at the Statue of Liberty. We eat dinner at Morandi, and my dad gives his leftover cacio e pepe to a homeless woman. We contemplate doing a boat ride, going to Coney Island or the Brooklyn Botanical Garden but decide there's not enough time. We see the new Boy George jukebox musical on Broadway that Paige got us house seats to. We eat Billy's Bakery chocolate cupcakes in our pajamas at my place as I tell them about Chasten. They sleep soundly and snore in my bed while I toss and turn on the pullout.

I'm exhausted.

It's three days before Paige's wedding, and we're sitting on the rooftop of my building, drinking rosé, eating cheese and admiring my new garden. My parents are impressed and as a gift had a park bench and a couple of small outdoor chairs delivered while Dad rigged a few strings of outdoor lights. They're beside themselves after I tell them what happened with Paige at the shower.

My mom is tipsy and she's getting angry with me. "I don't understand why you think Paige has you around as some kind of . . ."

"Pet," my dad says, finishing her sentence.

"I was gonna say 'accessory,'" she says to my dad.

"That's fitting too," he says to her.

"Thank you. I thought so myself," she says back.

"Okay, you guys don't understand," I interject.

"What the hell are you thinking? There's nothing to understand. You and Paige have been best friends since you were five years old. She used to stay at our house for *hours* before her mother called and told her to come home. You two were inseparable. You still are."

"Remember how she would always eat my secret stash of peanut M&M's," my dad says.

"The ones you kept hidden all over the house," my mom says.

"Yeah, I kept hiding them and she always found them."

"I don't know where you're getting this idea that you're

her . . . gay person she wants to keep around for her amusement. Just let that go."

"That sounds more like you're projecting how you see yourself onto her." My dad, the psychoanalyst, has a point. "Maybe you're just afraid to have the spotlight."

"You're not getting any younger. It's time you see yourself as the leading man in your own life for once," my mom says. "Live your best life."

This hits me. My parents know how to keep me tethered.

"And we're so glad you finally dumped Greg once and for all. That felt like years in the making," my mom adds.

"He was an idiot. Never liked him," my dad says.

"Tell us more about this Chasten," my mom says.

"He sounds fabulous," my dad says.

We eat, drink and laugh under the twinkling lights with the Empire State Building in the distance. Okay, you can't see the Empire State Building from my rooftop, but it sounded nice. The more I tell my parents about Chasten and see them react so positively to the idea of him, the more I realize something: I miss him.

chapter

THIRTY

THE REHEARSAL DINNER IS IN TWO DAYS, SET FOR 6:00 P.M. at Austin's restaurant. My stress levels are high. I haven't heard from Paige or Chasten since I was soaking wet, and I haven't reached out to them. Our group text has been silent. Now I suppose it's my responsibility to be the bigger person and message Paige since she's the one getting married and she shouldn't be upset on her big day.

But I can't just text Paige a joke, hope she'll reply and all is forgiven. For a minute, I consider maybe a Very Special Splunch, but with two days to spare, Paige won't have time for me and my apology tour. Her two sets of parents are also in town, so I'm sure she's prioritizing them.

My plan is to suggest something bigger than a Splunch. Something that not only redeems me in her eyes, but also can contribute to her wedding. The surprise that she'd asked me to deliver. A big idea came to me as I was sitting on the rooftop with my parents. But first, I have to meet with Chasten and say

my piece. As my fellow best man, he legally has to meet with me
before the wedding despite any differences we may have. That's
just wedding law. And if I'm honest with myself, there are some
bigger thoughts I'd like to express to him about the two of us
and what our future might hold.

I send Chasten a couple of music videos reflecting what I
want to say, but it's not until I half-jokingly send Madonna's
"Sorry" that he responds. After many long, drawn-out pauses
and one-word responses on his end, he finally relents and agrees
to meet me at Fonda, a cute little Mexican restaurant halfway
between us in Chelsea. I figure we could revisit chicken mole,
the chocolate dish we bonded over, and I'll win him back.

Wednesday night comes, and I'm waiting for Chasten at a
tiny two-top table in the window at Fonda, watching various
characters who populate Chelsea walk by: a Thor-looking muscle head carrying a tiny Chihuahua; a sixtysomething silver fox
handsome gay couple dressed to the nines, in a hurry; an old-
timer who's lived here since the dawn of time, slowly pulling his
small metal wire shopping cart full of Gristedes bags. Each person is like a slot machine image of my future spinning by.
Which one will I be lucky or unlucky enough to land on? And
then . . . Chasten approaches.

Jackpot?

Soon after polite hellos, a half basket of tortilla chips, and a
spicy margarita each, we're still avoiding any meaningful conversation by studying our menus. Or maybe I'm avoiding it and
he's just following my lead. The awkwardness is palpable. I've
never seen him this conflicted before. He's not his usual life of
the party. And I'm trying hard not to be my usual death of the
party. It hurts me knowing that I've hurt him to the point where
he seems unsure if he even wants to be friends with me. I finally

break the tequila ice by talking about a safe topic of conversation: Paige.

"Is Paige still mad at me?" I ask him.

"She's pretty upset," he tells me. "The whole argument kind of put a damper on the shower."

"Literally. I didn't think bridal shower meant an actual shower," I say. Chasten doesn't find this funny. Until he thinks about it for a second, then he finally cracks a smile.

"Damp John Cusack isn't your best look. I wish I had a photo of your face as you fell into the pool." He imitates what I looked like, and while it's both insulting and funny, I can't help but think how cute he is even when making a horrible face.

"Pretty crazy we both showed up as *Say Anything . . .*"

"Yeah, well . . ." His sorta-smile fades to a frown. He stares at his cucumber-ginger margarita with salt, deep in thought. Then takes a big swig. Our friendly server arrives, asking for our dinner orders. I tell her we probably need a few more minutes but I'll have another margarita. Chasten declines a second one. This is not a good sign. She sizes up the tension between us with a knowing smirk and goes.

"I don't think I meant what I said."

"Which part?" He looks up at me, one arched eyebrow, skeptical.

"The part where I said I didn't want to date you. I didn't mean that. Like, at all."

"Obvious next question: So, why'd you say that?"

I stare at him with clarity. "When Paige and I were in high school, I think I kinda broke her heart when I came out. And my whole adult life with Paige I've felt second banana–ish."

"Were you dating?"

"No. But we probably could've gotten married if the whole

gay thing wasn't baked inside me. She saw the rest of her life with me. Even at that young age. And so, I felt bad. In college, having a gay best friend gave her some cred with the theater crowd. In return she tried setting me up with guy after guy. So, when she suggested you and I—"

"So, you feel like you're Paige's accessory. I get that."

"Exactly. I don't wanna feel like a Barbie doll she can mix and match with her other Barbie dolls, ya know? Paige suggesting the two of us dating is the thing that finally broke me. If it happens, I want it on my own terms."

"Right." Chasten averts his eyes. Swirls the rest of his drink.

"I know she's always been slightly disappointed that I didn't fit her perfect idea of a gay best friend. Especially when she met you. You're her ideal gay best friend. She finally realized I'm not good at dresses or wedding rings or braiding hair."

"I don't think any bride-to-be would braid her hair on her wedding day."

"I rest my case."

"Why did you let her turn you into her sidekick all these years?"

I think about this.

"Maybe I felt bad for saying I wouldn't ever have a romantic interest in her. So, I let her."

"But you guys are actual best friends."

"True. But sometimes it feels uneven. So that's why I *said* I didn't want to date you. I didn't want Paige connecting her two best gay friends. I wanted to make that happen myself. I just don't want to be pigeonholed into her supporting character anymore."

Our server brings my fresh drink. I hold my glass out to clink with Chasten's near-empty one but he's not looking at me anymore. It feels like I've somehow lost him.

"Max, it's good you know how you feel about Paige. And I

think you should tell her everything you just told me. But I don't know what any of that really has to do with us."

I blink. Panicked. Have I said too much or too little? Before I can decide, he continues.

"I didn't meet you tonight just to talk about Paige," he says. "I thought we were here to talk about the two of us, not the three of us." He scoots his chair out a little. "I think I should probably just go, so . . ." He scoots his chair out even more and stands. "I'll see you at the wedding."

I open my mouth to protest but Chasten is already out the door, walking away like a cold stranger. The packed restaurant continues buzzing with people talking and laughing all around me, as if nothing just happened. As if what I thought could be my potential future didn't just disappear. I screwed this up.

Our server is the only one who notices anything. In fact, I'm realizing she saw the entire thing from start to finish as she walks by and stops in front of me and says, "What are you waiting for? Go run after him like they do in that movie." She's right. I realize at this very moment, I'm no longer the sidekick. This isn't about Paige anymore. This is about us. I'm the main character of my own story now and I need to tell Chasten how I really feel about him. I express my gratitude to the intuitive server, down my drink and pull out my wallet.

"I got this. You get him," she says like some kind of fairy godmother.

I head for the door, then turn around to ask her, "Wait— which movie?"

She looks at me like I'm an idiot. "All of them."

I smile and sprint outside, looking in every direction, assuming Chasten has hightailed it to Hell's Kitchen. I don't know whether I should hop in the subway, grab an Uber, hail a taxi or jump on the hood of a random moving car. Running down the street to snag the man of my dreams doesn't seem like an option right now until I sense something behind me. I turn to see my fairy godmother server pounding on the inside window of the restaurant with wide eyes. She's recruited two other servers and they're all wildly pointing at something. Quickly turning back, I spot Chasten at Billy's Bakery directly across the street, being handed a single cupcake and walking out the door. I turn back, put my hand on my heart and mouth "Thank you" to my match-makers. They all roll their eyes and shoo me away toward Chasten.

I hop into the middle of traffic, almost colliding with a noisy city bus, and run after the fast-moving Chasten down the side-walk. When I'm finally near him, he turns around, startled to see me right behind him. I'm out of breath and already breaking a sweat like a madman. I'm not wasting any more time so I launch right into it.

"You were right. I didn't ask you out tonight to talk all about Paige. This night was supposed to be about us. So I'm here to tell you a few things." I exhale and speak from my heart. "Your knowledge of fashion and food and social etiquette annoys the crap out of me. Whenever we're talking, your intense eye con-tact scares me. You have the most unrelatable hair. And you're competitive to a fault."

"Um. Okaaay," he says, not knowing where I'm going with this, clearly wanting to eat his cupcake and dart in the oppo-site direction.

"And by that I mean, I've never met anyone like you. You're magnetic. You make me nervous and excited and full of some kind of weird hopeful feeling that I've never experienced before. De-spite all of our differences, I feel connected to you on so many

levels. I get all fluttery every time I see you and realize when I'm
with you, I never want to be anywhere else."

Chasten's smile returns. The one that I hadn't seen all night.
The smile that I've missed. His eyes are on me, doing that thing
again where I feel like the only person in the universe. He
sees me.

"Your clothes are terrible. You're a total control freak but
don't realize it. And you're a basic midwesterner to the friggin'
core, Marge," he says.

"Again, I'm not from Fargo," I remind him. He laughs.

"But you make me laugh. You challenge me in a way no one
else does. You're smart, loyal and one of the realest people I've
ever met. You're sensitive and you have depth. And the first time
I laid eyes on you in that diner, under the daily specials, I knew
I wanted to know everything about you."

We hear someone across the street interrupt to yell, "Oh, just
take him home already!" We turn to see our server with her
three coworkers now outside, metaphorically eating popcorn,
waiting to see how this ends. We all laugh. Who am I to ruin a
good show? I lean in and kiss Chasten, right there in the middle
of Ninth Avenue as our audience cheers us on.

"Are you gonna eat your cupcake?" I ask. He holds up his
chocolate cupcake between us and we both take a bite.

How we get to his apartment feels like a total blur as we exit
the elevator and walk past the doorway to the rooftop where our
first, um, dalliance happened. Chasten unlocks his door onto a
clean, modern little foyer with a sizable round table in the center.

"Nice orchids," I say, admiring the deep pink beauty centerpiece.

"I got those for you," he says, not sure what I'm going to
think.

"Are you serious?"

"When you messaged me, I secretly hoped our night would lead to this," he tells me. That fluttery feeling has taken the wheel from me as I swivel my head from the orchids to Chasten, back to the orchids, back to Chasten. I'm moved that this guy went out of his way to buy me something that I love. My god. He did this? My smile is uncontrollable.

"Maybe we both really wanted this all along," I confess.

"And we just let everything else get in the way," he says.

This is the clarity we both needed.

Before I can take him in my arms, I feel Chasten's strong hand squeeze my shoulder, then another stronger hand on my other shoulder. He steps closer, lightly massaging me. I stand there, eyes closed, soaking it up. It feels like fireworks.

We stare into each other's eyes for what seems like an hour, our hands on each other's shoulders, chest, stomach. Lightly hairy forearms rubbing against very hairy forearms (mine) until our hands finally connect, gripping as tight as we can, squeezing and testing each other's strength. I feel the subtle callouses under his fingers, probably from lifting weights. We release our grips into a softer, gentler touch. We measure both of our right hands in the air, like synchronized swimmers, lacing fingers, a perfect fit.

Our faces are closer than they've ever been now. Closer than that first night we met. His breath on mine is sweet and welcoming.

Our mouths crawl toward each other, our lips teasing one another's until we are fully locked. Together. Our tongues meet each other for the first time, and I think how badly I've wanted this since the night we met. We kiss each other uncontrollably, like a faucet that's been turned on full blast. Two animals in the wild.

After several minutes of kissing like it was our last minute on earth, we slow it down, patiently savoring every second. Chasten pulls away, and just when I think he's going to stop this moving train, he grabs my hand and leads me through his apartment.

He switches on overhead lights, warmly dimming them to perfection, and I finally see his living room. It's stunningly beautiful, all shades of white, and highly decorated in the most comfortable way. His plush sofas invite me to sit on them, with hardcover novels and books about chocolate in his built-in shelves. Seeing all of his classics neatly lining the walls, I'm reminded that Greg never picked up a book. *Fuck Greg.*

We move past his modern kitchen equipped with everything you could possibly want, passion and love emanating from the apartment's core. Chasten's hand grips mine tighter as we enter his large bedroom, and his other hand turns music on with his phone. A rhythmic percussion surrounds us like we're by the pool at magic hour in Ibiza. The windows are open, and his curtains lightly blow in an unexpected deep-summer breeze.

Standing in front of the bed, we release our hands and stare at each other, daring ourselves to look away. But we can't. We see each other. Our mouths fall into place again, this time with more surprising twists and turns.

I lift the bottom of his shirt above his stomach, signaling for him to take it off, as we glide it past his head together. Without missing a beat, we take mine off together. Our skin-to-skin contact feels unreal as we kiss in an embrace, shirtless. He rubs his hand through my chest hair and I do the same to him. He lightly pounds on my pec, testing its strength, making me slightly insecure I haven't been to the gym, but neither of us cares. I pound his chest with both hands. Damn. His pecs win.

I feel the thick veins coursing through each of his baseball-sized biceps.

We fall into each other, into the center of the perfectly comfortable bed that engulfs us like a cloud, like a love cocoon. We roll around, me on top of him, him on top of me, and we kiss and kiss and kiss and kiss, and he tastes like tequila and chocolate and home. I brush my fingers through his thick dark hair, massaging his scalp, letting my fingers lightly float through the top spikes of his mane, feeling closer to him than ever. I feel his hands all over me, pressing, gliding, caressing, holding me like he would never let me go. It supercharges me all over.

With one quick move, he spins me under him, climbing on top of me. I push his hefty weight up to get a better look at his meaty pecs, feeling his flat stomach (not too many abs!), rounding out his broad, muscly shoulders.

"Your body is a wonderland," I jokingly say in a cheesy whisper that makes us both laugh, even though I'm dead serious.

"I enjoy your body a lot," he says and starts unbuttoning my jeans. "Is this okay?" Like he has to ask. I nod and help him before tearing off his pants. He falls back on top of me, both of us in boxer briefs, grinding against each other to the beat of the music, which seems to crescendo at the exact right moment. Before I explode and embarrass myself again, I pull his underwear off with my foot and he yanks mine off.

Now that we're both completely naked, I've never felt a more perfect fit.

Hearts racing, we go to town on each other.

Through a moan, he says my name like it's the most important word in the world. My toes curl and eyes fill with tears as I groan, ecstatic at how incredible this feels physically, but finally connected emotionally, fully.

We're left breathless, still embracing.

"That was so much better than the first time," he says into my neck. I just nod, sweat beading on my forehead. Grinning ear to ear.

After Olympic-level cuddling, building a fort out of each other's limbs, we lie side by side, reeling on the blur of a night.

"What are we gonna tell Paige?" he asks at the exact same time I think that.

"I thought this wasn't about Paige. But we can tell her the truth," I say.

"She'll be happy she brought together her two best gays."

"Are we together?" I ask, hopeful.

"I don't know. Are we?"

"Well, I am single now," I say. We smile together.

Chasten says, "By the way, I've been following you on Instagram."

I sit up slightly. I had no idea. "This whole time?"

"This whole time. Can't believe I finally got to have sex with the Real Robert Plant."

I'm shocked and flattered. He never gave up on me.

"I told my entire extended family and their friends to follow you."

"I wondered how I've been racking up so many followers."

"You're welcome," he says.

"So you wanna hear my big idea on how I'm going to help Paige with her wedding?"

"If you want to get on Paige's good side, I can help you."

"Okay, but we have to start first thing in the morning."

Before I can explain, I give him a manly smooch on his manly lips. We hop in the shower and do it all over again.

Austin and Paige's

REHEARSAL DINNER MENU

———

THE NIGHT AUSTIN PROPOSED TO PAIGE IN THE HAMPTONS
*Scallops, seaweed salad on
a bed of ocean pebbles*

PAIGE'S CHILDHOOD BACKYARD
*Wagyu beef served on a pillow
of fresh-cut grass*

10-YEAR-OLD AUSTIN'S INVENTION
Lobster roll ice cream

CHASTEN'S CHOCOLATES
Dark, heart-shaped

chapter

THIRTY-ONE

WHEN I SAID "FIRST THING IN THE MORNING," I MEANT pre-morning. We're up before the sun rises, and I'm totally spent but fully inspired by this new energy. His bedsheets are more expensive than I thought, now that I can see them in the daylight, and they're tangled at our feet as we snuggle awake.

After a third (fourth?) heated session, Chasten makes a power breakfast of oatmeal, fresh berries and scrambled eggs with orange juice, which he squeezes himself, as I reveal my plan to help with Paige's wedding and surprise her at the same time.

"Centerpieces," I say. He blinks, trying to decipher what I mean. "You know, for the tables." I can see the realization wash over him.

"Like flowers in vases or those floating-candles-in-water thingies?" he asks.

"Duh. *Plants*," I say, like he should've known. "Paige mentioned there were some problems happening with her florist." He thinks it through.

"Can you pull it off?"

"You've seen my Instagram," I say, looking at him dead serious.

My newfound confidence surprises me.

"That's actually brilliant," he says.

I don't even have time to admire Chasten's sun-filled apartment and how the shapes of the early morning light filter his already flawless features, because before I know it, we're off to the Flower District.

Paige's rehearsal dinner is tomorrow night at Austin's restaurant, so we only have two days to create the perfect centerpieces for the actual wedding. My mind races with ideas, and I sketch something out on a tiny pad of paper while we play footsie on the subway.

Emerging from underground into the sun-filled baby-blue skies on this Friday, I text my parents that I'll see them this afternoon, as my disguise, Chasten, texts Paige, asking her to put all of her trust in him to make magic happen with her centerpieces. Turns out, her wedding planner had had a miscommunication with her florist about what Paige was looking for and instead of settling, Paige asked if they could redo them all. So the florist rudely pulled out of the job. Paige's indecision bites her in the ass. She doesn't realize she's more of a plant person than flower girl anyway, which makes our surprise even more perfect.

I don't want to bother Paige with texts or calls, so I'll just have to show up to the rehearsal dinner and hope she can carve out a minute for us to reconcile privately.

Hopping from plant shop to plant shop with Chasten, I somehow instinctively know exactly the kind of centerpiece I'm going to create. It feels like we're on an episode of a plant reality competition show and I have one hour to make a dream wedding come true. Chasten watches my every move and smiles whenever I make a decision. My summer of sad plant collecting has possibly become my true calling.

After listing final instructions and items to one particularly helpful shopkeeper, I say, "Since it's a Labor Day weekend wedding, I think the theme should nod to saying goodbye to summer while leading us into fall." *Where did that come from?* The shopkeeper writes down everything I say like I'm some sort of pro.

I lead Chasten out of the store and he says, "Funny how the guy who claims he doesn't know a thing about wedding planning has become the wedding planner."

"I prefer wedding planter."

Walking the streets with Chasten, I involuntarily grab his hand and I feel that shock wave all over again. I want to show him off to everyone, especially my parents. But I know I have to slow it down and not try to rush into this.

We find ourselves completely making out in broad daylight, trying to tear away from each other for the day as I go downtown and he goes uptown. We're glue.

"I'll see you tonight?" he says. I nod. "These are gonna be amazing."

On the outside, I play it cool, throwing him a smile and tossing a casual wave. Inside, a million colorful flowers bloom, and I float down into the subway.

AROUND NOON I MEET MY PARENTS FOR A LIGHT LUNCH OF BAcon cheeseburgers, fries and three individual chocolate soufflés at Little Owl. We don't want to ruin our appetites for tonight.

It would be embarrassing having your parents meet you at the end of your walk of shame from a one-night stand, but this feels neither shameful nor like a one-night stand. As much as they think Chasten sounds like a catch, they're worried I'm putting too much of myself into him so soon after Greg.

"You don't understand. My relationship with Greg has been dead for years. I just never wanted to face the rotting corpse under my floorboards." They both go quiet, looking up from their burgers with concern.

"What do you mean? There's something rotting under your floorboards?" my mom asks naively.

"He's talking about him and Greg. It was a metaphor. I think," my dad says.

"Honey, no rotting flesh talk while we eat please."

I roll my eyes so hard it hurts. "The point is, I just hadn't realized how emotionally far away from Greg I really was until now. And I know, I'm not going to rush into anything with Chasten. I'm just ready for whatever happens next." I think of Chasten and smile big, still on my high from last night.

"Congrats on getting laid, Max," my dad says too loud, slapping me on the back as we all laugh.

"When are you gonna talk to Paige about all of this?" my mom says as she pours more salt on the warm fries and stuffs a handful in her mouth.

THE NEXT NIGHT, APPROACHING AUSTIN'S RESTAURANT ON Ludlow Street on the Lower East Side, my mom can't get over why there isn't a sign outside. She doesn't believe this is actually the restaurant.

"Mom? It's not a Denny's," I say, which doesn't amuse or satisfy her.

"Advertising only helps. I don't understand why you wouldn't want to have your name out front is all I'm saying."

"You can take the gal out of the Illinois . . ." my dad says.

An extremely tall, odd bird of a man with a long gray ponytail who looks like he moonlights as a vampire opens the door for us with a creepy grin, and we walk inside where we find . . . a completely empty restaurant. It's tiny, all muted grays, but elegant. The horseshoe-shaped sleek counter has twelve soft leather high seats and no settings. There's no music. Not a flower in sight. The only signs of life are six chefs in the gleaming open kitchen, bending over plates, using tiny scissors to cut fresh herbs and carefully placing them on top of tiny bites of food with tweezers.

"Right this way," our vampire host says with a flourish of his hand that guides us through another door into a wide service elevator. We step inside and, with his back to us, he pulls a heavy caged door shut. We jerk left and right until the elevator starts rising. My parents look at me suspiciously.

"Well, this is different," my mom squeaks out.

The antiquated elevator spits us out, and we walk through another door onto the rooftop of the building. This is not like any other rooftop I've ever seen before. Not to belittle my own recent handiwork, but there's an actual professional garden with a staggering number of vegetables including zucchini, radishes, tomatoes and every herb imaginable. It's a culinary mindblower.

Beyond the greenery is one long farm table decked out with dozens of purple hydrangeas and votive candles. Above the dinner setting are hanging mason jars strung around everywhere and filled with tiny LED lights made to look like fireflies. It feels like we're in the middle of the South of France on a cool summer night.

Paige holds court with her older sister Zoe and her stunning California family, her mom Nadine and Nadine's husband Ron, showing off her ring, looking casually elegant in all beige. Even at this distance, I can see Paige's mom immediately hijack the conversation to make it about herself because Paige has that familiar squished, pained look on her face. They all turn to see us walk in and I swallow hard. As we approach, Paige's mom lets out an excited shriek.

"The Moodys!" Nadine and my parents drifted apart after Nadine divorced her first husband, Paige's dad, but there's history there. After hugs, my parents fawn over Paige.

"Honey, you look amazing. I love your outfit," my mom says.

"Doesn't she look clean?" Nadine says weirdly, with a smile. She has a way of thinking she's being nice, but it usually comes out sideways. "And you all look so fantastic. How's sleeping on the cot at Max's place?"

"Oh, it's not a cot. Max gave us his bed and he takes the sofa bed," my mom explains in her cheery way.

"Ehhh, that still sounds like a cot situation to me," Nadine says to confused looks. "Ron and I are at the Carlyle and I feel like *I'm* the one getting married." Normally here is where Paige and I would exchange knowing looks, but Paige isn't giving in to me so easily. "Free breakfast every morning *and* it's continental," Nadine says like that's a thing we're supposed to be impressed with. "He treats me like I'm Princess Eloise," she says, then leans into Ron and nuzzles his neck inappropriately.

"Eloise wasn't a princess and she stayed at the Plaza," Paige corrects her, and then, finally, she's had enough. She turns to me. "Do you wanna—"

"I'd love to," I say before she can finish.

Paige and I stand alone in the kale section of the garden. You can actually see the purple-lit Empire State Building in the distance. I start. "I've been so excited for you. And I hope I didn't let you down by not stepping up the way you wanted me to."

"I just hope you'll forgive me for pushing you in the pool."

"You're a bridezilla. It's cool," I say. Paige laughs.

With so many years between us, we don't need to dwell on formal apologies. But there is one thing I have to get off my chest. "I'm sorry—I guess . . . I'm just sorry I didn't want to go to the Winter Formal with you."

"Winter Formal? That was so long ago," she says with a laugh, but I can see residual resentment still there. It's always been there.

"It just feels like there's lingering trauma for both us from that day I told you I wanted to go to the Winter Formal with Nate Gimbel. And as much as I try to be the gay you want me to be, I just may never meet your gay-xpectations."

"I realized forever ago you were never going to tell me how fierce I look or throw shade while we have a kiki or wear silly wigs with me or gossip about Bravolebrities or call each other 'gurl' while spilling tea, screaming show tunes at a drag queen lip sync—"

"Okay, okay . . ." I interrupt.

"I know planning this wedding wasn't exactly your forte. None of that is who you are, and that's why I love you." We exhale and smile. "Plus, that's why I have Chasten now." We both laugh. "You and me are lifers. Best friends forevs."

"We'll never get rid of each other no matter how hard we try," I say. And for the first time since, well, forever, I lean in and give Paige a very big, warm hug.

"Whoa. Touchaphobic is hugging it out," she says into my armpit. "You sure you're okay?"

"Maybe thank Chasten for reigniting my sparkle."

"What. He reignited your sparkle? Are you stealing him from me already? I need to hear about this later." Renewed, we hop over the garden together and head back to the party, where my parents are now talking to Paige's dad, Bruce.

The dinner is playfully personalized by the culinary genius Austin. At first, I'm skeptical of the overly nostalgic menu items, wondering if it's style over substance, but it works. Some of it sounds like a foreign language to me (a bed of ocean pebbles?) but it magically comes together for one of the most delicious and memorable meals I've ever had, ending with—my favorite—bites of Chasten's Chocolates.

It's fun to watch Paige and Austin loving on each other, and Nadine and Ron chug the expensive wine pairing you're supposed to sip, and it's especially heartwarming to see my parents buddy up to Chasten, laughing and swapping stories.

I snap a photo of the perfect tableau and send it to the group text between me, Chasten and Paige with a string of different-colored heart emojis to form a rainbow. Paige immediately texts back, That's the gayest thing you've ever said. The three of us look up at each other from across the table and laugh.

It's nighttime now. Through the laughter and the clinking of silverware on plates, the smell of the fresh soil from the garden wafts my way, reminding me of my centerpieces.

That's when I get a text from the shop owner saying they can't complete my order. And now I'm silently panicked, trying to figure out what I need to do next if I'm going to prevent Paige's wedding from becoming a total disaster.

Together with their families

PAIGE
GREENDALE

— *and* —

AUSTIN
BENCHLEY

INVITE YOU TO SHARE IN THEIR JOY ON

their wedding day

SUNDAY, SEPTEMBER THIRD

AT THREE O'CLOCK IN THE AFTERNOON

FISHERS ISLAND CLUB

WHICH HOPEFULLY

MAX MOODY

won't completely ruin

chapter

THIRTY-TWO

8:30 A.M. STANDING AND SWEATING ON A STREET CORNER in Brooklyn is not what I pictured I'd be doing on the morning of Paige's big day. I honestly don't know if I'm even going to make the wedding. The logistics of designing, organizing and delivering centerpieces were way more complicated than I'd imagined.

I'm outside GRDN, a hipster Brooklyn garden shop, after texting back and forth all last night during the rehearsal dinner with the shop owner of the original plant shop. They ran out of vases and plants and couldn't fill my order in time so they referred me to their friends here.

Last night I also never got the opportunity to fill Paige in on the extent of what's been happening with Chasten and me. She'll be okay with everything, Chasten and I decided.

"Max!" I hear my name and turn, thinking it's the shop owners, only to find a smiling, fresh-faced Chasten.

"What are you doing here?"

"I'm partially responsible for all of this. You think I'm going to leave you in charge?" We kiss hello. His lips are slightly wet and squishy and wonderful.

"I've been waiting for these people for an hour," I say. After fifteen minutes of debating if we should leave because there's no way we're going to make Paige's wedding bus to the ferry in time, a nice woman with keys dangling outside her jean shorts runs up to us, introduces herself as Selena and opens the shop, profusely apologizing.

Inside the shop, we find all the materials we need to create the remaining centerpieces. The Flower District store had already made four and shipped them to the location. We're charged with making six more to complete the ten tables. With no time to spare, the three of us get to work. I have to step in to help with Chasten's because he keeps messing up the arrangement, and we both can't get over how I'm suddenly better at this super-gay activity than him. Meanwhile, Selena can't stop gushing how much she thinks Chasten and I make "the cutest couple." Neither of us protests.

When all of the centerpieces are organized, packed and ready to go, we hug Selena and book home to grab our tuxedos. Paige's wedding buses have long gone, and while I'm at my apartment picking up my tux, I decide we're going to have to jam Chasten's tiny Mercedes full of centerpieces and drive to the venue ourselves. To save time, I'll have to meet him at his place. As I'm shuffling out the door, carrying my weekender bag, butcher paper full of giant leaves, three tall vases, and my tux, I realize something.

The jackhammer has stopped. I smile to myself and cab it to Chasten's.

11:20 a.m. Six giant glass vases rolled in paper and a mountain of greenery are stuffed in the back seat. We're stuck in traffic. Not moving. Chasten and I check the GPS, which tells us we're scheduled to arrive one hour and forty-five minutes late.

12:08 p.m. Traffic crawls. Momentary relief sets in. We move glacially. I play Tracy Chapman's "Fast Car" on Spotify.

1:37 p.m. A break in traffic. The ceremony starts in less than twenty minutes. We missed dress rehearsal. *Paige is relaxed, she won't mind*, we say. *We've been to weddings before, we don't need a rehearsal*, we say. *Fucking floor it*, I say.

2:04 p.m. Sitting in our car on the moving ferry. Gridlocked by Labor Day weekenders sitting in their cars. Everyone is Connecticut born and bred in their uniforms of pastel polos tucked into their khaki shorts. Chasten and I laugh as we struggle to change into our tuxes sitting in his open convertible. A woman in her seventies wearing large sunglasses and a pink golf visor watches us through the window of her generic SUV, scowling.

2:45 p.m. We land at the harbor, disembark the ferry and speed through the beautiful island, winding around bucolic, lazy scenery that mocks our panicked state. Chasten plays tour guide of the exclusive island off Connecticut where his even fancier cousins have been summering on since he was a kid. "There's only one ice cream store, one grocery store, one liquor sto—"

"Just drive," I plead, my stomach in (wedding) knots.

2:58 p.m. Screeching into the stately country club, in the middle of the pristine island, we hop out of the car and are greeted by two gangly teenage valets whom Chasten recognizes as "Chip and Mason." I joke that that's the name of my new gardening shop.

2:59 p.m. We race through the club and peek out onto the patio. The Atlantic Ocean in the distance, flanked by a perfect golf course. One hundred guests sit in neat rows on the green lawn, fanning themselves with paper fans that read "P & A" in cursive. Even with the ocean breeze, the heat is sweltering.

3:00 p.m. We duck back inside to find the wedding party, all dolled up, sitting in club chairs by the main indoor dining room. They all breathe sighs of relief. A wedding planner whose style could only be described as Zoë Kravitz Mother Earth chic and who is wearing a hands-free headset introduces herself as Joy (*really?*). She scolds us for being late. We apologize, and she quickly briefs us before stomping toward the guitarist and pianist, who start up "Oscillate Wildly" by the Smiths. I smile and think, *Is this my wedding?*

3:07 p.m. The bridesmaids and groomsmen line up, looking amazing, and walk down the aisle in pairs until finally it's just me and Chasten. We wipe the sweat from our brows, fix each other's ties and lock eyes.

We walk down the aisle that's layered with cream-colored rose petals, our hands occasionally brushing up against each other on purpose. The radiant guests fill us with love. We smile back, winking at our parents. My dad gives me a corny thumbs-up, and my mom holds back tears.

We wait at the altar, waves crashing just beyond us, for what seems like forever. The music changes to the overture of Sondheim's "Merrily We Roll Along." I laugh, knowing from Paige that this show is about three best friends, as Paige and her dad walk down the aisle. She looks otherworldly. Now I'm tearing up.

The ceremony is full of love, emotion, laughs, awkwardness, someone sneezing twice and ocean breezes, and it ends with a too-sexy kiss. As everyone cheers, Chasten and I catch eyes. I wonder if he's feeling what I'm feeling. We grab hands and give each other a quick kiss as we walk back down the aisle.

7:09 p.m. Chasten helped his brother plan the hors d'oeuvres and added a couple of our Splunch favorites. The mini mozzarella sticks are a thoughtful gesture for not letting me throw Paige's wedding in a diner. Cocktails are drunk, dinner is eaten and speeches are made. Now it's my turn to say something as Paige's man of honor. My usual panicky self would be anxiety ridden, unable to breathe. But with the warm glow of these jumbo round paper lanterns hanging from the ceiling of this cozy tent, filled with these people I love more than anyone in the world, I'm completely relaxed as Chasten hands me the mic.

7:10 p.m. For the longest time, I'd imagined I'd write a speech for Paige's wedding and read it off a piece of paper with shaky hands. Well, tonight, I'm just going say how I feel about Paige from the heart. Here goes:

"Thirty years ago, I met the person who would become my best friend forever. Mikey Petterelli." My opening line gets a big laugh, and I go on to list all the wild, funny, fun, weird, quirky, poignant, sad, talented, earnest things I love about my actual best friend, Paige. Staying in the unscripted moment feels good for a change and, I have to admit, it kind of brings down the house.

7:36 p.m. Either I spot a Steve Martin impersonator getting drinks for his lady friend or it's actually Steve Martin and Paige got the job cowriting his Broadway show.

7:38 p.m. Chasten's aunt Poppy corners me by one of the bars. "I'm mad at you," she says, lightly poking my chest. Do people really do this? She's either drunk or this is her personality. "You never called me after their engagement party. I still need someone to design my terrace garden."

"I'm so sorry. I thought maybe that was just cocktail party talk," I say, not wanting to reveal my little white lie.

"Chasten tells me you made these fabulous centerpieces, and I've gone through two garden designers since we met, so now I just *have* to have you. Can you please come next week to Park Avenue and whip my terrace into shape? If it works out, I have lots of friends I can refer you to, but me first." She's coming at me like a fangirl, and I'm having an out-of-body experience as my ad agency exit plan flashes before my eyes. I say yes.

7:43 p.m. Holding champagne, I meet Paige near the dance floor and finally get to see her up close for the first time since arriving. I tell her how "fierce" she looks, and we crack up to the point of tears, all of our stress finally released.

"Oh, did I tell you I got the Steve Martin thing?"

"I thought that was him by the bar! Holy Pink Panther. That's huge!"

"Pink Panther. Nice deep cut. Yeah, I invited him as a joke and he actually came."

"Proud of you. In so many ways," I say in all seriousness.

"Don't be a dork."

"What do you think of the centerpieces?"

"Love. Chasten did such a great job, right?"

"Ahem. You mean me. I designed them. Chasten merely helped transport."

"Get out. For real? Max, they're perfect."

We both scan the towering green centerpieces dotted among the tables, and Paige wants to know what's in them.

"The tall branches are lemon leaf with some seeded eucalyptus, peegee hydrangeas and a hint of lavender. Then around the base are just little echeveria succulents. For the bridal table, I added some baby's breath. You know, for future good luck." I turn to see Paige has tears in her eyes but doesn't want me to see. "Are you crying right now?"

"Maybe. I just get choked up hearing you say the word 'succulents.'" We laugh and hug like it's the most natural thing for us to do now. "How did you even do all of this? I'm so impressed."

"You wanted a surprise," I say.

"I want this for you too."

"The centerpieces?" I joke, knowing what Paige means.

"I want you to find love and happiness and all the cheesy, embarrassing things I probably made fun of all these years. You deserve all of this and more, Max." And now we're both tearing up.

Our moment is interrupted by Joy, who is anything but.

"Stealing her for a second," she says and motions to the band, which begins to play "The Origin of Love" from *Hedwig and the Angry Inch*, another one of Paige's favorite Broadway shows. Paige and Austin take center stage on the eighties vintage dance floor that's lit up with colored tiles.

"Our kids grew up too fast," I hear behind me as I turn to see Chasten standing there, smiling, his bow tie slightly crooked in the sexiest way possible.

"Didn't they though?" I rest my elbow on his shoulder as we watch Paige and Austin slow dance, whisper to each other and laugh. One by one, guests join them on the dance floor.

"Interesting song choice," he says.

"A little bit rock 'n' roll and a little bit Broadway. That's Paige."

He turns to me. "We did it."

"We sure did," I say, my heart bursting. I grab his hand and lead him to the dance floor. We hold each other close, our tux jackets tight around our bodies as we sway to the music. Eyes closed, I flash back to that first night we laid eyes on each other at the diner, our encounter at Barracuda, our awful first hookup, reuniting at the engagement party, Fire Island, the chocolate factory, the amazing night at his apartment.

I hear the opening chords of "This Charming Man" by the Smiths and, to my utter shock and thrill, turn to the stage where I see Paige, Eliza and Katie performing. With Paige singing, Eliza on guitar and Katie on drums, they've reunited their band Barbara and the Broccoli for a one-time-only performance. I pump my fist and smile at Paige while she sings and coolly winks back at me. All the couples around us break apart and bounce around, charging the entire tent with a brand-new high-octane energy as the rest of the guests flood the dance floor to shake their stuff.

Chasten and I continue to slow dance, still in our embrace, connected, the music guiding us, and I know the best is yet to come.

Vows

MAX MOODY and CHASTEN BENCHLEY

Max Moody, the son of Phil and Joanne Moody of Plain Ridge, Ill., and Chasten Benchley, son of Theodore and Gail Benchley of New Canaan, Conn., are heavily dating but not getting married anytime soon. Check back for updates.

ACKNOWLEDGMENTS

When I was eleven years old, I wrote a Choose Your Own Adventure book. For some bizarre reason, no one wanted to publish my masterpiece, but I'm thankful for the lifetime of encouragement it brought from my friends and family that led to this book.

A very special thank-you to my friends at Lit Entertainment Group, including my film and TV manager, Adam Kolbrenner, for your relentless loyalty, epic email therapy sessions, countless spinach and cheese omelets and making dreams come true. This book would not have been written before I turned seventy-five without you.

Huge thank-you to everyone at Writers House, including my book agent, Daniel Lazar, for your wisdom, patience and determination. Your intuition and thoughtfulness made this story better. You were right about everything.

One hundred pages of thank-yous to the entire Penguin Random House team, including Daniel Brount, Megan Elmore, Tal Goretsky, Heather Haase, Angela Kim, Angelina Krahn, Christine Legon, Dasia Payne and Sammy Rice. Thank you to Craig Burke, Kristin Cipolla, Loren Jaggers, Bridget O'Toole and Kim I. for your publicity and marketing magic. And the world's biggest thank-you to my editor, Cindy Hwang, for your enthusiastic notes, sparkling ideas and endless conversation about Broadway theater.

Thanks a million to Eric Brooks for your legal expertise and smart taste in novels.

Throwback thank-you to my high school English Lit teacher Mrs. Perry for wearing John Lennon glasses and playing Steely Dan while we wrote. Thank you to Jim Cash, my screenwriting guru and college professor who made us wait for an hour and a half that one time because you were on the phone with Tom Cruise. Boss move.

Theeeeeenks to my writers' group: Kathy Fusco, Pete Grosz, Jeff Hiller, Chris Kipiniak, Catie Lazarus, Mark Sam Rosenthal, Brian Sloan, Irina Arnaut and Sabrina Martin. You're all perfect. No notes.

Thank you for being a friend and/or early reader, Sari Knight, Emily Heller, Brent Smith and Robert Traynham, David Binder and Rob Bannon, Tami Brown Lucker, Melissa Roth, Jordan Feldman, Marc Porter and Jim Hennessy, Dan Jinks, Tom Mizer and Travis McGhie, Josh Borock, Lara Shapiro, Elizabeth Clark Zoia, Tom Coleman and Jaclyn Murdock. You all get Edible Arrangements.®

I'm eternally grateful to my brothers and sisters, Anita and Jimmy Benser, Jo Blake and George, Nick and Miriam Karger, Julie Willner and Billy, and Butch and Nancy Karger, for your unconditional love. Big hugs to my nieces and nephews, Ashley, Doug, Sarah, Ernie, Jessica, Matt, Ryan, Olivia, Kira, Jourdan, Taylor, Zach, Mollie, David, Michael, Nancy and your beautiful families.

Merci beaucoup to my real life rom-com, the one who inspires me every day, who loves a good pun, and always knows exactly the right thing to do in every situation, Jean-Michel Placent. Thank you for being the kindest person on the planet and for guiding me through the wilderness. Zelda and I are lucky.

How can I thank my parents enough? I'm forever thankful to Frank and Cookie Karger for your warm hearts, your senses of humor and your love of books. You ignited my imagination when you let me read any book and watch every scary movie, even when I was five years old. Thank you for teaching me how to read, write, laugh and love.

**Turn the page
for a sneak peek at
Sidney Karger's
next novel!**

PROLOGUE

MACKENZIE
Estacada, Oregon
May 2021

HELLO THERE! FIRST OFF, I'M VERY EXCITED THAT YOU'RE considering me as your egg donor.

A little bit about me: I have blue eyes and brown hair and I'm five eight. My grandparents are from Ireland, Germany and the Netherlands. My mom is a teacher and my dad is a commercial fisherman.

I had a 3.9 GPA in college, and currently I work as a medical assistant in a women's health clinic. I aspire to become a surgeon or an FBI agent.

My absolute favorite food is steak . . . by a landslide!

A unique quality of mine is that I can imitate a dolphin noise.

My favorite movie is probably *Mean Girls*. My favorite book is probably the entire Harry Potter series. My favorite TV show is *Yellowjackets* and I recently binged every episode of *Friends*. My parents told me about it and I couldn't believe how funny it was. My taste in music is all over the place! I love pop, alternative, hip-hop, rock and lots of country.

My role models include Audrey Hepburn and Steven Spielberg.

My friends and family would describe me as funny, kind, empathetic, loyal, compassionate and warmhearted. I love people and animals! I guess you can say I'm mostly an extrovert but I can sometimes be an introvert if that makes sense? I'm a huge advocate for the environment, I consider myself a human rights warrior and I like to promote mindfulness whenever possible. I've been told I have above-average intelligence and I'm a hard worker, fiercely independent and entrepreneurial. My family, friends and dogs are the number one top priorities in my life and I've never met a stranger. I'm a bit of a goofball, love corny jokes and generally enjoy being silly.

As far as hobbies and activities, honestly, I'm always on the go! I'm an active person and I'm very athletic. Ever since I was a little girl, I've been involved in various different sports. Throughout my life I've played soccer, volleyball, basketball, softball. I've done karate (green belt), gymnastics, ice skating and I love swimming. Recently, I've taken up snowboarding but I'm not very good.

When I'm not working, I'm usually spending time outdoors, enjoying all the fun things to do in my small town with friends, going on a hike, playing with my two husky rescues or just cozying up with a good mystery book on a park bench under a tree somewhere.

I also consider myself to be a very creative individual. For fun, I dabble in watercolor paintings and often make collages of random things like magazine cutouts, dried leaves or pieces of old clothing I wore as a child. My work has been displayed in several different cafés and independently owned craft stores in various parts of the Pacific Northwest.

Growing up, I had the perfect childhood. I have three younger sisters, and my parents weren't wealthy by any standards but we were comfortable, and like my mom always says, we were rich because we had a loving household.

My philosophy in life is "Don't sweat any of the small stuff" because, like the saying goes, it's all small stuff. Except if you're in a major life crisis or natural catastrophe, then you can sweat the big stuff. Do whatever feels right. Life is just too short.

Lastly, it would be such an honor for me to have the chance to help you on this crazy journey, whether you're growing your existing family or starting from scratch! I know what a long and challenging road this will be and I am here to say I hope everything goes as smoothly as possible. Choosing me as your egg donor would be an incredible experience for both of us because there's nothing more beautiful than bringing a child into this world.

What you're doing is brave and I become emotional thinking about how beautiful your child will be because they will have a dedicated family like you. Whether or not you choose me really doesn't matter to me in the grand scheme of things because I see you and I celebrate you for making your own path to creating a happy, healthy, loving family.

I wish you all the best.

ONE

IT'S CHEESY

WYATT WALLACE WAS STANDING ON A MASSIVE SET DE-signed to look like an upscale kitchen that belonged to a dad with a ten-year-old girl. He wiped his bleary eyes and sighed, exhausted from an unnecessarily long day of directing a commercial for cream cheese. If he never heard "It's cheesy AND creamy!" ever again, he would be a happy man. That line reverberated in Wyatt's brain like a bad song. After what seemed like several hundred takes, the demanding clients were finally satisfied with both actors' appropriate levels of energy and agreed that it was a wrap.

"Great shoot, everyone!" Wyatt's no-nonsense assistant director immediately shouted, ending the day before anyone could change their mind.

When the overly enthusiastic applause from the clients and crew faded, it was Wyatt's cue to leave. Not that people were clapping for him. Wyatt was just the director. The real star of that day's production was a semi-well-known stand-up comic who never once hid his disdain for any suggestion Wyatt made, and yet everyone was cheering for him. *This is how people become egomaniacs*, Wyatt thought. A group of adults giving a standing ovation to another adult who only had to say six sentences would turn anyone into an unbearable narcissist.

As the director and captain of the ship, Wyatt dutifully made his rounds, shaking the hands of every single member of the crew, thanking them for a great shoot. It was only the professional thing to do. He turned to where the semi-famous comic had been standing but the guy had already disappeared, probably back to his dressing room to smoke weed with his entourage, which they had been doing all day in between takes. Wyatt was relieved that he didn't have to pretend straight to the stand-up comic's face that working with him was a pleasure.

It was a breezy September afternoon with the golden sun shining through a cloudless blue sky, but Wyatt would never know that since he'd been stuck inside the massive, windowless studio in Jersey City for the last thirteen hours and wasn't able to leave just yet.

As he maneuvered his way past the three cameras, stepped over the thick strands of cables snaking every which way on the floor and passed through video village, which was now a ghost town full of empty director's chairs, orphaned water bottles and monitors where the clients sat and annoyed the shit out of him, Wyatt didn't think about any of the shots he might've missed today. Nor did he think about any of the subtle changes in performance he should've requested from the semi-famous comedian. There was no impromptu "You know what angle would look cool?" on this shoot, which would typically happen on every shoot. He wasn't concerned that this cream cheese commercial might advance his career or win awards—of course it wouldn't. For this one, all Wyatt cared about was the paycheck.

Ever since he and Biz had decided to have a baby, Wyatt had tried to squirrel away as many directing gigs as possible and had traveled to wherever the work took him. Just in the past month there was the Mucinex commercial he shot in LA, the Home Depot commercial in Atlanta and three commercials he shot back-to-back in Mexico City for some bank. Or maybe it was a credit union?

In the unglamorous production office, Jillian, his overworked line producer with a raspy voice, informed Wyatt that she had to take care of the ten-year-old actor's paperwork before his, since technically the kid had had a hard out two hours earlier and the budget couldn't afford more overtime. Wyatt shared a laugh with Jillian that this kid had more power than him. He was intimately familiar with the weird world of child actors. Wyatt's boyfriend, Biz, had left high school during his sophomore year in Cedar Rapids, Iowa, to costar on a short-lived Nickelodeon sitcom called *Yo, Dude*, about a group of kids living on a dude ranch. The emotional roller coaster of those three seasons became a cautionary tale that would later haunt Biz, the effects of which would eventually worm their way into all of his adult relationships.

Waiting to be released, Wyatt plopped onto the green corduroy couch and pulled out his phone, which had been silenced all day. He ignored all of his work-related missed messages and texted Biz to say he was sorry for being such a dick this morning; the stress of directing a long string of nonsense commercials was getting to him. Biz accepted his apology and asked if he wanted pasta for dinner tonight, Biz's specialty dish. Wyatt said he would love that and ended their exchange by asking Biz to give their Boston terrier, Matilda, a squeeze for him; he'd be home soon.

When the kid actor and her mom entered the room, Wyatt genuinely apologized for going over schedule and, even though it was the cream cheese clients' fault, Wyatt played the diplomat and took the blame. The mom was not the stage mom he'd half expected. She seemed to Wyatt like someone he and Biz would've hung out with when they met as freshmen at NYU.

"Thanks for being so wonderful with Daisy. You must have kids of your own?" the mom asked him. Something inside Wyatt couldn't help but feel a little proud that a stranger recognized his paternal instincts.

"Our first is on the way!" Wyatt said. He hoped that by the cheery way he'd answered, she didn't recognize any trace of the relationship issues he'd been having with Biz.

"So exciting!" the mom said with a bright smile. Wyatt held himself back, wanting so badly to elaborate. The mom's open and comfortable disposition made Wyatt want to admit to her that having a baby via the very complicated surrogacy route had put a strain on his relationship with Biz and they were having a few hiccups. He wanted to tell her all of the unbelievable ups and downs they'd been through to get to this place. If only he could unleash all of his problems onto this nice woman.

She also struck Wyatt as the kind of fun person who would laugh with him at how many times people in the fertility industry used the word *journey*. Where are you in the process of your *journey*? We're so happy to assist you on your *journey*. Has your *journey* been very *journey* as you and *Journey journey* into your *journeying journeylicious journey, Journey*?

What he really wanted to say to her is how incredibly lucky she was to have just one night of sex, then nine months later have a baby. That simple process wasn't possible for the gays. For Wyatt and Biz, it was three years of studying hundreds of egg donor profiles, meeting with a dozen surrogacy agencies, attending one conference called "Gay Men Having Babies," having four different surrogate candidates drop out for various reasons, and absorbing countless opinions from friends, family and that friendly but sometimes invasively curious barista at their local coffee shop in Brooklyn. Not to mention the costs. But Wyatt didn't want to complain. Despite the ongoing issues between him and Biz, Wyatt was all too aware of his current good fortune. And he didn't want to burden this nice woman.

The concerns about having a baby were fairly basic at first for Wyatt and Biz. At thirty-five, were they too young (in gay years)? All of their straight friends at that age have toddlers, so why can't they? Will they know how to change a diaper? What if it's a boy and they have to do sports? What if it's a girl and they have to do makeup? Do they really want to give up their exciting and busy life filled with dinner parties, gay bars, Broadway shows, off-Broadway shows, training at the gym, Fire Island shares, trips to P-Town, New Year's Eves in Puerto Vallarta and trying every new restaurant that opens in the city? Or can they have a kid and still do it all? They were the first in their group of friends to move in together as a couple in their twenties, so why can't they be the first ones to have a kid in their thirties?

But then the tension between them eventually grew deeper. Wyatt, always the organized one, wanted to plan every possible pre-baby milestone, from the color of the room to the baby's clothes to what preschool they should start applying to. Biz was the loosey-goosey one who wanted to determine the color of the room according to the baby's eventual personality, who shrugged whenever Wyatt brought up baby clothes and who didn't give a crap about which was the best preschool.

Once the production assistant pulled up to the front of the studio in the courtesy van that was headed to Wyatt's nook of Brooklyn, he hopped into the way-back seat even though the cast and crew kept insisting he should take the front passenger seat. He was the director, after all. But Wyatt was never interested in lording his power over anyone and happily sat behind two burly grips, the funky wardrobe stylist, a hipster electrician, the aloof head of the props department and the ten-year-old actor and her nice mom, to whom Wyatt gave the front seat. They stuffed as many people as they could into those dreaded courtesy vans.

The collective conversation during the drive back to Brooklyn sounded vaguely like politics, but Wyatt decidedly, effortlessly, tuned it out. He was spent from the day and done talking. As a director, all he did was talk. He told actors where to stand, how to speak and what to think. When he was done talking, he was answering questions.

Do you want to shoot this in a wide or a head-and-shoulder shot?

Do you want her wearing the green shirt or the polka-dot shirt?

Do you want him sitting on the exercise ball or standing next to it?

He didn't feel like answering any more questions and he didn't need to engage. He had clocked out of being the director for the day.

Staring out the window as the van crossed from New Jersey into Manhattan and toward Brooklyn, Wyatt thought of Biz and their future baby again. Since the beginning of their *journey*, Wyatt was never a hundred and ten percent sure that Mackenzie was the perfect egg donor, and that residual doubt was still nagging at him. Wyatt wasn't certain that they could ever fully know if Mackenzie was right, having to choose half of their baby-to-be's genes from a two-page essay and a three-minute video that she shot in her backyard in Estacada, Oregon. Some of her answers they thought were cringe (*dolphin noise?*) but she was smart, funny, beautiful, creative and heartfelt. Mostly, her personal statement addressing them at the end hit home, and they were hooked by her final message to them. None of it would matter once the baby was born, but they didn't realize that now.

Wyatt and Biz never asked the agency, but they were both convinced "Mackenzie" was a fake name. It was irrational to care about this, Wyatt told himself, but if all of these potential egg-donor women were pretending to have names like Mackenzie or Cornelia or Anastasia or Penelope, what other little white lies were they telling to sell themselves to desperate intended parents? That was another thing about Wyatt. He tended to indulge himself with irrational thoughts.

The van careened over the Brooklyn Bridge as droplets of water started appearing on the window, but Wyatt was so deep in thought that it took him a few minutes to realize that it was raining and that they'd turned onto his leafy street in Brooklyn Heights. The conversation between everyone was still going—something about the New York Yankees now—and Wyatt felt like the sullen kid in the back of his parents' minivan when they took road trips every year from his home in Midland, Michigan, to Disney World in Florida and talked about adults he didn't know.

He busied himself by texting Biz that he'd be home in two minutes.

Even though Wyatt hadn't let the crew pressure him into commandeering the front seat, the production assistant felt strongly about dropping off the director before anyone else.

Wyatt wanted that day to be over so badly that for this he would not put up a fight. When the van stopped in front of his building, he said, "See you on the next one!" to everybody and climbed out, breaking up the fourteen-hour family they had formed that painfully early morning.

It was a steady downpour now as Wyatt approached the steps of his brownstone, where he rented a sizeable three-bedroom on the second floor with Biz. As he walked, his thoughts naturally centered themselves around the most important thing: the baby was due in three weeks. They would fly to LA for the surrogate birth and their lives would forever change. But first, Wyatt and Biz had to work out a few lingering issues between them that were rooted in something they couldn't quite understand yet. Wyatt didn't want these three weeks to just sail by and then have the baby become the Band-Aid on their wounded relationship. He needed a plan to get them more in sync.

As he opened the tiny black gate and walked up the steps of his building, Wyatt was soaking wet, but he paused to relish in the great idea that had just popped into his head. Probably the best idea he'd had all day. He swung open the front door of their apartment to the sounds of "Goodbye Yellow Brick Road" by Elton John playing, while Matilda hopped around in circles on her hind legs and Biz grated fresh Parmesan cheese over hot plates of delicious-looking cacio e pepe, and made his announcement.

"I think we should go on a road trip."

SIDNEY KARGER is an award-winning screenwriter for film and television. He is a former writer / director with Comedy Central, MTV and AMC, among other networks, and a contributing writer for *Saturday Night Live*, *Billy on the Street* and *McSweeney's*. He currently lives in New York City with his partner and their Australian Labradoodle, Zelda. *Best Men* is his debut novel.

Ready to find
your next great read?

Let us help.

Visit prh.com/nextread

Penguin
Random
House